SAINTS OF NEW YORK

SAINTS OF NEW YORK

R.J. ELLORY

THE OVERLOOK PRESS
NEW YORK, NY

First published in hardcover in the United States in 2014 by
The Overlook Press, Peter Mayer Publishers, Inc.

141 Wooster Street
New York, NY 10012
www.overlookpress.com

For bulk and special sales, please contact sales@overlookny.com,
or write us at the address above.

First published in Great Britain in 2010 by Orion, an Hachette UK company

Library of Congress Cataloging-in-Publication Data
Saints of New York : a novel / R.J. Ellory. -- First edition.
pages cm
ISBN 978-1-59020-461-0 (hardback)
1. Police--New York (State)--New York--Fiction. 2.
Murder--Investigation--Fiction. 3. Corruption--Fiction. 4. Mystery
fiction. 5. Suspense fiction. I. Title.
PR6105.L65S25 2014
813'.6--dc23

2014017047

Manufactured in the United States of America
ISBN: 978-1-59020-461-0

First Edition
1 3 5 7 9 10 8 6 4 2

"Saintliness is also a temptation."
—Jean Anouilh

ACKNOWLEDGMENTS

Since the publication of *The Anniversary Man* back in 2009, I have been to a great many places – France, America, Dubai, Holland, Canada, the list goes on. I have made a great many friends, amongst them the crews at Sonatine, Overlook and de Fontein, people like Peter and Aaron, Jack and Emer, Veda, George Luca, Francois, Marie M., Marie L., Leonore (my little-big French sister), Arnaud, Xavier, Sophie, Fabienne, Susan, Catrien and Genevieve. In Dubai I was privileged to work with Isobel and her team, and then there were the extraordinary folks at the Southern Festival of Books in Nashville, those in Miami and Chicago and at Bouchercon in Indianapolis. Seems I have had the good fortune to meet some truly great people everywhere I've been, and I never cease to marvel at the warmth and generosity extended to me. It is a privilege and an homour to know you all, and to now count you amongst my dearest friends. My sincere thanks go to all of you for making this past year so memorable.

As always, my thanks to the team at Orion, to Euan, my agent, and to my own family, whose tolerance of my idiosyncrasies seems limitless.

And to you, dear reader, without whom this would all be kind of pointless.

Finally I would like to dedicate this book to the memory of Norman 'Bill' Bolwell (1938–2009). Bill was a Coldstream Guard, a Detective in the CID, the Anti-Terrorist Unit and in Special Branch; he was an accomplished musician, a wonderful artist, a true friend, and a great man. For a few too-short years he was the closest we ever got to having a father, and my brother and I will miss him greatly.

ONE

MONDAY, SEPTEMBER 1, 2008

Three Vicodin, half a bottle of Pepto-Bismol, early on a bitterly cold morning. Frank Parrish stands in the narrow bathroom doorway of a derelict apartment, his shirt unbuttoned to the waist, his earpiece switched off, and inside his shoes he has no socks. He cannot recall where his socks are. He knows they are covered in someone else's puke.

There is a lot of blood in the bathtub ahead of him, and amidst the blood are two people. Thomas Franklin Scott, sitting there, legs outstretched, out of his mind on something harsh, and his crazy bitch of a girlfriend, name of Heather, leaning against him, her back to his chest. Parrish was told her surname, but he can't now recall it. There's a wide gash in her thigh, cut with a straight razor. Her blood has been flicked around the place like this is some kind of performance art thing, and now Tommy Scott has gotten it into his head that they are going to end it all here and now. Is everybody in? he asks. The ceremony is about to begin. Acidheads and fuck-ups. Just what's needed at eight o'clock on a Monday morning.

Tommy, Frank Parrish says. Tommy boy. For fuck's sake. This is bullshit.

Is it? Tommy says. Bullshit you say? He laughs coarsely. B-U-L-L-S-H-I-T.

I can spell, Tommy.

It's all a scam, Frank.

Tommy laughs again, forced and unnatural. He's scared, he's hot-wired.

I know it's a scam, Tommy, but you're young. How old are you, for Christ's sake?

Twenty-four last count. He laughs again, and then he starts to gag like there's something stuck in his windpipe.

Twenty-four? Jesus, man, that's young as anything, you got time, Tommy. Look at me. Forty-something years old and I'm in a fucked-up state most of the time. You don't want to wind up like me—

I already did, Frank. I already wound up no good. There ain't nothing happening here for people like us. Right, Heather, sweetheart?

But Heather is bleeding out. Her eyes are half-closed and her head is lolling back and forth like a string puppet. Nuuuggghhh, she slurs, and Frank Parrish knows that she has maybe an hour, probably less. She looks terrible. Pale, real fucked up, thin and weak, her body ravaged by whatever the hell she's been chucking into it. Skag. H. Hardball. Sugarblock. All of it cut with baby laxative, Drano, talcum powder. She isn't gonna last long. No fight in her. Not anymore.

Tommy! For Christ's sake! How long we known each other?

You put me in juvy.

Frank smiles. Hell, you're right, man. I forgot about that. Shee-it, that's gotta count for something hasn't it? I put you in juvy. You lost your cherry with me. Fuck it, Tommy. Get out the fucking tub, get yourself cleaned up and we'll take your girl down the emergency room and go get some breakfast. You had any breakfast?

Nope.

So let's go get some. Bacon, some home fries maybe? You want some steak an' eggs? My treat.

Fuck it, Tommy says. He has the straight razor in his hand.

Nu-nu-nu-nuuuuggghhh, Heather slurs.

Tommy, man, come on.

Fuck it, Tommy says.

Frank can hear the earpiece crackling at the end of the wire. Don't use negatives, *they'll be telling him.* Don't tell him what he can't have, what he can't do. Tell him what he *can* have and do. Positive influence. Make him feel that the world wants him. Use first names. Eye contact. Find his level.

Fuckers. What do they know? Come live here for a week and tell me about positive influence, tell me how the world wants you so bad it's got a hard-on.

Tommy. Seriously now. Heather don't look so good, man. We gotta get her down to ER. They gotta put some stitches in her leg.

2

As if in response to Parrish's words Heather turns towards the wall and the scarlet mouth of a wound that gapes in her thigh oozes another quart of blood into the tub. Must have hit the femoral artery.

And Tommy is having a hard time sitting upright now. He's skidding, can't get purchase. He's got the straight razor in his hand and it's all going to hell in a hand basket.

He starts crying. Like a little kid. Like he bust a window with a football and he's been grounded and he's sorry, and there's no allowance for a month. He didn't mean to do it. Isn't there such a thing as an accident? It was an accident for God's sake, and now all this shit is coming down on him, hot and heavy, all this b-u-l-l-s-h-i-t . . .

Hey there, Frank says, his voice calm, soothing, comforting, paternal almost. Frank has kids. He says kids, but they're all grown up now. Caitlin and Robert. He's twenty-two, she's two years younger. They made it into college, they're doing good. At least when he last heard. Their mother is a nightmare in high heels and lip gloss. No, he shouldn't say that. He should be more tolerant. He should be more forgiving. Ah fuck it, she's a bitch.

So he says hey there, Tommy, his voice gentle and certain. Hey there, son. We can make it out the other side. It's gonna be okay, I promise.

You can't promise squat, Tommy says, and Frank notices how the razor catches the dull light through the window. The day is dull. A gray faceless nothing of a day. Not a good day to die.

You can't promise me anything, Frank. Whatever you say here means nothing. You're just gonna say whatever they've told you to say so I don't stick her, right?

Frank wishes he had his gun. Left it back there at the door. There were terms and conditions for getting this far. Leave the gun behind. Undo your shirt to the waist. Take that piece-of-shit listening thing out of your goddam ear. I don't want you having conversations with anyone but me. You get that, Frank? You get me on this one?

I get you, Frank had said, and he left his gun at the door, unhooked his earpiece, removed his jacket, unbuttoned his shirt . . . and out in the hallway there are maybe eight or ten other guys, negotiators, bullshit-artists of all descriptions, and they're all a hell of a lot more qualified to deal with this, and all of them are straight-up sober, whereas Frank is slugging his way through the shadow of three days of drinking. Enough Bushmills and he's sick like a baby. He doesn't have enough Irish blood in him to stand up against the onslaught.

But Tommy Scott has been arrested half a dozen times by Frank Parrish. Tommy knows Frank's name. So when there's a call about some asshole with a straight razor cutting up his girlfriend in a bathtub, when a uniform gets down here and calls it in, it's Tommy who says Get me Parrish. Get me Frank fucking Parrish or I'll stick her in the fucking throat right fucking now!

So here he is. Shoes without socks. Puke stains down the front of his pants. No gun. No earpiece. Early Monday morning after three days of Bushmills, and he feels like the Devil raked him a new asshole and turned his guts inside out.

Okay, so we're done playing games now, he says. He's beginning to fray at the edges. He wants out. He wants to go home. He wants to take a shower, find some clean socks, get a cup of coffee and a smoke. He's had enough of Tommy Scott and his dumb cooze of a girlfriend, and he wishes they'd get the fucking thing over with one way or the other.

And that's what Tommy does.

Fuck it baby one more time, he sings, and he pulls that straight razor right up against the side of her face, and then he jerks it round like he's pulling the whipcord on a chainsaw.

Blood – what little of it she has left – jettisons up the wall to Tommy's left, and sprays back against the shower curtain.

NO-O-O! Frank hears himself holler, but there's something so magnetic about what he's seeing, something so horrifyingly compelling, that he's rooted to the spot, right there in his puke-spattered brogues, and it's all he can do to lunge forward when Tommy Scott takes that straight razor and cuts his own throat.

Takes some fucking balls to do that, Frank will say later. Takes some stainless steel fucking balls to cut your own throat, and cut it deep like he did.

Tommy didn't bleed out earlier. Tommy ain't no sapling. He's gotta be five eleven, maybe one hundred and seventy-five pounds, and when he opens up his jugular it comes rushing out of there like a street-corner fire hydrant in the height of summer.

Frank gets a mouthful. It's in his eyes, his hair, all over his tee-shirt. Even as he's struggling to get a grip of the kid, even as he's trying to pull him up out of the bathtub and lay him on the floor so he can push some fingers into the wound and stop the blood . . . Even as he's doing this he's wondering whether Tommy Scott is HIV Positive, or if he's got AIDS or hepatitis or something.

Two minutes, maybe three tops, and Heather something-or-other will be as dead as it gets.

Frank Parrish manages to haul them out of the tub. Later he won't even remember how he did it. Where the strength came from. It's all a mess of twisted arms and legs. Blood everywhere. More blood than he's ever seen. He's kneeling over Tommy Scott, who's now on the bathroom rug twitching and gibbering like he's got his fingers in a socket, and the blood won't stop coming. Frank is holding the guy's neck hard enough to choke the poor bastard, but there's some horsepower back of this thing, and it keeps on coming, keeps on coming, keeps on coming . . .

Heather is gone. She's deadweight. Not a prayer.

Fuck it, Frank, is the last thing that Tommy Scott says. The words are choked through a throatful of blood, but Frank hears him good and clear.

He dies with a smile on his face, like he believes whatever is waiting for him is one hell of a lot better than whatever he's leaving behind.

Frank sits back against the side of the tub. He has blood all over him and it's starting to dry. The negotiator comes back to the bathroom, wastes no time telling him how he fucked it up, how he could have saved their lives.

Saved their lives? Frank asks him. For what, exactly?

And the negotiator looks right back at him with that expression they all do. Heard about you, that expression says. Heard all about you, Frank Parrish.

And Frank says Fuck you.

Once upon a time — he can't remember when — someone asked Frank Parrish why he chose the job.

Frank remembers how he smiled. How he said, You ever get the feeling that maybe the job chose me?

He pulls himself to his feet and goes in search of a smoke.

TWO

Frank Parrish makes a call from the corner of Nevins Street near Wyckoff Gardens.

'You in?' he asks.

Sure, sweetheart, I'm home.

'I'm coming over. Need a bath, a change of clothes.'

Where are you?

'On Nevins, maybe half a dozen blocks or so.'

I'll see you soon.

He pockets his cell, heads for the Bergen Street subway station and Flatbush Avenue.

'Jesus, what the hell happened to you?' she asks when she opens the door. As he passes her she wrinkles her nose.

He stops, turns, stands there with his hands down by his sides, his palms outward as if there is nothing she does not know about him, nothing he could ever hide from her.

'Kid killed his girl, then himself. Cut his own throat.' He feels the tension of dried blood in his hair, in his nostrils, his ears, between his fingers.

'I ran the bath,' she says.

He steps towards her, and smiles. 'Eve, my sweet . . . were it not for you, my life would be as nothing.'

She shakes her head. 'You are so full of shit, Frank. Now go take a bath for God's sake.'

He turns and walks down the hallway. There is music playing somewhere – 'The Only Living Boy In New York'.

He lies in the pink water, his hair wet, his eyes smarting with some jojoba extract shampoo that she buys for him. *Shadows are just shadows,* he thinks. *They can't hurt you until you start believing that they are something more than that. Once your mind* goes that way . . . well, you'll give them teeth and claws, and then they'll get you—

'Frank . . .'

'Come on in.'

Eve opens the door a fraction and steps sideways into the bathroom. She sits on the edge of the tub. She has on only her underwear and her robe. She reaches down and swirls her fingers through the water.

'Tell me what happened with this boy and his girlfriend.'

Frank shakes his head. 'Not now. Another story for another day.'

'You wanna drink?'

He shakes his head again.

'You wanna get high?'

Frank smiles. 'I grew out of that in my twenties. Besides, you shouldn't smoke that shit. Ain't good for the soul.'

Eve disregards the comment.

Frank draws himself up until his back is against the side of the tub. Now he's sitting just like Thomas Franklin Scott.

Eve passes him a towel. He rubs it through his hair, and then hands it back to her so he can get out of the tub.

He stands before her, naked and wet.

She takes hold of his dick, starts to massage it, even dips her head and puts her mouth around it.

Nothing's happening.

'You want something?' she asks.

'What? Like one o' them pills? Jesus, Eve, no. Day I start taking that shit to get it up I'll know my time is over.'

'You still love me, right?'

Frank smiles. He reaches out his hands, she takes them, and he pulls her to her feet. He holds her close, feels the warmth of her body against his damp skin. He shudders.

'You okay?'

He nods his head but doesn't speak.

He wants to say, *No, Eve, I'm not okay. Not exactly. Sometimes I have conversations with the ones that didn't make it. The ones I didn't find in time. The ones that slipped through my hands and wound up dead. That wouldn't be so bad if they didn't talk back, but they do. They tell me how pissed at me they are. How I fucked up. How I didn't figure out whatever the hell it was that happened to them, and now they're in limbo . . .*

'Frank?'

He leans back, looks right at her, and he smiles like its Christmas. 'I'm fine,' he says. 'Better than fine.'

'You gonna stay and have some breakfast?'

'No, I gotta go,' he replies. 'I have an appointment.'

'What?'

'Just a work thing.'

'Coffee?'

'Sure,' he says. 'Strong. Half and half.'

She leaves the bathroom.

Frank leans towards the mirror, tilts his head back and looks up his nostrils. He presses the ball of his thumb against the right, blows blood out the left at sixty miles an hour.

Looks down at the narrow spray of Tommy Franklin on the white porcelain.

Hindsight: the stark and obvious illumination of history.

He says the prayer, the one they all say in such moments: If nothing else, Lord, grant me just one more day.

Frank Parrish leaves a hundred bucks on the bureau near the front door of Eve Challoner's apartment. Three years he's been coming here, ever since he turned over a solicitation bust on her. Lost the paperwork, made it go away. Not because he figured he could fuck her for free, but because he felt something else for her. Sympathy? No, not sympathy. *Empathy.*

We're all fucking someone for money.

He closes the door quietly behind him and makes his way down the stairwell to the ground floor. It's ten after nine. He has a report to write about the Franklin fiasco, and then, if he's lucky, he can be late for his appointment. Half an hour late, maybe even forty minutes.

En route to the subway station he steps to the edge of the sidewalk and is sick into the gutter. He feels that burning in his stomach, his trachea, his throat. He figures he's got to get a check-up. Tomorrow. Maybe Wednesday.

THREE

'You're late.'
'I am.'
'I think you should try and be on time.'
'I did try.'
'Could you try harder?'
'Sure I could.'
'So take a seat, Frank . . . tell me what happened this morning?'
'You can read my report.'
'I want to hear it in your own words.'
'I wrote the report. Those *are* my own words.'
'You know what I mean, Frank. I want to hear you tell me what happened.'
'He cut his girlfriend's throat. He cut his own throat. There was so much fucking blood it was like a water slide at Tomahawk Lake or something. How's that for you?'
'Tell me from the beginning, Frank. From the point you got the call about how he was holding the girl hostage.'
'No.'
'Why not?'
'Because I can't be bothered, that's why. Jesus, what the fuck *is* this?'
'This is therapeutic counselling, designed to help you deal with the stress of your job and make you feel better. You know that.'
'You want to make me feel better?'
'Sure. That's what I'm here for.'
'Then come over here and take care of me.'
'No, Frank, I am not going to come over there and take care of you.'
'You married?'
'Is that important? '

'Maybe . . . I'm just thinking . . . you got no wedding band, but maybe you just don't wear it 'cause you kinda like burned-out alcoholic cops hitting on you.'

'No, Frank. I don't wear one because I'm not married.'

'Well, how 'bout that! I ain't married neither. So what say I come down here to your cozy little office, we draw the blinds . . . you know how it is. That's the kinda stress counselling I could really use right now.'

'Is that what you feel?'

'Damn right it's what I feel. And I bet you do too, *Doctor*. If only it wasn't for professional ethics, eh?'

'Whatever you say, Frank.'

'Now we're talking.'

'No, Frank, I don't think we're talking at all. You're trying to offend me, and I'm humoring you.'

'Is that what you think I'm doing? Saying shit that will offend you?'

'I do think that. You're trying to shock me. That stuff about coming over to take care of you, for example.'

'No, Ma'am, that's how I go about courting someone.'

'Well, if that's true, then I figure we're all pretty much safe from the charms of Frank Parrish.'

'That's funny. Now you're trying to make me laugh.'

'No, I'm not. But I *am* trying to give you an opportunity to release some of the stress and trauma that goes with your particular line of work.'

'Oh, shee-it. Save it for the rookies and the faggots and the female officers.'

'That's a very slanted viewpoint.'

'Hey, lady, it's a very fucking slanted world.'

'So you don't want to talk about Tommy Scott and Heather Wallace.'

'That a question or a statement?'

'Whichever.'

'No, I don't want to talk about Tommy Scott and Heather Wallace. What the fuck use would that be?'

'Sometimes people need to talk.'

'Sometimes people need to have other people urinate all over them. Don't mean it does 'em any good.'

'Why do you think you're doing this, Frank?'

'What?'

'Trying to offend me.'

'Lordy, lordy, little girl, you *have* led a sheltered life. You think that's so offensive? Hell, you should hear what I say to members of the general public.'

'I've heard about some of those things.'

'Well, this is me being polite, okay? On my best behavior.'

'Well, your *best behavior* has gotten you eleven verbal cautions, two written warnings, your driver's license suspended, and a one-third pay hold until Christmas. Oh yes – and a recommendation that you see me on a regular basis until your attitude improves.'

'And you think it'll do me some good? Coming on down here and talking to you?'

'I hope so.'

'Why?'

'Because it's what I do, Frank. It's my job, my purpose.'

'And you're a shrink, right?'

'I am a psychotherapist.'

'Psycho-the-rapist.'

'No, Frank, a psychotherapist.'

'I've met a few rapist psychos in my time.'

'I know.'

'You *know*?'

'Yes, Frank, I know some of the people you've had to deal with. I know about some of the things that you've seen.'

'And what does that tell you?'

'It tells me that you're a troubled man. That you might need someone to talk to.'

'Am I that obvious?'

'Well, yes, I think you are, Frank. I think you are that obvious.'

'You wanna know something we were taught in the Keystone Kops?'

'Sure.'

'Sometimes the obvious occludes the truth. And sometimes things are exactly as they appear.'

'Meaning what?'

'Well, it's real simple. I *appear* to be an aggressive, fucked-up, alcoholic loser with some twenty years on the career clock . . . and you can throw into that incendiary mix my dangerously low self-esteem and a taste for cheap women and expensive whiskey, and you wind up with someone that you really don't want to get involved with. And like I said, even though that is only who I *appear* to be, I think you're gonna find out it's exactly who I am.'

'Well, it looks like we're going to be spending a few really interesting weeks together.'

'You're worried I'm gonna go crazy, aren't you?'

'I don't like to use that term.'

'Oh for God's sake, when did everyone start getting so goddamn scared of words? It's just a *word*, okay? Just a fucking word. Crazy. Crazy. *Crazy*.'

'Okay, so I'm worried that you might go crazy.'

'Some people never go crazy. What truly horrible lives they must lead.'

'You think that?'

'Bukowski said it. You know Charles Bukowski?'

'He was a drunk, I believe.'

'He was a writer. A writer. Like I am a cop, like you are psycho-the-rapist. The booze doesn't define us lady, it augments the already rich fullness of our lives.'

'You are so full of shit, Frank Parrish.'

'Are you actually allowed to say that to me? Doesn't your professional ethical code prevent you from telling me that I am full of shit?'

'Go home and get some sleep, Frank. Come back and talk to me when you're in a better mood.'

'Hey, that might just be never, Doctor Griffin.'

FOUR

Somewhere on his desk – somewhere beneath the first officers' reports, the supplementals, the evidence submission slips, the body custody forms, the fingerprint dockets and the interview notes – was a cell phone. It rang now, with a harsh sound, almost bitter, as if accusing Frank Parrish of something.

There were few phone calls that did not have a dead body at the other end. Before the cell phone age those who attended to such matters could have been elsewhere, unreachable. Now the dead bodies found them wherever they were: no hiding and no heroics for the detectives of Homicide Unit Two, 126th Precinct, South Brooklyn. *We get there when the killing's done*, they say. They will also tell you that most murders are brief, brutal and uninteresting. Nine times out of ten they are also pointless.

Like the old saying *Tutte é Mafia in Italia,* everything – just *every*thing – is dead in Homicide.

Parrish located the phone, answered it.

'Frank, it's Hayes here.'

'Hey there. What's up?'

'You know a guy called Danny Lange?'

'Sure I do. Mid-twenties, weaselly-faced kid, did a three-to-five for robbing a drugstore.'

'Yeah. Well, he's dead. Someone put a .22 in his head. You wanna come down here and sort it out?'

Parrish glanced at his watch: it was quarter after five. 'Can do. Where are you?'

Parrish scribbled down the directions, then grabbed one of the uniforms to give him a ride in a squad car. The traffic was bad, jammed up and tight along Adams. They took a right after the Polytechnic University, made better time along Jay, and came out opposite Cathedral Place. Parrish could already see the red flicker from the black-and-whites. They pulled over sharply and Parrish got out, telling the uniform to head on back. To Parrish's left was an empty lot, a derelict coupe hunched like a sad dog, a handful of federal yellow flowers escaping from beneath the hood.

Back of the tapes Danny Lange was spread-eagled on the ground, head at an awkward angle, the expression on his face something akin to mild surprise. He was looking back towards the church at the end of the street. There was a neon sign up there, the light from its tubes subdued by smog and dirt, that Parrish knew well. *Sin Will Find You Out.* No shit, Sherlock, he had thought the first time he saw it.

'You turned him yet?' Parrish asked Paul Hayes.

'Ain't done a thing,' Hayes said.

'No change there then,' Parrish quipped.

'Go fuck yourself, Parrish,' Hayes replied, but he was half-smiling. 'There's a deli half a block down. You want anything?'

'See if you can get me some Vicodin. If not, aspirin. And a cup of coffee. Black and strong.'

Hayes disappeared.

Down on his haunches, Frank Parrish surveyed the body silently for some minutes, aware that darkness was dropping fast. He sensed the uniforms watching him from the black-and-whites.

Danny had leaked, just a little. That was not unusual for such a small caliber. It would be up to the ME to make a call on this as the primary or secondary crime scene. This was the drop, nothing more. Parrish put on latex gloves, went through Danny's pockets, found the better part of a hundred bucks which he tucked discreetly into his shoe. No ID, no driver's license, no billfold, no watch. Still, despite such missing artifacts, this was no robbery. Danny Lange was not a man to wear a watch or carry a billfold, or even a man who washed, for that matter. Dying had not tempered his characteristically rank odor.

The hole in his throat was the only wound. Entry, no exit. Looked like the .22 had actually been pointed upwards at a steep angle, leaving the bullet still inside his head. Those little slugs had insufficient power to make it a through-and-through; they would just ricochet around like a fairground ride and mush the brain. Number of times they collided with the internal wall of the cranium just pancaked the shit out of them. Difficult to pull any lands, grooves, striations. Parrish used his little finger to push up into the entry wound. It was still moist an inch or so in, telling him Danny had been dead no more than a couple of hours. Danny Lange was small time. No money, no future, little of anything at all. He would have pissed someone off, short-changed them, cut a deal with something obvious like baby laxative or baking soda, and that was that. It was all the same, and it was all war. Parrish knew his Cormac McCarthy. The old judge in *Blood Meridian* said, "It makes no difference what men think of war. War endures. As well ask men what they think of stone. War was always here. Before Man was, war waited for him . . . That is the way it was and will be."

The war had reached Danny Lange, and he was now one of its countless casualties.

Frank Parrish called one of the uniforms over, gave him some gloves, told him to help him roll the vic. They did. Danny had crapped himself.

'You call the DC?' Frank asked.

'Yes, sir, I did.'

'Good man. You wait here and keep an eye on him. Make sure he don't do a runner. I'm gonna go drink some coffee with my friend, and I'll speak to the deputy coroner when he comes down, okay?'

'Yes, sir.'

Hayes had made it as far as Starbucks. No Vicodin, only aspirin, but at least the coffee was passable. Parrish chewed a couple of tablets and washed them down.

'Anything?' Hayes asked.

Parrish shook his head. 'Usual shit. He must've upset someone. Someone said something. Like the Sicilians say, a word in the right ear can make or murder a man.'

'How many you got on?'

'Three,' Parrish replied.

'I already got five open. Can you take this one?'

Parrish hesitated.

'You take this one and I'll give you a credit on my next bust.'

Parrish nodded. 'Deal.'

'You got your partner yet?' Hayes asked.

'Tomorrow,' Parrish said. 'Some nineteen-year-old out of detective school.'

'Hope that works out for you.'

'Me I ain't worried about. It's whatever dumb schmuck they give me'll have the problem. He better be able to look round corners.'

'So, we're good? I'm away. Leave you to deal with the DC.'

Hayes walked back two steps, turned and disappeared. Parrish heard his car start around the corner and pull away sharply.

He drank half the coffee, tipped the rest into the road, dropped the cup into a basket at the corner, and walked back to Danny Lange.

FIVE

The Deputy Coroner came and went. Parrish watched the wagon take Danny away, and then walked to the nearest subway station.

Danny Lange's place was a flea-bitten rat-hole of a shit-house up on the ninth floor of some project building. Even as Parrish approached the entrance, he remembered an earlier time he'd been there. Two years ago, maybe three. He'd come away feeling the need to wash his hair and dry-clean his clothes. It was a sad day when a man lost his reason, sadder when he lost his respect. Danny Lange had lost both a long time ago.

The inner hallway smelled of piss and puke. A scattering of used hypodermics crunched underfoot as Parrish skirted the elevators and headed for the stairwell. The elevators were notoriously unreliable, the very worst kind of place to get trapped.

He reached the third and was already out of breath. He was alone. Shouldn't have been, but partners wore out quicker than they used to – last one took a permanent rain check. Parrish had done his first three years as a detective in Vice, the next six in Robbery-Homicide, and when they split the units he stayed with the dead people. Robbery was bullshit. Penny-ante liquor store hold-ups, some Korean guy dead for the sake of twenty-nine dollars and change. Junkies working for enough money to score pep-pills, trying to stave off the heebie-jeebies. Heebie-jeebies gonna getcha no matter how many stores you rob. That was just the way of things.

Fifth floor and Parrish took a break. He would have smoked a cigarette but he couldn't breathe. He stopped, tried not to think of Caitlin, his daughter, but she came at him every which way. *Get more exercise, Dad. Smoke less cigarettes. And don't even get me started on the drinking.* He wasn't winning.

She was almost done with her training, and he wanted her close – Brooklyn Hospital, Cumberland, even Holy Family down on Dean Street, but Caitlin wanted to go to Manhattan. St. Vincent's perhaps. She had gone for nursing; something her mother had always supported. And Caitlin's mother was Frank's ex-wife. Clare Parrish. Except now she'd reverted to her maiden name of Baxter. Fuck it. How did that ever go so wrong? Sure, they were married young, but it had been good. December '85 they'd gotten hitched. Robert was born just four months later in April of '86, Caitlin in June of '88. Good kids. Better than their parents. Such a great start. Difficulties, yes of course, but nothing major, nothing serious. How that deteriorated into a barrage of vitriolic accusations – unfounded for the most part – he would never know. Silent grievances saved up like bad pennies. He was aggressive, bull-headed, ignorant, forgetful. She was shallow, cynical, untrusting, dismissive of his friends. Friends . . . What friends?

And then it turned really bitter. He failed to understand *even the most rudimentary requirements for social interaction*. She *could not cook, clean,* she had *no culture, no passion*. Afterwards, the argument spent, they would get drunk and fuck like rampant teenagers, but it was never the same and they both knew it. Each had uttered sharp words, and between them – neither more guilty than the other – they had pricked the matrimonial bubble. Tolerance deflated. He had rented a three-room apartment on South Portland, started an affair with a twenty-seven-year-old paralegal named Holly. Clare started screwing her hairstylist – half-Italian with a ponytail – who called her *bambina* and left fingernail crescents on her ass.

Hindsight, ever and again the cruelest and most astute advisor, gave him harsh lessons in responsibility. He should have had a better attitude. He should have appreciated that his wife – despite the fact that she did not work in Homicide – nevertheless had an important job raising a family. All well and good now, after it had blown itself skywards. *Most guys*, she used to say, *you have to wait for them to fuck up. You? With you there ain't no waiting. You're a fuck-up before you arrive.*

Divorce had gone through in November 2001, when

Caitlin was thirteen, Robert two years older. Clare got them weekdays, Frank had them weekends. They got their diplomas, went to college, started to take their own bold steps in the world. They were undoubtedly the best thing that came out of it. They were the very best part of him.

Parrish reached the ninth and was ready to fold. He stayed for a while, leaning against the wall, heart thudding. A black woman opened the door of one of the apartments, looked him up and down like he'd gotten his dick out and shook it at her. She asked nothing, said nothing, closed the door again.

He tried a deep breath, headed down the hallway, and let himself into Danny Lange's apartment with the key he'd taken from Danny's pocket. Everything else he'd signed over to Evidence Control and left for Crime Scene to pick up.

The lights were on, and the place smelled ripe.

She wasn't yet old enough to show any wear on her face, not even in her eyes – eyes that looked back at him with the quiet and hopeful surprise so evident in all unexpected deaths. She was naked but for her underwear, her skin the color of alabaster; white, with that faint shadow of blue that comes a little while after the breathing stops. The thing that really surprised Frank Parrish was that he was not surprised at all. A dead girl on Danny Lange's bed. Just like that. Later, he even remembered he'd said something to her, though he could not recall what it was.

He pulled up a chair and sat for a while in silence. He guessed she was sixteen, perhaps seventeen. These days it was so hard to tell. Her hair was cut shoulder length and hung down around her face. She was beautiful, no question, and the care and precision with which she had applied red polish to her fingernails and toenails was something to behold. She was almost perfect in every sense, save for the livid bruising around the base of her throat. Confirmation of strangulation came when Parrish knelt on the floor and looked directly into her eyes with his flashlight. The tiny red spots of petechial hemorrhaging were there – present on her eyelids, and also behind her ears.

He had not seen Danny Lange for a couple of years. Then,

19

the guy had been a junkie and a thief, not a killer. But hell, times had changed. It wasn't that people did worse things than they had fifteen or twenty years before, it was simply that more people did them.

Parrish called it in. Dispatch said they'd inform the Coroner's Office and Crime Scene Unit. Parrish went around the apartment – the front room, the kitchen, the narrow bathroom, then back to the girl on the bed. There was something strangely familiar about her, and then he realized what it was. She looked like Danny.

Fifteen minutes later Parrish's suspicions were confirmed. He found a small bundle of pictures – Mom, Danny, the dead girl on the bed. A hundred-to-one she was Danny's baby sister. In the pictures she was no more than ten or eleven, bright like a firework, all smiles and freckles. Danny looked real, like he had yet to hit the dope. Mom and the two kids – a regular snapshot from the family album. Was there such a thing as a regular family, or did shadows lurk behind the front door of every home?

He pulled a clip-top evidence bag from his jacket pocket and dropped the photos into it. Then he went and sat back in the chair near the bed. He wanted to stay with the girl until everyone else arrived.

An hour and a half later Parrish was in a window booth in a diner on Joralemon Street near St. Francis College, a plate of food in front of him. He'd managed just a few mouthfuls, but that acid burning was back, somewhere low in the base of his gut. An ulcer perhaps. If he saw a doctor he would be told it was the booze. *Cut back on the booze*, the guy would say. *Man your age should remember that the body hurts faster, heals slower.*

Parrish perused the half-dozen pages of notes he'd taken in Danny Lange's place. There was nothing much of anything. Deputy Coroner had shipped the girl out, tied and tagged, and she would be autopsied tonight or, more likely, tomorrow. Coroner's initial findings at the scene accorded with his own.

'Thumb prints here and here,' he told Parrish. 'Fingers here and here and here. Marks are darker on the left side of her neck, which means whoever choked her was more than likely a rightie. You can't be absolute on that, but it's a strong possibility.'

The DC had checked beneath her fingernails for skin, combed her hair and her pubes for foreigns, checked inside her mouth, looked for cuts, bruises, abrasions, bite marks, needle punctures, indications of tape adhesive on the ankles and wrists, rope-burns, signs of restraint, subcutaneous hemorrhaging, external residues of toxic elements, semen, saliva and blood. She was pretty clean.

'I can do a rape kit, confirm COD, and get word back to you within twenty-four, maybe forty-eight hours,' the DC had said. 'Might be able to get a tox done, but that'll take a little longer. At a guess, she's been dead . . . I dunno . . . about eight hours, I'd say. Laking indicates that this is the primary. I don't think she was moved.'

They pressed latex and Parrish left.

So Parrish went to a diner and had tuna casserole, a bagel, some coffee. The casserole was good but the appetite was gone. He kept thinking back to Eve, to the fact that he couldn't get it up that morning. Seemed he was losing everything by inches. He was on the way out. He needed to take some exercise, cut back on the smokes, the drinks, the hydrogenated fats, the carbs, the shakes and chips and Oreos. He needed a vacation, but he knew he wouldn't take one.

His father used to say something: *What do you want most? And what would you do to get it?*

To this he could now add his own variation: *What do you fear most? And what would you do to avoid it?*

Right now, what he most wanted to avoid was another session with the psychotherapist.

SIX

TUESDAY, SEPTEMBER 2, 2008

'Why did you become a cop, Frank?'

'Why did you become a shrink?'

'I'm not comfortable with that term.'

'Like I'm comfortable with being called a cop?'

'Okay . . . why did you become a police officer?'

'Why did you become a headpeeper?'

'Very good, Frank. You seriously want to spend the next month playing games every day?'

'No, not really. I want to spend the next month solving murders.'

'Well, be that as it may, Frank, the fact is that unless you continue to see me on a regular basis then you're going to be suspended. That means either you can see me and continue to work, or you can refuse to see me and stay home. Which is it going to be?'

'The first one.'

'Good. So – I'm going to put my cards on the table. The particular aspect of therapy that I focus on relates, in the main, to parental relationships. We all know who your father was. We know his record and his achievements, and we know that he was a significant figure in your early life. This is something I want particularly to address with you.'

'You want me to talk about my father?'

'I do.'

'What if I want to talk about my mother?'

'Then there will be an opportunity to do so but, in the first instance, I will acknowledge you politely and ask you to talk about your father.'

'Seriously?'

'Seriously.'

'You don't want to know about my father.'

'Yes I do, Frank, I want to know everything you remember about him.'

'And you think this will have some value to me?'

'I do.'

'Well *I* can tell *you* it won't.'

'Naturally, I can't force you to talk about him, but I must stress that progress along that line will be my main interest.'

'And I will acknowledge you politely, and then tell you to go fuck yourself.'

'Okay, let's start somewhere else. Tell me why you became a police officer?'

'So I could find out all the things that my father never told me.'

'Go on.'

'Okay, Doctor Griffin . . . Marie . . . you don't mind if I call you Marie . . . You *really* want to know about him?'

'Yes.'

'Well, my old man was a ballbreaker. He was OCCB.'

'OCCB?'

'Organized Crime Control Bureau. He was there when they got The Cigar in 1979.'

'The Cigar?'

'A nickname. That's what they called Carmine Galante, 'cause he always had a cigar in his mouth. Even when he was shot dead he had a fucking cigar in his mouth.'

'Did your father tell you about this?'

'Sure. He told me all sorts of things.'

'About the work he did against organized crime?'

'Yes.'

'You want to tell me about that? Tell me about The Cigar?'

'What's to tell?'

'Whatever you like.'

'I'll tell you something about the famous John Parrish. How about that? How about we go straight to the jugular if that's what you really, really want.'

'Yes.'

'My father was a badass, through and through—'

'To you?'

'To pretty much everyone.'

'He's dead now, right? When did he die?'

'Sixteen years ago. End of September 1992.'

'And your mother?'

'She died in January of '93.'

'How was their marriage?'

'He treated her like a princess. He worshipped her.'

'You have brothers and sisters?'

'No.'

'So did he want you to be a police officer?'

'He wanted me to stay quiet and keep out of the way.'

'You don't think he loved you?'

'He loved me the way all Irish-American fathers love their kids. When I did good he didn't say a word, when I fucked up he gave me a good thrashing.'

'And if he were alive now, sitting right here, what would you say to him?'

'I'd tell him to go fuck himself.'

'Even though he was a decorated officer?'

'You checked up on him.'

'Briefly.'

'Then why give me the impression you don't know who the hell I'm talking about?'

'I need *you* to talk, Frank, that's what this is all about.'

'Oh yeah? If you're gonna put your cards face-up, then put them face-up. Don't bullshit me. Say, "Hey, Frank, your father was some big dick on campus wasn't he? He got Christ-only-knows how many citations, and by the time he was gunned down in the fucking street the Mayor of New York was all set to give him the Congressional Medal of Honor." Tell me that. Tell me what you know, and then I can fill in the gaps. If we're gonna get up close and personal here, Doctor Griffin – Marie – then we might as well be playing in the same freakin' ballpark.'

'Sure.'

'Good. So let's start over.'

'Your father was a decorated cop. He was involved in the Organized Crime Control Bureau and the New York State Organized Crime Task Force. I understand that he was instrumental in some of the most effective investigations into

corruption in the construction industry, waste haulage, JFK, and the fish and garment businesses—'

'You sound like you read an obituary on Google.'

'I did.'

'Well, whatever you might have read didn't include all the truth. He was a good cop, at least for the most part, and yes, he did all those things they write about. But he did a lot of things that they didn't write about, and maybe they never will. And those things went with him to his grave.'

'And are they things that you think people need to know?'

'God no! Let 'em believe what they want to believe. People have got to have faith in something. You can't take it all away otherwise we'd all be neck-high in shit.'

'Do you want to tell me about some of these things?'

'Why? You wanna hear old war stories from the day? You wanna hear how my father and his buddies kicked the Mafia out of New York in the Eighties? Or do you wanna hear the truth?'

'The truth?'

'Sure, the truth. What you read isn't so much as the tip of the iceberg as a handful of snowflakes.'

'He wasn't what they said he was?'

'My father? Jesus, no. He was anything but.'

'Do you want to talk about it?'

'Not today.'

'Why is that?'

''Cause I got to go see the Coroner and get an ID on a dead girl I found, and then I gotta figure out what the fuck Danny Lange was doing in an alleyway with a bullet in his throat.'

'Well, I'm glad you kept the appointment, Frank.'

'Hell, Doctor Marie, if I gave up on every girl after the first date I'd never get laid.'

SEVEN

'Rebecca Lange is the name we've got,' Deputy Coroner Stanley Duggan said. 'Crime Scene found her purse in another room, with a video rental store card in it. We traced her on the Child Services system. Picture they had confirmed ID. As best as I can determine, she was killed somewhere between eight and twelve hours before you found her. No secondary laking, so I think she died in that apartment, right there on the bed.'

They stood on either side of the steel table. Frank Parrish breathed slowly and silently, conscious of such a sense of sadness engendered by this dead girl. By the futility of a wasted life. There was something utterly desperate about her. About the red nails. Her hair. The fact that she seemed perfect and unblemished, except for the neck bruising. Unblemished except for that.

'Sixteen years old,' Duggan went on. 'Date of birth, March sixth, 1992, COD strangulation. Good possibility he was right-handed, like I said, and he had big hands. There was nothing under her nails, no foreign hairs in her pubic region.'

'Rape kit?' Parrish asked.

'She wasn't raped, but she'd had sexual intercourse recently. Found lubricant, spermicide, no semen. Hard to tell precisely when, but there's minimal bruising and no internal abrasions.'

'Drugs?'

'Some alcohol. Not a great deal.' Duggan reached in back of the shelves behind him and withdrew a half-gallon glass jar. Three or four inches of brownish, viscous liquid swirled in the bottom. 'This, and a bunch of fries, some hamburger and pickles.'

Parrish looked back at the girl. He could imagine her alive,

her eyes bright, her cheeks flushed with color, the wind through that hair.

Hey, Frank.

Hey, Rebecca.

Frank . . . didn't want to mention it, but you don't look so good.

I'm okay, sweetheart. Now you – you're one to talk.

I don't have to look good, Frank. I'm dead.

You wanna tell me about that?

Shit, you're starting to sound like Doctor Marie.

You're a funny girl.

I was, Frank, I was.

So we're not gonna talk about what happened to you?

Can't help you, Frank. It's the rules. The dead don't talk to the living. At least not to divulge the secrets.

'Detective Parrish?'

Parrish snapped to.

'Anything else you need me for? I got a half dozen bodies backed up.'

Parrish smiled. He reached out and touched Rebecca's hand. Red nails. Redder than blood.

'No,' he said. 'We're all done.'

'Good enough. I'll zip her up and put her on ice. You got maybe a week, and if there's nothing going on we'll turn her over to State Mortuary. Far as I can see there's no parents, no next of kin.'

'Aside from the brother, and he's dead too,' Parrish said, and then recalled the woman in the picture. Probably the mother. Where was she while her daughter was lying dead? 'The brother got done yesterday as well. GSW up through the throat into the brain?'

Duggan nodded in recognition. 'Yeah, yeah, I know the one. Their deaths are connected?'

'Hard to avoid the coincidence, but right now there's nothing that puts the scenes or the killings together. He died about three o'clock in the afternoon, she died somewhere between eight a.m. and noon on the same day.'

'You know what they say,' Duggan interjected. 'Sometimes the obvious—'

'—occludes the truth, and sometimes things are exactly as they appear.'

'Well, we'll do tox next, but any other tests you need, you have about a week.'

'Appreciated,' Parrish said.

He looked back one last time through the porthole in the door. Such a beautiful girl. Such a painful and tragic waste.

Walking away from the mortuary, Frank Parrish thought of Doctor Marie Griffin. She was a looker, no question. A little hardness around the eyes, maybe, like she'd seen – or heard – too much that upset her. A Police Department counsellor. Maybe he shouldn't have been so tough on her. All the psycho-the-rapist shit. He was an asshole sometimes. He knew that.

He remembered the last counsellor, fellow by the name of Harry something-or-other. He asked the question they all asked.

What do you see when the lights go down, Frank?

Darkness.

But inside the darkness. What do you see there?

I see your wife, Harry, and she's got my dick in her mouth.

Always the bravado. Always the wide swing that missed. Truth was, these counsellors had no fucking idea. Hell, *he* had no idea. Sometimes it took a fifth of Bushmills to put him down. Honestly, it didn't matter whether it was darkness or daybreak, he still saw the dead ones. Sometimes the women. And the teenagers, girls like Rebecca. All gone, smashed to fuck. But mostly it was the children. For the children there was no reason, no rationale, no excuse. And his father was always back of it – drunk-ass son-of-a-bitch that he was. No-one knew the truth about John Parrish. What he did, how he did it, how he covered up all that garbage with a clean white layer of virginal snow. Dead for sixteen years and Frank Parrish still couldn't exorcise the motherfucker. He didn't become a cop because of his father; he became a cop despite him.

Maybe he *would* share the stories with Doctor Marie: JFK Airport, the McClellan Committee report, Local 295 and The Teamsters. Jimmy fucking Hoffa and the New York State Investigation Committee. The Gambinos, the Luccheses, the Gottis, the Lufthansa heist in '78, the Kennedy Rackets

Investigation, Henry Davidoff, Frank Manzo and the Lucchese capo regime, Paul Vario. It was all there – *United States* vs. *International Brotherhood of Teamsters* – and Detective John Parrish was right in there with them, his citations for bravery and exemplary conduct falling out of his ass by the handful. Motherfucker.

Parrish got off the subway at Hoyt Street and walked to the precinct.

Homicide Division at the 126th was a blunt and brutal fuck of a thing. *Working here,* someone once said, *is like watching a slow-motion car crash. You know what's gonna happen but you can't stop it, and you sure as shit can't look away.*

It had been said too many times to be anything but true, but cop life was not a movie. The phone goes. There's a dead person somewhere. You find your car keys, you drive out there. Get there, no-one saw anything. No-one wants to see anything. The black-and-whites have rigged a perimeter, contained the scene. The Deputy Coroner is late. You stand for a while in the bitter cold or the aching heat. You need to piss but you can't leave. You smoke too many cigarettes. Eventually you give up waiting and walk over there with a flashlight and a pair of latex gloves. You take a look up close, you see the obvious, you look for the un-obvious. You go through the guy's pockets, or the girl's purse, or maybe if it's one of the transvestites downtown you go through *his* purse. You find gum, keys, a cell phone, bills, change, smokes, condoms, pens, subway tickets, bus tickets, candy wrappers, a watch. Sometimes a whistle or a can of mace, string, scraps of paper with scrawls of indelible handwriting, receipts, photos of kids, photos of husbands, wives, lovers, girlfriends, parents and friends. There is only so much to be found in the pockets of the dead.

When the Deputy Coroner shows up you help him roll the body, note any obvious signs of wounding from bullets, knives, chains, pipes, baseball bats, boots, fists; every once in a while something melodramatic like a nail gun, a non-recoiling ball-peen hammer or a heavyweight wrench – the kind that screws up the bolts on car tires so they won't come loose on the freeway. Then you walk the edges. You look for beer cans, wrappers, spent casings, blood spatter, brain matter, skid marks, tire treads, escape routes, vantage points for eyewitnesses, the impact of stray gunfire in concrete walls and wooden doors. You make copious notes. You start to feel the enervating tide of disillusionment as you add another name to the dead-file.

Under the direct aegis of the Crime Lab Director there are Supervisors, Criminalists, Scene Analysts, Firearms Specialists, Forensic Techs and Latent Print Examiners. In the Coroner's Office there are Deputy Coroners, Forensic Pathologists, Anthropologists, Toxicologists, Duplicate Testing Supervisors and the Peer Review Unit. The Firearms unit alone could determine make, model, caliber, serial number, indications of carriage and concealment, land and groove marks, striations, rifling, types of ammunition, marks from the firing pin and the breech-block face, weapon distance, the size and shape of powder particles around the entry wounds. All these things. Necessary things, important things – and futile if there was no weapon recovered, no bullet located. Futile if the deceased had been decimated with shells from a sawn-off Magnum at a range of four feet. Futile if funding cutbacks put the network out of reach.

This was not the movies. This was real. Here the bad guy got away. Nine times out of ten you didn't even know who the bad guy was and, even when you did, he walked on a technicality. It was always a day late and a dollar short.

Parrish was neither pessimistic nor cynical. He was pragmatic, methodical, realistic. He was not disillusioned, he was reconciled and resigned.

Homicide was simply about the dead, and more often than not there was little justice where the dead were concerned.

Now his concern was Rebecca, Danny Lange's sister, and why Danny would be dead in an alleyway when his kid sister had been choked to death in his rat-hole apartment. He remembered the money he'd taken from Danny's body. He dropped it into a cigar box in the lower drawer of his desk.

First thing was the parents. Secondly, go chase up some of Danny's contacts – Lenny Hunter, Garth whatever, the other one with the bad skin who looked like someone had dragged his face through a grater and put it back all wrong.

Parrish picked up the phone and dialed numbers he knew by heart. A stony heart – perhaps somewhat cold and unyielding – but a heart all the same.

EIGHT

Five o'clock he got a call to go up and see the Captain.

Jack Haversaw was ugly as sin. What was that old saying? *Face like a bulldog sucking a wasp?* Jack Haversaw made that boy look pretty.

'Sit down,' Haversaw said. 'How're you doing?'

'I'm okay,' Parrish said.

'How's things working out with the shrink?'

'Only got going yesterday. She seems fine . . . easy on the eye. I think I can do some time with her.'

'You don't have a choice, Detective. It's do or die this time. You don't wanna know how long it took me to convince Valderas *not* to deep-six you. And then Valderas had to convince Lieutenant Myerson. I invoked rank in the end. Enough said. Listen up, Frank. I want you here. I *need* you here, but the bullshit theatrics I can do without.'

Parrish didn't respond. He and Haversaw went back far too many years to do foreplay.

'So what's on your desk?'

'Got five. Latest is this Danny Lange killing, then his sister choked to death in his apartment.'

'And besides that?'

'The hooker from last Tuesday, the black kid from the Tech College, and the Transit Museum guy who got pushed under the subway train.'

'Right, right . . . I forgot about him. How you doin' on this stuff?'

'Same old, same old. The Lange murders interest me—'

Haversaw smiled. 'No problem, Frank, just ditch the tedious ones and handle the ones that give you a hard-on.'

'You know what I mean.'

Haversaw rose from his chair and walked to the window. He was silent for a little while, and then he turned, put his hands in his pockets and sat against the sill. 'Got you a partner.'

Parrish raised his eyebrows.

'Name is Jimmy Radick.'

'I know him. He was down in Narcotics for a while.'

'Well, he's in Homicide as of now, and I'm assigning him to you. He knows he's with you and he's okay with it.'

'Good for him.'

'Don't be an asshole, Frank. Treat the guy decent, okay? Don't fuck him up for everyone else. He's got the makings of a good detective.'

'I'll do my best,' Parrish said.

'Your best hasn't been good enough, pal. Squad Sergeant Valderas heard that even the Divisional Commander wanted to know what the deal was with you. You know what he called you?'

'Enlighten me?'

'An internal enquiry just waiting to happen.'

'I'm seeing the doctor woman, okay?'

'And I don't wanna hear that you went and screwed her and it's all a godawful mess, huh?'

'I ain't gonna screw her, Captain. Jesus, who the hell d'you think I am?'

'Frank Parrish, that's who. Son of John Parrish, one of the most decorated officers this Precinct ever saw, is ever likely to see.'

'We done, Jack?'

'We're done, Frank. Time are you finished with the shrink tomorrow?'

'Ten, ten-thirty.'

'Okay. Here, eleven o'clock tomorrow morning. You, me and Jimmy Radick.'

'You got a date.'

Frank Parrish got up and started for the door.

'You take care now, Frank, and take care of your new partner, you hear me?'

Parrish raised his hand in acknowledgement and was gone.

He still didn't have a lead on the parents. He went after Danny's known associates, found – inevitably – that numbers had been disconnected. He chased Verizon to get updates and changes. It was a ball-breaking, heartbreaking thing.

'Have a number here for Leonard Hunter, one-three-five, that's one-three-five Grant Street. Number's no longer connected. I wanted the new one.'

'I'm sorry, sir, that number was disconnected due to non-payment of charges. There is no secondary number.'

Same thing over again for Garth Fauser, and for the life of him Frank could not recall the name of the kid with the bad skin who used to hang out with Danny Lange.

Around him the Homicide Unit was busying up. Paul Hayes, who'd handed him the Danny Lange crime scene, Bob Wheland, Mike Rhodes, Stephen Pagliaro, Stan West and Tom Engel. All Homicide dicks. Good people. And then there was Squad Sergeant Antony Valderas, hard like a hammer, ample bark, more than sufficient bite to back it up. It was a tight crew, and they gave Parrish space for maneuver, space that he needed in order to stay sane in this fucked-up job. Brooklyn 126th handled the better part of twenty homicides a month, and up on the board at the far end of the room the opens were marked in red, the closeds in black. Those names stayed black for twenty-four hours just to keep everyone up on the fact that they did finish a case every once in a while, and then the slate was wiped and another red went up.

From where Frank Parrish sat he could see *Daniel Kenneth Lange 09/01/08 FP**, and *Rebecca Emily Lange 09/01/08 FP**. The asterisk beside his initials indicated that he was flying solo. As of tomorrow it would read *FP/JR*. Jimmy Radick. Frank remembered him. Remembered that he had liked him, the first impression at least. Jimmy was police family too – his father, his father before him – but they were never part of OCCB or the Brooklyn Organized Crime Task Force. He didn't have that part of the history to contend with. Reminded of his father again, Frank believed that it would do no harm to share a few of the war stories with Doctor Marie Griffin. Maybe it would exorcise a few demons, some ghosts, some memories. Maybe not. No harm in trying. Tomorrow . . .

Back on the phones, trying with all he possessed to remember the kid with the bad skin . . . Lucas, Leo, Lester . . . something beginning with 'L'. Louis. That was it. Louis

Bryan. Frank went through his Rolodex and found the number. It worked but it rang out.

Frank decided to make a trip down there; he spoke to the Squad Sergeant.

'You getting anyplace on these others?' Valderas asked him.

'The subway guy. I think that was a random. Some crackhead decided to push him for kicks. I figure he was wrong place, wrong time.'

Valderas shook his head. 'Transit Authority are all over me like herpes. You know how many we got last quarter just across Nevis, DeKalb, Hoyt and Lawrence Street?'

'Too fucking many, like always,' Parrish replied.

'Mother*fuckers*.'

'I'm out to see someone on the alleyway shooting.'

'Wasn't a suicide maybe?'

Parrish shook his head. 'ME says his crime scene was a secondary, and who the fuck shoots themselves in an alleyway?' He took out his gun, upside-downed it, held the butt in his hand with his thumb on the trigger. He put the muzzle of the gun to the uppermost part of his throat and tilted his head backwards. 'And like this? Angle's all wrong. Right side up you couldn't get your finger to the trigger.'

'Okay, go. Call in and let Dispatch know if you're not gonna be back tonight.'

Parrish went back to his desk and took a twenty from the cigar box.

A little after eight Frank Parrish found Louis Bryan. His skin was even worse than he remembered it, and he was still living with his bedridden mother. Every once in a while Mother would bang on the floor upstairs and Louis would have to hurry up and tend to her needs.

'She's bad man, real bad. Don't think she's gonna last much longer.'

'I'm sorry, Louis.'

'Hey man, it goes this way, you know?'

'You heard about Danny.'

'Sure I did.'

'You don't seem so upset.'

Louis smiled. His teeth, those that he still possessed, were junkie-yellow. 'I don't know what to tell you. Goes with the territory. If I kept count of the ones that went down I'd lose count in a month.'

'ODs I get,' Parrish said, 'but Danny got shot in the head.'

'So? You think some of these motherfuckers don't carry guns? Some of these assholes would pop you for a ten-bag. You know the score, man. You been around the block.'

'But Danny wasn't in with those kind of people, Louis, not when I last saw him.'

'And when the fuck was that?' Louis was scratching bad. Just watching him made Parrish feel like his skin didn't fit.

'I don't know, a year ago, eighteen months maybe.'

'Well, nothing changes faster than things, man. Six months you can go from bad to worse to worser.'

'What's the deal with his folks?'

'They're dead. Been dead forever.'

'What happened?'

'Car crash. Both killed.'

'How long ago?'

Louis shook his head, turned his mouth down at the corners. 'I don't know – four, five years maybe.'

'And his sister?'

'What about her?'

'You know her?'

'Know *of* her, sure. Seen her coupla times. Cute looking. She don't do no skag though. Hardest thing she done is Pepsi-Cola.'

'Not anymore.'

Louis looked worried. 'She got done too?'

'Yeah, she got done.'

'Same way as Danny?'

'Nope. She got herself strangled in Danny's apartment.'

'Shee-it!' Louis seemed genuinely surprised. 'She was a sweet kid, real sweet. Pretty an' everything. Who the fuck woulda wanted to off her? They do her as well? Like they raped her or what?'

'I don't think so. Just killed her.'

'That's them all gone then, ain't it? All the whole family gone. Mom, Dad, Danny and the kid sister. Shee-it, that's gotta fuckin' hurt when the whole family's gone.'

'You know who looked after the sister?'

'Some chick up in Williamsburg, as far as I remember. Don't know her name. Danny never really talked about it.'

'Any idea where she went to school?'

Louis shook his head.

'And you think Danny would have—'

Louis' eyes widened. 'Danny? No fuckin' way man. He loved that girl. Far as he was concerned she's walkin' on water. Said she was gonna be a model, you know? Me, I figure you gotta be five eight, five nine minimum to do that catwalk shit, but Danny wouldn't have it. She's gonna be a catwalk model and she gonna get herself all Calvin Kleined up an' earn some serious money. He's shootin' for the high-life, the penthouse suite, you know? He's a fuckin' dreamer man, but I don't say nothin'. You take away someone's dream, even if they's real foolish, and you take away their hope.'

'When did you last see him?'

Louis thought for a moment. 'What day we got? Tuesday . . . ? I seen him Sunday afternoon, maybe four, five o'clock.'

'Where?'

'His place. We did a smoke or two together. I didn't stay long, had some business to attend to.'

'And his sister?'

'She wasn't there, man. Didn't see her.'

'Did he say where she was?'

'Nope. He didn't say nothin' and I didn't ask.'

'And you haven't heard word around of what happened? Anything at all. Someone shooting their mouth off? Someone bringing it up in conversation?'

Louis shook his head. 'I don't make these things my business, man. You don't go lookin' for it then it ain't gonna find you, know what I mean?'

'Okay, Louis, okay. You keep an ear and an eye out for me, okay? You hear anything you give me a call.' Parrish took the twenty and gave it to Louis.

Louis took it. 'An ear and an eye I can do.'

Louis showed Parrish to the door just as Momma started banging on the floor again.

NINE

'Frank, I need you here on time. Twenty minutes and I have another appointment.'

'That'll work fine, 'cause I have an appointment in fifteen.'

'Seriously, I need you here on time. We can't get anywhere in fifteen minutes.'

'So what do you want? You want me to stay or go?'

'Stay. Sit down. We'll make a start. You were going to think about discussing your father.'

'I did think about it.'

'So are you willing to talk about him?'

'Where are you from, Doctor Marie?'

'I can't see what that has to do with anything.'

'Humor me.'

'Originally I'm from Chicago.'

'Another good gangster town, eh? So how long have you been in New York?'

'Three years this Christmas.'

'You know a lot about it?'

'Why?'

'Well, New York is a union town. Always has been, always will be. Democrats generally. Only exception was when they brought in Giuliani, who turned Republican in the Eighties. He served his time with the US Attorney's Office for the Southern District, became US Attorney himself, the big boss of the hot sauce, and then he was Mayor from January 1994 to December 2001.'

'I remember him from the 9/11 attacks.'

'Right. And you remember when he ran for the Senate, and then the White House? He was a tough guy, big heart, but up against more internal shit than he ever bargained for.'

'In what way?'

'Hell, Marie, you have to understand the nature of the city, some of its history, to really appreciate what happened. What's still happening.'

'I've got time.'

'You really wanna hear this shit?'

'I want to hear about your father. That's *really* what I want to hear about, Frank.'

'Well, if you want to hear about John Parrish then you have to hear all about the Saints of New York.'

'The who?'

'The Saints of New York. That's what they called themselves, bunch of egotistical assholes.'

'So who were they? The only thing I hear about your father is how many decorations he got, how he and his colleagues helped break the back of Mafia control in the city.'

'The truth and what you hear are never the same thing in this business, believe me. The Fulton Fish Market, the Javits Convention Center, waste haulage, the garment industry, the construction business . . . hell, they were into everything. Organized crime was so much a part of this city that no-one thought they could ever be separated. But that's what the OCCB and the Strike Forces and the Feds tried to do, and to a degree they succeeded. But even in their finest hour there was still so much internal corruption, so much money passing hands, that no-one ever really knew who was clean and who wasn't.'

'And your father?'

'You really want to know about him, then we'll have to begin at the beginning.'

'Then do that, Frank.'

'Well, okay, here we go. New York City. You got the five boroughs, okay? Manhattan, the Bronx, Queens, Brooklyn and Staten Island. We have one New York Police Department, but each borough has its own DA. Then there's the Department of Justice, and they have US Attorney's Offices in every federal judicial district in the country. There are two districts in New York, the Southern in Manhattan and the East in Brooklyn. The DOJ also has the FBI, and they operate independently of the US Attorney network. The FBI is responsible for investigating cases, the US Attorney for prosecuting them. It's supposed to be that simple. There are three FBI offices in New York City – or were back then – Manhattan, Queens and New Rochelle. Each one worked independently until the action against organized crime stepped up in the Eighties and these boys started getting smart, working together. So you got this system going on, right? The Feds raise the cases, the Attorney's Office prosecutes. You with me?'

'Yes, go on.'

'Okay. Then comes RICO. That's the federal act against racketeering and corruption, and it gave the Feds the authority to investigate anything – and I mean *anything* – that they felt might relate to organized crime. So the Feds started getting cases together and bringing them to the relevant US Attorney's Office, and then the US Attorney would bring them to federal court in the Southern or Eastern district. You follow me so far?'

'Sure, yes.'

'Well, the federal courts have judges who are appointed by the President of the United States, with advice and consent from the Senate. These boys, these judges, once they're in, they're in for life. They got life tenure. Now we go back down and look at the five District Attorneys. These guys get elected to four-year terms by the citizens of their boroughs, and they operate entirely independent from the Mayor's Office and the State Attorney General. They are not obligated to co-operate with one another, and they don't take orders from higher federal or state authorities. Co-operation has only ever occurred on a case-by-case basis.'

'The point being?'

'I'm getting to that. So you have the NYPD, the FBI, the DA's Office, the New York State Attorney General, the Organized Crime Control Bureau, the Brooklyn Organized Crime Strike Force, and the original remnants of the New York Task Force which had its headquarters in White Plains and field offices in Buffalo and Albany.

'Each of these groups is independent, and they all got their own snitches and CIs – confidential informants – and their own cases. And you wanna get this shit arranged in such a way as to bring about effective co-operation and the precise application of the law? Hell, we have enough trouble getting a bust for parking violations. These guys were fighting a losing battle even before they started. The degree to which organized crime had infiltrated the police and the courts was staggering. There are forty thousand officers in the NYPD alone, and they *react* to crime, they don't proactively investigate *potential* crime. That's the job of the Feds, but the Feds are limited to handling espionage, sabotage, kidnapping, bank robbery, drug trafficking, terrorism, and civil rights violations. You get a murder or two thrown in there, and unless the acting NYPD Homicide detectives can deliver probative evidence that the homicide was in some way related to one of those federal categories, they ain't got a hope in hell of getting FBI support.

'Well, the Mafia knew all this, and the bits they didn't know they could find out easily enough. They knew that the borough DAs didn't work together, so they dumped bodies along the borough divisional lines. Bullshit paperwork on which DA was responsible for that piece of territory could keep the case running for months, and then they get a judge who's on their payroll to dismiss it, based on the fact that the NYPD and the DA's Office were hounding and harassing the defendant unnecessarily . . . Some of the things that happened way back when you wouldn't believe. Anyway, in the Nineteen-Eighties all these legal organizations got wise, they started to get their shit together. Rudy Giuliani went into the US Attorney's Office Southern District in 1970. Three years later he was chief of the Narcotics Unit, and in 1975 he became an Independent and went to work for Gerald Ford. After that he went into private practice, and when Reagan was elected in 1980 he decided he was now a Republican. Reagan made him Associate Attorney General, and from that position he supervised all of the federal law enforcement agencies of the US Attorney's Office, the Department of Corrections, the DEA and the US Marshals Service. In 1983 he came into his own with indictments and prosecution of organized crime figures and he indicted eleven people through '85 and '86. That sorry bunch of motherfuckers included the heads of the Five Families, and

Rudy got convictions and hundreds of years of prison time for eight of them. He was the hero of the fucking century.

'Now the OCCB had been around since 1971, but it was in the Eighties under Giuliani that they really started to kick ass and take names. That's where you would have found the late John Parrish, forty years old and a cop since 1957. He's got a seven-year-old kid and a mortgage, and he has a network of CIs and allies in and around the Brooklyn area to support. So: he's taking money left, right and center any which way he can find it, and he's asked to join the Organized Crime Control Bureau, supposed to be the cleanest, most upright and honest crew in the city. These are the new Untouchables. These are the guys who are going to break the back of the Mafia in New York. He gets with them, and he finds out that a lot of these guys are no different from him, just regular humps trying to make a living and not get shot. They got wives and kids and mistresses, they have rent to pay, and they're as open to temptation as anyone on the street. But now the stakes are so much higher. You give information to the Mafia and the payback is huge. Where some cop would have gotten a hundred bucks for looking after some business-man who wanted to lose a truck full of TVs and claim the insurance, now he's given five or ten times that much for looking the other way. Such cops stayed there for ten years, never got so much as a caution or a written warning. They were the Saints of New York, you see, and they couldn't put a foot wrong.'

'And they were all like this? All corrupt?'

'God no, not at all. There were a good percentage that stayed clean, worked hard, got the job done. But my father, the big hero that everyone seems to have a hard-on for, the guy whose standards I have failed to meet on *every* level, he *was* corrupt, and as far as I can tell he was probably the worst of the lot.'

'And you resent it when people compare you to him?'

'Resent it? Why would I resent it. The motherfucker's dead.'

'I don't mean resent *him*, I mean whether or not you resent the fact that people talk about him as a hero when he wasn't.'

'People understand what they want, they say what they want. I haven't got the time or the inclination to change their minds. I think the fact that I know the truth is enough.'

'Is it? Do you really think that?'

'Well, I fucking well hope so, because I don't have anything else.'

'So, tell me what he was like. And these people, the Saints of New York.'

'They were all OCCB cops, and they were all crooked like fishhooks. A handful of them inside the Bureau were making life very easy for the mob at JFK Airport.'

'The Lufthansa heist? I've seen *Goodfellas*.'

'Well, you've seen the flag on the top of the mountain, sweetheart, but you ain't seen the mountain yet. I'm afraid that is gonna have to wait. I have a new partner to meet this morning.'

'Frank . . . hell, Frank, this is why you *need* to be on time. We start into something like this and we need to get to a good point before we leave it.'

'Life moves on, you know? I'm sure your day is filled with excitements just as mine is.'

'Well . . . We'll carry on tomorrow.'

'Sure.'

'And you're doing okay otherwise?'

'I'm okay, yes.'

'You sleeping?'

'On and off.'

'You want something to help you sleep?'

'Christ no. I start down that route I ain't coming back.'

'Okay, Frank. I'll see you tomorrow. You have a good day now.'

TEN

Radick and Parrish had not seen one another for a good two or three years. Radick had come from Narcotics, had hung in there until what he saw and what he heard went more than skin-deep. You could see only so many dead junkies, could interrogate only so many dealers, watch only so many cases fold up and die, before you started taking that shit home.

As far as Parrish was concerned, Jimmy Radick looked exactly the same.

To Radick, however, Frank Parrish appeared to have lost twenty pounds and aged a decade. He wore the spiritual bruises of the conscience drinker: a double or two to blunt the edges of the day's disappointments, another couple to soften the guilt about drinking. It went downhill from there. The worst cases came in still drunk from the night before, spent two out of five shifts with the medical officer. Whatever wagon they kept trying to get on had a slide fitted.

'I don't need to introduce you, do I?' Haversaw said. 'You already know one another.'

Someone was at the door. Haversaw hollered 'Come in!' and Squad Sergeant Valderas entered. Valderas was a career cop. Had never wanted for anything else, never *would* want for anything else. He ironed a clean shirt every night for the next day.

'Frank,' he said matter-of-factly, and then extended his hand to Radick, who rose from his chair. They shook, shared a wordless greeting, and Radick sat down again while Valderas leaned against the wall.

'Antony has a good team here,' Haversaw told Radick.

Radick glanced at Parrish. *The pep talk.*

'You got Frank here, then there's Paul Hayes, Bob Wheland, Mike Rhodes, Stephen Pagliaro, Stan West and Tom Engel. You know these guys?'

'Some,' Radick said.

'Well, you are in Two Unit with Frank here. Eight in all, four pairs, split shifts reversing every two weeks. Alan here will give the lowdown on the schedule. Overtime is frequent enough, time and a half for weekends if you're off-shift, double-time for public holidays if you're not booked in already. Easy enough to understand. You're not married, right?'

Radick shook his head. No.

'Ever been?'

Again a no.

'You supporting kids?'

'No, no kids.'

'Parents here in New York?'

'Both dead,' Radick said.

'So you're all alone in the big, bad world.'

Radick smiled. 'Sure am.'

'Well, you'll get along fine with Frank. Frank don't have no-one to care for him neither, do you, Frank?'

'We'll care for each other, right, Jimmy?' Parrish said.

'Yes sir, Mister Parrish sir,' Jimmy replied, with a military snap in his tone.

Valderas shook his head. 'Couple of firecrackers here,' he said. 'We'll see what damage they can do between them.'

'Take 'em away,' Haversaw said. 'They're your problem now.'

Down in the Two Unit squad room Valderas sat with Radick and Parrish, asked if Radick wanted coffee. He declined.

'Take it,' Parrish said. 'It'll be the last time he offers.'

'You are such a fucking wiseass,' Valderas said. 'Not so fucking clever when it comes to your stats.'

'I have a sixty-eight as of yesterday,' Parrish replied.

'And I have Hayes and Wheland with an eighty-two percent, Rhodes and Pagliaro with a seventy-nine.'

'And you give them the slam dunks.'

Valderas hesitated.

'See?' Parrish said. 'It's what I say. Give them the slam dunks, give me the ball-breakers and the heartachers. You are such a transparent motherfucker.'

Valderas looked at Radick. 'See what I have to contend with? Maybe a bit of your stabilizing influence might bring this guy around.'

Radick turned his mouth down at the corners. 'I don't know, Sergeant,' he said. 'I was told that you were the one who needed help.'

Parrish laughed.

Valderas rolled his eyes.

'Enough already,' Parrish said. 'We have work to do.'

'Your alley shooting,' Valderas said. 'Wasn't he a CI sometime back? Didn't he used to work for Charlie Powers over at the 17th?'

'No, that must've been some other Lange. This one I knew – didn't know his sister, but I knew Danny. He was just a user, a small-time thief. Seven-Elevens, liquor stores, shit like that. Did a coupla turns around the yard way back, but he wasn't someone to write a Report about.'

'Got anything?'

'On him or the sister?'

'Either.'

'Danny got a .22. I figure the slug will have pancaked, won't give us nothin'. I'm checking up on his friends, all bullshit so far. His sister I ain't gotten to yet. She got choked in Danny's apartment. Sixteen years old, real pretty.'

'He could've done it?' Valderas asked.

'I don't think so, no. If it'd been some rich girl in there, then maybe, just *maybe* Danny might've choked someone for enough cash, but his sister? Uh-uh, I don't think so.'

'And the parents?'

'Both dead, I heard. Car crash a few years back. Seems the girl had some woman looking after her in Williamsburg.'

'So what are you going to make some progress on today?'

'Well, far as I can tell, the subway guy just caught an opportunist psycho. I spoke to his wife, his kids, people at his work, everyone I could think of. He was just a regular schmuck. No gripes, no grievances, didn't drink or smoke, no hookers, no drugs. Sort of guy who'd die and his wife would forget him by the weekend.

'The hooker we got a lead on from a friend of hers, another girl who reported a john making noises about killing one of them for kicks. A real party boy, you know? The kid at the college – the one who got stabbed – seems he ripped off a coupla dealers. He wasn't the good little boy that his folks would have us believe. He took a couple of grand off of someone who was supplying the campus. Anyway, that's gonna resolve by the end of next week I'm sure.'

'So the only one you got right now that hasn't moved any place is the brother and sister?'

Parrish nodded.

'Get on that for today then,' Valderas said. 'Spend a couple of hours with Jimmy here. Take him round the place, show him where the john is, where he's gonna sit. The usual. Then get your lazy asses out on the street and find out who wanted Danny Lange and his kid sister dead.'

Parrish got up.

'And you,' Valderas said to Radick, as he rose to leave the squad room, 'it's good to have you here. You come with an honest reputation. Let's keep it that way, okay?'

ELEVEN

'Lange was just your regular mope,' Parrish said.

He and his new partner sat at facing desks. Radick was emptying a box of things into the desk drawers – stapler, pens, notebooks, pencils. The usual.

'He was bound to get himself put down sooner or later,' Parrish went on. 'He'll have crossed someone, short-changed someone, sold someone some crap, you know? The twist is the sister. That's what doesn't make sense. She gets herself strangled, he gets himself shot a few hours later? This is a coincidence I cannot ignore.'

'You got pictures?' Radick asked.

'Not yet.'

'Autopsy report?'

'We pick it up today.'

'You say he was shot under the chin up into the head?'

'Yeah.'

'More like an execution.'

'Sure, but these characters watch TV. They get creative. You know – theatrical.'

'Can we go see her?'

'No problem.'

Duggan, the DC from the call-out wasn't in. Parrish got someone else. He asked to see the Lange girl.

'You can wait ten? I got someone else doing something down the hall, and I'm gonna need to be with you.'

They waited twenty, paced up and down the corridor, hands in pockets, nothing much of anything to say.

The guy came back, showed them into Theater 4, walked through to the iceboxes and opened the drawer.

'She *is* pretty,' was Radick's first comment. He leaned close, his face inches from hers, almost as if he hoped to absorb the truth of her death from her skin.

Then he commented on her fingernails.

'Toenails are the same,' Parrish said. 'Professional job.'

'She was raped?'

'Nope. Had sex, no rape.'

'She wasn't turning tricks?'

'Can't see it. Not the way she looks, not unless she was a real newcomer. No hooker I ever saw looked that good.'

'But she looks younger than she is,' Radick said.

'You think?'

'My brother has three girls. Eleven, thirteen, fifteen. They spend all their time trying to look twenty-five. This hairstyle is young for sixteen, makes her look twelve or thirteen. Doesn't fit with the nail varnish. Her clothes?'

'Found her in her underwear,' Parrish said.

'She had clothes in the brother's place?'

'Dunno, haven't been back there. Got confirmation of COD yesterday, rape kit, stomach contents . . . there was nothing out of the ordinary there.'

Parrish zipped up the body bag, pushed Rebecca back in her slot and asked for the Danny Lange autopsy report before they left.

'Nothing that will help us here,' he said, after skimming through it. 'Slug was as flat as a shadow.' He folded it up and tucked it into his jacket pocket. 'Let's go see the apartment.'

Radick wouldn't do the stairs. 'Nine floors?' he said. 'No fucking way.'

They took the elevator, shuddered and stuttered all the way up.

Parrish still had the apartment key, though the word 'apartment' suggested something altogether more functional and appealing than the sight that greeted them.

'I still cannot understand how the fuck people can live like this,' Radick said. He snapped on latex gloves, started turning over greasy fried chicken boxes, empty cans . . . found a coffee cup with half an inch of coffee under an inch of mold.

'Girl wouldn't have been here long,' Parrish said. 'Very few girls would tolerate a place like this. She'd have cleaned it up some, I'll bet.'

'You think maybe someone killed her, then went after him because he could put her and the strangler together?'

Parrish didn't reply. He was on his hands and knees looking along the line of the carpet.

Radick shrugged. He walked on through to the bedroom where the murdered girl had lain. He produced a small digital camera from his jacket pocket and started taking pictures.

'You always take your own?' Parrish asked as he came through the doorway.

'Helps to have extras. Sometimes I can't wait for the crime scene snaps to be delivered.'

Parrish left him to it, saw the flash out of the corner of his eye every time it went off. He put gloves on too, started through the kitchen, rifling drawers, opening the cooker, the microwave. The cupboards were pretty much empty – one can of chili, another of adzuki beans, half empty pack of Uncle Ben's. In the fridge he found one egg and a carton of milk five days past, already swelling a little. On the shelf beneath was half a head of lettuce in Saran wrap and three slices of brown bread, stale and stiff and upright at the corners. How could people live like this, Radick had said. Easy, Parrish thought, considering that his fridge looked pretty much the same. He didn't know what he would find here, especially as Crime Scene had already been through, but he kept on looking regardless.

Half an hour and Radick was done.

'Got what I wanted,' he said. 'What d'you want to do with this now?'

'Well, we need to find this woman in Williamsburg, get Rebecca's school, talk to her friends, anyone she hung out with,' Parrish replied. 'See if a Missing Persons report has turned up.'

'You think she died because of him, or he died because of her?'

'He died because of her I should think, but hell, it's just guesswork until it's something else, right?'

*

Three hours and they had a name and an address in Williamsburg. They managed to trace Rebecca through Child Services to the Williamsburg Schools Register. They called Student Information, had them fax over a copy of her registration form, and there – top right-hand corner – was as clear a photograph as they could have hoped for. They called the school back, got the name and contact number for a Helen Jarvis, filed with the school as Rebecca's legal guardian: the woman they were looking for.

At five, Parrish and Radick sat in a delicatessen up on Prospect Street near the Manhattan Bridge. Parrish had pastrami, open-face with melted Swiss cheese; Radick had a bagel, toasted dark, with peanut butter.

'So Rebecca lives over in Williamsburg, Danny lives in South Brooklyn. They see each other rarely. She's a good girl, goes to school, grades are fine . . . and then she vanishes.'

'I think we go talk to this Helen Jarvis,' Radick said. 'I'm all for going now.'

'Sure,' Parrish said. 'Let me finish my food.'

The traffic was better than usual, and at a quarter of seven they pulled up outside 1256 Ditmars Street.

The woman who opened the door was the better part of forty-five, maybe older. Parrish immediately recognized her from the photograph he had found in Danny Lange's apartment.

Helen Jarvis knew who they were before the badges came out.

'It's Rebecca, isn't it? Has she gotten into some trouble with Danny?' She stood right there in the doorway despite the chill. She didn't invite them in.

'Could we come in please, Miss Jarvis?' Radick asked.

Helen Jarvis stepped back without speaking, showed them into the living room.

Parrish asked about her relationship with Rebecca, whether she was a family member.

'No,' she replied. 'I knew her parents . . . many years ago, of course. They're dead, you know. Tragic really. Car crash, both of them killed instantly. Anyway, Danny was eighteen at the time, Becky was eleven.'

'And she's been living with you since then?' Parrish asked.

'Yes, she has.'

'And you are her legal guardian?'

Helen Jarvis looked awkward. 'I'm in deep, right?'

Parrish frowned.

'Child Services?'

'I'm sorry, I don't understand, Miss Jarvis.'

'I knew this was going to happen. One day it had to happen, didn't it?'

'What, Miss Jarvis? What had to happen?'

'That it would be discovered that I'm not her legal guardian. I mean, I couldn't very well leave her to be looked after by Danny, could I? He was already . . . well, he already had his own problems to deal with. He didn't want a little girl hanging around the place, did he? And anyway, there was no money. What little there was got swallowed up with bills and God knows what else. Child Services came down here, asked Danny if he would take care of his sister. He was already eighteen by then, and legally he could do that. I told him to tell them yes, he'd take her, and they went away glad not to have the problem. I then told Danny to leave her with me. He went off to Brooklyn and she stayed here.'

'And you know she's been missing from school for a week, Miss Jarvis?'

Helen Jarvis bowed her head. 'Yes,' she replied. 'I know.'

'And you didn't file a Missing Persons Report?'

'Well, I called the school on Tuesday and the principal called me back and said that she hadn't been into school since the previous Friday. I called the local police down here, and they said I had to wait forty-eight hours before I could file a report. Then it got to Thursday and I thought that I'd give it just one more day, and then Thursday came and went. I called Danny, no answer, so I even thought of going down to Brooklyn to see if she was with him.

'She's done this before, you see, run off to Danny's . . . done it at least half a dozen times, but she always comes home. I just imagine that that's what has happened. I thought I'd give her until Saturday to phone. I knew she would phone eventually, and she will. She will phone and tell me what happened, and she'll be sorry for all the trouble she's caused. She's a good girl really. And Danny is a live wire, you know? Danny is always exciting, always has something going on, but I don't think he's a good influence – not that he's a bad person, of course. I wouldn't want you to think that he was a bad person by any account, but I don't think it's good that Rebecca looks up to him so much. And it isn't like she's incapable of taking care of herself. She's older than her years, if you know what I mean. And I trust her. I just assume she's run off to Danny's again . . .'

'And you last saw her when?'

'Monday morning. Early. She went off to school as usual.'

'And there was nothing strange in her behavior? Nothing out of the ordinary you noticed?'

Helen Jarvis shook her head. 'Nothing that I can think of, no. I mean, she's a teenager, and I know that sometimes teenagers can be difficult—'

'Miss Jarvis,' Radick interjected, and Parrish could see in that moment that she knew.

They always knew. When the police appeared on their doorstep, they knew. When the black-and-white pulled up outside the house, they knew. When the kids didn't come home from school, and friends didn't know where they were, and so-and-so wasn't having a sleepover, and there was no after-hours football practice, they *knew*.

Helen Jarvis had that expression. Defeat. Overwhelm. Pained resignation. Her words – nervous, too fast, all too eager to explain the what and where and how – had been merely a delaying tactic. She had spoken of the girl in the present tense, the past tense, the present tense once more.

'No,' she said quietly, her voice barely a whisper. And then again, 'No.'

'We found her in Danny's apartment,' Parrish told her. 'On Monday. We found Danny a few hours earlier.'

Helen Jarvis's eyes widened.

'Both of them,' Parrish said. 'Danny was shot at close range, and Rebecca had been strangled.'

'Strangled?' Helen asked, and it wasn't that she misunderstood the word, or was unable to appreciate the concept, it was that she was hit broadside by the image of *her* Rebecca choking to death with someone's hands around her neck.

She started to breathe then, fast and short, started to hyperventilate, and Parrish told her, firm but gentle, to stand up, to walk around, to take deep, deep breaths. He told Radick to fetch her a drink of water, but Helen said she wanted a glass of whiskey. It was there in the cupboard above the sink, the glasses to the right.

She sat down, she stood up again, and then she started to cry.

She cried for half an hour, her chest heaving, her voice strained, her eyes red and swollen and desperate. She kept looking at Parrish as if he could say or do something to make her feel better, but he could not, and she knew it.

Never once did she ask if she was in trouble. Never once did she enquire as to whether she would be under investigation from Child Services. That fact alone told Parrish that Rebecca could not have found a better home after the death of her parents.

As they were leaving Parrish held back a moment. He sent Radick on to the car.

'I need to ask you something about Rebecca's appearance,' he said.

'Her appearance?'

'I wanted to know whether she wore nail varnish.'

Helen Jarvis frowned. 'Not that I'm aware of. I mean, she might have done, but I don't recall ever having seen her wearing nail varnish. Why?'

Parrish shook his head. 'And her hair was cut short in back and then close in to her face, right?'

'No, her hair was quite long. Straight down her back, parted in the middle.'

'Okay,' Parrish said. 'Someone is going to be in touch with you, Miss Jarvis. Unfortunately, you might be the only person who can make a formal identification, and then there'll be the funeral arrangements to take care of.'

Helen Jarvis raised a handkerchief to her face.

'Is there someone who can come and be with you?'

Helen looked vacant for a moment, and then she shook

her head. 'I'll be okay,' she said, but Parrish knew she wouldn't.

Parrish reached out and touched her hand, and then he left her standing in the hallway and made his way to the car.

Radick drove, Parrish sat in silence. They would have to file a report with Child Services. Helen Jarvis, having spent the last five years caring for Rebecca, never once having made a claim for financial support from the county, would have to endure weeks of criticism from the very people who should have helped her. Parrish, having seen and heard so much of this, could not fault what she had done. So easy to judge from an objective perspective. She had convinced herself that Rebecca was with Danny. Rebecca was sixteen, and Parrish knew from personal experience how his own daughter had been at that age. At some point the parental chains had to come off. At some point you had to accept the fact that the world was out there, that it was waiting for them, and if they were going to make it . . . Well then, they would make it. Or they wouldn't. If you chose to collect them from school one day to ensure they'd get home safe, then it could be the following day that a hit and run might kill them at the crosswalk. Life had sharp corners and rough edges. Life had spikes.

Radick asked if Parrish wanted to be dropped at home.

'Precinct,' Parrish said.

'You've been on shift since this morning, Frank. You should go home.'

Parrish smiled. 'It is my home.'

TWELVE

'A dream . . .'

'A dream? More like a nightmare.'

'About the girl?'

'The girl and her brother.'

'Tell me.'

'What's to tell? It's just a dream. Doesn't mean anything.'

'It can do.'

'I don't agree.'

'You don't have to. Just tell me anyway.'

'She talked to me. She was beside me in the car, and she was talking to me.'

'What did she look like?'

'I don't know exactly. I couldn't look sideways at her, could only look directly ahead. And she asked me not to look at her anyway . . . she said she didn't look her best.'

'Because she was dead?'

'I assume so.'

'And what did she say to you?'

'I can't remember.'

'You want to try and remember?'

'It has no significance. I do not think that the solution to her murder is my dreams.'

'*Her* murder? What about her brother?'

'That's a casualty of war. Overdose and murder are just occupational hazards for people like Danny Lange. Anyway, that's not the issue right now.'

'You don't want to talk about this anymore, Frank?'

'No.'

'What do you want to talk about?'

'I was gonna tell you about JFK.'

'I looked up some stuff last night on the internet.'

'What you'll find on the internet and what I can tell you are not the same thing.'

'I know that. I was just reading up some of the history of it.'

'Idlewild?'

'Yes, Idlewild.'

'Well, that was what it used to be, and then, when it became JFK Airport, things didn't change a great deal aside from the scope of what they were getting up to. Even as Idlewild, right from the point it opened in '48, this airport was run by the Mob.'

'Your father used to tell you about all of this?'

'Sure he did. He told me the whole history of the Mafia in New York, how it all started, how it all ended up.'

'And how did that make you feel? When he talked to you about these things?'

'Made me feel he was the smartest guy in the whole freakin' world.'

'A saint, even?'

'The Saints of New York? No, that wasn't for years.'

'So tell me about it. Tell me some of the things he used to talk to you about.'

'Well, to tell you the truth, the height of the Mob's control of New York was from the Thirties to the Fifties, certainly as far as the docks were concerned. That was the International Longshoremen's Association. You saw *On The Waterfront*?'

'Marlon Brando. Yes.'

'Right, Marlon Brando. Anyway, that was all about that shit. The way the unions and the mob controlled which ships could get loaded and unloaded, and whether the crews were working down there. The largest ILA local, Brooklyn 1814, was controlled by a guy named Anthony Anastasio, but they called him "Tough Tony". Anyway, Tough Tony died in '63, and 1814 was taken over by a guy called Anthony Scotto, and he was a big deal. He was a great success in the ILA, and he was also a capo in the Gambino crime family. He had some of the most powerful political connections in New York's history.

'Now, the business coming through the ports and Idlewild

itself had been big, don't get me wrong, but in 1963 when Idlewild became JFK, these guys realized that JFK's traffic would make everything they'd done before seem like pocket change. They saw the possibilities there, not only because of all the merchandise that they could steal from the airport, but also the way in which the freight forwarding could be managed.'

'How do you mean?'

'Well, this goes back to the Fifties. The Teamsters. You've heard of the Teamsters, right?'

'Sure. Jimmy Hoffa and all that.'

'Yeah, Jimmy Hoffa. Well, Teamsters Local 295 was established back in '56 to represent the clerical guys, the dispatchers, and also the truck drivers and the warehousemen employed by the freight-forwarding and trucking companies that served the airport. The Lucchese family controlled 295, and the two guys that ran that show were Johnny Dio – John Dioguardi to give you his full name – and a guy called John McNamara who was the nominal president of 295. So McNamara and Johnny Dio get busted for conspiracy and extortion in '58, and there's this thing called the McClellan Commission set up to investigate all the corruption in this end of the business. Well, they dig deep, and they find out that Jimmy Hoffa created Local 295 and a couple of other paper locals—'

'Paper locals?'

'Sure, locals that just exist on paper, but they don't really exist. Anyway, they find that Hoffa created these outfits to milk as much money out of the freight-forwarders as possible, and that money was going directly to the Lucchese family, and they were supporting Hoffa's candidacy for President of the International Brotherhood of Teamsters. Anyway, there's so much corruption and so much money in all of this. It's a mess. No-one knows who to believe or who to trust. The New York State Investigation Committee gets involved, there's public hearings into racketeering at the airport, but it isn't for ten years that anyone is really charged with anything. That tells you how much they were all involved. Politicians, police, representatives of the Mayor's Office, the FBI, the SIC . . . they were all getting paid off. Finally, in '69, John Gotti takes a fall for three years for hijacking trucks. That was nothing more than a publicity stunt to give everyone the idea that they were really changing things down there.'

'And your father knew about this?'

'I'm getting there. Let me finish with the history. So, 1970, the Luccheses support the creation of Teamsters Local 851, and this outfit represents over two thousand truckers and warehousemen and fourteen hundred clerical people, all of whom were former members of Local 295. New name, old face, right? Anyway, this same old crap goes on. They are pulling merchandise and money out of the airport like there's no tomorrow. Finally, the US Attorney General, John Mitchell, has had enough. It's 1971, and he announces two antitrust indictments against a whole bunch of trucking companies and the entirety of the National Air Freight Association. The shit hits the fan. Everyone pleads no contest, the NAFA is dissolved, and they set up this commission to ensure that air freight price-fixing is prevented.'

'But I guess that doesn't happen, right?'

'The airport is fifteen miles from the center of Manhattan, it accounts for thirty percent of air cargo coming in and going out of the mainland United States. It covers five thousand acres, and there's endless runways, terminal buildings, cargo hangars, warehouses, high-security storage vaults, container stations and truck depots. It has forty thousand people working there. For God's sake, there's the same number of people working there as the whole of the New York Police Department. The thing is managed and run by the Port Authority for New York and New Jersey. The *Port* Authority, right? For New York and *New Jersey*. All the way back to the Fifties, when planes instead of ships started carrying America to the rest of the world, organized crime has been in charge of this stuff. The Luccheses already owned many of the port trucking firms, and they were the backbone of the Metropolitan Importer Truckmen's Association. It was just a matter of switching from one area of business to another. You think that something so insignificant as the US Attorney General and a few court cases are going to stop this shunt they had into the financial arteries of the airport?'

'And that was what your father was involved in?'

'Sure he was. That was what the Saints were all about. If these people needed help from the NYPD they would call the Saints.'

'So how did he manage to get all these commends and citations for his work against organized crime?'

'The Mob gave him people. They sacrificed people every once in a while. A bust or two. A small truck firm folds and somebody gets a couple of years. The trucks get confiscated, they are sequestered in a police compound somewhere, and six months later someone loses the paperwork and they are sold to another trucking firm for peanuts. That was the way it worked.'

'And you never thought to report this to—'

'To who? Report it to who? The police were taking more money than anyone else, and besides, you can't break the police. No-one ever has, and no-one ever will. Aside from the police closing ranks, aside from the fact that Internal Affairs, the very people who are supposed to investigate police corruption, are part of the police department themselves, it is highly unlikely that any congressman or senator would ever sanction the prosecution of anyone higher than a sergeant. Why? Because you can't have the people losing faith in the police. You understand this, right? I don't need to tell you why. You start to point the finger at the people in charge, and society gets very nervous.'

'And when you were younger, when your father was still alive, you knew he was doing this, taking money off organized crime people, turning a blind eye to thefts at the airport?'

'Turning a blind eye? Taking some bribes? Hell, they were doing a hell of a lot more than that.'

'Such as?'

'Well, let's say this. My father spent ten years in the Organized Crime Control Bureau, and then a further ten years in the Brooklyn Organized Crime Task Force. That's twenty years in the guts of this thing. Twenty years investigating these people, talking to them, arresting them. Twenty years up against the worst kind of temptation you could find. The money, the women, the booze, the drugs, the opportunities were limitless, and he and his friends, no more than ten or twelve of them, ran the most successful unit within the NYPD for all that time. They busted more people than anyone else. They secured the greatest number of convictions, the greatest numbers of years of imprisonment, but if you look closely, if you start to look beneath the surface, you'll find that the people they took down were just the foot soldiers, never the under-bosses or the bosses. This was the way it worked. Hell, these assholes even had a roster for who was gonna get busted next. It was part of the game. Three years out working the business, six months in prison. Five years living the life, a year or two in prison. These guys, these Mafia soldiers, even paid each other off to take the fall. So-and-so's wife was pregnant, someone'll take your turn on the roster, do your twelve months for you, but when it comes to his turn you have to take his charge and do his time.'

'And your father did some serious things?'

'He didn't just do them, he organized them. He was instrumental in some of the scams they pulled at the airport.'

'Such as?'

'You like this shit, don't you? You like hearing about this stuff, right? The war stories?'

'It's fascinating. Worrying, to say the least, but fascinating as well.'

'Well, I have to love you and leave you now, but tomorrow we'll talk about Lufthansa, and the better part of six million dollars they took from an airline hangar. Up to then it was the largest heist ever in the history of the United States.'

'And your father—'

'That was a Saints job right from the get-go. And that explains why they only ever recovered a hundred thousand dollars out of the six million, and why the vast majority of the people involved in it wound up dead, and no-one – not one single person – has ever been arrested or charged with those murders.'

'Okay, so you tell me tomorrow. And what is happening with your current cases Frank? The dead girl and her brother?'

'We have to go to work on that today. I have to find her friends, the people she spent her time with.'

'Here in Brooklyn?'

'Williamsburg.'

'She's important to you, isn't she? The girl that was strangled?'

'I don't know. Maybe. I'm not sure what to think about it. Yesterday I saw the woman who took care of her after her parents died. A good woman. She's gonna get some shit for not coloring inside the lines, but that's always the way with these situations. Someone gets hurt, and they can't just leave it at that. The people on the edges have to get hurt as well.'

'You sound like you're taking it personally.'

'No, not really. I'm just a little bitter when it comes to such things.'

'So she has become important to you. Finding out what happened, I mean. More than would be the case usually.'

'Maybe it has. Hell, she's turning up in my dreams, isn't she?'

THIRTEEN

The rain came without warning, and by the time Parrish and Radick reached the outskirts of Williamsburg it was pounding down on the roof of the car.

They sat for a while, hoping it would ease off.

'We do the school first, right?' Radick asked.

'Sure. I called the principal and he's expecting us.'

'And anything more on Danny Lange's friends?'

'Danny Lange didn't have any friends.' Parrish turned and looked at Radick. 'You did Narco, Jimmy. You know how this goes. Junkies are a breed all their own. Addiction is stronger than any loyalty. Friends, family, it all goes by the board. The only thing that will get any of his compadres or associates talking is money.'

'You have money?'

'Don't worry about it,' Parrish replied.

At eleven they left the car and hurried across the street. They checked in at the front lobby, waited for someone to come collect them, and then made their way through a maze of bi-colored hallways to the principal's office.

The principal got up as they were shown in.

'Frank Parrish. We talked on the phone.'

'Of course.'

'This is my partner, Jimmy Radick.'

Radick extended his hand.

'David Carlisle.' Carlisle walked around his desk. 'Please,' he said, 'take a seat.'

Parrish asked the usual questions. Carlisle wasn't defensive.

'I have six hundred students here, Detective. I do my damnedest to keep track of all of them, but it's simply not possible twenty-four seven. Rebecca didn't show for school on Monday morning—'

'She didn't show on Monday?'

'Right. She was here last Friday, and then didn't appear Monday morning.'

'And you contacted her guardian?' Radick asked.

'I'm afraid that's where we fell down, Detective. Strictly speaking we should have called, but we did not. We had a couple of teachers away on a course, we had subs in . . .' Carlisle shook his head wearily.

'But you called on Tuesday?' Parrish said.

'Rebecca's father called us.'

'Her *father*?'

'Yes,' Carlisle said. 'Her father called Student Reception on Tuesday, told them that Rebecca had been ill on Monday, would be back on Wednesday. Then later that day we got a call from this woman, Helen Jarvis, and she said she was Rebecca's legal guardian. That was when Reception informed me of the situation. I didn't tell Miss Jarvis that the girl's father had called, I just called the police immediately. They told me that they had some information on it, and they were waiting for the guardian to file a Missing Persons Report. I then checked our records and we had Helen Jarvis listed as Rebecca's mother, not her guardian. It's not that uncommon to find mothers and daughters with different surnames these days.'

'And did you tell the police about the call from the girl's father?'

'Yes I did.'

Radick was taking notes, and then he looked up at Carlisle. Carlisle was confronting the fact that he had a great deal more to deal with than a missing student.

'She didn't come in on Tuesday because she was already dead,' Parrish said matter-of-factly. 'We can only assume now that her killer called in and posed as her father to delay any alarm being raised about Rebecca's disappearance.'

'Dead?' Carlisle echoed. 'Oh my God . . .'

'She was dead on Monday,' Parrish repeated.

'Oh my good God almighty . . .'

'And whoever called on Tuesday saying that he was the girl's father wasn't her father at all,' Radick said. 'We need to know who you spoke to and at which precinct.'

'Yes . . . er . . . yes, of course. Oh this is terrible. This is truly terrible. I don't know what to say.'

'There isn't a great deal you *can* say, Principal Carlisle. The details of whoever you spoke to at the police precinct would be really appreciated.'

'Yes . . . I think his name was Trevitt. I'll see to it now.'

'So she leaves home at – what? – seven o'clock Monday morning? She comes down to Brooklyn. She's dead somewhere between eight and two. That's a pretty narrow window.'

'But nevertheless enough time to get a haircut and do her nails. More likely, to have someone do that for her, and that was done somewhere specific.'

'And the brother?'

Parrish shook his head. 'He has to have been involved, otherwise it's way too much of a coincidence.'

'Very fucking strange,' Radick said.

'Well, we have some questions to ask of Sergeant Gary Trevitt,' Parrish said, and got out of the car.

Williamsburg 91st Precinct – the same featureless building as a thousand other precinct houses. Radick and Parrish waited in the foyer for a good twenty minutes, and then Trevitt came down the stairs. He looked suspicious before they even introduced themselves. Perhaps he took them for IAD.

'Who?' he asked.

'Rebecca Lange. Sixteen years old. St. Francis of Assisi High School. The principal called you on Tuesday, guy by the name of David Carlisle.'

'Yeah, and the girl's guardian called as well,' Trevitt replied.

'And you told her she had to wait forty-eight hours.'

'Sure I did. That's standard.'

'But she never called back.'

'Couldn't tell you,' Trevitt replied. 'I was off yesterday. The girl showed up yet?'

'Yes,' Parrish replied. 'Showed up dead.'

'Oh fuck,' Trevitt replied. 'And you guys are from where?'

'Brooklyn.'

'And what the hell has this got to do with you?'

'She was killed in our neighborhood. Her brother too.'

'Well, sorry to hear it,' Trevitt said. 'You need anything from me?'

'No,' Parrish replied. 'We're done here.'

Radick drove them back to Brooklyn. The rain had done its worst. The streets were wet and greasy.

'If the brother hadn't been killed I would have said a straight kidnap,' Parrish commented.

'But with the brother in the mix—'

'Means they were involved in something. If it was the Danny Lange I know then it would have been drugs or money. Maybe he had the sister set up for something. It goes bad, she's dead, he does a runner. Whoever it is catches up with him and it's all over.'

'But it's all guesswork right now.'

'Always the way, my friend,' Parrish replied. 'Always the way.'

FOURTEEN

Later, so many more hours of talking this thing back and forth, Parrish sent Radick home for the night. Parrish took the subway to his apartment, called Eve when he got there and was directed to voicemail. That meant she had a client.

He finished a fifth of Bushmills by nine, and went out for another.

He watched TV when he returned. Thought to call Caitlin but decided against it. She would know he'd been drinking and bitch at him for his own good. If it was for his own good how come it felt so bad when she did it?

He tried to focus on Rebecca's motives, her methods, her opportunities. He tried to imagine what might have possessed her to skip school and come to Brooklyn. He knew it wasn't just her brother. He knew it was something else.

He fell asleep on the couch just after eleven. He didn't wake until five and the TV was still on.

FIFTEEN

'So what makes you think she was into something?'

'Her brother, and the fact that she took off from school and came here to Brooklyn. That, and the way she looked . . . her nails, her hair. Her guardian, this Helen Jarvis, said she never used nail varnish and her hair was cut long, but when she died her hair was short. I was up thinking about it last night, and the only idea I had was that maybe Danny got her hooked up with someone. Someone who had money. Maybe he was using her in some way . . .'

'He would have done that to his own sister?'

'You don't know junkies.'

'Okay, but why don't you think she was kidnapped–'

'Because kidnap victims are tied up and beaten usually, and the sex isn't consensual, it's forced. It's rape, and she wasn't raped. She'd had sex, but there were no signs of physical violence, nothing to indicate she'd been held against her will. Truth is, I don't know what to say. Maybe it was an older lover, a man with money . . . maybe there was someone who could afford to have her get a haircut and a manicure.'

'You just don't know, right?'

'I just don't know.'

'So what now?'

'Me and Radick . . . we get to canvass the beauty salons and hair salons and nail manicure places in Brooklyn and Williamsburg. We take a picture around and see if anyone recognizes her.'

'How's it going with your new partner?'

'He's okay.'

'Different from the last one.'

'They're all different. That's how people are.'

'The last one died, didn't he?'

'Yeah, he died.'

'Do you want to say anything about that?'

'No, I don't want to say anything about that.'

'Okay, Frank, I understand . . . So . . . you were going to tell me about the Lufthansa heist.'

'I was. But first I have to tell you about the airport system and the Saints themselves. You have to get a little bit of the back story on this thing otherwise it won't make sense.'

'Go ahead.'

'Well, all the industry on the eastern seaboard relies on JFK to ship their goods out and bring their materials in, right? It involves the shippers themselves, the airlines of course, the freight-forwarding companies who direct business to the airlines from the customers, and then there's the unions. The unions are basically two Teamster Locals, 295 and 851. The 295 has two thousand members – truck drivers, switchers, platform men, hydraulic lift operators, mechanics, garage people and fuelers. Local 851 represents the clerical guys. Here you have the office people and the dispatchers. Make sense?'

'Sure.'

'So, say you have a company. For example, you make shoes. You're gonna send your shoes to wherever in the world. You have however many thousands of pairs and you call up an agent who gets you in with a freight forwarder. The freight forwarder takes on the job, and he can arrange for packing, re-packing, marking, weighing, everything. You have three hundred forwarding companies down there, the majority of which use their own trucks and drivers to go fetch the goods from wherever you make the things and bring it to the airport. The freight forwarders make their money by charging you one rate, and then they pay less than that because they're shipping bulk through the airlines, right?'

'Like any business really. The forwarders are the middlemen.'

'Yeah, the middlemen. So you see how important the freight forwarders are to the airlines. Freight forwarders can make or break an airline by directing traffic their way or not. The guy in the freight forwarding company who has the say-so is the lead agent. He's the big boss of the hot sauce. He's the guy the airlines want to be in with. They got to keep him happy, got to make it worth his while to send the business their way. Well, Local 851 was owned by the Luccheses, and most of the lead agents were represented by 851. Lead agents knew what goods were in which trucks. They knew when it was three hundred tons of butter or six hundred cases of caviar. They knew everything inside out and back-to-front. These were the guys who would arrange the give-ups—'

'The what?'

'The give-ups. It's another kind of hijack. The driver is paid off to leave his keys in the ignition and go get a cup of coffee in a diner somewhere just outside of the airport. A hijacking is a straight thing, no prearrangement with the driver. A crew hijacks a truck they're gonna knock the driver down, steal his keys, whatever they have to do. They go in there with guns, right? With a give-up you have the co-operation of the driver and there's no noise or violence. The Luccheses had an entire network of cargo handlers, packers, drivers and airport security staff working on this thing. Millions and millions and millions of dollars' worth of goods went walking out of that airport into the hands of the Luccheses. The most famous hijacker ever was Jimmy Burke, and he had lines into the airport that told him about potential witnesses and government informants. His success was based solely on the fact that no-one actually ever made it to court to testify against him—'

'Why not?'

'Because he killed them, or at least arranged to have them killed.'

'And your father knew him, I suppose?'

'Sure he did. All the Saints knew Jimmy Burke.'

'So you were going to tell me about them. The Saints.'

'There were twelve in all, and one-for-one they were part of the Organized Crime Control Bureau or the NYPD Internal Affairs Division. They had all bases covered, you see? If a question was raised about the integrity or honesty of one of the OCCB officers, then IAD would investigate and come back with a clean bill of health. They called such things their annual medicals, and they came away like Snow White. A few times they talked about it in the house, treated it like it was some kind of a joke.'

'You met some of them?'

'Some, sure. Hell, I don't remember them all, and I never really spoke to them. A few of them are still around even now. Retired, but alive. Probably own sea-view properties in Pompano Beach, Florida or some such. I remember Don Hunter and George Buranski, and an Italian guy . . . Mario something-or-other . . . Gamba, Mario Gamba. And there was Art Billick and Shaun Beck, and a guy called Randall Kubis. They were the good old boys, you know? They used to come round the house, watch football games, have barbecues. I was a kid, all of six or seven back in the early Seventies, and I was in my teens when my father transferred to the Brooklyn Task Force. I was twenty when I joined the police. That was August of '84, and my father and I didn't see anywhere near as much of one another after that. I made detective in '96, and by that time he'd already been dead for four years.'

'Murdered, I understand.'

'Yes. As were three or four of the original twelve as far as I can work out.'

'How did you feel about that?'

'Feel? Jesus, *I* don't know. What the hell are you supposed to feel when your father is murdered?'

'Were you angry with him?'

'For what?'

'For being corrupt?'

'Angry? No. I don't think anger would have been the appropriate emotion, and I certainly didn't feel that at the time. I think I was just disappointed, you know? All those chances he had to be a decent guy, he just turned out to be an asshole.'

'And your mother died shortly afterwards. What happened?'

'Nothing *happened*. She just died . . . four months later. Went to sleep one night and didn't wake up. Autopsy said it was congenital heart failure, but she was one of those women who lived for her husband and when he was gone there was just no point carrying on.'

'Were you upset?'

'Sure I was. Far more about her than I had been about him.'

'And did she know what her husband was involved in? Did she know that he was corrupt?'

'Of course she did. God, they had more money than he ever could have earned as a cop. They had stashes of cash all over the place. Nothing was ever banked, and there were no records, no receipts, nothing like that. Just shoeboxes and paper bags full of money stuffed down the back of cupboards, and wedged beneath floorboards and under the insulation in the attic. And he kept moving it. Like he figured someone was out there keeping track of where he put it. Sometimes he would just go crazy, digging holes in the back yard and burying it, only to dig it all up again three days later and put it somewhere else.'

'Did you take any of it?'

'God no! I wouldn't have dared. He knew exactly how much was where at any given time.'

'And some of this money came from the Lufthansa robbery?'

'It must have done, yes.'

'How much?'

'I can only guess.'

'So guess.'

'About two hundred thousand dollars, I'd say.'

'And the other men?'

'There were half a dozen of them involved, as far as I could work out. They each got about the same. Two hundred grand, six guys . . . ? That's one point two million. They took the best part of six million, and only a hundred grand was ever recovered.'

'How come they got so much?'

'Because it was a big score. It took a lot of balls to pull that off. This happened in '78, and the case was immediately assigned to the OCCB. They investigated it, of course, and any time they found anyone who knew something, any time they got hold of someone who even *looked* like they might talk, they killed them. All of those guys who were involved, they protected their own interests, they protected Jimmy Burke. It was, as we say, a mutually beneficial arrangement.'

'Your father killed witnesses?'

'Witnesses, informants, all sorts of people. You think that a robbery of that magnitude isn't going to leave things wide open everywhere you look? There were people all over the place, through every level of the Lucchese family, who knew about Jimmy Burke and the Lufthansa heist. They couldn't afford to have anyone talking. Not only would they have lost their jobs, but they would have gone to jail and they would've had to give back the money. Back in '78 a couple of hundred grand was a huge amount of money.'

'So tell me what happened at JFK.'

'JFK? JFK was like a bottomless purse for these guys. They kept putting their hands in it, and back they came all full of money again.'

'I'd like to know more about your father. The people he worked with.'

'Well, you and I are going to have to talk about that tomorrow. I have to go trawl the hair salons and beauty parlors with Radick and show the girl's picture.'

'You know, Frank, you're supposed to be here for an hour every day, and mostly you stay for half of that. And you waste time going out to get coffee.'

'So what? You're gonna tell on me?'

'No, Frank, I'm not going to tell on you.'

'Well, you got me talking. Take a win on that, eh? Take a win on the fact that you got Frank Parrish talking about his old man. Keep this up and you'll have me crying like a baby on the couch and wanting to tell my mom how bad I've been.'

'I'll see you tomorrow, Frank . . . a little later. Say ten-thirty?'

'You work Saturdays?'

'Yes. And good luck with the girl.'

'Appreciated.'

SIXTEEN

It made sense to start in Brooklyn, so they did. Three blocks each way from Danny Lange's apartment. They stayed together, walking the streets and visiting beauty salons, boutiques, manicurists, pedicurists, hairstylists, even massage parlors, in the hope that there might be some small unit in back that filed and painted nails.

Once they had exhausted all possibilities, they drove north-east to Williamsburg and started all over again. Three blocks each way from Helen Jarvis's house, knocking on doors only to have those doors closed abruptly on them; asking questions; producing IDs, showing the picture – *What do you say her name was? Rebecca what?* – and then winding up back at the car no wiser than when they'd started. No-one had recognized Rebecca, seemed like no-one *wanted* to recognize her.

As far as Radick could see they had covered all bases. The school principal, Trevitt at the Williamsburg 91st Precinct, Helen Jarvis; they'd even submitted a request for a complete schedule of all calls received by Rebecca's school at the time in question. How many calls there would be Radick had no idea, or whether they'd have a prayer of isolating the one that came in from the girl's fictitious father . . . It was a futile activity, he knew that, but it was an avenue that had to be pursued.

'Her friends,' Parrish said. 'I'm going to go over to the school and talk to her friends. And I want to go alone.'

Radick questioned his decision.

'One is less intimidating, less official. These are kids we're talking to.'

Radick said he'd drive Parrish over there. They agreed that if anything came up in conversation with one of the kids then Parrish would have to get Radick back over there to witness any statement. If Parrish took it alone it would not be valid.

Parrish called David Carlisle, the principal, who was wary, but didn't refuse the request. He did say, however, he would have to have the school counsellor present for all interviews.

The partners drove to the school after lunch. They arranged that Parrish would call Radick to pick him up when he was done – if he didn't need Radick sooner.

Carlisle was good to his word, and had set aside an office for Parrish and the counsellor.

'Ruth Doyle,' she said, introducing herself with a firm and businesslike handshake. *I am here on the same terms*, that handshake said. *I can cut it with the best of you.* She had on a skirt suit – the kind of not-too-casual-not-too-smart outfit that said she was here to do a job, but she could still relate to the kids. Parrish had seen a hundred thousand such people – in Social Services, Child Services, Welfare – and they all said the same things and thought the same thoughts. They were servants of the bureaucratic machine and, however hard they tried to make a difference, they were still rigidly bound by a system that dictated they possess no initiative.

'We have a good two dozen,' she told Parrish. 'These are people that knew Rebecca by name, shared classes, some of the friends she hung out with. We appreciate the need for this, but the truth of the matter is that they are all pretty shaken up by what's happened. The principal said a few words to the whole school yesterday, and we've had a priest in from St. Barnaby's to talk to the ones that needed . . . well, the ones that took it hardest.'

'I really appreciate your help,' Parrish said, and he smiled as sincerely as he could. His head hurt from the night before. He'd chewed a couple of aspirin on the way over, and the bitter aftertaste hung there in the back of his mouth. He could have used a cup of coffee but he knew that getting one would be more trouble than it was worth.

First up was a frail and timid girl with thick-lensed spectacles. She spent five minutes trying not to look scared, and seemed extraordinarily relieved to get out of the room. Next was a dark-haired teenager who said he'd dated Rebecca.

'Well, kind of dated,' he added, smiling awkwardly. He had

braces top and bottom, his hand hovering in front of his mouth in an effort to hide them when he spoke. 'We were just friends really. But this was like six, twelve months ago, and we never really went anyplace, you know? We just hung out. We were into the same kind of tunes, that's all.'

Third was a girl not dissimilar in height and build to Rebecca, but her hair was darker, longer, tied back behind her head in a ponytail. She cried from start to finish, in her hand a balled-up fist of Kleenex, a metal stud in her tongue that seemed to make speech a chore.

After an hour Parrish was fading. Ten gone, thirteen or fourteen to go.

It was a young man called Greg Kaufman that changed things.

Like that other girl that my sister knew.

'I'm sorry?' Parrish said.

'The other girl. The other one who died last year. It reminded me of that. I mean, Rebecca I didn't know very well really. We took a couple of classes together and she seemed real nice, but when I heard about it I thought of the girl that died last Christmas, you know? I think she was strangled as well.'

'What girl?'

'I don't remember her name – Clara, Carla, Carly – something like that. My sister would know. My sister and her were real good friends.'

'And your sister is here at this school?'

'No, she's at Waterbury up near the Grand Street subway station.'

'And your sister's name?'

'Hannah, Hannah Kaufman.'

Parrish made a note of it.

One other girl provided something of interest. Brenda Grant said she and Rebecca had spoken about Danny, Rebecca's brother.

'Becca told me he knew he was in trouble about something or other.' She looked up at Parrish nervously. 'You know – um – I guess you know he was into drugs, right?' She asked the question hesitantly, as if this was somehow her fault.

'Yes, Brenda, I knew Danny quite well.'

'Well, I don't know if this trouble he was in was anything to do with the drugs, but Becca told me that she was really worried about him, that he might have gotten himself into some difficulties.'

'Did she say what kind of difficulties? Or who he might have been in trouble with?'

'No, sir, she didn't say anything specific, just that she thought he was into something deep, and she was worried about him.'

'Did you know that Rebecca used to run away from home to spend time with Danny?'

Brenda glanced at Ruth Doyle.

'It's okay, Brenda,' Doyle said. 'Detective Parrish is here to find out as much as he can about what might have happened to Becca. He's not going to get mad or anything like that, and you're certainly not in any trouble.'

'Yes, she told me that she would go there at weekends sometimes. Not every weekend.'

'And did she say what they used to do together?'

Brenda frowned.

'Like they would hang out, maybe go see movies, or go see a band? Something like that?'

'I don't know what they used to do. She just used to tell me that she'd been to see her brother at the weekend or whatever, and I would ask how he was, and she would say he was good, or he was doing better, and sometimes she would say he was doing worse.'

'And do you know if Rebecca ever took drugs?'

'No way, never in a million years. She wasn't like that at all. She was really serious about that kind of thing.'

'Okay, Brenda, this is really appreciated.'

'Is that all?' Brenda asked, and started to rise from her chair.

'One other little thing,' Parrish said. 'Did she ever use nail varnish?'

'Huh?'

'Nail varnish. To color her nails, you know?'

'No, I don't think she did. She didn't use a lot of make-up or anything like that. She had really nice skin . . .' Brenda hesitated. She seemed confused for a moment. 'She had really nice skin,' she repeated, and then it seemed to Frank Parrish that she was ready to cry. It seemed that perhaps she had put it all on hold, and finally – in that moment, having to remember so much about her friend – she had at last confronted the simple fact that her friend was dead. She knew then that Becca wasn't ever coming back because someone had choked her to death.

SEVENTEEN

Parrish left St. Francis of Assisi School at a quarter to four. He should have called Radick, had him drive over and pick him up, but instead he walked to the subway station and took a ride to Grand Street. He found the Waterbury School without difficulty, presented himself, his ID, asked to see the principal.

Principal Bergen, another capable, forthright, uncomplicated type, granted Parrish an audience without hesitation. She was an attractive woman, wore a wedding band.

'I am working on a murder investigation,' Parrish told her. 'A student from the St. Francis School was found strangled. I spoke to a friend of hers and she mentioned that you might have had—'

'Karen Pulaski,' Bergen said. 'That's who you're talking about.'

'What was the deal with that?'

'Last Christmas, couple of days after, the twenty-eighth I think, she was found strangled. She had only recently joined the school. Had been here – I don't know – six months, nine perhaps. It was a terrible, terrible thing.'

'And the case was never solved?'

'Not that I'm aware of, Detective. I haven't heard anything for a several months now. I can only assume that if it was solved the police would've had the courtesy to inform me.'

'Never guaranteed, Mrs Bergen,' Parrish replied. 'I can find out for you and let you know.'

'Don't trouble yourself, Detective. Perhaps it's better to go on assuming that it was resolved swiftly and expediently, but the relevant detectives have been so busy with other incidents that they just forgot to let me know.'

Parrish didn't reply. He knew the case was open. He just felt it.

'And the investigating officers on the case?' he asked.

Bergen shook her head. 'I don't remember now. They came up from the nearest precinct, over near Gardner and Metropolitan I think.'

'I'll find out,' Parrish said.

'You think your girl and ours were murdered by the same person?' Bergen asked.

Parrish shrugged. 'I shouldn't think so, Mrs Bergen, but I have to follow up everything I can, you see? Sometimes it's little more than a formality, other times it goes somewhere.'

Bergen rose and walked Parrish to the door.

'Appreciate your time,' he told her.

'You're welcome, Detective. Good luck.'

Parrish called Radick from a payphone.

'Go on home, Jimmy,' he said. 'I'm still over in Williamsburg. I'll get the subway back. You take off, have a good evening, and I'll do the Active Invest report when I get back.'

'How d'you get on over there?'

'Not a great deal of anything. Couple of things to check up on, but nothing positive as yet.'

'Thanks for doing the report, Frank.'

'Sure. No problem. See you tomorrow.'

Parrish walked three blocks and found a diner. He was starving hungry, freezing cold.

The special was some kind of mystery meat stew. A lot of carrots, little substance. He ate it anyway. After that he took the subway from Grand to Jefferson, walked up Flushing Avenue to Stewart, took a left and walked the six blocks to Scholes. Here he turned right and found the Williamsburg 91st Precinct on Gardner and Metropolitan.

They were helpful enough. The desk sergeant found him a uniform, the uniform showed him where Actives were stored, and by seven Parrish was seated in the station house canteen with the Karen Pulaski file open in front of him.

Everything seemed to be present. Records of date, time of dispatch, dispatch number; number of the city ambulance unit that responded; name, unit and number of the first officer at the scene; the incident tracking number, the name of the attending Homicide detective – Richard Franco – the

ME's report. The crime scene pictures were there, and the Q&A sheets from the initial canvass; lists of evidence-bag numbers for her shoes, her clothes, her belongings; the crime lab report, and reference numbers for the skin, hair and blood samples for later DNA comparisons.

Karen had been sixteen when she died. From her crime scene pictures she seemed not unlike Rebecca – fresh-faced, youthful, blonde. There were similar abrasions, bruising and ligature marks around her neck and throat, but Karen had not been strangled manually. A quarter-inch rope, Parrish guessed, perhaps even a cable.

There were indications of recent sexual intercourse, even semen deposits, but the DNA report and coding analysis from January of 2008 indicated that the sample had not matched anyone on file within the New York database. Karen appeared to have been an only child. Her parents – Elizabeth and David Pulaski – lived about eight or nine blocks south on Troutman Street. Both employed, the father a management accountant, the mother a receptionist for a local orthodontist. Karen had gone to see friends on the 26th, the day after Christmas. By all accounts she had boarded a bus on Irving Avenue opposite Bushwick Park, and vanished into nowhere. Two days later, approximately four in the afternoon of December 28th, her body had been found in a dumpster behind a hotel on Humboldt Street. Detective Franco had been thorough. He had traced the bus driver, and then a couple of other passengers had come forward as a result of a newsflash on the 29th, but then it went quiet.

Karen's friends, her boyfriend, her parents, even the girls she knew from a local mall, seemed to have shed no light on what might have happened. She had far better than average grades at school, seemed happy at home, was pretty and popular. If she had run away she hadn't made it far. Time of death, though rarely accurate, said she drew her last breath between eight and midnight, night of the 27th. The dumpster where her body had been left was the secondary, and no primary had been found. Six, twelve, even twenty-four-hour TOD spreads weren't uncommon. Unless liver temp. was taken on site the DC would've had to have gone by rigor. Rigor is evident in the smaller facial muscles and the ends of the fingers within a couple of hours, but rigor sets in, dissipates, and then returns over a more substantial time frame, and thus accurate determination of the victim's time of death from rigor has to be done twice over a span of some hours. And an external crime scene is far more difficult.

Even with an internal, crime scene evidence starts to deteriorate as soon as it becomes a crime scene. A homicide detective who appreciated this fact would deal with the body last. The body was going nowhere, no-one would touch it, whereas fibers, hairs, footprints, anything transient, would vanish fast. Inside, you didn't have to deal with inclement weather, the wind and rain wiping away all traces of who'd been there. With a property you could ascertain ownership: was there forced entry, and if no forced entry then the possibility that the perp was perhaps known to the vic? You might have an apartment block where people were aware of the comings and goings of their neighbors, curiosity occasioned by an unfamiliar face. The physical evidence left by a killer was far easier to isolate in an enclosed room than in a snow-covered tenement alleyway littered with broken bottles, spent needles and garbage. What was absent was often as important as what was there. And the more police that were present, the more difficult it became to control the scene; even experienced people made mistakes, and sometimes the DC – the individual whose job it was to authorize the movement of the body – often came in and made his initial examination before the detective had finished.

The Holy Trinity – physical evidence, eyewitnesses and confessions. Without the first two it was rare to obtain the third.

In the cases of both Rebecca Lange and Karen Pulaski, there was little physical evidence, no eyewitnesses, and thus no-one to interrogate.

The similarities between the two cases were the approximate age and appearance of the girls, and the fact that they had been strangled. But Rebecca had been choked by hand, whereas Karen had been strangled with a rope.

Parrish closed the file and returned it to the office from where he'd taken it.

He left the 91st a little after eight, walked back to Jefferson, took the subway to Lorimer Street. Here he changed lines and headed south to Brooklyn – Broadway, Flushing, Myrtle-Willoughby, Bedford-Nostrand, south-west to Clinton-Washington, and then a handful of minutes walk along Lafayette until he reached Clermont.

He stopped at the liquor store on the corner of DeKalb and bought a bottle. He was hungry again, wondered if there were any frozen pizzas left in the apartment. He took a gamble and skipped the Seven-Eleven. He could always come back if there was nothing at home. Come to that, he could always have another couple of glasses and forget about eating altogether . . .

He waited for the elevator, aware that one of his neighbors waited too. He did not acknowledge her until the elevator door opened, and then he realized it was the woman from the floor beneath. Mrs Langham, he believed. Her daughter was with her, couldn't have been more than six or seven years old. Parrish held the elevator door, allowed them entry first, and he smiled at Mrs Langham. The woman did not smile back. She either knew he was police and disapproved, or she didn't know and disapproved anyway. The bottle in his hand perhaps didn't contribute to the atmosphere. She more than likely knew he lived alone, and in this building – perhaps not a great deal different from many other buildings across the city – people didn't feel comfortable with a police officer as a neighbor. Until they got burgled, or someone tried to mug them on the stairwell. Then you became the most important person in the world.

Parrish was aware of the little girl staring.

He looked down and smiled at her.

The little girl beamed back at him – such enthusiasm, such lack of preconceptions.

Parrish opened his mouth to speak, but was cut short by the mother, invoking maternal authority in a forced whisper.

'Grace . . . stop staring. It's rude.'

Parrish watched the little girl's smile vanish, and then the elevator stopped, the doors opened, and Grace Langham and her disapproving mother stepped out.

The little girl turned as the doors came to, and she raised her hand in farewell.

Parrish waved back, and they were gone.

Frank Parrish was in his kitchen by eight-forty-five. He was a third of a bottle down by nine-thirty, and he made do with a can of tuna that he found at the back of the cupboard.

EIGHTEEN

Parrish awoke before nine. From his bathroom window the sky was five shades of gray and lent the day an air of disappointment before it had begun.

He remembered the report he was meant to have completed, the Active Investigation Summary. Squad Sergeant Valderas would read him the riot act if it wasn't done by noon, but Parrish could not take his attention from Rebecca and, behind those thoughts, Karen.

Last night he had reviewed all these things. The trouble with the clear-headedness of a drinker was that the brief and brilliant moments of clarity did not survive. Sometimes because there were just too many thoughts, other times there seemed to be a single idea that overwhelmed all other considerations. The explosion that caps an oil fire.

During his deepest hours Frank Parrish would resolve his marriage, the disillusionment of his career, the conflict with Caitlin, even his own *raison d'être*. All these things would appear simple and straightforward – until morning.

Sometimes the drink turned ideas into dreams, but more often into nightmares.

He knew he had changed, become bitter, cynical even. As if the person he used to be was trapped somewhere else, pacing back and forth across the span of some unknown room – waiting, expectant.

He seemed possessed by some strange obligation to peer into the darkest and most hidden recesses of the world. Not only that, but to reach his hands inside and bring the darkness out. And this had fixed him where he stood, while the rest of the world had moved on. Clare, Caitlin, Robert:

they had all moved forward, yet he continued flogging himself on the same treadmill.

Frank Parrish began each case with renewed hope. A hope as big as Christmas. All homicide investigations were reactive. Nothing happened until someone died, and then everything happened. Get to twenty-four, forty-eight hours from the event and already things were growing cold and dry. Potential witnesses had second thoughts; the human instinct to tell what you saw, even what you *thought* you saw, was transformed into the fundamental instinct for self-preservation. Better to say nothing. Better not to get involved.

Some truths had been so well-hidden they became sacrosanct. Some cases would never be solved.

He thought often of those who survived, who somehow had navigated the awkwardness of childhood; of those who suffered falls from high places with nothing to show for the experience but bruises and vertigo. People endured the pain of broken love affairs, disastrous marriages and shattered families. Too many years he had spent breaking up the kind of domestics where violence was always the first port of call. Fight first, talk later. Or just keep on fighting and never talk at all. Crimes of passion, of opportunity, of human error. All this they survived, only to be killed stone-dead by a drunk driver or an opportunist mugger. One moment they were there, and then they were gone. The scene was processed, the tapes rolled up and stowed away, the Fire Department hosed down the sidewalk and the world was back to rights. And more often than not those deaths were without rhyme or reason. Rare was the killing dictated by malice aforethought. The psychos and serial killers were in the minority. The motive and rationale back of most murders was simple: for love, for money, for nothing. Only a few were murdered for a killer's gratification.

Sometimes he sat on the subway and looked at people. He would watch them unaware, and wonder who might not make it to Christmas. Even as they reviewed the complications of their own lives, considering possibilities, formulating plans, those complications were pointless and redundant. They would be dead before they saw another birthday.

Perhaps his behavior betrayed a pessimistic nature, but it served to remind him of the fragility of things. And he had yet to find so much darkness that it stopped him looking. Perhaps the more he found, the more he became inured to it, so that he stopped perceiving darkness, but simply saw shadows . . .

As far as homicides were concerned, the first twelve hours were vital. Beyond twelve hours the dead stopped talking. Evidence was destroyed, conspirators collaborated on a common and plausible alibi, weapons were dispatched to the unrelenting depths of the East River or Maspeth Creek. Speed was of the essence, and yet speed sometimes sabotaged thoroughness and attention to detail. The secret was in the balance, and so many times the balance was anything but right. And later, in those moments of quiet reflection, there was always time to consider what he might have done better. What was it Jackson Browne used to sing? Something about not confronting him with his failures, that such things were never forgotten?

When Frank Parrish was married it was a matter of pushing it all aside. Drinking. Pain pills. Starting with three or four, then another and yet another until whatever was keeping him awake was subdued.

Face the truth, Frank. No-one ever got better from drinking.

The echo of Clare's voice in his head.

And then the children came along, Caitlin especially. Caitlin had been his conscience, his salvation, his redemption, and yet a mirror for his guilt. Caitlin was the darkest of all his nights, the brightest of all his days. The most brilliant light always cast the deepest shadows. And *those* shadows . . . ? The shadows of his own failures as a father? For him there was no darker place than that.

That morning he did not eat breakfast. He left the apartment shortly before nine and took the elevator. Once again he coincided with Mrs Langham and Grace, and once again Grace was reprimanded for staring.

Grace went on looking at Parrish as if he carried all the secrets of the grown-up world in the creases of his face.

Mrs Langham, however, looked awkward, as if to say, *I'm sorry for my daughter . . . she isn't embarrassed, and neither are you, but for some reason I am.*

Parrish just smiled at her, and when he stepped back to allow them exit from the elevator he said, "Bye, Grace. You have a good day, okay?'

He walked from the apartment block and took the subway to Hoyt Street.

In the Homicide Division squad room, he found the week-end-shift detectives – Paul Hayes, Bob Wheland, Mike Rhodes and Steve Pagliaro. Mumbled greetings, the odd jibe, and Parrish was then in back surveying the case board. Date initiated, detectives assigned, a series of boxes that were checked as the administrative requirements were fulfilled – Crime Scene, DC's Report, autopsy, rape kit, tox, a box headed Suspect/s which was only checked if someone was brought in on a realistic possibility of charge and arraignment – and over on the far side, a box that was filled with a number that increased each day the case remained active. If the case was closed that box was filled with a black "X". Black Xs were the thing that Lieutenant Myerson and Captain Haversaw required in a daily report from Squad Sergeant Valderas. The Active Investigations Summary Report was completed by each lead detective after a complete shift, whether it be three days, five days, or two and a half hours in the case of overtime. It was a laborious process, the re-defining of each homicide, a paragraph or two detailing what had been done thus far – the people interviewed, whether or not the investigating officer had reason to consider them a suspect, the in-office interrogations that had been undertaken, the results of those interrogations, and on and on. Parrish still had active cases, but for him it was simple.

Rebecca was not a hooker or a dealer or a thief. She was never meant to survive the same occupational hazards as the others. You got yourself involved in the sex-for-sale industry and you were a magnet for flakes and psychos. And if you came up from the projects with your pockets full of crack, if you fronted for someone, if you gypped someone, then it was all too understandable if you wound up with a five-inch paring knife in your throat. Such eventualities went with the territory. Danny Lange was a junkie. With junkies it was not *if*, but *when*. Not *whether*, but *how*. An overdose, an accident while stoned, a hallucination that put you wandering in the Colorado mountains when really you were jaywalking into six lanes of traffic on the Brooklyn-Queens Expressway. Once again, occupational hazards.

But Rebecca was different. Rebecca was the only one that really mattered. And it wasn't simply that she reminded him of Caitlin. It wasn't that she was orphaned or had a piece-of-shit junkie brother. It wasn't that her St. Francis of Assisi friends considered her quiet and funny and sweet and pretty. It was something else. A reminder that if there was no-one there to look after you, no-one to keep an eye on things, then the world and all its wonders would devour you in a heartbeat.

You were there, and then you were gone.

Why had she run to her brother? Why had she left Williamsburg for Brooklyn? Why did she have her hair cut and paint her nails? Who did she have sex with? Was it consensual?

He wondered whether the tox test had ever been done. He picked up the phone and called the Coroner's Office. He gave the case number, Rebecca's name, waited while the attending receptionist looked her up.

'No tox,' she came back. 'Don't have one scheduled. You need one done?'

'Please, yes,' Parrish replied. 'I was told we would get one but I never heard back.'

'Well, someone screwed up then, didn't they? I'll book it, but it won't be until Monday now. I don't have the people here to handle backlogged tox tests.'

'What's your name?'

She gave it.

'I'll call you Monday afternoon and see what the deal is.'

'You do that, Detective, and have a good weekend.'

Parrish hung up, made a note in his diary to call on Monday.

He completed his report, dropped it in the basket by the door, and then retrieved the rest of the cigar-box money from the lower drawer of his desk.

'You outta here?' one of the uniforms asked as Parrish came down the corridor.

'Not a prayer,' Parrish replied. 'Here all day.'

'You still off the road?'

'Yeah, until January. I get my license back after the New Year.'

The uniform made some comment, but Parrish didn't hear it as he went down the stairs to Marie Griffin's office.

NINETEEN

'You've heard of the Valachi papers?'

'It sounds familiar.'

'Joseph Valachi. First guy to ever really break ranks in the mob. His testimony opened up the whole thing, gave people a look inside something that had only ever been a myth. It all went back to a guy called Joseph Masseria back in the early Thirties. Masseria said that any underworld figure from a place called Castellammarese de Golfo in Sicily was to be killed. What followed was called the Castellammarese War. One faction was led by Masseria, the other by a guy called Salvatore Maranzano. Other gangs allied themselves to either one or the other. Vito Genovese, Lucky Luciano, Dutch Schultz and Al Capone supported Masseria, but in 1931 Masseria was assassinated by order of Luciano, and that was the end of the war. Maranzano called together about four hundred people from all the different families in order to establish some kind of structure for their activities and territories. Maranzano himself was also assassinated a few months later, but the structure he put in place still holds to this day. They started infiltrating legitimate businesses right from the get-go. You've heard of Arthur Miller, right?'

'Playwright Arthur Miller, who married Marilyn Monroe?'

'That's the guy. Well, as early as '51 the *New York Daily Compass* commissioned him to report on Senator Estes Kefauver's hearings on organized crime, and it was already coming to light that the Mob controlled the unions on the city's waterfront. Columbia, Union Street, the Red Hook district . . . that's where Capone and Frankie Yale and others from Murder Incorporated came from. Even then they had already instituted something called the "shape-up".'

'Which was?'

'Basically, it meant that a dockworker or a longshoreman

didn't have a working contract. It meant that he had to show up for work at the docks every day, and he had to be hired newly each day. That kept everyone on their toes. Made people grateful to work. Made them accept lower wages. A lot of these guys remembered the end of the Depression, and if they didn't know it personally, they knew it from their fathers. Within fifty years there were twenty-four different organized crime families operating in the US. A city usually had one family running it, but New York was the only city that had more than one. There were five here: Genovese, Gambino, Lucchese, Bonnano and Colombo. Back in '83 a guy called William Webster was the Director of the FBI. He testified before the President's Commission on Organized Crime that there were approximately seventeen thousand soldiers and about seventeen hundred made men.'

'Made men?'

'It's a rank, a status if you like. It's awarded to a guy by the family he works for. A made man cannot be killed by another family without the express authority of the head of the made man's family. So say you have a Gambino who wants to kill a made man in the Colombo family. Well, the rules say that he can't do that unless a Colombo boss gives the go-ahead.'

'And the families had complete control over running the unions and the docks?'

'They ran a great deal more than that. They were into clothing, construction, furs, flower shops, the entirety of the Fulton Market. They had butchers, funeral parlors, barbershops, milk delivery companies, box manufacturers, window cleaners, and an entire network of taxicab firms that spider-webbed across the whole neighborhood. They ran everything, inside and out, so when someone came along and said they were going to turn the old Idlewild Golf Course into an airport, well what better business could they get into? Fifty thousand staff, ten thousand car-parking spaces, five thousand acres just to begin with. The payroll at Idlewild was half a billion, and that was in the mid-Nineteen-Fifties. These guys came from East New York, South Ozone Park, Howard Beach, Maspeth and the Rockaways. Everyone wanted a piece of the pie, and the truth of the matter was that the pie was so fucking big they could keep on taking and keep on taking and it would never run out.'

'So what about the police, the authorities who ran the place?'

'What about them?'

'Well, didn't they have security in place? Didn't they have the local police taking care of security for the airport?'

'The Port Authority had over a hundred uniformed police on the airport grounds every day. They had customs inspectors, FBI, additional police from the 103rd Precinct, but you're talking about five thousand acres of land and buildings. Take, for example, the US Customs building. I don't remember how many floors it had – ten, twelve, something like that. Huge place. People in and out. No security to speak of. And here were the pigeonholes that carried the consignment notes and bills of lading for every shipment that came though the airport. In the early Sixties there was thirty billion dollars' worth of stuff coming through Idlewild. So the airport loses thirty million dollars' worth of traffic, that's only a tenth of one percent. Even three hundred million is only one percent. They claim it off the insurance, the insurance pays up, the insurance company hikes the premium, but all in all it's a hell of a lot less hassle than hiring more security – managers and stuff – and the cost of it, you know? As far as the airport was concerned, it was par for the course.'

'And the police that were there . . . they took bribes as well?'

'Of course they did. Police, Customs people, even some of the federal guys. Take airline tickets, for example. Guys would come down with dozens of stolen credit cards and buy up a bucket-load of tickets. Then they would get cash for them, sometimes sell them at a discount. Frank Sinatra did a national tour on a wad of stolen airline tickets.'

'You're kidding—'

'Absolutely true. He had a manager called Dante Barzottini. He bought fifty thousand dollars' worth of airline tickets off of someone that had paid for them with stolen cards. He used them to transport Frank Sinatra and eight other people around the country. Barzottini got busted for that and they put him away.'

'And no-one ever came forward and testified against these people?'

'They tried to, of course, but people got killed. Informants, witnesses, as many as a dozen a year. And the thing that made the most money for these guys was the hijackings. They were kings of hijacking. You remember I mentioned Jimmy Burke? Well, he was so damned good at hijacking that the Colombo family in Brooklyn and the Luccheses in Queens shared his services. That was the first and only time I'm aware of where one guy ended up working for two different families. He had people in his own crew – people like Tommy DeSimone, Angelo Sepe, another guy called Skinny Bobby Amelia – but the real prize was Jimmy Santos. Santos was an ex-cop who got busted for armed robbery. He did his time and then he went over to the bad guys. Well, Jimmy Santos knew everyone. He knew who was good and who wasn't, and who would take money, or who wouldn't. He knew which guys had mistresses and which were stretched with alimony payments. He knew which cops gambled, and out of those who owed the most money. He got word out through his contacts in the PD, and he got the people he wanted transferred over to the airport detail. By the time they were through they had maybe half the police on the airport working for them, and that's how come my father got involved.'

'He knew Santos.'

'He knew of him. My father was already a sergeant in '67. He was here in Brooklyn, ran the department that processed all the paperwork for inter-precinct transfers. He had a couple of guys in his own precinct who wanted to move to the airport, which had become JFK by then. Anyway, he thought this was strange, two of his best people wanted out to the same detail within two or three months of each other, so he dug a little and found the connection to Santos. And what did he do? He went to Santos directly, said he couldn't have the men, not without paying up. You ask me about my father, you ask me what kind of man he was? That's who he was. A crook. No question about it. Santos started giving my father a monthly amount, just a couple of hundred dollars to make the transfers go smooth. My father would

get the tip-off on which transfers were Santos's, and he'd
hurry them through. That arrangement went on until my
father moved to Organized Crime Control Bureau in 1972.
Then they had the airport as their territory, and right at the
top of their jurisdictional and operational priorities was
cleaning up the scene down there.'

'But they didn't, did they?'

'They cleaned up, that's for sure, and my asshole of a father
was right inside of it all. Just in the ten months from the start
of '67 to October, two point two million dollars' worth of
goods went out of JFK. That was the actual value of goods
taken right out of the storage bins and security rooms of the
Air Cargo Center. TWA also lost two and half million dollars'
worth of stock, and those figures don't take into account any
of the goods that were hijacked beyond the airport limits.
Believe me, Doctor Marie, the stuff that was stolen out of JFK
was pocket change compared to what they took once the
trucks had left the perimeter.'

'These were the hijacks and the give-ups?'

'Yes. Well – one of the difficulties the OCCB and the police
had at the time was that the New York State Legislature
hadn't officially codified hijacking as a felony. Anyone who
got busted for hijacking actually had to be charged with
robbery or kidnapping, maybe firearms offences or possession of stolen property . . . stuff like that. And because
hijacking a truck wasn't in the statute books yet, there was a
loophole for these guys. They had the money to buy up the
best lawyers, and they paid off the courts to delay hearings
and postpone arraignments. I heard one time that one case
was kept rolling back and forth between the courts and the
DA's Office for eleven years, and by the time it actually came
to court they fined the guy two hundred and fifty dollars.'

'Which brings us to Lufthansa.'

'Yes, it does, except—'

'Except you have to go now.'

'I'm afraid I do.'

'Well, if nothing else it's been interesting, Frank.'

'Tomorrow. We talk about Lufthansa tomorrow.'

'Tomorrow is Sunday.'

'Monday then?'

'Monday it is.'

'You going to manage without me for a whole day?'

'I'm sure I'll cope somehow, Frank.'

'Well, you have my file there, and my phone number's got to be in there somewhere. You feel like you need to talk to someone then you give me a call, okay?'

'That's very good of you.'

'You take care now.'

'You too, Frank, you too.'

TWENTY

As if all the parts had been put together by a clumsy child, the seams of his life gaped wide and would not close with time. This was how Parrish felt sometimes.

Other times he felt driven by a purpose, incandescent and fierce. *Blood on the teeth*, the Scandinavians said. You caught the scent. The case had a hook and it pulled you. You pulled back and it started to unravel like a ball of twine. Back in the Forties sometime, at least from Parrish's perspective, the law and justice seemed to diverge. The law served its own end, and then it served the lawyers. Justice, once fast and cheap, was laborious and expensive, as rare as a prize diamond. People read fiction, they watched movies, they wanted life to be like that, but it was not. The good guys did not always win out, and the bad guys stayed bad and free. Frank Parrish believed himself one of a dying breed. Someone who gave a damn. He did not believe himself an arbiter of justice or a staunch testament to the law, but there were cases he had pursued in his time that had resolved through sheer persistence and an indomitable sense of purpose. And it was always children. As he had so long considered, for the children there could be no reason, no excuse. And though neither Rebecca nor Karen were children, they were young enough to be unaware of the snares and pitfalls that lay in wait. The dark spirits of the city had been out in force, and they had been too naïve, too innocent, to see them. And if Frank Parrish didn't care what had happened, then who would?

He carried a notebook in his pocket, and sometimes he wrote down thoughts that came to mind. Seated in a coffee house three or four blocks south of the Precinct, somewhere down near Schermerhorn, he scribbled down a line he remembered from a Tom Waits song. The one about how there wasn't really a Devil, that it was just God when He was drunk.

He drank his coffee. He waited for Jimmy Radick to come meet him. He thought of Rebecca, of Karen, and he tried so very hard to believe their deaths were unrelated. But he was unable to convince himself. It was then that he decided to go out and see Karen's parents.

Radick was there just after eleven-thirty. Parrish told him what he wanted to do.

'And you want to go alone again, right?'

'I think it's best. This is now crossing precincts—'

'And what was her name?'

'Karen Pulaski, P-U-L-A-S-K-I.'

'And you really think there's a connection between her and the Lange girl?'

Parrish shook his head. 'Instinctively, yes. In reality? Probably not. But I've got to check it out. It'll bug the hell out of me until I do.'

'OK. I'll head back to the squad room. What do I tell Valderas?'

'Say you don't know where I am. Tell him we're meeting later, that we're starting the shift late, that you've just come in early to do paperwork or something.'

Radick got up. 'Call me if you need me, okay?'

'Sure I will,' Parrish replied.

Parrish left Brooklyn at noon. He walked a while and then took the subway at Nevis Street. Between Fulton and Clinton-Washington he instinctively looked left towards his own apartment. A woman sat facing him and to the right. She was reading *Trying To Save Piggy Sneed*. She glanced up at Parrish, and Parrish smiled. He opened his mouth to say something about the book, but her expression cut him dead. *I don't know you. Don't even think about talking to me. Say one fucking word and I will scream until your ears bleed.*

He wondered when it had changed. The world. But *had* the world changed, or was it simply his perception?

After alighting at Broadway, he took another subway to Myrtle Avenue. He remembered the Pulaskis' address, up there on Troutman Street, and he found it without difficulty.

The place, a three-storied brownstone walk-up, looked cold and empty, as if vacant, but he went on up and knocked on the door anyway.

It was when he heard the voice from within – *I'll get it!* – that he fully realized what he was doing.

The woman that opened the door was dark haired, five-four or five, wide in the shoulders and slim in the waist. She had on sweat pants and a tee-shirt, over that a loose-fitting gray cardigan sweater. She had socks on her feet but no shoes, and she stood there for a moment just looking at Parrish as if he was some long-lost relative finally returned.

'Police,' she said matter-of-factly.

Parrish nodded. He had his hand around his pocketbook, was ready to show his ID, but who he was seemed such a foregone conclusion there was no point.

'Detective Frank Parrish,' he said quietly. 'I've come up from Brooklyn, and I wondered whether you might have a moment or two to answer some questions.'

'Karen?'

'Yes, Karen.'

'You haven't found the guy who killed her, have you? If you had you wouldn't have more questions—'

'No, I'm sorry, I haven't found the guy who killed her, Mrs Pulaski, but I have lost another girl—'

'*You* have lost another girl? What d'you mean, *you*?'

Parrish felt foolish all of a sudden. 'I don't mean . . . I don't know, er . . . I'm sorry, it's just that sometimes I tend to take these matters personally.'

'Well, Detective Parrish, I'm glad someone does, and it's reassuring to know that the investigation is still going on after a year. Come in. My husband's upstairs. I'll fetch him down.'

Parrish followed her into the front room of the house, stood there on a colorful rug, looked at the wall, and found Karen looking right back from a photograph that couldn't have been taken much before her death. He felt bad. The Pulaskis would now think he was working on their daughter's murder, and he was not. He imagined – in all likelihood – that the death of Karen hadn't been looked at for a good seven or eight months. It was one of the Williamsburg 91st Precinct ghosts.

The father appeared, the management accountant. Mid-forties at a guess, graying hair, bespectacled; the kind of guy who wore an old football shirt without ever having played football in his life. He had on a wristwatch with multiple dials and a black rubber housing. Why did desk jockeys always wear Navy SEAL watches?

'Detective,' he said calmly. 'I'm David Pulaski. You've come to tell us something about Karen?'

'No, sir, I'm afraid not. I'm actually working on another case that may be related, though that is not certain right now.'

David Pulaski looked at his wife. The disappointment was evident in both their expressions. They wanted to know that their daughter's killer had been found, that he had been shot by the police as he tried to escape, that even now he was experiencing the most excruciating agony, lying in a pool of his own blood in a filthy alleyway somewhere. The medics would take their time. There was no reason to hurry. I mean, why should this guy deserve any care at all? But they would step in at the last moment, they would staunch the blood-loss, ferry him to hospital, fix him up sufficiently for trial, conviction, for some interminable prison sentence, and then a prolonged and terrifying execution. This was what they wanted to hear, but this was not what Parrish would tell them. This was real life; it only worked that way in the movies.

'Another girl?' Pulaski asked.

Parrish nodded.

'Sit down, Detective.'

Elizabeth Pulaski asked if Parrish wanted coffee. He declined. He didn't want to be here any longer than was absolutely necessary.

'I just wanted to know if there were any further details that you might have remembered,' Parrish said.

Pulaski shook his head. 'I don't know, Detective, I really don't. Karen was here, and then she wasn't. She was a grown-up, even at sixteen. She knew what she wanted in life, she knew where she was going. She was responsible, polite . . .'

He paused, glanced at his wife. 'She often stayed with friends, always had lots of friends, and it was Christmas. She went over to see them on the 26th. They live up on Willoughby. She arrived about ten in the morning, was with them until four-ish. Then she walked down the road, got on the bus, and that was the last anyone saw of her. Whether she got off the bus before she reached home no-one knows. Whether she made it all the way home and was abducted before she reached the house . . .'

'Or if she never intended to come home?' Elizabeth Pulaski ventured.

The question silenced her husband.

Parrish understood that they knew no more than they had already told the police.

'And the only reason I have ever considered that was because of her clothes,' Elizabeth added.

'Her clothes?' Parrish asked.

'When they – er – found her . . . when they found her she was wearing clothes that she would never have worn.'

Parrish's nostrils cleared, as if someone had given him ammonia. 'Would never have worn?'

'A short skirt,' Elizabeth said. 'Very short. And high-heeled shoes. I mean, Karen had high-heeled shoes, but only for dances, only for special occasions. She dressed in jeans and sneakers and sweatshirts, things like that. She hardly ever wore skirts, and even if she did they were long, down to her knees or longer. A short skirt and a halter-neck top, and high-heeled shoes . . .' She shook her head. 'That wasn't like Karen, not at all.'

'And you told this to the investigating officers?'

'Yes,' David Pulaski said. 'We told them everything. It should all be on record.'

'I'm sure it is,' Parrish said, remembering no note regarding Karen's clothes in the file. 'However, this is a Williamsburg investigation whereas my investigation is Brooklyn.'

'And the case you're investigating might be—'

'This is standard,' Parrish interjected. 'The investigation of your daughter's death will remain open until the perpetrator is found. The detectives working on it will never close it, and though you might not hear from them for weeks, even months at a time, it doesn't mean they're not giving it due attention.'

'We understand,' Pulaski said, and in his tone Parrish recognized the resignation. Pulaski knew that Parrish was telling him what he wanted to hear, and that this may not necessarily be the most accurate of truths.

Elizabeth Pulaski rose from the chair. She looked at Parrish, then at her husband. 'The sad thing is that after all the work we put in . . .' She shook her head slowly.

'Sorry?' Parrish asked.

'Karen was not our daughter,' David Pulaski said. 'Not by blood. We adopted her when she was seven. She was not doing well, not well at all. It took a good three or four years to really get her to settle down. '

'You *adopted* her?' Parrish asked, attempting to subdue the surprise in his voice.

Pulaski smiled awkwardly. 'It's not so uncommon, Detective . . .'

'No, of course not. I'm sorry. No, that's not what I meant. That just ties into something else I am investigating.'

'Something else you are investigating?'

'Another case. I'm sorry. I don't mean to sound insensitive, but it just drew my attention to another unrelated matter I am looking into.'

Parrish knew he sounded unprofessional. He stood up, perhaps a little too quickly, and it was obvious to both the Pulaskis that he was now ready to leave.

He thanked the couple for their time, he wished them well, and when he crossed the road and started down the facing sidewalk he did not look back towards the house. He felt their eyes on him, and he wanted them to forget as much of their meeting, as much about him, as possible. He had said nothing for a very simple reason: If he had stressed the significance of the adoption, then he had no doubt that they would have been up at the 91st asking questions of Detective Richard Franco and his colleagues. *Did you know that a girl was murdered in Brooklyn? A detective came to see us, and he told us that the girl from Brooklyn had also lost her parents, just like Karen? Did you know this? Was this part of your investigation when you were looking into the murder of our daughter?*

He did not wish to be caught stepping on anyone's toes, least of all another homicide detective from an entirely different precinct.

Parrish took the subway at Myrtle and headed back to Brooklyn. As far he could recall, the Records & Archives Division of New York County Child Services was over on Manhattan. Whether they were open on a Saturday or not he wasn't certain, but if they were he wanted to get there before they closed.

TWENTY-ONE

The offices of the Records & Archives Division was open, and would be until four-thirty that afternoon. Access to what he wanted was easy and swift. He showed his ID, he told them what was needed, and they came through with files on both Karen Pulaski and Rebecca Lange.

Karen had been a McDermott at birth, her parents unmarried. The father was the victim of an apparent hit-and-run when Karen was four, the mother had overdosed when the child was six. A year or so later David and Elizabeth Pulaski – registered as potential adoptive parents with the County Adoption Agency for three years – took delivery of their new daughter, a recalcitrant and difficult seven-year-old who had started out with two strikes against her.

CAA and Child Services visits were monthly for the first six months, quarterly for the next twelve, and then once a year, those visits finally becoming a formality. Mr and Mrs Pulaski, according to the reports on file, had done a remarkable job with their adopted daughter. Karen had become a happy, well-balanced, socially-oriented girl, and had stayed that way until someone strangled her with a cable and pushed her body into a dumpster.

Parrish turned to Rebecca. It seemed from a number of notes in her file that Child Services were well aware of Helen Jarvis, and understood that she was really the one who would be taking care of Rebecca. On paper Danny was the guardian; in reality he had little to do with the girl until she began visiting him in Brooklyn.

On the face of it, there seemed to be no connection between the girls aside from the fact that they'd lost their parents early and had been adopted – officially in Karen's case, unofficially in Rebecca's.

Cross-referencing the files, Parrish found no common

denominator in assigned officer or supervisor, either from the CAA or Child Services. One hailed from South Brooklyn, the other from Williamsburg, but CAA and Child Services also dealt with Bedford-Stuyvesant and Ridgewood, their jurisdiction stretching as far north-west as Brooklyn Heights, as far south as Gowanus and Red Hook. If there was a connection then Parrish could not see it, which left it open to coincidence. And Coincidence did not sit well. It never had. Coincidence defied Frank Parrish's natural sense of order and prediction. Then there was the short skirt, the halter-neck, the high-heeled shoes and, in Rebecca's case, the haircut and the nail varnish. Again a coincidence, the fact that in both cases the perp was a re-clother?

What now interested Parrish was the possibility that there might be others. Missing girls, re-clothed, hair cut, fingers and toes painted, perhaps wearing clothes that were out-of-character. Girls overlooked in the general manner of investigation because they were never seen as anything other than isolated cases, but – as had been said so many times – once was happenstance, twice was coincidence, but a third time was conspiracy.

Notwithstanding the possibility that the cases were isolated, unrelated, completely devoid of connection, it was Rebecca's face that still haunted Parrish. He remembered his own daughter at sixteen, and that simple image reminded him that Rebecca had been someone's child, and if he didn't pursue the truth of her death then who else would? Danny? Danny was dead. Helen Jarvis? Hardly . . .

It was four o'clock by the time he once again sat behind his desk in the 126th Precinct. Radick had left a note. *Shooting Range*, it read. *Call me if you need me, otherwise see you tomorrow.* Parrish had eaten no lunch, but whatever hunger he should have felt was absent. A drink, though . . . a drink would have been good.

He accessed Divisional Records on his own system, ran a search for missing persons and homicides, limiting it to the previous twenty-four months, age range between fifteen and twenty. Girls only. He fetched some coffee while the machine did its work.

When he came back he had seventeen names on the screen. Only one of them was his. January 2007, a nineteen-year-old called Angela Ross. Parrish remembered the case. Originally filed as a Missing Person, Angela had been found the following morning. She'd been stabbed eleven times – three times in the neck, twice in the side of the head, the remaining wounds to the upper torso. The perp had never been found, and the reason for her murder had remained completely unknown, never so much as guessed at. Parrish knew from his own investigation of the case that there was no connection to Child Services. Both Angela's parents had been blood; Angela had been the youngest of four children.

He looked through the other sixteen cases. Five had been assigned to Hayes and Wheland, three of them closed; seven to Rhodes and Pagliaro, six of them closed; finally four to Engel and West, two of them closed. That gave Parrish five unsolved and still extant cases, three of them Missing Persons, two of them straight homicides, all females between fifteen and twenty, all of them from within the 126th Precinct's jurisdictional territory. He jotted down their names and the case numbers, and headed down to Records to pull the relevant files.

It was the photographs that did it. For some considerable time he did nothing but sit there, the pictures laid out before him. Two homicides, three apparent runaways. Five girls, all young, two of them at the end of their lives before those lives had even begun. In one instance – seventeen-year-old Jennifer Baumann – the body had been laid out carefully on a motel room bed, restful almost, as if a consensual sacrifice. There were signs of bruising and restraint on the wrists and ankles, and the motel room had been confirmed as the secondary crime scene. Jennifer had not been murdered there, simply left there for someone to find her. Another – Nicole Benedict, also seventeen – was found dead in a mattress bag on an apartment block stairwell. Her head had been twisted back at an extraordinarily sharp angle. Parrish stared at the picture for quite some time, the image jarring and unsettling. It seemed physically impossible that such a thing could be done to a young girl, but it had been, and the photographs were there to prove it.

Parrish gathered up the files and returned to his office. After an hour he had found only one reference to Child Services – merely a footnote that Hayes had made, inconclusive, as to whether Jennifer Baumann had been in the care of Child Services, or she had a friend in care who needed to be questioned. Parrish did not intend to pursue the question with Hayes. His decision – certainly contravening protocol if not procedure – was to say nothing about his interest in these cases.

He put the files in a lower drawer, the two homicides uppermost, and before he left he took one more look at the face of Jennifer Baumann. Her eyes were just sadness personified, a sadness so deep it made Parrish feel hollow. He now had four dead girls – Rebecca, Karen, Jennifer and Nicole, perhaps unrelated, perhaps entirely irrelevant, but it would do no harm to keep hold of them for a while. The dead ones seemed important. The runaways? Well, they could be dead too, but right now they weren't, at least not on paper.

At six-thirty Parrish was seated in a corner booth in Clay's Tavern. He couldn't take his mind off Caitlin. He knew there was no reason to be more worried about her welfare today than any other day, but the pictures he had looked at had disturbed him enough to exacerbate that worry. She resented even the slightest attempt on his part to give advice or interfere with her life, and he needed to learn to leave the girl alone. He needed to let her go. She was old enough to sink or swim by herself.

Parrish didn't worry about his son anything like as much. With Robert it was different, as was always the way with sons. Robert challenged and argued and debated and raised issues. Parrish had even told Robert about Eve, and Robert thought it was *most cool* that his cop dad had a relationship with a hooker. Both Robert and Caitlin had a key to his apartment, but Robert was the only one who'd ever shown up unannounced and unexpected. Frank knew his son had a little more devil-may-care in him than his daughter, but with

Robert it had never been a question of his physical welfare and safety. But Caitlin . . .

Parrish let go of the thought. Caitlin was fine. It was just the case that had got to him, he told himself. The photographs, the consideration of dead girls in motel rooms, on stairwells, girls with handprints on their necks . . .

He bought another drink. The money he'd taken from Danny Lange was burning a hole in his pocket. He'd forgotten to drop it off, would take a walk back the way he'd come and deliver it before he went home for the evening.

Within an hour he was joined by a regular – ex-police Lieutenant Victor Merrett, old-school, old-time, a veteran of the day. He sat down with Frank, they talked of nothing in particular for a while, and then Merrett mentioned Frank's father.

'Have to be honest with you, Frank,' Merrett said, 'and meaning no disrespect to his memory, but I never did see eye-to-eye with your father.'

'Well, Victor, I can tell you that what people saw and what he really was . . . hell, let's not even go there eh?'

'Don't get me wrong, Frank, I'm not saying he wasn't a good cop. He was as good as they get—'

Parrish smiled wryly. 'You on the books, Victor? Were you ever on the books down here?'

'On the books?'

'Taking an income from my father's crew, you know?'

Merrett frowned. 'What the hell you asking me that for, Frank? What kinda question is that?'

'A straight question, Victor. A straight fucking question. You can't answer a straight question?'

'You're drunk, Frank. Jesus, I come here to be sociable, come to say hi, how ya doing, and you give me this shit. What the fuck is wrong with you?'

'Ain't nothing wrong with me, Victor. Something wrong with a whole bunch of other people though, and I just wondered if you were one of them.'

Merrett got up. He looked down at Frank and shook his head. 'Think you should go home,' he said. 'Get whatever the hell is going on with you slept off.'

Parrish leaned forward and picked up his glass. 'Well,

before you go, Victor, let me tell you something about my father. The only people he ever saw eye-to-eye with were the ones who were taking money off of him, the people he had something over, right? If you weren't on his side, then you were an enemy.'

'But his reputation—'

'Bullshit reputation, Victor. John Parrish was as crooked as they come and that's the truth.'

Merrett looked alarmed. 'I don't think that's something you should go shouting your mouth off about, especially in the state you're in—'

'Why? Why shouldn't I say what the fuck I like? It's the truth, Victor, the fucking truth. He was a bullshit artist just like the rest of them. He didn't do anything but stick his hand deep in the honey pot and take just whatever the hell he wanted for the whole of his working life. And you can't tell me that people didn't know. You can't ever convince me that the people who were above him didn't know what he was doing. But they let it slide, Victor, they tolerated it because he brought in enough small fishes to keep the net heavy. That's what he did. And even those guys, even the ones he brought in, he didn't bust them, Victor. He didn't do the work. Those guys were given to him by the Mob, and he wheeled them in and his superiors were happy, and the Mob was happy, and everyone slapped everyone on the fucking back and went home with their skims and kickbacks. That's the way it was, Victor, and that's the way it will always be.'

'Christ Jesus, Frank, I never heard you talk like this. What the hell has gotten into you?'

Parrish smiled enthusiastically. He was drunk and he didn't give a fuck. 'Therapy,' he said. 'I've been having therapy.'

'Well, Frank, I have to say here and now, that I think it might be a good idea if you got another therapist. Doesn't seem the one you've got is doing you much good.'

Merrett started towards the door.

'You're leaving?' Parrish asked.

'I have to make a move, Frank, yes.'

'Well, seems to me the least you can fucking do is buy me a drink before you go.'

Merrett stood there for a moment looking down at Frank Parrish. 'Think maybe you've had enough,' he said quietly, and then he turned his back and walked away.

TWENTY-TWO

Frank Parrish woke late Sunday morning. He could remember little of the night before.

On the kitchen counter was a half-opened can of chili. He had never gotten as far as putting it in a pan to warm up.

He made some coffee, sat for a while in the kitchen, looked through the window at nothing in particular. He thought to call Caitlin, decided against it. He wondered whether he should have Radick check up on her. He thought of the dead girls, and when he pictured their faces he saw nothing but their naivety, their vulnerability, the utter pointlessness of their deaths. Caitlin wasn't so much older. She traveled back and forth to work, sometimes late at night, alone and in the dark. How much distance was there between her and a dumpster? Very little, in all honesty. And was it always opportunist? Was it always just random – the way these guys just snatched girls from the street, used them for whatever purpose they saw fit, and then disposed of them? Parrish did not believe so. He believed that the files in his desk drawer would provide him with something more than just dead and missing girls. Besides Rebecca and Karen, if even one of them had been adopted, had been processed through the County Adoption Agency or Child Services, then he was going to pursue it. He would speak to no-one. He would employ his own energies, his own contacts, his own resources, and if it came to nothing then nothing would have been lost.

But now it was Sunday, and he would not be going to the office. He would go and see Robert, perhaps Caitlin, and he would try and get through the evening without a bottle of Bushmills. The likelihood was slim, but he would try.

He took a straight route to his old house, the one where the bitter ghosts of his marriage still resided, stopping en route to spend a handful of minutes in St. Michael's church. He spoke to nobody, merely walked the length of the aisle, deposited the remainder of Danny Lange's money in the donation box, and then left.

Arriving in front of the house where so much of his life had been spent, he paused on the sidewalk and hesitated before climbing the steps and banging on the door.

'You don't look so good,' were her first words.

'Hi, Clare. How are you? How have things been? You know something, it must be the better part of three weeks since I last saw you, and *you're* looking pretty damned good, Clare, even though it pains me to say it . . . you're looking pretty hot.'

'Fuck off, Frank.'

Parrish smiled. He went back down the steps and stood on the sidewalk. He buried his hands in his overcoat pockets and looked left.

'You gonna ask me in,' he said, 'or are you going to stand there and watch while I come in anyway?'

'What do you want, Frank?'

'I came to see Robert.'

'He's not here.'

'You know where he is?'

'He's gone for the day. He has a girl now, but you wouldn't know that because you don't give a crap about what's happening with him, do you?

Frank didn't rise to the bait.

'So he's not here and I don't know when he'll be back, and *if* and *when* he does come back I'll tell him that you called for him, okay?'

'That's very good of you, Clare.'

'I know.'

She slammed the door and Frank Parrish stood there until he could no longer hear her footsteps.

It was always the same tune, the same exhausting aggression and bitterness. He couldn't understand why she held onto it with such ferocity. Surely now, after all this time, they could converse without the tension and angst and melodrama?

Frank Parrish walked back to the subway.

Today was not turning out as planned.

An hour later he stood in the hallway outside Caitlin's apartment and knocked for the third time. She was not in. He knew that now, but he had nowhere else to go and nothing else to do. He waited patiently, fool that he was, and then he knocked once more. Finally he conceded defeat.

He arrived home mid-afternoon. He called Eve and it went direct to her answer phone. She was with clients, or she was out, or maybe she was visiting her mother upstate. Eve's mother believed that her daughter was a Human Resources Manager for Hewlett Packard. She would go on believing that until she died. Whether she suspected that your average Hewlett Packard HR manager did not look like her daughter no-one would ever know; and if she did, it would never go further than suspicion. There were some things it was better not to know, even when you knew them.

Frank Parrish turned on the TV, sat patiently for fifteen minutes, and then he could take no more.

He put his coat back on, headed out of the apartment, and made for Clay's. At least there were people down there. At least there was Tom Waits on the jukebox. At least there was a bottle of Bushmills and a clean glass, and no-one to tell him he couldn't.

TWENTY-THREE

'It's just a feeling, nothing more.'

'Don't you trust your feelings?'

'As a cop no, not really. They talk about hunches, about intuition sure, but I don't give a great deal of credence to such stuff.'

'Maybe you should.'

'There's a great deal of things I *should* do, and using my intuition is somewhere down near the bottom of the list. I've used intuition before and it's gotten me in trouble.'

'I was thinking about you yesterday, Frank.'

'Okay, so here we go. I knew this was coming—'

'Frank, listen to me. Joking aside now.'

'Sense of humor is very therapeutic, isn't that so?'

'I was thinking that you have to learn how to trust yourself.'

'What?'

'Perhaps re-learn. Perhaps it's not learning, but re-learning. It happens with a lot of people who have gone through divorces, who've had difficulty with their children . . . all the important things in life, you know? Those things start to go wrong, or don't turn out the way they intended, people can start to doubt their own ability to make the right decisions. Does that make sense?'

'You wanna know what happened on Saturday?'

'Saturday? Sure, tell me what happened on Saturday.'

'I met someone in a bar, an old-timer, someone who knew of my father. You know what I told him?'

'What?'

'The truth. That's what I told him. What my father was really like. The kind of asshole he actually was.'

'And what did this person say?'

'He said that maybe I shouldn't drink so much, refused to buy me another, didn't seem to find what I was saying too interesting.'

'And how did you feel when you said these things?'

'I don't remember. I think I was drunk.'

'Hardest thing that people have to face is the truth, Frank. I'm sure there are a lot of people who saw your father as a role model, as an example of what it's like to be a good cop, and they don't like to have that ideal taken away.'

'His whole life was a lie.'

'I know that, Frank, but I can imagine there are many people who wouldn't want to hear you say that. Some of them because they were involved with him, others because they don't want to lose their ideals.'

'But I can say what the hell I like to you and it never leaves the room, right?'

'That's right, yes. And I think it's a good sign that you said these things to this person.'

'Why?'

'Because it signifies that you're now willing to face up to some of the truth about your father.'

'I've always known the truth about him, about what he was really like.'

'Sure you have, but you've never said anything. You've had to defend him.'

'*Defend* him? I don't think so. It was more a case of being ashamed for who he was.'

'I see . . .'

'So what do you want me to talk about today?'

'You were going to talk about Lufthansa, remember, and your father's involvement in that, but we don't have to. We can talk about whatever you like.'

'I do want to talk about that, but I have this case on my mind.'

'Okay, tell me about that first.'

'I just want to say some things out loud. Just me talking and you listening, that's all.'

'Okay . . . what do you want to say?'

'This case I have going on, the girl that was strangled. I

went to her school to speak to some of her friends, and this guy tells me about someone up at Waterbury, this girl who had a friend who was found strangled last Christmas. I went and spoke to this someone, and I get a line on this dead girl. I go see her parents and I find out that this dead girl from last Christmas was also adopted, also processed through Child Services, and for some reason I cannot get this out of my head.'

'You think they're connected?'

'I . . . maybe, but . . . I don't believe they are, no.'

'I sense some hesitation there, Frank.'

'Well, the first girl, the junkie's sister . . . she had her hair cut and her nails were done with colored varnish. And this girl from Waterbury, she was dressed in clothes that her mother said she would never wear.'

'I see. And is there something else?'

'Well, I got interested in other missing girls, you know? I did a search and went through all the disappearances and homicides that fitted the same demographic, and I ended up with five more girls – two homicides, and three apparent runaways.'

'And they went through Child Services as well?'

'I don't know for sure. I haven't followed them up yet.'

'But you're going to.'

'Yes.'

'And they're all your earlier unclosed cases?'

'No, they're not *my* cases. Never were, still aren't.'

'Well, won't it cause trouble between you and your colleagues?'

'If they find out, yes.'

'But you're not going to tell them.'

'Only person I'm telling is you.'

'Well, Frank, I don't know what to say. I'm a therapist, not a detective, but in your circumstances I think it might be a good idea to tell the original investigating officers that you're taking over their cases—'

'I'm not "taking over" their cases.'

'What would *you* call it?'

'Homework.'

'Seriously, Frank, you cannot forget the situation you're in.

You have a dead partner, you've had your drivers' license taken from you, you're assigned to see me every day until further notice, and you're on a one-third pay hold until the end of the year.'

'Good that my shrink comes for free then, isn't it?'

'Frank, I really don't see how you can afford to be so facetious—'

'Look, Marie: if I tell them, it becomes official. These old cases become new workload. If I get nowhere with them I wind up with another five unclosed cases on my list, and that doesn't look so good. If I say nothing and nothing happens with them, then it's not a problem. No-one loses. I also avoid any possibility of generating ill-will with the other guys.'

'And if you solve the cases?'

'Well, I would hope that my fellow homicide detectives would be big enough to recognize that a solved case is a lot more important than who did it or how.'

'I imagine your superiors would think that, but I'm really not at all sure your colleagues will agree with you.'

'We'll see. The only important thing right now is whether or not the cases come to anything, whether there is a link between them.'

'Are you hoping that there is?'

'You're damn right I am.'

'So you can get a commendation?'

'No! For God's sake, you think this is what it's about?'

'I don't know what this is about, Frank. That's why I'm asking.'

'It's about my job. It's about what I'm in the PD for. Because there's actually very little that's more important than stopping the people who do this kind of thing.'

'You believe that?'

'Sure, don't you?'

'We're not asking about me.'

'Sure I believe it. If I didn't, then I wouldn't do the job. I would have quit by now, especially after all this recent bullshit.'

'What, particularly?'

'All of it. My partner . . . all of this crap during the past six months.'

'Do you feel angry about it?'

'I don't feel angry, no. Disbelief perhaps . . . disbelief, and the same thing that everyone goes through when . . .'

'When what?'

'When something happens, something like this. Going back over it time and again. What could I have done? How could it have turned out differently? Over and over and over in your mind.'

'Have you been made to feel that you were responsible for what happened to your partner?'

'Sure. Well, no . . . not like that. Not directly. I *was* responsible, we both were, but this is what we do. This is what the job *is*.'

'But the people that evaluate liability in these situations are police themselves. These are people who've also been in the firing line.'

'Sure they have, I know that, but until you're there, until you're right inside the situation you can't make a judgement. Every situation is different, and no-one is equipped for the kind of decisions you have to make in such scenarios.'

'So you do what you think is right at the time.'

'Yeah. And then you review and regret and repent at your leisure, after the fact.'

'Do you regret the decision to leave him back there by himself?'

'How can I? I didn't have a choice, did I? Whichever way I look at it, I don't see there could have been a different outcome. That doesn't change the fact that I'll be thinking about it forever. But I know two things for sure. First, because of what we did, two people are dead and thirty-four are alive; and the second thing, the most important thing as far as I'm concerned, is that if the positions had been reversed then he would have done the same.'

'You're sure of that?'

'Absolutely.'

'Do you want to tell me what happened that day?'

'No.'

'Because?'

'Because we still have to talk about Lufthansa. We're

talking about my father, and until we're done talking about him I don't really want to talk about anything else.'

'Okay. So start talking.'

'I can't. I'm real sorry, but I have to meet Jimmy Radick, and we have a squad briefing at ten.'

'Tomorrow then.'

'Tomorrow it is.'

'One question before you go.'

'Shoot.'

'How much did you drink over the weekend?'

'Oh, I don't know . . . probably just about enough to get me through 'til today.'

TWENTY-FOUR

Parrish picked up the phone, chased the Lange tox test again. He wanted to ensure that it got done before she was sewn up and shipped out to the big hereafter.

Jimmy Radick seemed agitated, and as soon as Frank came off the phone he told him that Valderas had been snooping around.

'Saying what?'

Radick shrugged. 'The usual shit, you know. How is the caseload? How is Frank? What are you working on? When do we see daylight on some of these files? The stuff all squad sergeants say.'

'And you told him what?'

'The non-denial denial. We're following up leads, had something promising and it turned out not to be so good . . . got things to move on today. We should have something solid before too long. I didn't say anything about Karen Pulaski.'

Parrish leaned forward. 'By itself, I don't see where this thing is going to go. I have one other guy I want to speak to, an old-time friend of Danny Lange's. He lives over the other side of the expressway. I thought of him when I was coming in this morning. He goes way back to when Danny was just a corner boy. We go see him, and if that comes to nothing then we're going to have to go wider.'

'Let's get out of here then,' Radick said. 'Anything's better than sitting around waiting for Valderas to come back and bust my balls.'

Wayne Thorson, called Swede for as long as anyone could recall, lived in the kind of place that most people rarely saw. A mess of semi-derelict tenements amidst Harper Street, Dean and Van Sneed. A place where the smell of the piers and Upper New York Bay, that rank and fetid funk, came away on your clothes, in your hair, in your mouth. The kind of place if people were born there they got out fast, and if they didn't make it they spent the whole of their lives wishing they had. Parrish had not been down there for a year or more, Radick for longer. He sat in the car, quiet, a thoughtful expression on his face, once again trying to understand how people could live like this. This was just another image he would try so hard to forget but knew he would always remember.

'What shoes you got on?' Parrish asked. 'Needles all over the stairs. You don't want to go down there with sneakers.'

'I'm okay,' Radick replied. 'Proper shoes today.'

'Let's go then.'

Swede wore green Marine Corps pants and a tee-shirt that had forgotten how it was to be clean. Opening the apartment door just an inch or two sent the stench of overflowing ashtrays, stale beer, weed, puke, sweat and apathy out to the hallway.

'Aah fuck, now what? Frank motherfucking Parrish. Can you not let it alone?'

Parrish smiled. He raised his hand and pushed on the door and Swede stepped back to let him in.

'A year,' Parrish said. 'Has to be. Jesus, you look good, Swede. Man, you look well. Best I ever seen you look. And you remembered my name? I'm honored, Swede, real honored.'

'Fuck off, Frank.'

Radick went in after Parrish, down the narrow, lightless hallway into a room that was nothing more than stripped walls, dirty windows, mattresses on the floor. A cheap stereo box sat in the corner, surrounding it a small army of empty bottles, burger cartons and newspapers. There was nowhere to sit aside from the stained and damp mattresses.

'So I'm looking out for Danny,' Parrish said.

'Heard he got done.'

'You heard right.'

'And you think I know who did it?'

Radick watched Thorson. His eyes were narrow and furtive, his complexion junkie-yellow, the skin raddled with sores and pockmarks. His right ear lobe had been pierced, and then stretched with a black hoop through which Radick could see the filthy window behind him. He carried the kind of look that said everything thus far had been a disappointment.

'I don't think anything, Swede. You know me better than that by now. This isn't a shake-down, my friend, this is merely a social call.'

Swede sneered contemptuously. He looked at Radick. 'Who's your new punk bitch?'

'This here's Jimmy. Jimmy's one of the good guys, Swede. Jimmy ain't a knucklehead, okay? You don't need to be disrespectful.'

'Whatever, man. I don't know nothin' about what happened to Danny, okay? I ain't seen Danny for two, maybe three weeks—'

'You meet his sister?'

Swede smiled. It was a nasty expression. 'I seen her, yes. What about it?'

'When did you see her?'

'Coupla times. Three weeks ago maybe. Saw her when I last saw Danny.'

'They came here?'

'No, man, they didn't come here. Saw them in the diner near where Danny lives. Near the park, you know? Saw them there.' Swede smiled again.

'What?'

'Cute piece of ass that one,' he said, leering.

'Cute piece of dead ass,' Parrish replied.

'Wha—'

'She got herself whacked too, Swede. She got herself strangled last week in Danny's place. And this isn't something I'm gonna forget about, you understand? I'm gonna keep pushing on this until something gives.'

'Man . . . what the fuck . . . What the fuck *is* this? Jesus Christ, man, she get herself killed as well?'

'Sure did. Deader than Elvis. Sweet girl. I don't see that anyone had a reason to kill her, and I'm thinking it could only have happened because of something Danny was into. That's why I wanted to come see you. See if you might have an idea or two. He owe anyone any big money? He rip someone off? He get himself involved with someone he shouldn't have?'

It was the hesitation that gave Swede away, gave him away but good.

He looked at Parrish, at Radick, and then back to Parrish. He opened his mouth as if to speak, and then closed it again.

'What?' Parrish prompted.

Swede shook his head.

'Speak to me, Swede, or I'm gonna be down here on a daily basis 'til I get you for possession, and then you're going away for good. You got two strikes, my friend, and you cannot afford a third.'

'Aah, fuck, no,' Swede said. He backed up and sat down on a mattress. He pulled his knees up to his chest and wrapped his arms around them. He looked like a twelve-year-old, yet had the eyes of an old and dying man.

'Swede, for God's sake tell me what you know,' Parrish said, his voice resigned to the inevitability of this game they would now play.

'You cannot do this, man. You cannot hold this shit over me. I don't know anything, okay? I hear this, I hear that. I don't know Danny Lange any better than any of the other junkies that come down here. They're all full of wild ideas. You know that. They're all on this plan and that plan. They all got something going on that's gonna get them out of the life. They've all got some shit going down that's the big fucking rescue from this. You know how it is, man, you seen it for as long as I have.'

'So what did Danny say? What did he have going on?'

'It's all bullshit. It's all fucking pipe dreams—'

'What was it you thought about when you heard he'd been killed? Hey? What was the first thing you thought about?'

'It was nothing, man. The same old bullshit these mother-fuckers always come out with—'

'Tell me what it was, Swede.'

Swede looked up. His eyes were shadowed. He looked like three weeks from dead. There was something in his face, something like a quiet and perpetual wonder – whether each new day would be anything more than its own particular brand of bullshit. Once you went with this life it owned you.

You got out and walked, or you braced yourself for the inevitable collision.

'Swede—'

'Hey, man, enough already.' Swede looked up. Hurt and anger and hatred flashed in his eyes. 'You can't keep pushin' on me. Push on someone enough and they snap.'

'I haven't been here for a year, maybe more,' Parrish said. 'Give me a break, for God's sake. I'm trying to find out who did your buddy. '

'He wasn't my buddy. I knew him from around and about. We didn't have any special fucking relationship, you know?'

Parrish sighed resignedly. 'Swede, tell me what the fuck you know or I'm taking you in.'

'What?' Swede started to get up. Radick stepped forward aggressively and Swede sat down again.

'What the fuck you gonna take me in for?'

'Abusive behavior. Suspicion of possession. We came in here with probable cause. We smelled weed from the hallway. We tried to speak with you, you got violent, right, Jimmy?'

Radick nodded but didn't speak. He continued looking directly at Swede.

'You're a cocksucker, Frank Parrish, a no-good fucked-up—'

'Tell me what you know, Swede, or we're taking you in.'

'The porno,' he said suddenly.

'The what?'

'Danny's sister. I heard she was gonna do a porno.'

'Danny told you this?'

'Sure he did. He told me she wanted to do a porno. She wasn't no sweetheart like everyone thought. She wasn't no clean-cut all-American schoolgirl. She was a nasty bitch, Frank. She wanted to do a porno, and Danny already had this thing going with this guy—'

'What thing?'

'Danny had a sideline, you know? Least he said he did. Had a thing with some guy who was always on the lookout for the younger ones, just the wrong side of legal. Fifteen, sixteen, whatever.'

'And Danny Lange was going to let his kid sister do a porno with this guy?'

'He wanted the money, man. She wanted the money too, but she was into it big-time. She was into doing this thing more than he was. She didn't have a fucking clue what she was getting into. She had some wide-eyed fucking Hollywood thing going on. She was gonna blow some guy and everyone would take her for Carmen fucking Electra. Sad fucking state of affairs, but she was really fucking determined to do this thing.'

'Danny told you this?'

'Danny and the sister. Last time I saw them.'

'And it didn't occur to you that this might have some bearing on Danny's death?'

'Hey, man, you know the way this goes. You do what you do, I do what I do. You think I'm gonna go running to the callbox and call you up because I think that maybe I have a tiny fucking idea about some junkie scumbag from Brooklyn? We're on different sides here, Detective Parrish, or hadn't you realized that?'

'Who was the guy?'

'I haven't a single fucking idea,' Swede said emphatically.

Parrish nodded, looked at Radick. 'Cuff him,' he said. 'We're taking him in.'

Swede got up fast. 'What the fuck are you doing? I told you what I know, I answered your questions.'

Radick stood with his cuffs.

'Tell us the guy, Swede,' Parrish said.

'I don't know the guy, okay? Seriously, man, I don't know who the fuck it was. He just said *some guy*. That was all. Just some guy.'

Parrish looked directly at Swede. Swede didn't flinch, didn't look away, stood there resolutely.

'Okay,' Parrish said eventually. 'You know anyone who might know which guy?'

'No, I don't,' Swede said too quickly.

Jimmy Radick stepped forward, reached out to take Swede's hand.

Swede snatched his hand away, stepped back.

125

'You don't wanna test me,' Parrish said. 'Seriously, you don't want to fucking test me today.'

'Go see Larry Temple.'

'And who the fuck is that?' Parrish asked.

'Two blocks east. Big high-rise place. Something *tower*. Third floor, apartment six. Tell him if he helps you out then he and I are quits. And just ask him the fucking question, okay? Don't go busting him, eh?'

Parrish nodded. 'Third floor, apartment six, Larry Temple.'

'Right, right. Larry. Go ask him, see if he knows who the guy was.'

'And what makes you think he might know?'

''Cause he watches that shit, man. Young girls, all that stuff. He's into all that sick shit, man.'

Parrish started towards the door. 'I find you held out on me, Swede, I'm gonna come back here and kick your ass all the way to Staten Island.'

Swede didn't say a word. He just stood there watching them, willing them to leave.

TWENTY-FIVE

On the drive over Frank Parrish tried to blank out the thought of Rebecca doing a porno. He tried not to think about her brother selling her for dope. Some police believed that the nature of the work didn't have to set the tone of your life. All they were saying was that they hadn't done the work for long enough. Give them another couple of years, five at most, and they'd sing a different tune.

Parrish thought about Eve, and then he thought about the ever-present discomfort in his lower gut. He wondered once again if he was sick, not just a flu or a virus or something, but proper sick.

'You know this Larry Temple guy?' Radick asked as they pulled over against the curb.

'Name's familiar,' Parrish said, 'but I can't place it.'

'Let's go see whether you're old friends then, eh?'

Larry Temple was no different from the rest of them. They all had bad skin. They gave off a smell – body odor, cheap disinfectant, the underlying decay that came with their pre-dilection. As if they were deteriorating from within, dying from the inside out, the odor escaping through their pores.

He was predictably resistant until Parrish mentioned Swede, told him if he answered questions he and Swede would be quits. With that Larry Temple stepped back and allowed them entry to his apartment. Here there was no scattered garbage, no greasy burger boxes or damp mat-tresses; here was a man who at least was trying his best to *appear* normal. An upstanding citizen. One of the good guys.

'You owe Swede?' Parrish asked.

Temple shrugged.

'You know who we are, you don't want us in here, I

mention his name and you're Mister fucking Sociable all of a sudden?'

'I don't have anything to hide,' Temple said.

Parrish looked at Radick. Radick smiled.

'How many times you been inside, Larry?' Parrish asked.

'Just the once,' Radick interjected.

Parrish's eyes widened. 'I remember you now. You got busted for kiddie porn a ways back. You lived over in—'

'That was a long time ago,' Temple said. He was nervous. He kept smoothing his hand over his hair.

'And you're not like that anymore, right?' Parrish asked. 'You're not into that shit anymore, eh?'

'No,' Temple replied. 'I got some help. I'm all clean now, all clean.'

'Not what we heard.'

'From Swede? Swede don't know shit—'

'Swede?' Parrish asked. 'Where the hell did that name come from? Hey, Jimmy, did you mention Swede?'

Radick turned his mouth down at the corners. 'I didn't mention Swede, no—'

'You just told me—' Temple interjected. 'You motherfuckers. You're messing with my head. What the hell is this?'

'We were telling you that we heard a few things, Larry.'

'From who?' Temple asked. 'If it's not Swede, then who's been saying shit about me?'

'Doesn't matter,' Parrish said. 'We got someone who's trying to work himself a deal downtown. He wants to give up on some people, you know? Lessen the burden he's carrying an' all that. Your name got mentioned, a few things of interest, and we figured we'd come over, say hi, chat for a while, see what's happening in your neck of the woods.'

'You ain't got nothin' on me,' Temple said defensively.

'We got word about a girl who was up for a porno. Kid sister of someone you know.'

Temple opened his mouth to speak, and once again he hesitated.

'You shouldn't do that if you don't want any trouble, Larry,' Parrish said.

'What? Shouldn't do what?'

'Look so fucking guilty.'

'Look guilty? I don't look guilty.' His complexion warmed. His eyes were back and forth from Parrish to Radick, real deer-in-the-headlights.

'Tell us about Danny Lange,' Parrish said matter-of-factly.

'Oh w-wait a fu-fucking minute here,' Temple stuttered, and started backing away. Radick took a step to the right and blocked him. He had cuffs in his hands.

'Wait a goddamned minute here,' Temple said. 'I heard about that. I heard about Danny and his kid sister, but you don't have anything on me and the—'

'Who said anything about a kid sister?' Parrish asked.

'You did. You said someone's kid sister was up for doing some porno . . .'

Parrish frowned. 'Did you hear me say anything like that Jimmy?'

Radick shook his head. 'Nothing like that, Frank. I think you were talking about the weather or something.'

'Oh fuck off! What the fuck is this shit? What the fuck are you doing here? You can't pin this on me. Who the hell do you think you are?'

'Couple of cops doing our job,' Parrish replied. 'I went to see Swede on this Danny Lange double homicide, he mentions your name, we come over here to just check things out and all of a sudden you bring up Danny Lange's kid sister and how you were going to do a porno with her.'

'*What?* What the fuck—'

'Heard it loud and clear, right, Jimmy?'

'Loud and clear, Frank.'

'You guys—'

'Start talking, Larry.'

'About what? Talking about what? What the fuck does this have to do with me?'

'You're into this shit up to your neck,' Radick said. 'You've already got a bust for this kind of business on your sheet. You know who's who. You know who's in the market at the moment, what they're doing, where they're working from—'

'I don't know *anything* like that,' protested Larry, almost hysterical now.

'Larry,' Parrish said. 'Larry, let's calm the fuck down for a minute, eh? Take a seat. Let's talk this out all civilized, okay?'

'Talk what out? There isn't anything to talk out . . .'

'Larry, sit the fuck down right now!'

Temple dropped into a chair and looked up at Parrish and Radick.

Parrish sat facing him. Radick stood to the right.

Larry Temple – wide-eyed, anticipating the worst – swallowed audibly.

'This is really, really simple, Larry. You know who we need to talk to. Danny Lange was setting up his kid sister for doing a porno, and you know who he was talking to.'

'Wha—'

'Just cut the crap, will you? You know who we need to talk to, Larry. Tell us who we need to talk to or I'm gonna leave Jimmy here with you while I go get a search warrant for your place, you understand?'

'You can't do that—'

'Try me.'

Larry Temple inched forward on the chair and then sat with his hands on his knees, his head bowed. He stayed that way for a moment or two, and then he looked up at Frank Parrish.

'I heard something,' he said quietly. He waited for Parrish to respond, but Parrish said nothing.

'I heard word of something, just a maybe, but this was some time back. Only reason I mention it is because Danny said something when I last saw him and it might have been connected.'

'When d'you see Danny?' Parrish asked.

'I don't know . . . three, maybe four weeks ago.'

'And you spoke to him?'

'Some, yeah.'

'And what was it he said?'

Temple hesitated, and then he looked away towards the window. 'He said he had a good score going on. He said he was gonna do a thing that would make a difference.'

'And what made you think there was some connection to what happened with him and his sister?'

'What he said after that.'

Parrish raised his eyebrows.

'He said he had someone lined up to do a skin flick, that he was gonna get some serious money for it—'

'And you thought that this might have a connection,' Parrish said sarcastically.

'Hey, this is like a month ago. I'm just shooting the shit with the guy and he says he might have someone for a skin flick. He didn't say anything about his sister, he just said that. It was only when I heard that he'd gotten himself killed, that his kid sister was killed too, that I wondered if she was the one that he might have lined up for it.'

'And if she was?'

'Then . . . well . . . then something must've gone wrong.'

'A bit of a fucking understatement, Larry.'

Larry Temple lowered his head again.

'So who would Danny Lange have gone to if he was selling his sister into this shit?'

'You know as well as me,' Temple said.

'This isn't small-time shit, Larry. This is someone who's into it deep enough to kill two people.'

'How the fuck would I know?'

'Because this is your world, Larry. This is what you do. These are the people you go hang out with, the other sick fuckos who watch this—'

'It's an illness,' Temple interjected. He looked confounded and hurt. 'It's a mental illness. It's something you're born with. It's not something you can just turn on and turn off whenever you feel like it.'

'Don't give me the fucking sob story, Larry, just tell me who Danny Lange might have been talking to.'

'I don't know, Detective Parrish, I really don't. I've told you what I know, and that's *all* I know. I'm not so close with the crowd anymore. Things have changed.'

Parrish was quiet for some time. He believed Larry Temple. There was just something in his expression, something in his eyes; Parrish had seen enough liars to know what they looked like. And he knew Danny Lange for what he was, so much the same as so many others. Big ideas, all mouth. I'm doing this, I'm doing that, today will be different, today I have *a thing*, today I'm gonna get out of the life. And they never did, and they never would. Addiction was addiction.

Did Parrish believe that Danny Lange might have sold his sister to do a porno? Yes. Did Parrish believe that Rebecca might have been into it? That Danny sold her on the idea that it was a cool thing, that she'd wind up with money, and her name in lights? Sure. It changed his perspective on the girl, but he was no stranger to this kind of thing. This shit went down all the time. And then what happens? She winds up dead, Danny either wants his money or he's going to the cops, and he gets whacked too.

Parrish rose to his feet.

Temple watched him stand, braced himself for a beating. The beating never came.

'You hear anything more you let me know,' Parrish said. 'You know how to get hold of me. I track some other line on this and find out you didn't tell me something, well I'm gonna come back here and I ain't gonna knock on the door, know what I mean?'

Temple didn't speak, but the recognition of what Parrish meant was in his eyes.

Parrish led the way, didn't speak to Radick until they reached the stairwell, and it was Radick who spoke first.

'You think he gave us everything?'

'Yeah, I think so. He knows the same names as me. I don't think there's some big fish that he's aware of that we don't know about.'

'So who do we start with?'

'I want to go back to the office first,' Parrish said. 'I want the tox results before anything else.'

TWENTY-SIX

The tox test on Rebecca Lange's blood and urine came back negative, but there was a note to say that hair had been sampled and would be processed before the end of the day.

Parrish sat at his desk, aware of the stack of files in his drawer and feeling some sense of urgency, a need to look further, delve deeper. He needed to pursue the possibility of any Child Services connection to Jennifer Baumann and Nicole Benedict. He had no reservations about the competence of Hayes, Wheland, Engel or West, but something such as this would have been so easy to overlook had they not known what they were looking for. The smallest fragment of information could change perspective utterly.

Parrish was frustrated that he'd not had these names before his visit to Child Services Records and Archives. It required time, but he didn't want to get Jimmy Radick in deep. Not yet. Not until there was something more substantial. Too many times he had fixated on a case, come to some wild conclusion, and chased it relentlessly, only to find out that the conclusion was a figment of his too-fertile imagination. This time he didn't want to go that route. Discretion and tact had never been his strong points, but now – in the current climate – it seemed that to ignore caution would be to court further criticism and censure. It was either tread carefully or get handed an official suspension. His only assigned homicides were Danny and Rebecca Lange, the hooker, the subway death, and the campus stabbing. The last three wouldn't go away, and yet Parrish felt no compelling duty to pursue them. For a moment he wondered if he could convince Radick to work them, but he knew that wouldn't fly.

Nonetheless, apart from Rebecca, it was those earlier homicides he was interested in – Karen, Jennifer and Nicole.

With Rebecca, that gave him four girls, two aged sixteen, two of seventeen. The first – Jennifer – had been found in January 2007; the second – Nicole – in August of the same year; Karen was found in that December, and finally Rebecca. Karen's body had been in clothes she wouldn't ordinarily have worn, and Rebecca's hair had been cut and her nails painted. Parrish knew little of the other two, save that Jennifer was found in a motel room, Nicole in a mattress bag with her neck broken. The circumstances of their disappearances had been as unremarkable as those of Karen and Rebecca. They just went somewhere, and they never came back. Somewhere between one and three days later they were found dead.

Parrish told Radick to start familiarizing himself with the different report forms that needed to be completed for on-going cases. While he was distracted with this, Parrish spent a couple of hours going through the files again. Wheland's unmistakable scrawl, Engel's cryptic notes that only Engel would ever understand. They were standard open cases – the canvass, the preliminary reports, the autopsy, the friends and relatives Q&A. Autopsy was of the greatest interest to Parrish, both Jennifer and Nicole having been found within twenty-four hours of their respective TODs. Jennifer's death was caused by strangulation, apparently manual, and in Nicole's case it had been a clean break between the second and third vertebrae. *As if she'd been hung*, the medical examiner reported, but there were no outward abrasions or ligature marks to the neck that a hanging would have left.

A severe contusion on the right side of Nicole's head suggested that she had been hit with something – or against something – with sufficient force for the neck to break. *Against* was the considered opinion of the ME, simply because there was no indentation, no shape to the injury as was usual when an object was applied with external force. This contusion showed just a flat and even impact, as if her head had been slammed against a wall. However, it was a neck-related injury that had occasioned the death of both girls – of all four girls.

There were no notes in these files regarding manner of dress, alterations in usual outward appearance, or other such things that might have alerted Parrish to a similarity to the others. Of course, they may have been present, but gone unnoticed. It was not, however, those outward signs that had grabbed his attention, but several other similarities common to all four cases. First, there was height, weight, coloring and age. Then the fact that each had engaged in sexual intercourse some short time before death, yet in no instance were there indications of rape. The fact that they all came from within a couple of miles' radius of one another was possibly significant. The fact that each body had just been left for someone to find. That no attempt had been made to hide the victims from the eyes of the world was an aspect that intrigued Parrish particularly. Criminal psychology was a field all its own, but homicide touched on it periodically. Parrish was not a profiler, but he understood sufficient to be aware of the four types of killer as detailed in standard texts. One man, or four different men, it didn't matter. Four dead girls. Four open cases, three in-house, and one that belonged to Richard Franco at the Williamsburg 91st.

Was there even the slightest possibility that they were connected?

Parrish's thoughts were interrupted by the telephone.

'Got your tox results on the Lange girl,' he was told. 'You ready?'

Parrish took a pencil, a sheet of paper. 'What you got?'

'She was benzo'd. A heavy dose.'

Parrish felt the kick in his gut – the feeling that something was becoming something else. How had he known that this would happen with this girl?

'Specifically?' Parrish asked.

'Flunitrazepam. Rohypnol, right? Roofies I believe they call it now.'

'How much?' he asked.

'Well, considering that recreational use averages somewhere between one-point-eight and two-point-seven, she was hit with about five or six as far as I can tell. It metabolizes very fast. That's why it wasn't apparent in the urine or the blood.'

'But the hair?'

'You can take it from the hair for up to about a month.

Depends how much was in the system, but about a month and you can still find it.'

'Anything else?'

'No, just the roofies. You want I should send the report on up to your office?'

'Yes, please. Soon as you can.'

'No problem.'

Parrish hung up. Karen, Jennifer and Nicole were out of the ballpark as far as new tox tests were concerned. Blood and urine would have been checked as standard, but hair was done only on request. Had he not asked for it in Rebecca's case it would have remained unknown. This threw a new slant on the thing. She was drugged, heavily, and she was probably fucked while she was out of it. She wouldn't have been capable of resistance. There would have been no fight in her at all. Truth was, she wouldn't have even been aware of what was happening, and if she had survived, she wouldn't have remembered a thing. Her brother? Someone her brother sold her to? And was this porno something else entirely? A snuff movie? Fuck a teenage girl while she's dying of a benzodiazepine overdose, or maybe fuck her once she's dead? Stick it on a DVD and sell enough copies to buy yourself out of a lifetime of addiction? Was *that* what Danny Lange had planned?

Parrish switched on his computer and pulled up the number for the Williamsburg 91st.

He introduced himself to Richard Franco, gave him a brief on what he was working on, and asked about Karen.

'Standard stuff,' Franco told him. 'Sure we did the tests, but I don't recall there being anything unusual about her, nothing that would have prompted me to ask for anything beyond blood and urine. You got a similar up there?'

'Maybe. I'm just following on the adoption connection on another case from last week.'

'Hell, I don't know what to say. It was the best part of a year ago now. I don't really remember much about it. You want I should dig up the file and send it over to you?'

'I already saw it. I came over a couple of days ago and had a look through it.'

'Well, that's all there is, I'm afraid. Anything else I can help you with?'

'I don't think so, not at the moment. I'll call you if I think of anything.'

Parrish thanked Franco and hung up.

He sat back and considered the conversation. It was a sad state of affairs when the death of a teenage girl occasioned such comments as *I don't recall there being anything unusual about her*. Nothing beyond the fact that she was sixteen and found dead in a dumpster.

Radick appeared. 'I'm outta here,' he said. 'You want a ride?'

'Sure, if you don't mind. I want to stop by and see my daughter on the way back if that's okay.'

'Sure, if you're not going to be long.'

TWENTY-SEVEN

Shortly after six they were over the other side of Flatbush. Radick came to a stop on Smith Street near Carroll Park.

'You don't have to come in,' Parrish said.

'It's fine. I don't mind.' Radick came out of the car, waited for Parrish to show him the way.

Caitlin Parrish shared an apartment with two other trainee nurses, but Parrish found her alone.

'Jesus, Dad, you should call before you come over. I'm going out.'

'Hey, sweetheart,' Parrish said. 'Good to see you. How are you? I'm fine. And how are you? I'm good thanks. Come on in, why don't you? Have a cup of coffee, take a weight off.'

'Okay, okay,' she said. 'We can do without the sarcasm.'

Radick appeared back of Parrish.

'Oh, this is Jimmy Radick. He's my new partner.'

Caitlin – brunette, five-five, slim and bright and sharp as a pin – extended her hand and shook with Jimmy Radick. 'Good to meet you,' she said. 'For your sins eh?'

Radick frowned.

'They gave you my dad as a partner for your sins.'

'Seems that way.'

'So come in, both of you, but I *am* in a hurry. Like I said, I'm going out. You want coffee then you're going to have to make it yourself.' She hurried down the hallway and disappeared through a doorway on the right.

'Where are you off to?' Parrish called after her. He stepped into the apartment hallway, waved Radick in, closed the door behind him.

'I'm going out to meet my pimp, and then I'm going to have sex with three different guys, and after that I figured I might get some crank and sit up all night smoking and talking shit with black people.'

'Caitlin—'

She appeared in the hallway, her blouse untucked, her feet bare, her hair loosely pinned back.

'Dad, seriously, you have to stop asking . . . and more importantly, you have to stop worrying yourself about what I might be doing and where I might be going.'

'Force of habit,' Parrish replied.

'Well, get another habit, for God's sake. A year or so and I'll be in Manhattan, either that or London.'

'London?'

'I'm kidding, Dad. Lighten up.' She disappeared back into her room.

'Coffee?' Parrish asked.

'Sure,' Radick said.

Parrish made himself busy in the kitchen. Radick walked on through to what must have been the girls' communal lounge room. A TV, a stereo, a couple of bookcases. *Peanuts*, *The Tommyknockers* by Stephen King, *Introduction to Diagnostic Medicine*, DVDs of *Scrubs*, *Grey's Anatomy* and *24*. Predictably diverse, at the same time appropriate.

Caitlin came into the room. She approached Radick hurriedly. The expression on her face was somewhat awkward.

'How long have you been with my dad?'

'Yesterday,' Radick replied.

'He drinks. You know that, right?'

Radick didn't reply.

'He drinks and he gets morose. There's a lot of history between him and my mom and he doesn't deal with it very well—'

'Miss Parrish . . . I don't know that you should be tell—'

She pressed a slip of paper into Radick's hand. 'That's my phone number here, my work number and my cell. Call me if he gets too fucked up, okay? Call me if you start worrying about him.'

'Miss Parrish—'

'Seriously. Call me—'

'Coffee,' Parrish said, and Caitlin turned suddenly. She smiled as he came into the room.

'I thought you were getting ready,' Parrish said.

'I am. I just came in here for a barrette and I cannot find it.'

139

Caitlin passed her father and left the room.

Parrish handed Radick a coffee cup, told him to take a seat.

Radick stuffed the slip of paper into his jacket pocket and took a chair near the window.

Parrish set his coffee cup on the table, said he'd be a moment.

Before long there were raised voices in back of the apartment. This was some father–daughter thing that Radick really didn't want to be involved in. He drank his coffee, sat patiently, tried not to listen but it was difficult. Frank was going on about her job, where she was going to be working. Sounded like he wanted her to be one place, she wanted to be another. Sounded like the sort of discussion that would only ever become a disagreement, an argument, a bone of contention. To Radick she seemed more than capable of making up her own mind, deciding where she wanted to live, where she wanted to work. But what the hell did he know? He was twenty-nine. He wasn't married, never had been, had no kids, no relationship. This was way beyond his territory, and he was glad of it.

Ten minutes and Parrish was done. He reappeared, that apologetic expression on his face that people wore when they felt guilty for having subjected a stranger to some of their life issues.

He didn't apologize however, merely told Radick that they were leaving.

Radick set his cup down. He followed Parrish to the door.

'Thanks for the coffee, Miss Parrish,' he called back, but there was no answer.

He dropped Parrish off at his apartment building, glanced in the rear-view as he pulled away from the sidewalk. Parrish stood there for a moment as if he was trying to remember something important, and then he seemed to shrug his shoulders disconsolately before walking up the steps.

Radick drove home. He was not averse to a few shots of something-or-other himself, but he knew if he started with Parrish they would wind up in a bar someplace, Parrish telling Radick his life story, feeling sorry for himself, starting down the slow decline. Radick wanted definition between work and personal. He didn't want to be Frank Parrish's drinking buddy. He wanted to be his partner. He knew of John Parrish – the *mighty* John Parrish, stalwart of the OCCB and the Brooklyn OC Task Force. The man had been a beast, and if his first couple of days with Frank were anything to go by he reckoned John would have been a little disappointed how his son turned out. But Frank Parrish *had* been good. One of the best, or so the rumors went. The man could teach you things. He had seen things, done things, solved crimes that no-one else had. He was a small legend, but a legend all the same. He was not his father. Hell, no-one was like John Parrish. But even if Frank had taken a percentage of his father's brilliance, and if that percentage was watered down five times and then five times again, even that would be enough for Jimmy Radick.

Parrish stayed home for no more than half an hour. He should not have walked out to DeKalb Avenue, but he did. He stood there at the corner, looked back towards his apartment on Willoughby, then left to Clay's Tavern. He vacillated. He always vacillated. He went left. He *always* went left.

Frank Parrish was a loyal drunk. He was loyal to Bushmills, loyal to his corner booth, loyal to the tunes he chose from the jukebox. Tom Waits' 'I Hope That I Don't Fall In Love With You' and 'Shiver Me Timbers'; Miles Davis' 'It Never Entered My Mind'; Stan Getz's 'Desafinado', and finally, predictably, so predictable that someone would call it from the bar . . .

Hey, Frank.

What?

Do it.

Do what?

Play Misty for me.

And Frank would smile, and amble to the jukebox, and drop a quarter in and punch the buttons, and Errol Garner would lull them all into a hazy, drunken sense of nostalgia.

Frank Parrish would stay until eleven, sometimes eleven-thirty, and then he would find his way home.

His father had drunk here. It wasn't Clay's Tavern back then, it was The Hammerhead, but a change of name hadn't changed the decor, the atmosphere, the reminders. Talking with Doctor Marie Griffin was proving easier than he'd imagined. Yeah, maybe it *was* time to talk. The asshole was dead, after all.

He found his corner booth. He ordered a double and collected it. He waved a 'hi' to a couple of regulars propping up the east wing of the bar. Retired cops. Guys who eased out the last two or three years of their thirty back of a desk someplace, and now spent their time talking about the *good old days* and wondering why they'd been so desperate to leave. Spend thirty years a cop you're gonna die a cop. There was no easy way out of it. It was not a job, it was a vocation. After that it became a passion, an addiction, a crutch, a belief. Either that, or you got out. Cops didn't marry well. They were lousy fathers. They walked out of the house into a world that no-one else could see, as if only they could perceive the thin veneer that lay between what people believed was reality and reality itself. Reality was behind the crime scene tape. Reality was found at the tip of a stiletto, down the muzzle of a .38, back of a sawn-off Mossberg pump-action shotgun as it unloaded its guts into half a dozen diners in a restaurant on Myrtle Avenue. Reality was a stabbing, a beating, a strangulation, a drowning, a suicide, an overdose, a hanging. Reality was twelve-year-old junkies, fifteen-year-old hookers. It was stealing and running and hiding, and backing up into a corner while the world looked for you, and knowing full well that soon the world would find you and it would all be over.

Reality was people like Rebecca Lange, a girl who wore red nail varnish and reminded Frank Parrish of Caitlin. That was what it had come down to – a dead girl who reminded him of his daughter, a daughter he could still argue with about nothing at all.

And then there was John Parrish, the Saints of New York, the whole fucked-up mess of Frank's own history that had somehow followed in the wake of his father – a man who wore one face for the world, but was someone else entirely.

Three double Bushmills and Frank Parrish realized that the road he had started walking down with Marie Griffin was long and winding, and it didn't really have a destination.

And he thought of his father, what he should have said to the man:

No, I don't love you. I don't even respect you. I know who you are. I see the rosettes and the plaques, the medal ribbons, the citations and commends, and I listen to you and your buddies talking your smart shit over Schlitz and hot dogs in the back yard, and I see right through you all. I see right through the host of motherfuckers that you really are. And it isn't the money that pains me. It isn't the cheating, the backhanders, the bribery. It isn't even the killing. The thing that pains me is that you spent all your time lying to people, and you didn't even admit how much you were lying to yourself. At least I know I fucked up. At least I possess enough humility to see that. I screwed up my marriage, screwed up my kids, but hell, I can at least admit it, you know? That's what galls me. That's what makes me ashamed to be your son.

And he thought of Caitlin, and he wondered whether he really should ask Jimmy Radick to keep an eye on her. Just for her own good. Just to make sure she was staying on the right side of the road.

Eleven-thirty Frank Parrish made his way home to his apartment.

Arriving in the austere and undecorated living room, nothing more than a sofa, a table and chair by the window, a TV set and an old stereo unit with a turntable, he resigned himself to the fact that whatever he had started with the counsellor woman would now have to go on. His father had been dead for sixteen years. That did not seem so long ago until he realized that Caitlin had been four years old at the funeral. To consider it this way made it seem like forever.

The TV did not distract him, and so he turned it off. He sat at the table, the drapes inched apart, and through the window he looked down towards Willoughby Avenue. Directly west, no more than three or four blocks, was Brooklyn Hospital. North-west, again little more than half a dozen blocks, was Cumberland. Caitlin could work at either. He could see her every week, perhaps a couple of times. They could meet for lunch in Auburn Place or St. Edwards. They could pretend that they were close until they became so. They – *he* – could make up for the past ten years of noise and bullshit that had pulled the family apart.

Frank fetched a bottle from the cupboard above the sink. He poured three fingers, returned to the window, tried to focus on Rebecca, the manner of her death, the reason, the rationale, the possible resolution.

Her face haunted him. The short hair. The painted nails.

He wondered if she had known her life was going to end, or if she had been strangled as she slept, waking only in those last handful of seconds before everything guttered and was extinguished.

He wondered if she had seen her killer's face, or if he had tied a scarf around his face, had worn a baseball cap tipped down low so she saw nothing but the muscles in his jaw line as he tightened his grip.

He wondered if Rebecca had tried to fight back, even though against someone so much stronger she had possessed no hope at all.

He wondered if she had pleaded, begged, prayed even . . . prayed to God for respite, for release, for forgiveness for whatever she might have done that had brought this upon herself.

Honestly? Frank Parrish would have liked to believe in God, but he felt that faith should be mutual. It should be reciprocated. And he knew, with certainty, that God did not believe in him.

He fell asleep on the sofa shortly before two. He was still dressed – pants, socks, shirt. An empty bottle sat on the floor, beside it a glass.

He seemed to remember waking near to dawn, but he made no effort to move. He just rolled over, buried his face in a cushion, and tried to push away the images of a dead Rebecca.

TWENTY-EIGHT

'Marty Krugman was small time, a wig salesman. He ran a wig store someplace and he had these late-night TV commercials, but beyond that he ran bets for people. Every once in a while he got something going with someone that added up to a few bucks. One of these people was a guy called Louis Werner. Lou was not a smart gambler. He was impulsive, went on the fly, and he wound up owing Marty something like twenty grand. This is 1978 now, you understand. This is a lot of money. So Marty is giving Lou a hard time about this money, and Lou is thinking of every which way he can get Marty off his back, because Marty is the kind of guy that just gets onto you and he won't let go.'

'Frank, I thought you were finally getting to Lufthansa today.'

'I am. Lou Werner was the Lufthansa cargo supervisor. There was nothing, just *nothing* that Lou didn't know about Lufthansa's traffic, in and out.'

'So what does this have to do with Marty?'

'Lou buys off Marty with a tip about Lufthansa and the money, and Marty takes it to Jimmy Burke, king of hijackers. Jimmy acts nonchalant: he might be into it, he might not. He doesn't want Marty to know he's interested because he hates the guy. I mean, *really* hates him. Jimmy was an insomniac, and sometimes when he was watching late-night TV, he would see Marty in these wig commercials himself, and he bitched about the fact that Marty had money for TV ads, but not for protection money for his store. Apparently Jimmy had tried to get Marty to pay protection, but Marty threatened to go to the DA. After that Jimmy never trusted him.

'Regardless of that, the amount of money that Marty was talking about, what could Jimmy Burke do? Was he going to pass up on something like that because of a wig salesman? He had his buddy Henry Hill speak with Marty Krugman, and Marty dealt with Lou Werner. Everything was distant, everything was twice-removed. Jimmy didn't even want Marty to know that he was going to be doing the airport job himself. But there it was, the biggest robbery in history. This was US dollars, all random and unmarked, coming in from West Germany. This was money spent by American servicemen and tourists over there. It comes back here on Lufthansa flights, it's stored overnight in the cargo bays, and then it gets moved out to the banks.

'Lou Werner gives them the names of all the employees and guards. They know the name of the terminal's senior cargo agent, the name of the night supervisor, the only employee with the right keys and combinations to open the double-door vault. They know there's a primary door, and if the secondary door was opened before the primary door was closed, then a silent alarm would be activated at the Port Authority police office. They knew everything.'

'And what did they get away with?'

'Five million dollars, cash. And then another eight hundred and seventy-five thousand dollars' worth of jewelry. And Burke kept it very tight to his chest. He shut everything down once they hit Lufthansa. No-one said a word, no-one breathed a word, that was his order. No-one spent anything, no-one discussed it in their homes, their cars, their back yards.'

'But it didn't go as planned?'

'Oh, the robbery went as planned. The robbery went exactly as planned. They had the place down cold, they knew it off by heart because of Lou Werner's detailed information, and they were in and out in an hour. The difficulty was that this was now a very high profile case, and all over the news. December 1978, five million dollars? I can't even begin to imagine what that would translate to now. Anyway, Jimmy was paranoid. He knew that with the number of people involved, and the very long sentences that would come down if they were caught, there was always the possibility that somebody might strike a deal with the DA to keep themselves out of jail. Organizationally, he had managed things well, and there was only one person who had ever met Lou Werner face-to-face—'

'Marty Krugman.'

'Well, no. The only one of Burke's gang that ever met Lou Werner was a guy called Joe Manri, but Marty was the mouthpiece. He was the one making all the noise, and so Burke killed Marty Krugman first. And once he'd killed him, it sort of set the precedent for anyone else who said anything out of turn. Jimmy Burke had connections into the OCCB, one of which was my father, and he let it be known that if anyone came in blabbing about the Lufthansa heist he needed to know about it. All told, there were ten murders as a result of Lufthansa, and though the general belief is that Jimmy and his people killed them all, I can tell you that that was not the case.'

'Your father—'

'My father knew all about it. He condoned it, and even if he hadn't had to kill anyone himself he would have assigned people to do that for Jimmy Burke.'

'And Jimmy Burke paid him?'

'Yeah, he paid him.'

'How much?'

'I have no idea. A hundred grand, maybe two hundred and fifty grand. Burke had five million dollars. He had however many accomplices who were vanishing at a rapid rate. I'm sure that Jimmy Burke wound up with most of that money all to himself.'

'And the investigation?'

'Well, the Feds sent in a hundred agents in the first forty-eight hours. They had police from the NYPD and the Port Authority; they had insurance company investigators; people from Brinks, Lufthansa's own internal security crews. Everyone was down there. The FBI got Burke's name somehow – not enough evidence to arrest him, but enough to put surveillance on him and a few of the others who had done the robbery – but Burke and his people managed to lose the helicopter traces by driving into FAA restricted flight zone areas at JFK. The Feds bugged their cars, but they had whispered conversations in the back seats with the radios turned up full volume.'

'Did they get any of them?'

'Well, they knew right from the get-go that it had to be an inside job. Burke's crew had hit precisely the correct warehouse out of a possible twenty-two on a three hundred and fifty-acre site. The cargo agent and the night supervisor told the investigators that the gunmen had known their names, the layout of the building, known about the vault doors, the whole works. Lufthansa's security people had given over Lou Werner's name within hours of the robbery because he'd already been a suspect in an earlier foreign currency robbery. That time there had been insufficient evidence against him, but this time Werner had actually stopped the Brinks security truck from collecting the five million dollars on the previous Friday night. He told them that he needed the signature of a cargo executive to let them take the money, which was not the usual procedure, but he forbade them to take the shipment and kept them waiting for an hour and a half. They were eventually ordered to continue their round without the Lufthansa cash, so the Feds knew that not only had Lou arranged that the cash was still there, but he was pretty much the only person who knew it was still inside the vault.'

'They arrested him?'

'Well, they put surveillance on him, they bugged him, they interviewed people he knew. They spoke to his wife, Beverley, who had left him some time before, and she told them that Lou had called her up, told her that he was coming into a great deal of money, and that she would seriously regret leaving him. Lou also told his best friend about the robbery a month before it even happened, and agreed to give him thirty grand for his taxicab business. Then he found out that this best friend was actually having an affair with the ex-wife, and he called up this guy and said he could go fuck himself as far as the thirty grand was concerned. Once the robbery was all over the newspapers, Lou told his girlfriend all about it, how clever he was, how proud she should be of him, but she panicked, told him that he would wind up in jail. Lou was really upset about her reaction. He hoped she'd be impressed with what a smart guy he was, but she went all crazy and hysterical so Lou, all down and depressed, goes to his favorite bar and tells the barman all about it.'

'So he was not the smartest guy in the world.'

'Well, he was an amateur. He wasn't Jimmy Burke, that's for sure. And this old buddy of his – the one that was screwing Lou's wife – well, he was so afraid that his own wife would find out about his affair with Beverley Werner that he agreed to help the FBI any which way he could. It was a straightforward job from there. They got testimony from half a dozen different people that Lou Werner had spoken to and took him in.'

'And he informed on Burke and the rest of the people?'

'Well, that's what they thought he would do. The assistant US attorney who was heading up the case, a guy called Ed McDonald, got the name of a Lufthansa cargo employee called Peter Gruenewald. Word was that Werner and Gruenewald had put the plan together. McDonald interrogated Gruenewald, who denied everything, but they found out that Gruenewald had applied for tickets to Bogota, and then on to Taiwan. Then they found one of the guys that Gruenewald had approached as a possible contender for carrying out the job that he and Werner had planned. They had enough to tie Gruenewald in with Lufthansa, so he elected to co-operate with McDonald.

'Well, McDonald thought that Werner would just roll over on everyone involved. He'd talked about nothing else but Lufthansa before he was arrested, but the moment they took him in he closed up like a clam. He said he had nothing to do with the robbery, that he had merely boasted about it to his wife and his girlfriend to satisfy his own ego. Until they confronted him with Gruenewald. Werner damned near had a heart attack right there and then, but he still insisted that he knew nothing about the robbery. Regardless, with testimony from Gruenewald, from Beverley Werner, from Lou's girlfriend, from the bartender, McDonald went to trial. May 1978, a ten-day trial, and Lou Werner was found guilty of organizing the Lufthansa robbery. Now Lou could go one way or the other. He could give up Joe Manri, and Manri could then give up Jimmy Burke and the rest of the crew, or he could keep his mouth shut.'

'What did he do?'

'Well, he didn't get a chance to make a decision. The same night a squad car unit in Brooklyn found the dead bodies of Joe Manri and another colleague of his, Robert McMahon, in a car on the corner of Shenectady and Avenue M. Both had been shot with a single .44 in the back of the head.'

'You're going into a lot of small details, Frank. Why is that?'

'Because . . . well, because I think . . . Well, if my father was involved directly in any of this, then I think it might have been that. I think he might have killed Manri and McMahon and prevented Lou Werner from ever giving Ed McDonald the connection he wanted to Jimmy Burke.'

'You actually believe he might have done that?'

'I think so, yes.'

'Why?'

'It was April of '79 when Lou Werner was tried. I was nearly fifteen years old, and I remember my father coming home that evening. We'd been following the thing on the TV. It was a big deal, you know, and they'd been going on about it for days. Anyway, he came home, and there was some feature or news program, and the guy was saying that Werner had been convicted and was waiting sentence, and there was a possibility he might cooperate with the US Attorney's Office in an effort to reduce his sentence.'

'And your father was watching it with you?'

'He was. It was some hours before the report came in about the two dead guys in Brooklyn, and my dad just smiled to himself, like I wasn't even there, and he said that it didn't matter what happened now. He said that it didn't matter what Lou Werner said now, that they would never get the guys who did it. And I looked at him right after he said it, and there was this expression on his face, you know? I thought then, and I think now, that he was the one who shot those two guys in their car and got Jimmy Burke off the hook for Lufthansa.'

'Oh my God—'

'You don't need to tell me. This was the guy with all the citations and commends. This was the guy, the hero, who headed up the Saints of New York.'

TWENTY-NINE

Parrish took a walk after his session with Marie Griffin. It was a little after ten. Radick had not yet arrived, and there was no message at the desk. Ordinarily, Parrish would have chased him up, but this morning – this of all mornings – he wanted some time and space for himself.

It took him twenty-five minutes to reach St. Michael's. He stood outside for a few moments, and then he made his way in, staying back behind the pews, traversing left and walking down the outside aisle. He stopped halfway, took a seat, and listened to the sound of nothing.

Father Briley saw him from the chancel, nodded in acknowledgement, and just when Parrish believed he might be left alone the priest started walking down towards him. Briley was an old man, late sixties perhaps, or early seventies. Parrish understood that he'd been offered a transfer elsewhere many times, and each time he'd refused. Briley had been here since Parrish was a child, when his father had brought him to church some Sundays because he, John Parrish, was a just-in-case Catholic.

'Frank.'

'Father.'

'I can sit?' asked Briley.

Parrish smiled.

'You are well, Frank?'

'As can be.'

'Seems we speak too infrequently these days, don't you think?'

'Yes, Father, I do.'

'You are working too many hours, I imagine.'

'The work doesn't stop. You know that as well as anyone.'

Briley smiled. He reached out and gripped Parrish's forearm. 'We appreciate your generosity, Frank, as always.'

'I do what I can.'

Briley hesitated, and then he looked at Parrish directly. 'You have about you the air of a man defeated.'

'Defeated?' Parrish shook his head. 'Frustrated perhaps, defeated no. They haven't broken me yet.'

'You must take better care of yourself.'

'Why do you—'

'Frank, I see what I see. I've been here too long to be fooled anymore. You do not eat well. I imagine you do not sleep. And there's the drink . . .'

'I'm doing what it says in the Bible, Father.'

Briley laughed. 'That old line?'

'You know it?'

'Of course I do. Proverbs thirty-one, chapters six and seven. "Give strong drink to him who is perishing, and wine to those in bitter distress; let them drink and forget their poverty, and remember their misery no more." You can't be the priest in an Irish community and not have heard that line a hundred thousand times before, believe me.'

Parrish looked away towards the end of the pews.

'And your family?' Briley asked. 'How are the children? Clare?'

'Clare is Clare, and my children are so far from children it's hard to imagine that they ever were children. They survive in their own ways, as we all do.'

'And you are troubled by your work?'

Parrish was silent a moment, thoughtful, before he answered, 'Yes, I suppose I am, to some degree perhaps. We see the worst of it after it's been done, you know?'

'And the burden grows heavier with time I should think.'

'Either that, or you become inured and weathered to it all.'

'Like your father?'

Parrish looked up at the priest.

Briley nodded. 'He came here alone sometimes. Not for mass, not for anything but a little peace and quiet. I spoke to him on a number of occasions, and he looked like you look now.'

Parrish frowned.

'As if he was carrying the same kind of burden.'

'I can tell you now that he was carrying an entirely

different kind of burden,' Parrish replied. 'More a burden of guilt than anything else.'

'Why do you say that, Frank?'

'Because he was not an honest man, Father. He was a corrupt and self-serving man. He knew his job well enough to see the lines, but he chose to step over them.'

'You know this?'

'Yes.'

'And you've always known?'

'Pretty much, yes.'

Briley leaned back. He took a deep breath and exhaled slowly. 'How do you deal with something like that, Frank? When someone so close is believed to be a paragon of decency and honesty and you believe they are not?'

'I don't think that you *can* deal with it.'

'And you feel differently about this now than you have in the past?'

'I'm trying to feel differently about it. I'm talking about it with someone. I've never talked about it before.'

'Talking is good.'

'I'm sure it can be. Right now it's doing little more than making me angry at him. It reminds me of all the reasons I had for hating him.'

Once again Briley gripped Parrish's forearm. 'Hate—'

'Is one of the seven deadly sins?'

'No it's not, Frank. It was a close runner but it didn't make the last hurdle.'

Parrish smiled.

'Hate is a powerful emotion,' Briley went on. 'Sometimes justified, I am sure, but in my experience it tends to do more harm to the hater than the hatee.'

Parrish laughed. 'Well, the hatee is dead, so I don't think there's a great deal more harm that can come to him.'

'Yet sometimes the memory of the man is more powerful than the man himself. The strength of reputation, of what other people think of him.'

'It wouldn't do any good to dispel the myth. As you know, my father was a self-proclaimed Samaritan and all-round good guy.'

Briley smiled sardonically. 'I know he was neither one of those,' he said.

'I think the only person's well-being he was interested in was his own—'

'You don't need to tell me, Frank, you really don't.'

'I feel like I have to tell *someone*. Someone other than—'

'No,' Briley interjected. 'You don't have to tell me because I already know.'

Parrish raised his eyebrows.

'Don't look so surprised, Frank. Really, you'd be amazed the things people will tell a priest, even outside the confessional box. Your father was here a month or so before he was killed, and he alluded to certain things, certain events, that troubled him.'

'L-like what?' Parrish asked, his voice catching in his throat, his disbelief evident in his expression.

'Nothing specific. No names, no dates, no places. I don't remember precisely what he said. This is – what? – fifteen, sixteen years ago? He began with the usual explanations and apologies for missing Mass and Confession. I asked him if he wanted to confess, and he said he didn't, that it was too late. He said that he had done some things, that he had abused his position of trust, that he had taken advantage of the fact that he was a police officer. He said that he had taken things that did not belong to him, that evidence had been suppressed, even destroyed, and people who were guilty had walked away as free men.'

'And what did you say?'

'What could I say? I acknowledged him. I told him to seek repentance. I suggested he take Confession, that he attend Mass, take Communion . . . that he should work to rectify the wrongs and make good.'

'And did he? Come to Mass, confess . . . ?'

'Not as far as I know. He certainly didn't come here again. Like I said, it was only a month or so before he was killed.'

'And when you heard he'd been killed?'

'Well, I pondered on what might have brought that about. Whether he had finally been overcome by his own torment and put himself in a situation where he could be killed, or if he had tried to change things . . .'

'Change things?'

'I wondered whether he'd said or done something that worried those around him, those who wanted to stay in whatever business they were involved in. I wondered if he'd said something that made them feel he couldn't be trusted anymore.'

'You think he might have done that?'

'Honestly?' Briley shook his head. 'He might, but I don't really believe so. I think when I saw your father he was long gone. I think he'd walked so far down that road that there was no turning back.'

'And you never told anyone?'

Briley smiled. 'The church is a sanctuary, Frank, you know that.'

'And me? You never told *me*. All those conversations we had when Clare and I were breaking up, and you never thought to mention the fact that my father came and spoke to you about what he'd done?'

'What good would it have done, Frank? What good is it doing you now? You have your own difficulties to deal with, and they're enough for any man.'

Parrish started to get up from the pew. 'Seems like I should have said something . . . seems like you should have said something—'

'I *couldn't* say anything. You know that. And you? What would you have said, and who would you have said it to? We draw lines everywhere, and then we stay inside them. That's the way we stay alive, Frank, especially in our line of work.'

'I don't know . . . I just don't know . . .'

'Don't know what?'

'I don't know what to think. I don't know what to feel about this.'

'Nothing. These things have occurred, my son. It is too late to do anything about them now. The sins of the father should not be carried by the son. You are not your father. He wasn't you. However, unless there's a great deal about you that I don't know, then it seems to me that you have not taken such a different path than him . . .'

'You don't know what you're talking about,' Parrish interjected. 'There is a world of difference between me and my father.' He got up from the pew and stepped into the aisle. 'I have to go now,' he said quietly.

Briley rose. He stepped ahead of Parrish and gripped his shoulders. 'I am here,' he said. 'I've been here for a long while, will more than likely be here for a good while longer. You know where I am.'

Parrish said nothing. He turned and walked back down the aisle to the front door.

As he left the church he felt that gnawing pain in his lower gut once again, but this time he couldn't tell whether it was fear or hatred or something altogether more insidious.

THIRTY

Radick was waiting for him in the office. He didn't ask where Parrish had been, and Parrish didn't ask why his partner was late.

'Today?' Radick asked.

'I need to go back to County Records and Archives and chase up some possible connections to Child Services.'

'Valderas has been down here,' Radick said. 'I think I should stay, do some work on these other things. It doesn't need both of us to go over there does it?'

'No. Makes sense.'

Radick got up, started to put on his jacket. 'I'll drive you,' he said.

'No, I'll get the subway. I'll be fine.'

'You sure?'

'You spend some time on these other things. Call me if you need to go out and see people. I won't be more than a coupla hours anyway.'

Parrish left, relieved that he was alone, relieved that it had been Radick's suggestion. Could he trust Radick? Hell, in all honesty he didn't know the guy from any other suit. The fact that he did good someplace else was no testament to his reliability or trustworthiness.

He made good time into Manhattan, was there just before noon and aware only then that he had not yet eaten. He stopped at a deli and had half of a pastrami sandwich. He couldn't face any more, but sat on in the corner booth a while, one eye on the street, another on the TV on the wall. A pretty girl in little more than her underwear urged him to drink Miller Lite. Right now. Right this minute.

Parrish tried not to think about Father Briley. He tried even harder not to think of his own father. It used to be that there were two parts to his existence: his work, and his own life. A single door separated the two but, after a while, even with the greatest effort, you became aware of the voices from the other side. They grew louder and louder, until finally, inevitably, whatever side you were on was populated with voices from the other. At home he would think of the dead. While he communed with the dead he would think of home. His marriage had suffered greatly, but perhaps this was the pattern for all marriages: a wide road, seemingly endless, that yet narrowed unnoticeably, until at last both husband and wife were trapped in a lightless cul-de-sac of bitterness . . .

Seated in a small windowless office on the second floor of the County Records building, something came to light that raised the hairs on the back of Frank Parrish's neck. Had he not somewhere been convinced that there would be a connection, he believed he would not have found it. Had he not been certain that there was something more to the deaths of these girls than locale, he would have overlooked the tiny thread that showed itself.

It concerned a girl called Alice Forrester, the stepsister of Nicole Benedict. Nicole's parents – Steven and Angela Benedict – had divorced. Steven had then married a woman called Elaine Forrester, and with her came her daughter, Alice. Parrish found Alice's file without difficulty, and there learned that Alice had been an only child, her father having died before she was born. Angela Benedict had been an alcoholic, and thus – unusually – the father, Steven Benedict had been granted custody of Nicole. The details of this soap opera were in Alice Forrester's file, and this was where Parrish found Nicole. Steven Benedict, now married to Elaine Forrester, had legally adopted Alice, and thus the link was incontrovertible. Anyone looking at the Alice Forrester adoption files would have come across Nicole. Her picture was there, her personal details, a brief report on her attitude towards having a 'new' sister. Alice was the responsibility of the CAA, but she had not wound up a victim. The stepsister had become a victim, and solely because her picture and her details had been there in Alice's file and someone had seen them.

Parrish leaned back in the chair and slowly exhaled. Same district, same jurisdiction, same offices that had dealt with

Rebecca, Karen, and now Nicole. But no Jennifer. He spent a good while searching out Jennifer but found nothing. That didn't necessarily mean there was no connection, but simply that the link could have been even more tenuous.

And then he remembered the runaways, the three girls that had gone missing.

Searching his pockets, Parrish found the notebook in which he'd scribbled their names. Shannon McLaughlin, reported missing on Thursday, February 1st, 2007; Melissa Schaeffer, missing since Wednesday, October 11th, 2006 and, most recently, Sarah Burch, who left home to meet with friends at a local mall in the early evening of Monday, May 21st, 2007 and not seen since. Melissa was seventeen, the other two sixteen.

There was no sign of Shannon or Sarah in the records, but it wasn't long before Parrish found the next one with a CAA connection. Melissa Mockler. Adopted at the age of four by a young couple named Steven and Kathy Schaeffer. Parrish remembered the file back at the office. He recalled her face. Rhodes and Pagliaro had taken the case, had worked the usual lines, canvassed the street, spoken to the neighbors, the boyfriend, the girls who shared her classes. As was always the case with such disappearances, the first forty-eight hours were crucial. Beyond that the likelihood of success faded rapidly. A week, and you could pretty much kiss goodbye to ever seeing the runaway alive.

Parrish left the office and took the files down to the lobby. He asked if there was someone who could assist him and was asked to wait.

Ten or fifteen minutes passed, then a young man approached him from the elevator.

'Detective Parrish?' he asked.

Parrish rose to his feet.

'Hi, I'm Jamie Lewis. Someone said you needed help with something.'

'Yes, I do. I don't know if you can help me, but I had a couple of questions. Is there somewhere we could go that's a bit more private?'

Jamie Lewis led them to a narrow room back of the lobby and Parrish outlined the four cases he was dealing with. He stressed that there was no official inquiry into the Child Services or CAA connection, that this was merely something that he was pursuing as a possibility.

'You realize that you're crossing jurisdictions now,' Lewis said. 'Of course, six months ago it wouldn't have been that way—'

'Six months ago? What do you mean?'

'The whole thing got turned inside out at the start of the year. They'd been talking about it for ever, certainly as long as I've been here, and finally they did it.'

'Talking about what, Mr Lewis?'

'The management system. The way the cases are dealt with. Up until the start of the year everything was dealt with through two main departments that acted as co-ordination points between Child Services and the Adoption Agency. They called them Family Welfare North and Family Welfare South. North District handled Manhattan, the Bronx, and everything west of the river, whereas the South District handled Brooklyn, Maspeth, Williamsburg – everything to the east. Then they divided each one into eight separate departments, each with its own jurisdiction.'

'So the cases that I have here—'

'Would have all been in the original South Zone.'

'And the CAA and Child Services maintain separate records for each case?'

'Yes, they do, and it's the job of the Family Welfare Departments to co-ordinate and liaise between the two.'

'So regardless if you were in South or North you would have access to both sets of records and would know where these kids were at all times.'

'Yes, you can access information at every level of the childcare and adoption process.'

'And how many people were employed in each of the original offices?'

'Oh Christ, I don't know. Maybe seven or eight hundred in each office.'

'Seven or eight hundred?'

'Yeah, easily. Could have been more. They covered a hell of a lot of cases across a huge zone, Detective.'

'Right. Sure. And if I wanted to get a list of every employee of the original South office how would I do that?'

Jamie shook his head. 'I should think that we'd have it somewhere here. Probably Personnel.'

'And they'd also have records of which people from South Welfare went to whichever of the new departments?'

'I should think so, yes. They go by zip code now. Personnel could give you a list of all those offices and their addresses as well.'

'Okay. That's been a great help, Jamie. I really appreciate your time.'

'You think it's someone working for Family Welfare who's done this to these girls?'

Parrish shook his head. 'I have no idea. There might be no connection at all. It could simply be a coincidence—'

'I'm not a great believer in coincidences,' Jamie interjected. 'Never have been.'

'I'm the same, but until there's something more substantial to connect them it *is* nothing more than coincidence.' Parrish got up. 'I'll go see Personnel,' he said. Pausing at the door he added, 'You appreciate that what we have discussed here is strictly confidential. No water cooler chatter with your colleagues. I really cannot stress that enough, Jamie.'

Jamie smiled. 'I'm not one for rumors and hearsay, Detective, don't worry, though if it does turn out to be someone in-house it'll turn things upside down, don't you think?'

'For sure it will,' Parrish replied, 'but let's hope that's not the case, eh?'

THIRTY-ONE

Parrish left the County Records and Archives building clutching a sheaf of papers that detailed over nine hundred names, all of them original employees of Family Welfare South. He also had a print-out listing all the new North and South District offices. The nearest one to the 126th – District Five South – was literally a handful of minutes' walk across Fulton. The feeling he had was one of quiet resolution, yet beneath that a sense of overwhelm. The first thing he would have to do was separate out the men from the women. This business – aside from rarities like Carol Mary Bundy and Aileen Wuornos – was a predominantly male province. Whether Family Welfare South was the link between Rebecca, Karen, Melissa and Nicole he did not know, but it could not be ignored. And if there *was* a connection, and if these girls had been selected not at random, but from files and records held within the administrative co-ordination units of the county's Child Services network, then the ramifications would be staggering. And if this was the case then Parrish believed there would be more. Teenage girls with unstable family backgrounds, perhaps chosen from photographs, even interviews, with a Child Services or Adoption Agency counsellor . . . chosen in the belief that they would never be missed, that no-one would care, that they were expendable?

Had this been the selection process for a sex killer? Or was he chasing a fragile thread of coincidence that would merely serve to alienate his colleagues and superiors further, and finally remove any possibility of real repatriation within Homicide and the Police Department?

Was it worth it?

Parrish didn't think that such a question even justified consideration.

*

He took the subway back across the river from Canal Street to DeKalb. As he walked towards the station house he felt an unexpected and immediate hunger. He had forgotten how it was to have an appetite. He stopped at a diner on Livingston and ordered a tuna mayo sub, some fries, a cup of coffee, and when he was done he had more coffee and a pecan Danish. He left nothing on his plate, and when he left the diner and walked up the street towards the office, he believed that he might get through the rest of the day without a drink. Something had changed. It was subtle, almost unnoticeable, but he recognized it for what it was: This was how a case had felt when he first made detective. Like there was a point.

Radick was at his desk. He asked how Parrish had got on over in Manhattan.

'It was okay,' Parrish replied. He held up the sheaf of papers. 'I might have something here. I'm looking at the possibility of a link between Rebecca and some older cases.'

'You serious?'

Parrish raised his hand. 'Hold on there,' he said, and smiled knowingly. 'Don't go all puppy-dog on this thing, Jimmy. It may be nothing. I got a bunch more questions that need to be answered before I come to any conclusions.'

He sat down, asked, 'So how did you get on with these others?'

'Think we have something on the campus stabbing. I have an APB out on someone.'

'And the subway?'

'Frank, seriously, nothing's gonna happen on that. No witnesses, no-one has come forward, nothing from his friends or family. The likelihood of that ever closing is a million to one.'

'I figured so,' Parrish replied.

'On the Rebecca Lange case, shouldn't we be following up on whoever Larry Temple was talking about? People who could've been doing a porno with her? He said that you and he knew the same names for that kind of thing.'

'There's two or three possibilities,' Parrish replied. 'I think one guy went out to LA, but there's still a couple here that we could chase up.'

'You wanna do that today?'

Parrish glanced at his watch just as the phone rang on an adjacent desk. 'I don't know,' he said. 'I just need to look at where our time is best spent.'

The phone kept ringing. Another three or four rings and it would transfer through to every phone in the office.

They waited – Radick and Parrish – for they knew that if Engel or West didn't appear in the next handful of seconds it would be their pick-up.

'Fuck it!' Radick said, snatching the receiver from the cradle and pressing 1.

'It's Radick,' he said to the operator. 'What's up?'

He motioned for a notepad and took a pen from his inside jacket pocket.

'Again,' he said, and started writing down an address. 'Okay, we're on the way.'

Radick hung up.

Parrish raised an eyebrow questioningly.

'Dead girl in a cardboard box back of Brooklyn Hospital.'

It was close enough to walk, and had Parrish been alone he would have done. They made their way across Fulton and Flatbush, took a left on Ashland, and then stopped at the corner of St. Edwards and Willoughby. A couple of black-and-whites had already taped the entry to a narrow alleyway that ran between two sections of the building. To the left was Fort Greene Park, and already a few stragglers and hangers-on had started to gather. Had there been forewarning they perhaps would have brought the kids, some sandwiches, a blanket to sit on. Parrish shared a few words with one of the responding uniforms. The Deputy Coroner and Crime Scene had already been alerted and were on their way. Parrish learned that the original call had come in from a janitor who had responsibility for the dumpsters at the far end of the alleyway. They were filled and emptied daily, and apparently it was not uncommon to find other trash dumped there. This time someone had put a large cardboard box halfway down the alley. The janitor had taken a look inside, and there she was. Right now he was in back of the building with a nurse and another uniform. He was an elderly man. Seemed his heart wasn't so good at the best of times.

The two detectives started down the alleyway towards the box. The buildings on each side were at least seventy or eighty feet high, and there was limited light. Parrish squinted into semi-darkness, wondering how many shadows he was bringing with him. This was where everything he knew had the most relevance. This was where the specialized knowledge that played no part in any other aspect of life was the most vital thing of all. The smallest things became the biggest things, and the obvious became meaningless.

Grateful in some small part for the relative cleanliness of the alleyway, Parrish paused for a moment and orientated himself. At one end was a small car park belonging to the Brooklyn Hospital, at the other an L-shaped bay where the trash dumpsters were kept. The alley was actually a sixty or seventy foot cul-de-sac with a single secure fire exit set in the right hand wall approximately ten feet from the end. The cardboard box was a good thirty feet into the alleyway, and while Radick surveyed the ground at the alley's mouth, Parrish took a deep breath and walked on down to see what had been left for him.

Five feet from the box he put on latex gloves. He felt the first few spots of rain and inwardly cursed.

'Jimmy!' he called back down the alley. 'You wanna get a couple of torches and a tarpaulin from somewhere. It's about to rain. Speak to whoever, and find out who collects the dumpsters. We need the driver from this morning back here. And find out where the fuck Crime Scene are.'

Radick raised his hand in acknowledgement, and made his way back to the car.

Parrish hesitated again. Without a torch it was difficult to clearly see the ground around the box. He waited until Radick appeared at the mouth of the alley once more, and walked up to meet him.

'Tarpaulin's on the way,' Radick said, and handed over a torch.

Parrish went back the way he'd come, and scoured the ground around the box, but saw nothing of any significance. Stepping to the edge of the box, he looked closely at the uppermost flaps where a serial number was crudely stenciled in black ink, noted the standard heavy-duty metal staples along the seams; the box could have housed a refrigerator, perhaps a piece of furniture. Measuring five foot high, but only three and a half feet wide, either the girl was very small, or she had been folded awkwardly, perhaps even dismembered. 'Her face,' was all the uniform had told him. 'The janitor says he opened the box and saw her face.'

Did the box contain all of her, or just her head, Parrish wondered, but when he saw her eyes he knew. When he reached into the box and felt through the darkness for her hand, he knew.

She was not beaten, not bruised. There was no blood, no vicious gouges torn from her shoulders or her breasts or her arms. She had not been hog-tied, or gagged, or blinded. There was nothing about her that suggested the nature of her death aside from the indication of ligature around her neck – a rope, a cord, a length of fabric perhaps – and the hemorrhaging visible in her eyes.

She looked at Frank Parrish as if she was relieved to see him. As if she was at peace. She was slight but perfectly proportioned, her hair dark and cut short at the back, and Parrish estimated she was five-two or three, perhaps a hundred to a hundred and ten pounds. Age about sixteen. Perhaps younger. He stepped back and took a deep breath. From all appearances she could not have been dead more than six or eight hours.

More than anything, it was her hands that made an impact. The colored nails, so perfectly varnished, not a smudge, not a mark not a blemish. Just like Rebecca.

Parrish was quiet inside. Not a sound, not a thought, just nothing at all.

Until they knew her name she was no-one, except to Frank Parrish.

Because he knew she was one of them. She had to be.

THIRTY-TWO

When you're young you have your dreams, all the things you could do, everything you could be. Parrish had accomplished none of those things, and now he was out of time. He felt the emptiness like a raw tooth socket. The memory of what he had wanted to become was as inherent and inescapable as his own blood: self-replenishing and permanent. His life was as predictable and unchanging as the progression of days. He thought *Every day in every way I am not getting better*. Whatever slim thread of optimism might have wound its way through his thoughts earlier – the feeling that he might make it through the day without a drink – had vanished.

He stood at the end of the alleyway, drinking cheap, burned coffee from a paper cup and waiting for Crime Scene and the Deputy Coroner to complete their scene-work. He impressed upon the DC the need for results on blood and tox.

'Rohypnol,' he told him. 'That's what I'm looking for. That or any other kind of benzo.'

It was after five by the time the DC left with the body. A few minutes after that, the lead Crime Scene analyst emerged from the shadows of the alleyway and told Parrish what he did not want to hear.

'No clothes, no evident signs of a struggle, no teeth-marks, no finger-marks on the neck, just the ligature, but we have a few fibers from her hair. There's no readable prints on the box. The surface is too rough. The number on the box is a classification code for the box itself, not the product it carried. I called it back to the office and someone checked up on the manufacturer . . . comes out of China, and they ship in excess of forty million of that size into the US annually. They are delivered all over the country, more than twenty-five percent of them along the east coast. They're used for furniture, air conditioning units, automotive parts, everything you can think of. We're taking it with us, but I don't know that lab time will give you anything more than we already know, which is basically nothing.'

Parrish thanked the analyst, watched patiently as he and his crew packed up their circus and disappeared.

He walked down the alley, Radick following, and then they stood in silence for a good while until Radick eventually spoke.

'We got the dumpster collection firm,' he said. 'There's two guys that come down here – the driver, and the one who hooks the dumpsters to the back of the truck and makes sure they up-end correctly. They didn't see the box down there, saw nothing out of the ordinary. We have names and addresses, a contact at the company, but I don't think they can give us anything more than we already have.'

Parrish didn't reply. It was as he had expected.

Little more than three hours had elapsed since the discovery of the girl, and now – looking back down the alleyway – no-one would have been any the wiser. It was as if she'd never existed, either in life or in death.

All victims are not created equal.

It was something his father had once said, back before OCCB, back before everything. It was only now – twenty-four years in the PD – that Parrish finally appreciated the depth of that statement.

'Frank?'

'I'm going to get a picture from the ME,' Parrish said. 'I'm going to print up a whole bunch of them and walk them through every department of Child Services and County Adoption if I have to. If she isn't on their system, then . . .' He shook his head, looked down at his shoes, said nothing more.

He walked on past Radick and back towards the car.

Forty minutes later Parrish and Radick had prints and pictures from the ME. Parrish sent Radick to run the prints for fingerprint identification, and he walked across Fulton to Family Welfare, District Five South. By the time he arrived it was closed, and though he spoke with the security people inside the lobby there was nothing they could do to help him. The place was locked down and empty until morning.

It was en route back that he took a call from Radick.

'We have a name,' he said, woodenly. 'Kelly Duncan. Sixteen years old. Father is dead, mother's alive, registered with Child Services two years ago.'

'A definite?'

'Yes, it's a definite. We had her prints on record from two assaults.'

'Who assaulted her?'

'Father. He was around until just over a year ago. He OD'd in July of 2007.'

'And she was still living with the mother?'

'Yeah, looks like it.'

'Where?'

'Seventh Street, down by the canal.'

Parrish didn't reply right away: Seventh Street was no more than three or four blocks from where Caitlin lived. And the girl's body had been found back of Brooklyn Hospital, the same approximate distance from his own place on Clermont.

'Frank?'

'Yeah, I'm here. Pick me up outside the office. We'll go down there and see her now.'

Janice Duncan was an ex-junkie. There was no question about it. The state of her teeth, her skin, the condition of her hair – the telltale signs of a heroin habit.

Her reaction to the news of her daughter's death didn't surprise Frank Parrish. She seemed philosophically resigned to the inevitability of such a thing.

'Shit,' she said matter-of-factly. She sat down on the sofa and lit a cigarette. Parrish sat on the only other chair in the room; Radick remained standing.

'What happened?'

'We believe she was murdered, Mrs Duncan. An autopsy is being performed right now—'

'Murdered,' she said, but it was not a question.

'We believe so, yes,' Parrish replied. 'Can I ask when you last saw her?'

'She came over Sunday,' Janice Duncan said. 'She was here

most of the day. Said she was fine. Didn't seem to be a problem.'

'She came over?' Parrish asked. 'She doesn't live here?'

'Lives with her grandma most of the time,' Janice Duncan said. 'We've always had issues. She was Daddy's girl, no question, but he was an asshole to her anyway. I didn't know what to do with her. She was always dropping out of school, hanging around with people too old for her. Then her father died last year, and she went to stay with her grandma. She came over a coupla times a week, but sometimes I wouldn't see her for two weeks straight . . .' Her voice trailed away. She was looking at Parrish but she wasn't seeing him.

'So her grandmother would have been the last person to see her?'

'I reckon so. You want her address?'

'Please, yes.'

'If you want to go see her now, I'll come with you. I can stay with her. She won't take it so good, you know?'

Janice Duncan got up and went for her coat in the hall.

Parrish turned and looked at Radick. Radick's expression said everything that needed to be said. *How do people get like this? How does the welfare of their own children become so unimportant?*

The grandmother's place was three blocks away on West Ninth. Here the response was entirely different. Parrish and Radick were there for an hour, much of it spent listening to Janice Duncan as she tried to console her mother. All they gleaned from the grandmother was that Kelly had returned there from the mother's place on Sunday evening, and then left for school on Monday morning as usual. They took the name of the school. Parrish guessed that Kelly had been a no-show on Monday, but they wouldn't be able to check that until morning. Had Kelly come home from school on Monday? No she hadn't, but she had called to say that she was going to her mother's place for the night.

Janice Duncan said that there had been no such arrangement. She didn't see Kelly on Monday.

Where had Kelly called from? From her cellular phone, Grandma presumed.

The detectives left a little after eight.

'Phone records,' Parrish said when he got in the car. 'What teenage girl doesn't have a cell phone these days?'

'I'll get onto it first thing,' Radick said.

'Not just Kelly – Rebecca. And the others as well. Melissa, Nicole and Karen.'

'You really think they're all the same perp?'

'I have no idea, Jimmy, no idea at all.'

Radick dropped Parrish on the corner of Clermont and wished him goodnight.

'Want an early start,' Parrish said. 'Eight-thirty, okay?'

'Eight-thirty,' Radick echoed, and pulled away.

Parrish walked on down to the apartment, entered the lobby just as Grace Langham and her mother came from the other side of the street. Parrish held the door and waited for them.

The little girl was in tears and being carried by her mother. Parrish recognized the symptoms – tired, cold, more than likely hungry – and Mom wouldn't get a break until the kid was fed and slept. As a parent, there were some things you never forgot.

Parrish smiled as Mrs Langham entered the elevator. Again that awkwardness of expression, the slight embarrassment – not only from the proximity of someone she had no idea how to relate to, but that instinctive sense of needing to apologize that all parents experienced when their children were potentially troublesome to others.

'What's this then?' Parrish asked. He directed his question at Grace, but got no response. But, with her head on her mother's shoulder, and Parrish right in her eye line, there was no way the child could ignore him.

'Gracie?' he asked, and received a momentary flash of acknowledgement.

'So you are listening to me, eh? Well, I have a question for you.'

Grace just stared at him, tears in her eyes, her breath hitching.

'You ready?'

Her eyes widened.

'How old are you, Gracie?'

'S-Six,' she said. 'Six and a quarter.'

Mrs Langham half-turned to look back at Parrish. The expression on her face was one of bemusement. She understood in that moment she may as well not have been there.

'Six and a quarter? Well, let's see. That's what? That's two thousand, two thousand one hundred, two thousand two hundred . . . and eighty-something. Two thousand, two hundred and eighty days. Roughly. That's how old you are.'

Grace nodded. She'd stopped crying.

'Well, here's a game . . . before I get out of the elevator you have to think of your favorite day out of all of them.'

'Favorite?'

'Sure. The best, best, best day of them all.'

'Disneyland!' she said suddenly.

'Disneyland? No way! You've been to Disneyland?'

'Yes! I went to Disneyland!'

'And how good was that?'

The elevator bell rang, it slowed and came to a halt.

'The best! The best day ever!' Grace said, and she started to laugh.

The elevator doors opened.

'Next time you can tell me all about it,' Parrish said. 'Now you go get something to eat and get to bed, okay?'

Grace was still laughing as she exited the elevator with her mother.

Mrs Langham glanced back as she reached her door. *Thank you*, she mouthed, and the elevator doors closed.

I saw Mickey and Minnie! Parrish heard Gracie shouting as the elevator started up to the next floor.

Back in his apartment, Parrish shrugged off his overcoat and jacket, went to the kitchen, and poured himself two fingers of Bushmills.

Back in the sitting room, he called Eve Challoner; the line was busy.

He thought of Caitlin. No matter the line that bisects a circle, the two halves will perfectly match. If he called her now she would ask him about the booze. She didn't understand it; hell, no-one really understood it. Like Mitch

Hedberg said, *Alcoholism is the only disease you get yelled at for.* He said that before he overdosed.

Caitlin – the brightest of all his days, the darkest of all his nights. And a dead teenage girl no more than three or four blocks from where she lived.

He picked up the phone and dialed Eve again. Answer service. He hung up and went back to the bottle in the kitchen.

THIRTY-THREE

'How are you this morning?'

'I'm okay actually. Feeling okay.'

'How's the case?'

'We had another yesterday.'

'Another girl?'

'Yeah.'

'And . . . ?'

'We're waiting for tox. If she was drugged then I think we're going in the direction that it's the same killer. This girl is physically the same type as the others, same paint-job on the fingernails. She *felt* like the same guy, you know? And if it's someone different then it's one fuck of a coincidence.'

'How old was she?'

'Sixteen.'

'And you had to tell her parents?'

'Mother. Dad's dead, OD'd a while back. He was a beater. Mom's an ex-junkie, if ever there was such a thing—'

'Meaning?'

'Meaning that there is very rarely such a thing as an ex-junkie. If they're really *ex* then they're usually dead.'

'I see . . . Right, well let's get back to you, Frank. Last time we spoke—'

'We talked about how my father might have killed a couple of guys to keep them from testifying.'

'Yes. And how have you been feeling about it since you told me?'

'Just dandy. Couldn't be better.'

'Seriously.'

'How do you think I feel?'

'I can't tell you that, Frank. You have to tell me.'

'Hell, truth is it doesn't matter how I feel. The past is the past. It's gone. No use hanging on to it.'

'I'm not suggesting you hang on to it. All I'm saying is that in order to let go of it you have to understand it.'

'What's there to understand? He was a crook, guilty as any man he ever arrested. The fact that he managed to maintain such a good reputation was a combination of his own brilliance and the corruptness of the system he was a part of. If the system had been clean then he would never have been able to do it.'

'I know you really believe he killed those men, Manri and McMahon, that he was really capable of such a thing. But what do you believe his motive was? Money?'

'Yeah, money, but also to protect himself, to protect his superiors, to make sure he didn't get caught in the line of fire somewhere . . . it really doesn't matter what reasons, he still killed them, and if he killed them then he was a murderer who got away with it.'

'But he didn't. He was murdered himself.'

'The best part of a decade and a half later. He got away with it for that long. And I can't imagine they waited that long to kill him because of Manri and McMahon. I'm sure there were other things going on. Fifteen years is a long time.'

'Do you think he deserved to die?'

'Probably, yes.'

'Do you believe in the death penalty?'

'As a deterrent no, as a punishment, yes.'

'So some people deserve to die?'

'Yes. Don't you believe that?'

'This isn't about me, Frank, this is only about you.'

'Sounds like a great foundation for a relationship.'

'Don't go off the subject. I want to talk about that. I want to know who you think deserves to die.'

'Well, for a start, we have this guy here – if it *is* one guy – the one that's drugging, fucking and strangling teenage girls. He'll do to begin with.'

'If you knew who it was would you kill him?'

'If I knew who it was I would arrest him, read him his rights, lock him up and let the DA prosecute him.'

'Do you have faith in the system?'

'Sometimes.'

'How do you feel about the people who walk on technicalities?'

'I have learned to be philosophical.'

'In what way?'

'Guy I knew, did a couple of armed robberies. One time he killed a girl. She was twenty-three and pregnant. Had an eyewitness who saw him go into the bank before he put his ski-mask on. Saw him walk right on in there with a sawn-off. Once inside they had nothing but video footage of him with the mask, so the whole thing depended on the eyewitness statement. Well, the witness had a stroke about three weeks before trial and the DA had to drop the case. The perp went to the court to meet with his lawyer and the judge, and he got the news. So he leaves the court, he walks three blocks and he hails a cab. Then he steps off the sidewalk and he gets hit by a truck. The guy was mystery meat for a block and half.'

'Karma.'

'Whatever you want to call it, he got his dues.'

'You think that happens to everyone?'

'One way or another, eventually, yes.'

'So you're a closet Buddhist?'

'If you like.'

'And what do you think is going to happen to you?'

'Me? I have no idea.'

'You think it's going to work out fine, or do you think—'

'I try *not* to think about that.'

'So where now with the case you're on?'

'We get the blood and tox tests, we find phone records for all of the girls. We start to dig a little deeper on this connection to Child Services and Adoption.'

'And if they *are* connected?'

'Then there's going to be a shit storm.'

'And how are you sleeping?'

'On my back usually.'

'Frank!'

'I'm okay, Doc, seriously. I'm sleeping fine.'

'And your diet? Your drinking?'

'The diet ain't so good. Hasn't been for a long time.

Sometimes I want to eat, most times not. And I want a drink most of the time.'

'There are pills you can take for that.'

'The ones that make you sick if you drink? No thanks. I hate pills. You start down that road and you never come back.'

'Well, I can't force you to take anything, but do you feel any better at all than when we first started talking?'

'I feel . . . I don't know how to describe it. I feel . . . uh . . . I feel sort of agitated.'

'Agitated? In what way agitated?'

'Like talking about this stuff has made me aware of the fact that I have plenty to be pissed off about.'

'Better to have it out there than all bottled up inside.'

'So I'm told.'

'You don't believe that?'

'Undecided as yet.'

'Okay, Frank, I understand. I'm not going to keep you any longer today. You need to make progress on this case, and I think work is the best therapy for you right now.'

'Yeah, for sure. Finding dead teenagers always lifts my day.'

THIRTY-FOUR

On Parrish's desk was a note that Father Briley had called. Would Parrish please call him? He threw the note in the trash. Hell, he was already dragging through everything with Griffin, he really didn't need a priest on his case as well, especially one that seemed to see no difference between him and his father.

By eleven Parrish had learned from Kelly's teachers that she had in fact made it through to the end of school on Monday. That gave him a time-window. Refuse collections from the rear alleyway of Brooklyn Hospital were made between nine-thirty and ten each morning. Now all he needed was the autopsy report, and hopefully that would tell him how long she had been in the box, how long she'd been dead.

While he and Radick waited for those results they worked on tracking down records for each of the girls' cell phones. They contacted available family members, and with each one there was the recognition that this was something they should have done before. But the possibility of some slim connection between them had really only come to light in the past day or so. And even now it was nothing more than intuition and assumption on the part of Parrish. If there was a connection, however, it was somewhere waiting to be found.

Two hours' work and they started to make headway. It appeared that records for Kelly and Rebecca were obtainable, though it would take several more phone calls and the requisite paperwork to get them e-mailed over. Karen, Nicole and Melissa – due simply to the length of time that had elapsed since the last account activity – were out of the ballpark. Parrish even tried the Alice Forrester name, taking a flyer to determine if someone might have contacted Nicole through her stepsister, but that was a blind hunt down a dark alley. They would have to work with what they could get, and until that time they could only hope that it would give them something.

Antony Valderas came down at two o'clock, haunted the room for a few minutes. He surveyed the board, he made some notes on a piece of paper, and then he rounded on Parrish and Radick in his inimitable style.

'So I understand that you have these things connected?' he asked Parrish.

'It's a real maybe,' Parrish replied. 'We're waiting on some tox tests for the Duncan girl and a couple of phone records that we've asked for. If she got benzo'd then we're playing in the same league. If what I think is on the phone records turns up then we're definitely on a straight line to someone within Child Services or County Adoption.'

'As a killer or a fixer?'

Parrish shook his head. 'I don't know. It could just as easily be someone feeding someone else as the man himself.'

Valderas turned to Radick. 'And your APB on the campus stabbing suspect?'

'It's still running. We've had a couple of reports, but they turned out to be someone else.'

Valderas shook his head. He inhaled deeply, exhaled again as he looked back at the board. 'I need some movement, guys, I really do. You have a lot of red names up there, and I need some black ones.' He looked at Radick again. 'Good impressions are made fast, Radick, remember that.'

'Sure, Sergeant, sure,' Radick replied.

'So get onto whatever you have to get onto, but do it quicker, okay?'

Valderas left. Parrish looked at Radick but said nothing. Radick held his tongue.

The call from the Medical Examiner's office came just before three. Kelly's results were ready. The ME himself, Tom Young, had done the blood work and he would be down there for another couple of hours if they wanted to speak with him.

Radick drove them the four blocks and they parked in back of the building.

'She was benzo'd,' Young told Parrish before they'd even reached the end of the corridor. 'He got her good. A very heavy dose. From what I can determine it would have happened late afternoon, early evening of Monday.'

Young held open the swing door for the detectives. They walked the length of the theater, and there she was. Naked. The Y-incision scarring her torso, her hair still wet from where they had finally washed the body. Her arms were slim, her hands delicate – and her nails were red.

Parrish stood for a moment in silence. She looked so much like Rebecca. Too much like her.

'Dead somewhere between four and eight on Tuesday morning, I'd say. Rigor is harder to determine, but I'd say she was in the box for four or five hours. She was found at one, right?'

Parrish nodded.

'That gives you your timeframe. Picked up and drugged late afternoon Monday, dead in the early hours of Tuesday morning, say around five, in the box pretty much right away, dumped around ten-thirty.'

'After Tuesday's refuse collection had already been made,' Radick said.

Parrish said nothing. He was looking at her face, then at her hands, then at her bright red toenails. She seemed so small, so fragile. She seemed like nothing at all.

'COD?' Radick asked.

'The strangulation,' Young said. 'No doubt about that. A scarf more than likely. Not a rope or a cord. A scarf or a length of fabric, but twisted tight. There's no tearing, no indent of a thread. And it looks like she didn't struggle. There are no additional abrasions or bruising, nothing beneath the fingernails, no defensive wounds.'

'Was she raped?' Parrish asked.

'No signs of rape,' Young replied. 'She had intercourse – anal as well as vaginal – there's bruising in the rectal passage, but nothing beyond what would ordinarily be expected from intercourse. Nothing in either orifice except Nonoxynol-9 spermicidal agent and some lubricant.'

'He used a condom,' Radick said matter-of-factly.

'For sure.'

Parrish looked at Radick. Radick's expression said all that needed saying. Same MO, same type of vic, and the connection to Child Services or CAA.

They thanked Young, and made their way to the car behind the building.

They sat in silence for a few moments, and then Parrish turned to face his partner.

'This will not be straightforward,' he said. His voice was measured and calm. 'Right now, there's a chance we have more than one victim from the same perp. Melissa – the runaway – she may not be a homicide, because we haven't found her body. That was assigned to Rhodes and Pagliaro. Jennifer was Hayes and Wheland, but we don't know if she's one of them because I haven't found a CAA or Welfare file. All I have on her is similar physical attributes to the others, and the same manner of death. Nicole was Engel and West, Karen was Franco at the Williamsburg 91st. Rebecca and Kelly are ours.

'Okay . . . All of them, except for Jennifer, had direct or indirect involvement with Family Welfare South, the office that co-ordinated all administrative records for Child Services and the County Adoption Agency. The offices separated into different districts a while back, and there's now sixteen in all. They were all handled by the old South office, but Rebecca and Kelly would have been transferred to the new district office. What we need to know now is *which* district office. If we discover that they were dealt with by the same office—'

'Which is the closest office?' Radick cut in, all too quickly understanding what such a discovery would suggest.

'District Five,' Parrish told him. 'It's just across Fulton.'

An hour later they left the District Five office with nothing. Whichever way it went, they didn't have a warrant. Welfare Office records were confidential. Back at the office Parrish had Radick start on the request paperwork while he went to speak with Valderas.

'I want a let-up on the other actives,' he told the Squad

Sergeant. 'I think I have a multiple, and some of those cases were originally taken by other teams.'

'How many?'

'Three of them. Rhodes and Pagliaro, Hayes and Wheland, Engel and West. One of them is a Williamsburg 91st case and I want that as well. Six in all.'

'I really can't do it, Frank.'

'Because?'

'Because the other actives will just get dropped if you don't handle them. Who the hell else am I going to give them to?'

'You could have Radick handle them, and I could work this thing alone—'

'Not a prayer, Frank, not a prayer. I have strict instructions to keep you on a short leash from now on. Hell, man, you've got a Duty Review Board in the New Year. You might not even have a job in the second week of January.'

'Tony – I really *need* you to get me the other four cases.'

Valderas shook his head. 'I don't know, Frank, I just don't know. You're going to have to put something substantial together to swing it. I need something a little more credible than a Frank Parrish hunch to get them reassigned. And even if I get ours turned over to you, I don't see how we can get the one from Williamsburg.'

'Okay, okay . . . do what you can for me, would you? I got Radick filing for a warrant on some Child Welfare records. Can you at least push that through for me?'

'On who?'

'Rebecca Lange and Kelly Duncan, the last two. They're both ours.'

'That I can do.' Valderas looked at his watch. 'It's nearly six. You're not going to see anything today. I'll do what I can to get it processed before noon tomorrow. You can put some time in on the other cases while you wait for it.'

'Yes, sure.'

But Valderas knew he wouldn't. It was there in Parrish's expression as he turned to leave the room.

'Frank?' Valderas called after him.

Parrish paused.

'How is Radick?'

'He's okay. He'll make a good detective someday.'

'Don't spoil him before he has a chance, okay? You have a tendency to break the things you're given.'

Parrish didn't reply. He closed Valderas's office door behind him and hurried down the hallway.

THIRTY-FIVE

THURSDAY, SEPTEMBER 11, 2008

'Did you drink last night?'

  'Yes, I did.'

  'How much?'

  'Enough.'

  'Enough for what?'

  'Enough to stop me thinking about you.'

  'I'll ignore that, Frank.'

  'Please yourself.'

  'I want to talk about this now.'

  'What?'

  'The drinking.'

  'What do you want to say about it?'

  'I want you to talk about when you started drinking, what was happening in your life at the time. I want you to just tell me whatever comes to mind.'

  'This is like proper psychoanalysis now, right?'

  'No. It's just you and me talking about some things, and then maybe in amongst the things you say I might find something we can look at more closely . . . analyze, you might say.'

  'So it's just guesswork.'

  'No, it's not guesswork.'

  'Sounds like guesswork to me.'

  'I think you should stop evading the issue now, Frank.'

  'I don't know what to tell you. I started drinking when I was a teenager. A coupla beers with my friends, some shots maybe. Same as anyone that age.'

  'And you carried on drinking after you joined the police.'

  'Like all the guys. It was never an issue. You're on shift, you cut back on the booze the day before. You come off shift, you tank it up some. That's the nature of the beast.'

'And you drank because you wanted to?'

'Sure.'

'So when did you drink because you *needed* to?'

'Since I started visiting with you.'

'Enough being cute already. Answer the question, Frank.'

'God, I don't know. I was married maybe. The kids came. The job got tougher.'

'And your father's death?'

'What about it?'

'Did you drink more after he died?'

'I don't remember.'

'Try, Frank. Try and remember.'

'I remember the funeral. I remember the number of crews that were there. Seemed like everyone he'd ever known from Brooklyn Organized Crime and the OCCB and the precincts he'd worked, all of them . . . even a couple of Federal suits and some reporters from *The New York Times*. They had a big picture of him, just a head and shoulders shot, on an easel up at the end of the church where his coffin was. He was looking back at everyone, and there was that same expression on his face.'

'What expression?'

'Like everyone but him was a schmuck. Everyone but him was two-bits' worth of bullshit. He looked like that a lot, like he *knew* he was smarter than everyone else.'

'But he wasn't?'

'Wasn't so smart that he could avoid getting whacked.'

'Did you have any ideas about who killed him?'

'Sure I did.'

'Any that still stand up after sixteen years?'

'Hey, it's like all of these things . . . the longer it goes on the more theories you get.'

'Were there any theories that scared you?'

'Like people in the department? That kind of thing?'

'Yes, that it might have been someone in the department who was protecting their own interests.'

'That's very cynical of you.'

'But very credible, perhaps? Considering what he was involved in for all those years.'

'I was being ironic. Of course he was killed by someone in the department, or at least someone who was set up to do it.'

'You're a conspiracy theorist?'

'Everyone is a conspiracy theorist, but I know he was murdered. He took and took and took all of his working life, and finally someone decided to take something back.'

'Well, I guess it wasn't as a result of Lufthansa. I don't think someone would have waited all those years to get him for that.'

'Unless someone was inside for all those years, and then got him after they were released.'

'So it could have been someone other than a police officer.'

'It could have been anyone. It doesn't matter now.'

'So – do you remember drinking more after he died?'

'No.'

'After your divorce, maybe?'

'No.'

'What about when your partner was killed last year?'

'I don't want to talk about that.'

'I think we need to talk about it.'

'Need and want are not the same thing.'

'I think *you* need to talk about it, Frank.'

'I'm not going there, Doctor.'

'Why?'

'Because it's finished. It's the past. I don't see the point of dragging everything out into the daylight only to realize why you packed it away so tight.'

'You're talking about your father. That's the past, too.'

'So?'

'And you said you felt better as a result.'

'I said I didn't feel worse. I can't say that I feel a great deal better.'

'What was your partner's name?'

'You know his name.'

'I want to hear you say it.'

'Why?'

'Because it's a start.'

'Michael Vale.'

'There, that wasn't so hard, was it?'

'Don't patronize me.'

'How old was he?'

'Younger than me.'

'How long had you been partners?'

'Four years. Back since May of 2003.'

'And you were both Homicide right from the start?'

'Robbery-Homicide until the fall of 2005, and then Homicide.'

'And he was Gold Shield too?'

'He was, yes.'

'He got his shield before you?'

'A month later.'

'Were you competitive?'

'This is a homicide unit, not a college fraternity.'

'So there was no rivalry between you?'

'No, there was no rivalry. Where the hell did you get that idea from?'

'I'm just asking.'

'I think you've asked enough for today. I have six dead girls to deal with.'

'I understand, Frank.'

'What's that supposed to mean?'

'It means that I understand, Frank. There's only so much time that you can spare.'

'So why make it sound like I'm finding reasons not to be here. I have a lot of work to do. A helluva lot of work—'

'I apologize. I know you have a heavy workload, I really do. I just wish that you'd be a bit more forthcoming when you're here.'

'Hell, Doc, how long have we been meeting?'

'We started on September first, so ten days, give or take.'

'Well, in a week and a half you've got more out of me than my wife did in sixteen years. You should take that as a compliment.'

'Okay, Frank.'

'I'll see you tomorrow, okay?'

'Tomorrow it is.'

THIRTY-SIX

There was another message on his desk from Father Briley. Did the guy not have better things to do? Once again Parrish threw it in the trash.

There was still no progress on phone records. Parrish believed that such information might be unavailable for Melissa, Jennifer, Nicole and Karen due to the length of time that had elapsed, but he still held out a thin hope for Rebecca and Kelly. Obviously those two girls' clothes and personal effects – cell phones included – had been taken by the perp, and more than likely been destroyed. It was simply a question of how long their phone companies retained an account record once the customer ceased using the service. One month? Six? A year maybe? The fourth victim had died in December of 2007, eleven months earlier. Nicole had been dead fifteen months, Jennifer twenty-two, and Melissa had vanished off the face of the earth more than two years before.

The warrant for access to Family Welfare records came down at eleven-thirty. Parrish and Radick walked together to the South Five office, where it took little more than half an hour to determine that Kelly had been dealt with by the new South Two office. Rebecca featured as nothing more than a filed note regarding a possible transfer back to Williamsburg's office, South Nine. The South Two offices were up on Adams near the High Street Metro station. Parrish stayed where he was while Radick walked back to fetch the car from the precinct.

'You could walk with me,' he told Parrish. 'Use the exercise, you know?'

'Single most common cause of premature death is exercise,' Parrish replied. 'If you knew the number of people who got seizures and strokes while jogging and weight-training you'd never go in a gym again.'

Parrish made small-talk with the security guy in the lobby, until his partner pulled up to the curb. He got in the car, and Radick turned right onto Adams at the end of Fulton. Borough Hall on the left, the Polytechnic on the right, a little way further and they passed the Supreme Court building across from NY Tech. Made him think of Caitlin; an exam she'd taken a while back at one or other of those colleges.

'So Kelly was dealt with by the South Two office, but Rebecca was dealt with by South Nine over in Williamsburg,' he said, reviewing the state of play. 'And we know that the earlier four were all dealt with by the original Family Welfare South District Office, as it was before they all split up. Which means, perhaps, that our guy was in the original South section and is now in either South Two or South Nine . . .'

Just before Adams became the Brooklyn Bridge, Radick turned left and came back on himself down Cadman Plaza. He parked up, put a Police notice in the front window, and he and Parrish walked across to the South Two building.

By a quarter after twelve they had the undivided attention of the unit's deputy supervisor. Supervisor was attending a 9/11 memorial for two City Family Welfare staff who had died in the North Tower collapse, but Deputy Marcus Lavelle seemed all too eager to assist with whatever questions they had.

Ten minutes of Lavelle's time, and they had further confirmed that Karen Pulaski, Nicole Benedict, Melissa Schaeffer and Rebecca Lange had all been under the aegis of the original Family Welfare South District.

'Of course, not all of them would have wound up with us here at District Two,' Lavelle explained. 'As my colleague explained to you, and as you have learned with Rebecca, it all goes by zip code now.'

'We found a file note over at District Five regarding Rebecca. I didn't really understand what it meant.'

'Let me take a look,' Lavelle said. 'As deputy supervisor I have access to the entire system regardless of district.' He typed, paused, scrolled, paused again, and then he nodded his head. 'This explains it. Rebecca should have been transferred to Williamsburg, which is South District Nine, but her brother was registered as her legal guardian and he is South

Two. The note was from someone who thought she should go to Nine. What was decided was that she should stay in Two because of the brother. We kept tabs on him because he was adjudicated a risk. According to this it seems he had a drug problem.'

'And how many employees do you have here?' Parrish asked.

'A hundred and nineteen,' Lavelle replied.

'And of those, how many are men?'

'Including myself and Supervisor Foley, forty-eight.'

'And do you have temporary staff?'

'God no,' Lavelle said. 'This is all strict security clearance stuff. We manage records for thousands and thousands of minors. Once you're in it's very hard to get fired, but it's even harder to get taken on in the first place.'

Parrish was quiet for a moment. He breathed deeply, wondering how much he really wanted to tell Marcus Lavelle.

'I am going to tell you a couple of things,' he began, 'but you have to understand that I am telling you only because I need to, and that I am relying on you to maintain the utmost confidentiality.'

'I can assure you, Detective—'

Parrish raised his hand and Lavelle fell silent. 'This is a tough deal, Mr Lavelle, a really tough deal, and you might not want to hear this, but you're going to, and you have to really understand the importance of keeping this to yourself.'

Lavelle nodded. His expression was sober and matter-of-fact.

'We have six girls,' Parrish said. 'Five of them are dead, one of them is missing, believed dead. Three of them were registered with the original Family Welfare South District office – directly in the case of Melissa Schaeffer and Karen Pulaski, and indirectly in the case of Nicole Benedict who was connected to South through her stepsister, Alice Forrester. Nevertheless, Nicole's personal details and pictures were held in Alice Forrester's file so she might as well have been here herself. As you have just told us, the last two victims – Rebecca and Kelly – were both registered with you here at the new South Two office. Then we have one more, a girl called Jennifer Baumann. Now, we haven't yet been able to trace

Jennifer on file, but she fits the physical attributes and MOs of the others. You understand what I'm saying?'

Lavelle had noticeably paled. 'You're saying that someone who used to work at the original South District Office now works here in South Two, and they're a murderer?'

'Not definitely, no. Someone in the office could be passing information to someone outside, and that person might be the perpetrator. However, the fact that the last two girls were dealt with here suggests that this is where he works.'

'But what about supervisors? Supervisors have access to files all over the system regardless of district?'

'I've considered that since you mentioned it,' Parrish said, 'but the fact that both Rebecca and Kelly were in your zone implies otherwise. It tells me that the connection is right here.'

Lavelle was silent for some time. When he looked back at Parrish he was visibly distraught. 'This is horrific. This is utterly unbelievable. God . . . I don't even know what to say. I don't even know what to think about this . . .'

'We don't want you to think anything,' Parrish said. 'This is a standard investigation. It is slow, thorough, often laborious, and many times it comes to nothing. We are assuming a great many things here. We are *assuming* that this is one of your employees, but we could be completely wrong. It could be someone who has tapped into your computer system, or someone who once worked for Family Welfare and has information on how to access your data. We don't know, and the very worst thing we can do in such situations is assume further and take action based on hunches and intuition. That is why it is so vitally, vitally important that you say nothing to anyone, not even your supervisor. I will come over tomorrow and speak with him personally, and in the meantime we are going to work out a precise course of action to vet your employees and determine whether any of them are potential suspects. This will be done with the utmost care and discretion, not only to avoid upsetting innocent people, but also to ensure that we do not tip our hand too heavily to whoever might be responsible, if in fact he does actually work here.'

'And it would definitely be a man?' Lavelle asked.

'The perpetrator? Yes. There is always the possibility that

we have a woman inside the office feeding information to someone outside, but the likelihood of that is extraordinarily slim. Women who murder very rarely tend to be organized and premeditated. They also tend to stick with shooting and poisoning. The vast majority of female killers, and I'm talking in excess of ninety percent, are those driven by jealousy or passion to kill in the heat of the moment. Those who act with premeditation, and certainly anyone who could be classified as a serial killer, are invariably men. As of this moment we are looking for a man, and that will involve the forty-eight of you in this office.'

'Forty-six,' Lavelle said, somewhat sheepishly. 'Surely you don't think that I, or Supervisor Foley, have anything to do with this?'

'I'm sorry, Mr Lavelle, but I'm afraid you're going to have to fall in with this program the same way everyone else will. If I exclude anyone then it will appear to be selective, and that I cannot have. Also, the courts may work on the philosophy of innocent until proven guilty, but as far as a homicide investigation is concerned we have to be a little bit Napoleonic about the whole thing and assume that anyone could be guilty until we have ruled them out.'

Lavelle nodded understandingly. 'And those who have nothing to hide won't fear inquiry,' he said.

'Either that, or they're so self-confident and organized they believe there's nothing that can connect them. I have seen it go many ways, and one thing I am certain of is that you can never second-guess or predict the outcome of an investigation.'

'And so what do I do now?'

'You can check one thing for us,' Parrish said. 'You can look up Jennifer Baumann on your system and tell us whether she was ever in the care of the County Adoption Agency or Family Welfare.'

'Of course, yes,' Lavelle replied. 'How do you spell—'

'B-A-U-M-A-N-N.'

Lavelle went to a keyboard and typed in the name. He waited for a moment, opened files, scrolled, opened more files, and then turned and looked at Parrish. 'You won't find a file,' he said.

Parrish frowned.

'A file isn't retained unless there is cause to consider that the case will be ongoing. A girl called Jennifer Baumann was interviewed by the police in December of 2006, but she was an apparent material witness to a sexual abuse case. The victim of the sexual abuse was in the care of Family Welfare, and so Family Welfare had someone present at the interviews. Jennifer wouldn't have a file in her own right, just the interview notes and her photograph. Seems that the case went no further and was dropped. The notes and the pictures would have been filed in the Miscellaneous Interviews for that month.'

'Does it say who was present at the interview?'

'Yes, it was Lester Young. He was one of our longest-serving staff.'

'Was?'

'Yes, he went into the Probation Service.'

Parrish nodded at Radick. Radick was already writing down the name.

'And now?' Lavelle asked.

'Nothing,' Parrish replied. 'You do nothing, you say nothing. I'll speak with Mr Foley tomorrow, and we'll go from there.'

Lavelle showed them out through the lobby, watched them as they made their way around to the side of the building. Once back on Cadman Plaza, Parrish told Radick he wanted to co-ordinate with Valderas, get Rhodes and Pagliaro briefed, and reinstate the Melissa Schaeffer Missing Persons investigation.

'And this Baumann girl,' Radick said. 'Interviewed in December of 2006, dead in January of 2007. Now we've confirmed that she's connected to Welfare we have a whole new case to open up. I'll start checking on this Lester Young guy.'

'I know a Fed as well,' Parrish added. 'He might give us a hand on this, get us a profile that will help eliminate some of these people at South Two.'

'We're assuming that he's inside that office,' Radick said.

'We are,' Parrish replied. 'It makes sense. Too much for me to ignore.'

THIRTY-SEVEN

Valderas didn't buck the request to reinstate the Melissa Schaeffer Missing Persons, and he told Parrish that he would brief the other detectives. They had all dealt with one or other of the victims, and the last thing he wished for was a rash of political in-fighting.

'I'll give you all the cases,' he said. 'I'll tell them that they'll get a note on their file to say that the case wasn't transferred due to lack of diligence, but because new information came to light and their own workload precluded the possibility of picking it up again. That should keep them quiet. I'll try and work an APB on the Schaeffer girl, but it'll be more like a few uniforms out canvassing her neighborhood. She went absent when?'

'October of 2006,' Parrish replied.

'Ain't gonna happen, is it?' Valderas said. 'I mean, it's very fucking unlikely that anything new will come out the woodwork two years on.'

'I know, I know, but hell, we have to try, right?' Parrish said. 'Maybe someone who knew something back then is no longer connected up here, and they can speak without fear of direct reprisal. I've seen it happen.'

'Leave it with me. What are you going to work on now?'

'The phone records, as many of them as we can get. That's more than likely another dead end, but who the hell knows, eh? We don't look, then we don't find.'

'Keep me briefed,' Valderas said.

Parrish sat down at his desk. He took the case files from his lower drawer and set them in front of him. No need to hide them now. The only one missing was Detective Franco's from Williamsburg, and then it struck him: Karen was from Williamsburg, and that's where Rebecca had lived when she was with Helen Jarvis. He'd known this, of course, but it was only in that moment that he wondered whether it possessed any significance. Perhaps it was a line to follow, but a secondary line. There was nothing to suggest a connection, whereas with Family South Two there was every possibility that the man they wanted was right there in amongst the forty-eight employees.

Seated there at his desk, once again the faces of the girls before him, he believed that such moments as these would ultimately define his life. People would always die, and others would always be responsible. Parrish believed that fear of dying was there within everyone, inherent and inescapable. Those that said they were not afraid were merely more afraid of showing it. Like a virus – subtle, insidious, gentle even – this fear invaded people such as himself, those who visited with the dead in the subsequent hours, the narrow window of warmth before all signs of life had evaporated. Despite arm's length or latex gloves the gentle airborne virus was absorbed through the tear ducts, the pores of the skin, the breath, and it started its work. It began – at first – to kill the personal things. First to die was the ability to speak of what was seen. Emotional transparency began to cloud over. Next to go were such things as hope, a belief in some fundamental and universal justice, the certainty that everything would turn out okay in the end. And finally the virus would take love and passion; it would take relationships, empathy, fellowship, fraternity. Wasn't it true that from the moment of birth we were in fact dying? Work such as Parrish's merely served to accelerate a process that was as natural as breathing. When all was said and done, there was nowhere to go but where you came from.

Some people's lives were bold statements. Parrish believed that his life would never be anything more than a parenthesis. There had to be something wrong with people like himself, people who did this work – a psychological fault line. It was this fault line that gave them the eyes, the stomach, the nerve to go on looking when any rational person would long since have turned away.

He believed he would die alone. Perhaps in a bar someplace between the jukebox and the next Bushmills. People would

remember him, but they would more easily forget. And then
– only then – would he truly discover what he had always
been looking for in the narrow spaces, the darkest shadows,
the awkward corners: he would know for himself what really
happened when the lights went out.

'Frank?'

Parrish looked up to see Radick staring at him. The expression on his face was something akin to concern.

'You okay?'

'I'm fine,' Parrish said. 'I'm going to call Franco at Williamsburg 91st. You chase up the phone records.'

Franco was as helpful as Parrish could have wished.

'The file you can't have, of course,' he said, 'but there's
nothing that says you can't have a copy of everything. I'll get
it done and sent over. One thing . . . if you break this, then
don't make me look like a dick, okay?'

Parrish gave his word, and Franco hung up with a promise
to have the papers at the 126th the next morning.

Radick was not so fortunate. There were no phone records
for Melissa, Nicole or Karen. Yes, both Rebecca and Kelly had
active cell phone accounts, but accessing those records
would take a warrant. However polite and insistent Radick
had been, they hadn't budged.

Radick started on the paperwork while Parrish went back to
the files to look for what he had so far failed to see.

At quarter to five Radick sent his warrant application over to
the courts by courier. In all honesty he would be unlikely
to get a response before Monday. Parrish called Valderas,
explained the situation, and Valderas said he would have
words with Captain Haversaw. They needed the Divisional
Commander's authority to prioritize and expedite, but
Haversaw's backing would at least be useful. Maybe, just
maybe, they would get the thing back before close of business on Friday, and then it was simply a matter of walking it
over to the respective cell phone companies' offices and
asking for the information. And what would they find? A
million texts to the girls' friends about boys and music and
Facebook; endless calls to organize rides from their folks and
rendezvous at the mall. The odds of finding a number that

bore some relation to their disappearance? Such a thing would be incalculable. Nevertheless, it could not be overlooked. There could be something there, however small, and if there was even the slightest fragment of connection between Rebecca and Kelly, it would serve as confirmation that these were in fact the same case.

What Parrish really needed was Melissa. He needed to find her – dead or alive – and once found, he needed to rule her in or out as a related case. Perhaps she would turn out to be nothing more than a runaway. What he hoped, and he hoped this with such sadness in his heart, was that she *was* related, and that she *was* dead, and that on her person would be something that would help them find the perp. There was a strong possibility that she might have been the first of the murders, and often – in the case of a serial – the definitive MO that made them a serial had not yet been fully formulated. The later victims were strangled. Perhaps the first one had been shot or stabbed, perhaps battered to death. It was true that the more dramatic the manner of death, the more potential there was for evidence and subsequent profiling. A simple strangulation said little more than the need to see the victims' faces as they died, to watch closely as the life-light faded from their eyes. A cord, a rope, a scarf, anything but their own hands. But perhaps there had been something *else* about the first one – something special, something unique – and it would give them an edge, a means by which they could narrow down their suspects at South Two. Everyone below five-eight and above six-two, everyone with fair hair is out of the picture . . . that kind of thing. You lose fifteen percent of your suspects. Now you only have forty-one to deal with.

Parrish smiled to himself – a rueful and sardonic smile. He knew he was fooling himself into thinking this was going to be straightforward, when – in truth – it was anything but.

He glanced at his watch. It was twenty to six.

'Take off, Jimmy,' he told Radick. 'I don't see there's anything more you can do now. We have to wait for the warrant, and then we go get phone records, but that's gonna happen earliest tomorrow, more likely Monday, unless Haversaw throws some weight at it.'

Radick rose, gathered his jacket. 'You okay, Frank?' he asked Parrish.

'Never been better,' Parrish replied.

'You gonna go home, eat out, what?'

'Go home, more than likely,' Parrish replied. 'Why? You gonna to ask me on a date?'

Radick shook his head. 'Not that desperate,' he said, and headed for the door.

Parrish watched him go, and he smiled. He knew what he would do. He would go get a take-out near Caitlin's and surprise her.

THIRTY-EIGHT

Parrish hoped that the girls who shared Caitlin's apartment would be out. He needed to talk to her; he needed her to finally and forever understand that his interference was paternal, parental, and – from his perspective – vitally necessary. At twenty years old you didn't just think you knew everything, you *knew* you knew everything. Sure, the world had changed – 2008 was not 1968 – but no-one could argue that it had changed for the better. It had not. Sure, the madness was there twenty, thirty, forty years before, but with TV, and now the internet, everyone got to share in the madness so much faster and so much deeper. And what had that done? It had given people ideas. Parrish was convinced of it. When he was a rookie cop there were ten ways to skin a cat. Now there were ten thousand.

He got off the subway at Carroll Street and walked a half block to a Chinese take-out he knew. He ordered crispy chili beef, fried rice, won tons, a whole bunch of stuff, and while they prepared his order he went up the street to a liquor store and bought a half dozen bottles of Corona.

A few minutes after seven he was knocking on the door at Caitlin's place, waiting patiently.

When he heard her voice, the sound of her laughing, he was disappointed. She was not alone. They were good girls, the ones she lived with, but tonight he could have done without them. It would feel awkward. Maybe he would just leave the food and the beer and go. Make it seem like he'd brought it up for her and her friends to enjoy. A peace offering.

Caitlin opened the door, and her expression changed so quickly from surprise to concealed anxiety that Parrish knew something was wrong.

'Hell of a way to greet your old man,' he said, intending

to sound light-hearted, but it came out all wrong. Sounded bitter, like an accusation.

'Dad . . .' she said, and it was half a question.

'It is,' Parrish replied, and held up his packages – a bag stacked with take-out boxes in one, a bag of bottles in the other. 'Figured we could have some dinner—'

'I'm going out to eat,' she said, and it was evident that this wasn't true. She said it too quickly, too eagerly. *I'm-going-out-to-eat* like it was just one word.

'So I'll eat a little, we'll drink a beer, we'll stick the rest in the refrigerator for tomorrow's breakfast for you and the girls.'

'Dad – I'm not alone . . .'

'I know that. Hell, there's enough for everyone—'

'The girls aren't here,' she said, and Parrish started to smile.

'Aha,' he said. 'A young gentleman is courting my daughter—'

'Caitlin?' a voice called from within the apartment, and Parrish saw his daughter flinch.

'What's up?' the voice asked, and Parrish felt something strange and cold and awkward surfacing in his thoughts.

He knew that voice. He recognized that voice.

'Radick?' Incredulity and disbelief were evident in his tone. 'Radick is in there?'

Caitlin tried to close the door as far as she could while she still remained between the edge and the frame. 'Dad,' she urged. 'Please, Dad. Don't make a scene. It's nothing, Dad, really. He just called me the day before yesterday because I was concerned about you—'

'What do you mean, concerned about me? You are *concerned* about me? What the fuck does that have to do with my partner? What the fuck is my partner doing coming over and talking to my daughter about me for?'

Parrish dropped the bag of take-out on the floor. It landed heavily but the boxes didn't spill out onto hallway.

He stepped forward and pushed the door, taking Caitlin by surprise, and the door flew open and banged against the wall. It rebounded with such force that it swung back and closed again.

Parrish strode past her even as she grabbed his jacket and tried to stop him.

Jimmy Radick stood there in the middle of the room.

'What the fu—' Parrish started, but Radick raised his hands and interrupted him.

'Don't read anything into this, Frank,' he said matter-of-factly. He was obviously agitated, but doing his best to maintain some semblance of calm.

Caitlin was behind Parrish. 'Dad,' she said. 'Enough already. There's no need for you to be mad at him.'

Parrish dropped the bag of beer bottles. One of them broke and beer spilled out along the edge of the carpet and made its way beneath the sofa.

'Frank, seriously, this is too much now,' Radick said. 'You listen to me before you say another word.'

Frank Parrish saw a great many things in that moment, and none of them were common sense. He took another step forward and even as he raised his hand to grab Radick's jacket lapels, Radick sidestepped and pushed him. Parrish lost his balance and fell into the armchair. As he tried to get up Radick was over him, his face challenging, his tone decisive.

'Frank,' he said. 'You listen to me now. Enough of this bullshit, okay?'

Parrish jerked his foot upwards. Radick saw it coming and turned to block it with his knee. He stepped back as the pain hit him, and Parrish was on his feet.

Now Caitlin went for her father, hands flailing, slapping his shoulders, the back of his head, the side of his face, and it was in that moment that Parrish saw nothing but his daughter and his partner conspiring against him, talking about him, denigrating him, finding him a source of pathetic humor. Suddenly he saw Clare in Caitlin's eyes, and the rage boiled inside him.

He hit her. Never in twenty years had he hit his daughter, but he hit her then. It was an involuntary and reactive swipe backwards, nothing more than an attempt to stop the whirlwind of hands that was coming at him, but her arms were down in that moment, and the side of his forearm connected with the side of her face and she went over like a ten-pin.

In the moment of shock, the handful of seconds it took to

truly comprehend what he had done, Parrish became aware of nothing but his own stupidity and ignorance. Radick was behind him, had both his arms pinned back with such force that Parrish couldn't even resist.

'You asshole, Frank!' Radick said. 'You dumb fucking asshole!'

'Caitlin? Caitlin? Jesus, I'm sorry . . . Jesus, Caitlin, I didn't mean to . . . Caitlin? Honey?'

But Radick was marching him to the door, pinning his arms behind him in a vice-like grip, and as he used one hand to open the door, he used the other to shove Parrish out into the hallway, before slamming the door shut.

Parrish heard the lock turn, the security chain slipping into its mooring, and he knew there was no going back.

'Caitlin!' he shouted. 'Caitlin! Jesus, I'm sorry! I didn't mean it! Caitlin!'

Radick's voice came then – firm and certain from behind the door. 'Go home, Frank. Cool off. You go home and calm the fuck down or I'll call the Precinct and have them lock you up for the night.'

'Fuck you, Radick—'

'Frank! Listen to me now! You go home and cool the fuck off or I'm calling Valderas and having your ass in lock-up for the night! You hear me? Back the fuck off, okay?'

Parrish took a step backwards. His heel connected with the bag of take-out boxes on the hallway floor, and in one last moment of outrage he let fly with the hardest kick he could muster.

Food exploded along the hallway and up the walls. Noodles, rice, pieces of chicken; a carton of sweet and sour sauce unloaded its contents down the uppermost risers of the stairwell, and Parrish watched it all in slow-motion, his heart racing, his fists clenched, and it seemed for a moment that he was standing outside of himself, and even he was laughing at the idiocy of his actions.

He knew then that Radick would not listen. He turned and pressed his ear against the door. He could hear Caitlin sobbing, could hear Radick consoling her, and he wondered whether this was now the beginning of the end. Caitlin would tell Robert, Robert would tell Clare, and the degree of estrangement he had already caused in his family would be magnified a thousand-fold. Radick would report it to Valderas, Valderas would speak to Haversaw, and Parrish would find himself without a partner once again. Perhaps this time they would can him for good. They would look at his desk and there they would find another six unclosed cases. That was besides subway, hooker and campus. The board would not look good. He could even be charged with assaulting his own daughter . . .

Parrish paused for a moment, unable to breathe. He wanted it all to end. He wanted the whole world to vanish, leaving behind himself, his daughter, and few minutes of silence to explain himself.

He looked at the mess around him – the spilled cartons, the food on the walls and the stairwell – and he couldn't face it a minute longer.

He hurried down and out of the building before anyone else saw him.

THIRTY-NINE

A gambler feels safe only when he has nothing left to lose.

Parrish had gambled with his marriage, his family, his career, his whole life.

Every day in every way I am not getting better.

He found a watering hole, some place on Baltic Street. He could have been anywhere, for such places were all the same – a weathered wooden bar, a sodium-colored atmosphere that made everyone look sick; a place that served merely to remind you of the very things you wished to forget.

Bad cop. No donut.

He wore his fears like a scar. He wore his heart on his sleeve, and that heart was broken and bleeding, raw and hollow.

Emptiness like a raw tooth socket.

After three Bushmills he believed he was forgetting what he had done.

You're unaware of what's important until it's gone.

After the fourth he made his way to the jukebox and put on Art Tatum.

I drink because I am lonely. I drink because I am afraid. I drink because of my father. Always the same old reasons: a liar never varies the story.

He tried to recall what had happened in Caitlin's apartment. He tried to remember how hard he had hit her.

And you were the darkest of all my nights, the brightest of all my days.

But he could not. He knew his mind had closed down somewhere back there, and anything that was in his memory would not be available for some time to come.

Change here for everywhere, and everywhere else as well.

He felt like the worst kind of human being. Less than that. Less than a human being.

Oh, Frank, your mother must be so, so proud of you . . .

And he wondered what tomorrow would bring. Wondered if Radick would speak to Valderas, if it was all over, if the world as he knew it had now drawn to a close and there was no longer a place on the stage for Frank Michael Parrish.

Lord God, if nothing else, just grant me one more day.

Five, six drinks, and he knew he should leave now, take a cab, go home and sleep it off.

And so he did. He paid his tab, left a ten-buck tip, and found his own way to the street.

In his years as a policeman, Parrish could have counted on one hand the times he'd been woken by nightmares.

Such was the power of the images and emotions that assaulted him that night that when he woke he believed he was still dreaming.

The pictures were there at the very forefront of his mind; the emotions were in his gut, his chest, his heart; there in the sweat on his hands, in the dampness of his sheets, his tee-shirt, his hair.

The door that had once so decisively divided the two parts of his life was no longer a door. It was a curtain – thin as gossamer thread – and through it he could not only hear the voices of the dead, he could now see their faces.

Kelly, Rebecca, Karen, Nicole, Jennifer – even Melissa, because something told him that she was also dead, and it told him with certainty.

And in amidst their faces was Caitlin, looking back at him – at one moment sympathetic, in the next accusing. In her eyes he could see Clare again, and he wondered what his ex-wife would say to him next time he saw her. Maybe she wouldn't wait; maybe he'd get a call from her . . .

You fucked up your own life, Frank, and you fucked up mine. Can I please ask you to stay away from the kids so you don't fuck theirs up as well? Is that too much to ask?

But . . . but . . . but . . .

Enough already, Frank. Like I've said so many times, some people you have to wait for them to fuck things up. But you? With you there's no waiting. You're a fuck-up before you arrive.

Parrish got up. He filled the bathroom sink and held his face underwater for as long as he could bear.

He drank some orange juice. He tried to make himself throw up but he couldn't.

He went back to bed, and somewhere between agitated wakefulness and restless sleep he spoke with the girls one by one. He listened to what they had to say. He knew it was nothing more than imagination, but it possessed power sufficient to make him believe that they were right there beside his bed explaining all that had happened to them.

Girls with lives that had never really started. Drugged and bound and fucked and killed. Left in a hallway, left in a motel room, left in a cardboard box for the janitor to find. What a waste. What a terrible fucking waste.

The pain woke him, and it was a real pain, not something from his dreams. That awful cramping in his lower gut again. The pain that had come back enough times for him to think that perhaps he should really attend to it, see someone, get a check-up.

But he knew he wouldn't. Knew he wouldn't do anything until he'd found the truth of these killings. There was just one dimension left to everything. The whole of his life was now collapsed into learning what had really happened to Rebecca and Kelly and the others. And why was it so important? Why this case above all others? Because these girls were like Caitlin? Because they represented every failure he had perpetrated with his own daughter? Because Caitlin could so easily have been a victim too? Because if this man wasn't stopped, there could be so many more?

Someone out there knew the truth. Someone in Family South Two. Lester Young, perhaps? A man who had transferred to the Probation Service, and could even now be making the lost and forgotten disappear from the face of the earth . . .

There was too much of a coincidence, too much of a connection for him to ignore it. One of those forty-eight men knew these girls' names, knew their faces, their phone numbers, their personal details. These girls had been chosen by someone to serve some purpose. Perhaps for nothing more than sex. Perhaps for photographs. Perhaps they had been dressed to look younger, and those images were now being circulated in the community that paid for such things. There was a depth of degradation and depravity out there that the vast majority of people could not even comprehend. Whatever could be imagined, people had already done it. Beyond that, they spent their time figuring out how to push the limits even further. Whoever had taken these girls from their families, whoever had drugged them and killed them, well they were nowhere near the bottom of the food chain. How did Parrish know that? Because they had been found. Not only that, they had been found intact. Those killers even more base in the scale of things would have broken up those bodies, torn them to pieces and buried them or scattered them to the four corners; they would have pushed them into waste pipes and garbage disposal units, into the river, the New Jersey marshes. And they would never have been found.

He thought of the age-progressed photographs in the classified sections of the newspapers: *This is how our son would look now. Have you seen him or anyone who looks like him? Please call 1-800-THE LOST. Thank you. (This item funded by The National Center For Missing & Exploited Children.)*

Thousands of them. Tens of thousands. Where were they? Where did they go? Why?

Parrish did not sleep again. He waited patiently until morning broke through the bedroom drapes, and then he rose and showered and shaved and dressed.

A new day, and yet a day like all the others.

FORTY

'I fucked up.'

'I know.'

'Radick told you.'

'He did.'

'And he told Valderas and God knows who else as well, right?'

'No, he didn't, and he says he's not going to.'

'And his reasoning behind that?'

'Ask him.'

'I'm asking you.'

'He considers that what happened last night is between you and your daughter, not between you and the department.'

'Well, that's very noble of him.'

'I don't think you can afford to be sarcastic, Frank.'

'I fucked up, okay? I already told you I fucked up. I'm not being sarcastic, I'm being straight with you.'

'Honestly, Frank, I think that that's one thing you haven't been.'

'What the hell is that supposed to mean?'

'Take a look at yourself. He doesn't want to work with you, you know that? He knows he doesn't have a choice, but he's putting in an application to transfer again. He's looking at staying on in Homicide but moving to another precinct.'

'You serious?'

'Of course I'm serious. You physically attacked him, Frank. You broke up your daughter's place, you kicked Chinese food down the stairs—'

'I was pissed—'

'Pissed or not, Frank, you have no right to do that kind of

thing, and considering the situation you're in I'm amazed that common sense doesn't dictate some sense of balance to your actions.'

'He is twenty-nine. My daughter is twenty—'

'And what does that have to do with it?'

'Goddammit, he's a cop, Marie . . . he's a fucking cop. This is not the sort of thing I want for her.'

'What? You think he was over there trying to sleep with her? You think that's what was going on? Honestly, Frank, I don't see how you could have been any further from the mark on this one.'

'You're telling me he wasn't over there trying to fuck my daughter?'

'Yes. He was not over there trying to sleep with your daughter. He was over there because *she* gave him her number, and *she* wanted to speak to him privately, and let's see if we can guess what she wanted to talk to him about, eh, Frank?'

'No need for the sarcasm—'

'You, Frank. You are the what and the who in everyone's life right now. Your daughter, your partner, me. Frank Parrish has gotten everyone wrapped around a pole, worried sick about what he's going to do next. Does he still have a job? Are his kids going to stop talking to him? Is his partner going to move to another precinct just to get away from him? It's all about you, Frank, so I think you've succeeded in that much at least.'

'Succeeded in what?'

'Getting yourself up there in the limelight. Getting everyone to see what a mess you've made of everything, but you're convinced that it's not your fault. I think we all realize that now. I think we're all willing to accept the fact that no-one can help Frank Parrish but himself, and he's the last person in the world who's going to do that.'

'Seems to me that you're saying things that you really shouldn't be saying—'

'Why? Because I'm your therapist? Though right now I don't see that I'm doing you any good at all.'

'So what? You're going to quit on me?'

'You're running me to the limits, Frank, and I don't know

how much longer I'm willing to let you do that. I have so many more people to see, and all of them, without exception, are a hell of a lot more forthcoming and straightforward than you. Thing about this job is that people actually appreciate what you do for them – at least most of them do. but it's almost impossible to overcome the difficulty of trying to help someone who just doesn't want to be helped.'

'You're bailing out on me? That doesn't show a lot of persistence now does it?'

'Persistence? I'm not sure you're the best judge of persistence—'

'Don't even go there, okay? Don't tell me about persistence. Persistence is pretty much the only thing that keeps me doing this job. The few people you manage to take off the streets, the ones that aren't kicked right out of court on some bullshit technicality, are replaced by their brothers, their cousins, their neighbors. You get older, they stay the same age. And the law? What the fuck is that? The law and justice are not the same thing, haven't been for fifty, a hundred years. Now the law plays out for the lawyers and the perps, not the victims or their families, and definitely not for the police. What do we represent for your average citizen? We're a fucking joke, that's what we are. They know we're not going to catch anyone, and in the rare case that we do then the asshole is gonna get the best defense that the taxpayer can buy. The guy that got robbed is paying taxes to defend the guy who robbed him. What do they hope we can do? They hope we can be some sort of legal revenge, that's what. They hope that we'll chase down some guy, and that guy'll kick and scream and resist arrest, and hopefully he'll have a gun or a knife and try something, and we'll get a chance to blow him away. That's what they hope. They want us to kill the perps so they don't have to carry the burden of guilt themselves.

'And the basic difference between the cops and the people out there? We run towards the trouble. That's what we do. Gotta be something wrong with us for doing that, but there it is. That's gotta say something about the kind of people we are, wouldn't you say?'

'Frank, I understand your frustration . . .'

'The hell you do! I'm one of those people who doesn't have new days. I just have old ones, okay? And the longer I live the older they get. Every day it's the questions for us. The cases we're working on are nothing but questions. Mostly it's who. Sometimes it's how or why. Every once in a while it's all three. It gets into your mind, and then it's in your blood, and you find yourself thinking about it even when you're talking to someone about some completely unrelated thing. You start to think that other people know, others besides the perp. Someone in a coffee shop, maybe, or sitting on the subway train. Random people. You think they know more than you do. You believe that if you could just find the right person, and just ask them one question, they would open up right there and tell you everything you need to know to close the case down.'

'Frank—'

'You start thinking that the dead can talk to you. You start imagining that the face of their killer is printed right there on their retina, and if you could just get close enough you'd see it. You start talking to yourself . . . in your head at first . . . and then one day you look up from where you're sitting in a diner someplace, and you realize that people are watching you because you've been talking to yourself for the last half hour. You tell me I lack persistence, and I tell you that doing what we do takes more persistence than pretty much anything you can imagine.'

'I'm not talking about your job, Frank, I'm talking about everything else.'

'What else is there? What the fuck else is there? I *am* the job. The job is me. If we're gonna talk about anything at all then it has to be about the job, because frankly, in all fucking honesty, there isn't anything else left right now.'

'Okay, let's talk about the job then.'

'I'm leaving.'

'Sit down, Frank. Sit down and let's talk.'

'No, I don't feel like it. I've said all I want to say. It's Friday. Let's just take a weekend without each other, okay?'

'You think that'll help?'

'Help me? Probably not. I'm thinking that it might help you.'

FORTY-ONE

By the time Parrish reached his desk, the copied file for Karen Pulaski had arrived from Franco at Williamsburg. Radick was nowhere to be seen.

Parrish left the office and took the subway on up to see Raymond Foley, the Supervisor at South Two on Adams.

Lavelle was there, sat in on the brief discussion. Foley listened patiently while Parrish explained the scenario.

'So you're going to want to interview every one of the forty-six male employees of this office?'

'I am, yes,' Parrish replied. 'And I'll need to ask you and Mr Lavelle some questions of course, simply because you're here too.'

'Well, go ahead,' Foley said. 'No time like the present.'

'There's a couple of things we need to verify before we can ensure that we have all the questions we need,' Parrish said. 'But that won't take long. I was wondering if we could start on Monday. I wish we weren't up against the weekend right now, but—'

'There's a good half of them here tomorrow,' Foley interjected.

'On a Saturday?'

'Sure, we have a covering staff on a Saturday. There'll be a good twenty or twenty-five of them here tomorrow.'

'Well okay, we'll start tomorrow.'

'I won't be here,' Foley said, 'but Marcus will, and he can take care of things for you.'

'That would be very much appreciated,' Parrish said.

'And you really think it's best to do it here?'

'Yes, if that can be arranged. They're certainly not under arrest, and I don't even want them to feel as though they're under suspicion. It's just a request for help from the police department, and their assistance with anything they know is going to be very much appreciated.'

'Sure, but the fact remains that you have a number of dead girls, and one of my people could be involved.'

'Yes, that is so,' Parrish replied. 'How many girls we don't know, or to what extent someone here could be involved. But this is what we're trying to establish.'

'Shit fuck God almighty,' Foley said. He rose from his desk and walked to the window, his back to Parrish and Lavelle. He was quiet for a good thirty seconds, and then he turned slowly.

'I don't know what to say—'

'You don't have to say anything, Mr Foley.'

'I mean, well . . . about the fact that it could be someone I know.'

'Though it might not,' Parrish interjected. 'It is not altogether impossible that someone has a line into your database, and they're taking the information they want from it.'

'You understand that the people here are quite strenuously screened before they're employed.'

'Yes, I do.'

'Though no system is foolproof, right?' Foley said. 'I bet you've had some awkward moments with police officers, right?'

'You better believe it,' Parrish replied. He thought of his own father. He thought of the way in which bad apples were overlooked, ignored, hidden from public view.

'Jesus . . . son of a bitch,' Foley said forcefully. 'Fuck.' He shook his head, walked back to his desk and sat down heavily. 'And you'll be doing the interviews?'

'Yes. Me and my partner.'

'So what can I do to prepare?'

'You can have a look at the names for me first and foremost,' Parrish said. 'Take a look at these cases and see if there's one employee who is connected to all of them.'

'Fire away,' Foley said. He leaned forward, turned his monitor to an angle, reached for the keyboard on his desk.

Parrish gave him the names. Foley typed them in one after the other, and then let the system do whatever it had to do.

'Three of them are from the original South unit, one was interviewed as a possible material witness to an abuse case we were investigating, and then the last two were from District Two, right here. You know that?'

'Yes, I was aware of that. I was also given the name Lester Young.'

'He's not here anymore. As far as I know he went over to Probation—'

'We're following that up separately,' Parrish said.

Foley read things, clicked, scrolled, read more things, and then he leaned back and looked directly at Parrish. 'No,' he said. 'There doesn't appear to be any common link between these cases. All of them have been dealt with by numerous counsellors, other people from CAA, from Child Services itself. We act as the co-ordination point for all records, and that's all we do. There doesn't appear to be any individual name that occurs more than once in any of these cases.'

'Was a long shot,' Parrish said.

Foley smiled wryly. 'When is it ever a short shot?'

Parrish got up and extended his hand. Foley rose also and took it.

'Appreciate your saying nothing until we show tomorrow,' Parrish said.

'Is there paperwork for this? Do you have to have a warrant?'

'To look at your records, yes,' Parrish said. 'That one we have already. To talk to your people, no. We're just making inquiries, nothing official as yet. We get some leads then maybe we'll need more warrants, but we'll jump off that bridge when we get there.'

Foley saw Parrish out. A couple of the desk jockeys seemed curious as to what was going on. Anyone with an average IQ would have known Parrish for a cop, and now he'd been here two days consecutive. There would be questions around the water cooler. Such rumors as would be circulating would serve Parrish well. If the perp was here, even the guy who gave up info on these girls for the perp – well, they would be on edge, already sweating by the time they got into an interview.

Parrish headed back to the subway, and took the train to Hoyt.

On his desk was a scrawled message from reception. Clare Baxter had called. Could he call her back?

He dialed a number he still knew by heart.

'Frank?'

'Hey there. What's up?'

'I'm gonna talk now, Frank, and you're gonna let me. This is about as much truth as you're going to get, and I think you should listen.'

Parrish closed his eyes resignedly.

'There's no-one, just *no-one*, who confuses and upsets me as much as you do. Sometimes I wonder if you've ever considered anything in your life, or if you do whatever the fuck comes to mind just to see what might happen. You did this to me for sixteen years, Frank, but I had a choice to get out and so I did. But Caitlin? Caitlin is your daughter, and so she feels there is an obligation to love you and to trust you. She doesn't have a choice the same way I did, Frank. She feels she has to listen to your bullshit because you're her father. Well, let me tell you now that I will be having a heart-to-heart with her about who you *really* are. Once that's done she can make up her own mind about whether or not she wants anything more to do with you. In the meantime, you just stay the fuck away from her, Frank, or I'm gonna spend every waking hour and every cent I can find making it illegal for you to see her—'

Parrish hung up the phone on his ex-wife. He took off his jacket. He wondered where the hell Jimmy Radick was.

FORTY-TWO

Jimmy Radick appeared just before noon. In his hand he clutched a sheaf of papers.

He sat down facing Parrish. At first Parrish said nothing, and then when he opened his mouth Radick cut him short.

'Yesterday was bullshit, Frank,' he said matter-of-factly. 'If I was a more aggressive man I would take you into the car park and beat the crap out of you. But actually, it's nothing to do with me. Whatever issues you have with your daughter are your own business, and the only mistake I made – the *only* mistake I made – was agreeing to speak with her about her concern for you. First time I met her she gave me her number on a piece of paper, and you know what she said to me?'

'What did she say, Jimmy?'

'She told me that you drink and you get morose. She said there was a lot of bullshit going on between you and her mom and you didn't deal with it very well. She told me to call her if you got too fucked up.'

'And you called her?'

'No, I sure as hell did not. She called me again. Yesterday. She asked me how you were getting on, how I was handling working with you, and I told her that it really wasn't any of her business and that I really didn't think it was appropriate for us to be having this conversation.'

'So what the fuck were you doing over there?'

'She asked me to go over there, Frank. She asked me to go over there because there was something she wanted to talk to me about and she didn't want to discuss it on the telephone.'

'And what was that? What was it she wanted to talk about?'

'I haven't a fucking clue, Frank, and you know why? Because you turned up and did what you did.'

Parrish lowered his head. He didn't feel ashamed. He just felt stupid. He didn't know whether Jimmy Radick was telling him the truth, though he suspected he was. Any lie that Jimmy told him now would be easily discovered with a few words from Caitlin – if she ever spoke to him again. Radick would know that. Radick was not aware of the threat that Clare Baxter had made.

'I'm sorry for—'

Radick raised his hand. 'I spoke to the doctor lady. That's all. I told her I was going to put in for a transfer, but I've decided not to do that. I want to stick with this, Frank, but there has to be some ground rules. You have to stop being an asshole, okay? You really have to just stop being a fucking asshole, and we'll get along fine, okay?'

'I can do that,' Parrish said.

'You sure you *want* to?' Radick asked.

Parrish didn't reply. He merely looked at Radick with a resigned and worn-out expression.

'Enough already,' Radick said. 'We have work to do.' He put the sheaf of papers on the desk. 'I have not been able to find this Lester Young. I got his name over to Probation and they have no-one by that name in their system. I'll keep at it. However, what I do have is phone records for Kelly, Rebecca and Karen. Nothing for the others, their accounts are too old.'

An hour and a half later they had something. Karen had taken two calls from a number – one on Wednesday, December 19th, 2007, a second just five days later on Christmas Eve morning. Kelly had taken a call on Friday, September 5th, 2008, from a very similar number, and then Rebecca had called the same number as Kelly from her cell phone on Thursday, August 28th, just three days before her murder. Information gave them what they wanted: the Karen Pulaski number was the original South District switchboard, the second number was the new South Two office.

Parrish called Foley immediately, learned he was out, got Lavelle instead.

'Mr Lavelle, Frank Parrish here. I just wanted to know if it was possible to find out where a call had been directed to when it came in to your receptionist.'

'I have absolutely no idea, Detective Parrish. Let me put you through to reception and see what they can tell you. Come back to me if you don't get an answer.'

Parrish did get an answer, was put through from there to the Communications Supervisor, who – though helpful – couldn't tell Parrish what he wanted to know.

'I'm sorry,' she said. 'We don't track calls like that. We have a central switchboard. All calls coming in go to the same number. Dealing with the sheer number of people we deal with, it proved unworkable to have each desk with a separate extension. There had to be some kind of filter or these people would be swamped with unwanted calls all day every day. From their desks they dial for an outside line, and then they can call direct. Incoming calls go to the same central number, and then they are transferred through to whoever they're for, but we don't keep a record of them. I'm sorry I can't help you with this.'

Parrish thanked her and hung up.

'Never straightforward is it?' Radick said.

Parrish told Radick about his meeting with Foley, that half the male employees would be in the following morning.

'I'd go alone,' Parrish said, 'but Valderas will consider it unacceptable protocol—'

'No question,' Radick replied. 'I'm coming with you. We need to speak to these people together.'

'Appreciated,' Parrish said. He glanced at his watch. 'You ever eaten at that diner down on Livingston and Elm?'

Radick shook his head.

'Let me buy you lunch, okay?' Parrish got up.

'You don't have to, Frank.'

'I want to,' Parrish said. 'Humor me, okay?'

FORTY-THREE

George McKinley Wintergreen had pushed a cart for as long as anyone could recall. Even when he slept, that cart was tethered to his right ankle with a makeshift chain of boot-laces. Cut that cord and you could have stolen the cart, but it would have done you no good. The entire shifting spectrum of George's worldly possessions were in that cart, but they were worthless to anyone but him. Bottle caps – a whole sack of them – everything from Coca-Cola and 7-Up to Seagram's, Crown Royal, Jim Beam, Jack Daniels, and even a small baggie of wood and cork stoppers from Labrot & Graham's Woodford Reserve. Next came cotton reels, bobby pins, buttons, photographic film canisters, eye-droppers, batteries, discarded keys, foreign coins, empty matchbooks, ring-pulls, barrettes, teaspoons, and a thick wad of postcards, all of which had come from England to the many and varied relatives left behind by American tourists.

Dear Ma. We saw Buckingham Palace. Lucy thinks she saw the Queen of Britain at the window.

Jimmy. We're having a great time, though a can of Pepsi is nearly two bucks!

Granddad. Hope you are well. Uncle David says we're going to see someplace called Madam Two Swords today. Sounds like a bordello!

Other such sentiments.

George Wintergreen was a jackdaw, a hoarder, though the rationale behind his collecting, what current or future purpose these things would ever serve, was unknown to anyone but himself. He guarded them ferociously, but was just as likely to decide that some item was no longer of value. During his fifteen years of vagrancy he had abandoned combs, lengths of string, padlocks, broken wristwatches, cigarette packets, computer discs, lipstick tubes, plastic forks and ballpoint pen refills.

Wintergreen haunted the edges of South Brooklyn – Carroll Park, the Gowanus Canal – sometimes crossing beneath the shadow of the expressway into Red Hook. He slept in doorways, derelict buildings, abandoned storefronts; and every once in a while took advantage of the narrow floor space available in a deconsecrated church near the James J. Byrne Memorial Park. Here, amidst the flotsam and jetsam of Brooklyn, those that walked the streets unseen like ghosts of New York's past, he slept for a handful of hours away from the bitter cold. Come daylight, he would disappear again into whatever world existed through his eyes. He pushed his cart, he collected his necessaries, he spoke to no-one.

One time George had been married. One time he'd understood the vagaries and vicissitudes of the international money market as well as any man, alive or dead, but then something happened. A chasm opened up. George fell headlong, and he kept on falling until he hit the dirt and – in preference to trying to claw his way out – he decided to stay there.

But however deep that chasm might have been, George still possessed sufficient common sense and connection to reality to understand that the dead body of a teenage girl was something he couldn't just push his cart away from and forget.

Early evening of Friday the 12th, perhaps a little before six, George made his way across the corner of Hamilton and Garner and headed beneath the expressway. He intended to skirt the Red Hook recreational area, make his way back along Columbia as far as Lorraine, and then turn right, follow Lorraine to Creamer and Smith, and then north again around the line of the canal towards Fourth. Had he completed his circuit as planned, he would have been no more than two or three blocks from Caitlin Parrish, perhaps the same distance from Kelly's home. But he didn't complete his circuit. In fact he got no further than the end of Bay Street, for it was here that he wrestled his cart between a dumpster and a rusted metal trash can. Snagged momentarily, George used all his strength to push the cart through the narrow gap.

What he didn't realize was that his cart was caught on a length of heavy wire that had been used to secure the lid of the trash can. In shoving his cart through the gap he brought the can over, and the wire, corroded and brittle, just simply snapped. The can went over, the lid broke loose, and the remains of a much-decomposed human being spilled out into the alleyway.

Unable to comprehend, unable to correlate this to any prior point of reference, it was some moments before George Wintergreen realized what he was seeing. Once two and two had become four, he backed up, left his cart right where it was, and hurried to the street. Fortunately, it took him no more than five or six minutes to flag down a black-and-white, whose occupants he directed, almost wordlessly, to the scene in the alleyway.

The younger of the two patrol officers turned gray-green and walked back to the car to call it in; the older officer, Max Wilson, crouched low and shone his flashlight right in there. He saw the purse at the bottom, saw whatever it was covered with, saw the last vestiges of fluid and flesh and rotted human being that was once a person, and from the presence of the purse and the size of the trash can he figured that it must have been a girl, no more than a teenager. He couldn't be certain, and he assumed nothing. Along with Crime Scene the DC had been called, and between them they would determine what had been discovered

The younger officer, Will Rathburn, headed back to deal with George Wintergreen. George sat on the sidewalk, maybe ten or fifteen feet from the overturned trash can, his cart beside him, his gaze unerringly fixed on the ground between his feet.

George didn't smell so good, and Rathburn hoped like hell they wouldn't have to take him in the squad car back to the precinct. Though he also knew to assume nothing, it seemed obvious that the old guy had merely pushed the trash can over with his cart. How long it had been there, and who was inside – well, that would be a job for Crime Scene. Right now it was simply a matter of containing the scene, preventing any further contamination of evidence, closing up each end of the alleyway and waiting for further instructions.

Crime Scene and the Deputy Coroner arrived simultaneously. They got the purse out of the bottom of the can and opened it up. Thankfully the purse was made of some artificial leather, more than likely a polyethylene-based fabric, waterproof at least, and amidst the remnants of gum wrappers, an undamaged cell phone, eye drops, and a single unwrapped condom, there was a wallet. Inside it was a student ID card, and that gave them a name: Melissa Schaeffer, d.o.b. 06/14/1989, her pretty face looking back at the DC like so many other lost daughters and mislaid girlfriends. The trash can had not been completely airtight, the extent of decomposition was such that there was little smell left, and when they tried to up-end the can the base broke away with corrosion. The thing had stood against all weather and wind for some considerable time, held merely by the strength of the metal and the fact that it had not been disturbed. Now it was simply a matter of determining whether the name on the ID card matched the body in the can. Then it would be a question of who she was, where she had come from, when had she gone missing, and who might still be looking for her. Sometimes people just stopped looking. Sometimes it was simply that a detective somewhere wished for nothing more than to resolve a question and close a file. Other times it was the end of someone's endless search, and their very worst fears confirmed.

FORTY-FOUR

Friday evening Parrish and Radick parted company amicably enough. Lunch had been brief, relatively laconic on both sides, and the hours until the end of their shift had been spent going back through files, through photos, through dates and names and Missing Person reports.

Parrish's conclusion, unavoidable in its simplicity, was that beyond Lester Young and the people at South Two they had no-one. If these enquiries came to nothing then they were back at square one.

That evening, willpower mustered to stay away from Clay's, Parrish watched TV for a couple of hours. Then he dragged out a box of letters and pictures that he kept beneath his bed. Robert and Caitlin as kids. Clare – young and pretty and still free of the antagonistic bitterness that seemed to be her stock-in-trade these days. At the bottom were photos of himself as a child, photos of his mother, his father, of graduations from high school and the Police Academy. His whole life in a box no more than ten by twelve.

He thought of going over to see Caitlin, of trying to explain himself. He imagined standing there outside her door, the feeling in his lower gut like an awkward teenager collecting his prom date. He hadn't felt this anxious since Caitlin's birth, before that Robert's, before even that the night he'd asked Clare to marry him. But that night he'd been drunk. Drunk also when Caitlin had been conceived. Hell, if his adult life was a road trip he'd done pretty much all of it DUI.

His thoughts of loss and loneliness like weeds that had taken root simply through neglect, Parrish wondered where it had gone off the rails. You worked so hard at so many things, you made decisions based on what you believed to be right, and more often than not it came out wrong. He understood that life was not meant to be easy, but how come it could be so hard?

Shrugging off the temptation to let himself get morose and nostalgic, Parrish packed up the letters and pictures and slid the box beneath the bed. There was something about this case that had really crawled beneath his skin. The sense of innocence abused, the feeling that someone somewhere had taken advantage of the trust and dependence afforded them by these girls. That was what it looked like, and that was what it came down to. Someone had said they would do one thing, and then they had done another. Someone had assumed a position of responsibility and guardianship, and then violated that agreement. Hadn't he done the same thing with Clare, with Robert, with Caitlin? Yes, for sure, but he hadn't murdered anyone. He might have killed a marriage, he might have suffocated any chance of real reconciliation between himself and his daughter, but he hadn't ended any lives. He considered his discussions with Marie Griffin, the details about his father – wondered whether John Parrish *had* in fact been guilty of the murders of Joe Manri and Robert McMahon that night in the spring of '79. He believed he had. He had felt sure of it. And it wasn't until now that he had allowed himself sufficient space to consider how that made him feel. Guilty? Not for the killings, but for saying nothing? For being sure of something and saying nothing? No, not even that. So what was it? It had to be that same thing: violation of trust, the agreement to carry the burden of responsibility, and then to do something else entirely. His father the lawman, the keeper of the peace, the one who was supposed to protect and serve . . . well, he protected and served the very people he was meant to stop. What was that if not betrayal?

So where did that put him? Right in the middle of this mess, right there in plain view, and he could make a decision to see it through, regardless of consequence, or he could call it quits, pack up his stuff, and walk.

The man he had always hoped to be would see it through, but what about the man he really was?

At quarter past eight Parrish left his apartment and walked

over to Clay's. He told himself he would have only one drink, but he was a liar, and he knew it well enough not to try and convince himself otherwise.

FORTY-FIVE

For no other reason than to satisfy his own curiosity, Parrish went by Marie Griffin's office on Saturday morning. It was locked, lights out, no-one home. Why this gave him a curious sense of satisfaction he did not know, but it served to assuage his guilt. He had suggested they take a break from one another, more for her benefit than his own, and she had done just that. He had made her feel awkward, challenged her position – personally and professionally – and yet he was not sorry. Whatever he was experiencing was real, very real indeed, and she was either up to dealing with it or she was not. He would see her Monday, and he hoped that by then he would have made some progress on the case. Perhaps with some forward motion on this thing he would be able to think about other things – what to do with Robert and Caitlin, how best to deal with Clare. Seemed to him that it was others' problems with him that caused the difficulties, not the problems he had with himself. But such things could be shelved for some other day. Today, Saturday the 13th, they would begin their interviews at South Two and see if there was a child-killer in Family Welfare.

Radick appeared just before nine, and Parrish had already prepared the files on each girl to take with them.

'How do you want this to go?' Radick asked him.

'Keep it simple at first. Names, addresses, how long have they worked there, where did they work before. Then we ask did they know any of these girls, have anything to do with them directly. That kind of thing. Once we've got whatever we can get from these guys, then we run our own checks on them, all the standard stuff – who has yellow sheets, who doesn't, you know. Like I said before, there's a guy I know in the FBI who might just be willing to do a search on them for us, if he's still there, and if he's in a good mood. For me, it's a matter of getting in front of some of these characters and seeing if there's anything that shows up. The over-confident ones, the dismissive ones, the nervous ones. There's bound to be a couple that stand out. We know that both Karen and Kelly took calls from Family Welfare in the days before they were murdered, and Rebecca called into the office herself. What that gives us I don't know, but it's a hook, you know? It's a coincidence, and I don't like coincidences.'

Radick agreed, couldn't see any better way to go, and they left for South Two just after nine-thirty.

Marcus Lavelle had been good to his word. He had set aside an office, even provided a coffee machine, a plate of Danish.

'We only eat donuts,' Parrish said, deadpan, and it was a moment before the strained and anxious expression on Lavelle's face eased.

'Lighten up,' Parrish told him. 'We're not orthodontists.'

Lavelle poured coffee, one for himself as well. He sat down with Parrish and Radick and asked them how they wanted to do this.

'Initially, we're going to need maybe ten or fifteen minutes with each one. How many staff do you have in this morning?'

'Twenty-six, twenty-seven if you include me. Guys, that is. We have some of the girls but I know you don't want to speak to them.'

'We may do,' Parrish said, 'but that'll be later. That'll depend somewhat on what comes up in our initial interviews.'

Lavelle was silent for a moment, his fingers tying invisible knots, his eyes wide, his breathing audible.

'What is it?' Radick asked.

Lavelle shook his head.

'If you have anything you feel we should know, Mr Lavelle . . .'

'It's nothing. Well, I say it's nothing, but it has been bothering me and . . . well, I don't know if it means anything but it struck me as odd, and at the time I didn't pay a great deal of attention to it, but in light of what has happened . . .'

He paused. He looked at Parrish, then at Radick, and back to Parrish.

No-one spoke for a considerable time.

'A while back, when we moved offices, when everything changed, you know?' Lavelle inhaled audibly. His fingers tied more knots, untied them, tied them once more. 'Well, obviously when we moved we had to take everything with us, all the old files, the records, the computers. We did leave the furniture behind . . . you know, desks and stuff . . .'

Lavelle smiled weakly, almost as if he was trying to convince himself that he was doing the right thing, that there was no option but to say what he needed to say.

'I was there during some of that work. We had contractors in. They broke up all the old furniture that was worthless, and the stuff that was still in reasonably good condition was shipped out to a warehouse somewhere. I think the city was going to sell it on, or perhaps use it some other place. Anyway, we had these lockers, and they were just regular lockers, the kind of thing you find in gyms and schools and whatever, with a little combination lock on the front, you know? Nothing much as far as security is concerned, but they served the purpose. People put their books and umbrellas and lunchboxes in there, stuff like that. Anyway, the contractors were breaking up these lockers and there was one locker with some magazines in there. Two or three of them, and they were just like your regular skin mags, you know? One of the contractors made a joke about it and he threw them into one of these big waste sacks they had, and I went over there, curious, you know? I went over there and had a look, and they weren't just regular magazines; at least they didn't seem that way to me. The pictures in them were of young girls . . . not like little children, but young girls. I don't know, maybe fifteen or sixteen or something, but too young to be taking their clothes off and having their pictures taken for magazines like that.'

'And did you know whose locker they came out of?' Parrish asked.

Lavelle nodded.

'Their name?'

'I'm not going to . . . I mean, you're not going to say that I said anything about this, are you?'

'No, not at all. This is strictly confidential, Mr Lavelle. It just gives us a heads-up on a possibility with one of the staff.'

Lavelle paused a moment, then said, 'Richard McKee. His name is Richard McKee.'

'And how long has he worked for Family Welfare?'

'Ten, twelve years,' Lavelle replied, 'and he's very good at his job, no question about that. He's never been in trouble. He's actually a model employee really. He works very hard. He's one of those that's here because it's his vocation, not for the paycheck. And I know there's nothing illegal about having magazines—'

'Depends on what they are,' Radick said, 'and how old these girls were.'

'Yes, yes of course, but in itself, you know? I mean, I don't—'

'It's okay, Mr Lavelle,' Parrish interjected. 'We really appreciate your telling us about this. Now, I think it's probably best if we make a start with these interviews, don't you?'

'Yes, of course. Sorry, I didn't mean to ramble on. I'll get the first one now.'

Lavelle left the room and Parrish set out a notepad, a couple of pens, a digital recorder. Radick put the files on the table ahead of him, stacked in date order – Melissa beneath, then Jennifer, then Nicole, Karen, Rebecca and Kelly. Parrish also made a note to ask about Alice Forrester, Nicole's step-sister.

The door opened, the first interviewee came through, and Parrish cleared his throat.

FORTY-SIX

Richard McKee was the fourteenth interview. He was in his late thirties, well-dressed, his hair immaculate, his shoes shined. He had on the kind of frameless, non-reflective spectacles worn by those who wished to appear as though they weren't wearing spectacles at all, but every once in a while he turned his head and the light reflected violet and pale blue off the surfaces and obscured his eyes.

It was nearly two in the afternoon. They had questioned a little more than half of the employees, and – as yet – there had been nothing significant, nothing that raised the hairs on the nape of Parrish's neck. They all seemed willing to assist, understanding of the need to maintain confidentiality, genuinely concerned that there might be a link between their own office and the deaths of at least five young girls, all of whom were in some way already unfortunate, disadvantaged, even lost.

'Seems such a sad state of affairs when someone who's already a victim is victimized again,' was the comment made by one Harold Kinnear, a fifty-three-year-old veteran of the business. 'Been dealing with adoptees and runaways and state wards and abandoned kids for nearly thirty years,' he went on. 'It wasn't easy in the Eighties, and it's even harder now. Seems the more civilized and sophisticated we become the less able we are to look after our own children.'

Parrish felt that Kinnear's last comment could apply to him, perhaps one of the world's very worst parents.

Parrish found McKee immediately concerned and co-operative. Yes, he had heard about the murder of Jennifer Baumann. Lester Young had told him. Lester had been the case officer for the girl they were interviewing about the possible sexual abuse.

'I can't remember the girl's name,' McKee said. 'The one

that had been abused. Lester was her case officer, I know that much. I remember the one that was murdered though. I remember when he told me about it. He went out there with the police to see the Baumann girl, and then he found out someone had killed her. It really shook him up.'

Radick looked at Parrish. Parrish felt like his heart had dropped into the base of his gut. Lester Young's name had come up for the second time . . .

'But Lester doesn't work here anymore. He went over to the Probation Service.' McKee sighed audibly. 'I try and remember all the cases, but it's difficult. So many names and faces and files, and we're advised not to make any of it personal.' He looked away for a moment, and then he smiled with effort and looked back at Parrish. 'You try and make it impersonal, businesslike you know, but sometimes you just can't help it.'

McKee had also heard of Karen Pulaski, though he hadn't been aware of her murder.

'Of course, anything I knew is now very old,' he said. 'And what I did know, well I don't see that it would be relevant now.'

'And the others?' Parrish asked him. 'Melissa Schaeffer, Nicole Benedict, Alice Forrester, Rebecca Lange, Kelly Duncan?'

McKee shook his head, and again the light played off the front of his glasses and obscured his eyes. 'No,' he said, but there was a heartbeat of hesitation in his voice.

'You're sure, Mr McKee?' Radick said, leaning forward, and Parrish sensed that Radick had picked up on the hesitation also.

'Like I said, it's hard to remember every face and every name,' McKee said. 'I deal with hundreds of cases every year, some of them closely, some of them in a supervisory capacity, some of them simply because I'm on the referrals check-list. I even do reviews for case officers in training. I look over their files before they are submitted for examination. It's a lot of people in any given year, and these girls . . . well, they go back two years . . .'

'I just want you to take a moment and think, Mr McKee,' Parrish said, and he repeated the girls' names – each one

231

slowly, carefully, all the while watching for the slightest shift in McKee's expression.

'No,' McKee said, his tone definite, his expression unchanging throughout. 'I really can't say that any of those other names ring a bell with me. Of course, if anything comes to mind later I'll let you know.'

'That would be very much appreciated,' Parrish said, and he took out his card and slid it across the table.

There was silence between Parrish and Radick after McKee had left the room.

Radick broke it. 'I didn't get anything from him,' he said. 'Okay, so he may or may not have had some skin mags way back when. What the fuck, eh? Most people would think it abnormal if a guy didn't have a few skin mags at some point.'

'Well, I figure that's sufficient grounds for arrest,' Parrish said, and he smiled sardonically. 'Fact of the matter is that he wouldn't have appeared a great deal different from anyone else we've spoken to, but we had those few words from Mr Lavelle and all of a sudden we're biased.'

'I didn't get anything from any of them so far. They all seem like decent, concerned people, trying to do a really, really hard job in a really fucked-up system.'

Parrish leaned forward. 'I agree, but we've spoken to – what? – fourteen of them. Another twelve to go today, and then there's the other twenty-odd on Monday.'

'I need a break,' Radick said. 'Seriously.'

Parrish looked at his watch. 'We need to get done,' he said. 'I want to get through these today, and then we can run checks on them tonight and tomorrow. Then we start afresh on Monday with the rest.'

Radick couldn't disagree, and so he didn't argue. This kind of work did not wait. Word would be out among those who had not yet been interviewed, and if their man was one of them, and in his answers there was something incriminating, then they could not afford to give him any leeway. Let him go home, now apprised of the investigation, and he could remove evidence. The likelihood that this would happen was slim, but often the thinnest thread was attached to the strongest lead.

Radick and Parrish pressed on – different faces, same

questions, over and over with the girls' names. It was as Parrish had suspected. To all intents and purposes these people were good-hearted, somewhat jaded, a little exhausted with the frustrations attendant to any profession where a desire to help was the motivation, but on the surface they appeared to be nothing more nor less than what they said they were. By the time they were finished he could remember only Harold Kinnear and Richard McKee, Kinnear because of the telling comments he had made, McKee simply because of what Lavelle had said about the skin mags.

Lavelle was last. It was past six. The office was now empty and both Parrish and Radick were mentally battered.

'I don't know what else to say,' Lavelle began. 'I've been out there talking to them. Some of them remember the girls, others don't. I don't think I dealt with any of the cases directly, couldn't say I've ever spoken to them, but a couple of the files have crossed my desk from a referral perspective, you know? The thing is . . . well, you never expect something like this to happen, and there's no way of predicting who might get into trouble, so you can't help but deal with all of them in exactly the same way. Truthfully, certainly for the majority of us, there's no one case that's any more important than any other.'

'And from your discussions this afternoon, both with those that we had interviewed and those that were awaiting interview, is there anything that was said by anyone that appeared odd or unusual? Anything on your radar, so to speak.'

Lavelle shook his head slowly, as if answering the question before he'd even considered it. 'I don't think so. No-one seemed stressed or overly anxious. There's a couple of people who've had homicide cases before. A ten-year-old who was beaten to death by her stepfather, a young boy who was killed by his mother, but it was years ago. Nothing to do with the current investigation. I think the general view is that the world is so fucked up that, well, something like this is bound to happen at some point. It's the career, you know? It's obvious in your case, but there's a lot of professions that deal with the less fortunate members of society, and they're going to touch the edges of this kind of thing every once in a while, aren't they? They're bound to I suppose, one way or the other.'

'Okay,' Parrish said, tired now of hearing the same thing a hundred different ways. 'We just need your full name, date of birth, Social Security number, address, work history prior to your employment here, and then we're done.'

Lavelle gave them what they wanted to know, just as all the interviewees had. Not one of them had objected. No-one had even inquired as to whether or not a lawyer or someone from Family Welfare's own legal department needed to be present. Helpful, co-operative, concerned, interested, eager to divulge anything that might help. It was all too easy to forget that the decent people were the majority. Perhaps there was a bad seed here, and perhaps they would find him on Monday.

Parrish and Radick thanked Lavelle. They shook hands, left him behind to turn out the lights and lock up the building.

'We have to find Young,' Radick said. 'Lester Young is going to be my priority right now.'

It was as they reached the car that Parrish was paged. It was Pagliaro. Parrish called him back immediately.

'I'm at the City Morgue,' Pagliaro said. 'I think we've got your runaway.'

FORTY-SEVEN

What little remained of the victim from the trashcan was spread out on a steel operating table. Remnants of clothing and personal possessions sat on an adjacent trolley, and it was from these that Pagliaro extracted the purse – in it the cell phone, gum wrappers, eye drops, condom – and showed it to Parrish and Radick. It was Radick who held up the plastic baggie, within which was the student ID card.

The forensic pathologist, a genial, red-faced man in his mid-forties, introduced himself.

'Andrew Kubrick,' he said, and then added with a grin, 'No relation to Stanley.'

'So who do we have?' Parrish asked, looking at the ID card. 'Is this Melissa Schaeffer?'

'I don't know yet,' Kubrick said, 'but what I *can* tell you is that skull morphology and femoral bone dimensions give us a Caucasian female, approximately five-three in height, somewhere around one hundred to one hundred and ten pounds.'

Kubrick picked up the skull, already detached from the spinal column. 'There's a connective tissue joint between the frontal and parietal bones of the skull. As we get older that joint closes up. How far that suture is closed can give us approximate age. This young lady? I'd say somewhere between sixteen and nineteen.'

'Any indication of COD?' Radick asked.

'Strangulation,' Kubrick said, tone matter-of-fact.

'How can you tell?'

'Know what the hyoid bone is?'

'In the throat?'

Kubrick pointed to a spot on his own neck. 'Horseshoe-shaped bone, only one that isn't articulated to any other bone in the human body. Sits between the chin and the thyroid cartilage. It's a delicate little bone, and it's fractured in about thirty percent of all strangulations. This young lady was strangled, no question. There's no other broken bones, no indication of any damage to the skull.'

'And how long has she been dead?' Parrish asked.

'I'd say two, maybe two and a half years. The trash can wasn't airtight, that's for sure. She just broke down in there, much as she would have done had she been buried. Clothes rotted, flesh decomposed. Water got in there, did its work.'

'Can was found in an alleyway at the end of Bay Street,' Pagliaro said. 'Some bum pushed it over with a shopping cart and the lid came away. It had been wired, but the wire corroded. Soon as it went over the base of the can came away, and there she was.'

'Is it realistic that a trash can like that could have been in an alleyway for two years with no-one any the wiser?' Parrish asked.

Pagliaro answered with a 'who knows' expression; Kubrick shrugged, and said, 'I have no idea. Can could have been there all this time, could have been there a week. The lid was wired shut, as your colleague says, but if it was down there with other trash cans and dumpsters I don't think anyone would have necessarily identified the smell of decomposition. Wiring the lid down prevented rats getting in there, that's for sure, but aside from that, well . . . hell, it could have been there all this time without anyone knowing about it.'

'So how do we formally identify her?' Radick asked.

'We don't,' Kubrick said. 'We could get a forensic anthropologist to try and reconstruct her face over the skull, but there's little chance of getting approval to do that. We'll do dental, but as far as I can see she doesn't seem to have had any significant work. Teeth are in good condition, no irregular spacing, no major cavities, no overcrowding. She just happens to be one of the very few who wasn't dropped into the orthodontist's chair at three years of age.'

There was silence for a while – Pagliaro, Radick and Parrish on one side of the table, Kubrick on the other, the broken-down remnants of somebody's daughter on the smooth stainless-steel surface between them.

'Is there any hope of determining whether or she was given drugs?' Parrish asked. 'Rohypnol primarily, or any other kind of benzodiazepine?'

Kubrick was shaking his head before Parrish had even finished the question.

'Not a prayer,' he said. 'You can pick it up in the hair for a month or so, but beyond that no. It passes very rapidly through the system.'

'I figured so,' Parrish said, unable to hide his disappointment. 'How was the alley?' he asked Pagliaro.

'Crime Scene went through it thoroughly but there was nothing there beyond the usual crap you find in such places. Nothing that related to this. What we have is the body, the trash can, the purse and its contents. I'll ask for the phone to be processed and we'll get whatever's on the card downloaded to see who she was calling, who might have been calling her. That should give us the owner of the phone, but that doesn't confirm that the dead girl and the owner of the phone are the same person, just like the ID card doesn't confirm that this is Melissa.'

'I can take care of the phone,' Parrish said. 'Effectively this is my case now, isn't it?'

'And you're welcome to it,' Pagliaro said, 'though God knows what you're going to do about formal ID and informing next of kin and all that.'

'I'm going to proceed on the basis that this is Melissa, certainly as far as the investigation is concerned. I'm not going to speak to her family, not yet . . . hell, maybe never. We can't exactly ask them to come down and ID her—'

'I'll see what I can do on the forensic anthropologist front,' Kubrick said. 'Sometimes we get graduates from the university down here who do some work for free. For the experience, you know? They're properly supervised so it won't be bullshit, but I can't guarantee anything.'

'That would be good,' Parrish said. 'I really appreciate that. Anyway, we'll get the phone sorted out, and we'll go from there. I think it's her. I feel in my gut that it *is* her. I don't see her purse and her phone being put in a trash can with some other girl's body, do you?'

'Who knows?' Pagliaro said. 'I stopped being surprised by any of this shit years ago.'

Parrish thanked him. Pagliaro left. Kubrick said he was off-shift imminently, and he needed to close up the place.

Parrish took the phone, signed for it, called Valderas as they were leaving.

'I need you to authorize some work on a cell phone, and I really would like to get it done tonight or tomorrow.'

Valderas said he'd do what he could.

Parrish told Radick to take him to the Precinct, drop him there. He planned to start running backgrounds on the employees from South Two.

'I'll come do it with you,' Radick said. 'And I can see if there's any trail on Young at the same time.'

'It's okay. I have nothing to do this evening. You go do whatever. I've wrecked one evening for you already, so I'll check on Young as well . . . can't be that hard to find some-one who's worked both for Welfare and Probation.'

Radick hesitated, and then said, 'The thing with Caitlin—'

Parrish shook his head. 'Forget about it. I was being an asshole. I can be an asshole far too often and far too loudly. It means a great deal to me that you didn't speak to anyone about that. I'll sort things out with her.' He smiled wryly. 'Issues, you know? We all got issues.'

Radick let Parrish out at the 126th, watched him as he hurried up the steps, carrying the notepads and files, the cell phone in a baggie, and he wondered if he would ever be as alone as Frank Parrish.

He called Caitlin, shared a few words, and then turned around and headed directly down Hoyt towards Smith Street.

FORTY-EIGHT

Parrish found Valderas, turned over the cell phone.

'You got the Schaeffer girl, I hear.'

'We are assuming it's her, yes.'

'Not enough left of her to give you anything?'

'Enough left to tell us she was strangled. That's all we've got.'

'And how did your interviews go?'

'As expected. We've done a little more than half. There's another twenty and then the supervisor himself, and we'll deal with those on Monday.' Parrish nodded at the phone in Valderas's hand. 'That would be good, you know? If you can get someone in Tech to download the card and tell us who she was calling.'

Valderas looked at his watch. 'Honestly? I don't think we'll even get a look in until Monday morning.'

'Whatever you can do,' Parrish said. He held up the stack of paperwork from South Two. 'Going to start running backgrounds on these guys, see if anything turns up.'

It was nearly eight by the time Parrish sat at his desk and spread the interview notes out in front of him. He typed in every name – all twenty-six of them, twenty-seven including Lavelle; dates of birth, Social Security numbers, the bare minimum that was needed to get the process started. He let the computer start working, and left for the upstairs canteen.

Seated at a corner table, cup of coffee between his hands, he looked out through the window to the street below. Saturday night. Fulton Street busy with traffic, people heading somewhere other than where they'd been for the week. Himself? Not a hope. He was where he'd always been, perhaps where he always would be. He smiled to himself. Today, sitting there listening to the South Two employees tell their little stories, he had noticed Jimmy Radick – how he looked, his mannerisms, his expressions. He had started to show the signs of wear. You could see his vocation in his eyes: eyes that looked for meaning in shadows. It would not be long, and then the line between who he'd been and what he'd become would blur and disappear. It was the effect that dead teenage girls in trash cans had on you. That was all it was.

An hour later – Parrish surprised at the amount of time he had spent thinking of very little at all – he returned to his desk to check progress on the backgrounds.

Two of them were flagged. The first was Andrew King. The face was there on the screen, but Parrish didn't recognize him from that afternoon's interviews until he realized that the assault charge that had put King in the system dated back to March of '95. It was then that Parrish recalled the man – thirty-four years old, suited, clean shaven, polite, and presentable for any occasion. The picture on file was of a long-haired, unshaven twenty-one-year-old. Appeared that King had gotten into a fight with a grocery store clerk who'd accused him of stealing something. King had hit the guy twice in the face and run, leaving behind his wallet and his groceries. King had turned himself in within half an hour, perhaps to ensure that he got his wallet back. He was arrested, arraigned and brought up. Judge gave him a community order, sent him back to the grocery store to work it off.

And then there was Richard McKee. Appeared that McKee had been handed a caution for violation of a City Building Ordinance. He'd applied for a permit to convert his roof space but began work before the permit arrived. The permit was approved and, in the end, no-one pursued the case, but it was still there in the paperwork.

And that was all he had. Two people. Two bits of paperwork. Nothing substantive, nothing incriminating. But what had he expected?

He ran a search on Lester Young, found four of them – three DUIs and a GTA. They all had work records on the system, and none of them were registered as having been employed by the City in any capacity. So the Lester Young they were after had never been arrested. That was all the system could tell him.

Parrish called it quits. He packed everything up and put the files and reports back in his desk.

Once again he thought of trying to speak with Caitlin, but it was Saturday night. She would more than likely be out with her friends, and if she was not, then she'd have made the definite decision to have a quiet night at home. If either was the case then Parrish would have found himself superfluous or unwanted. He took the subway to DeKalb and walked home. He bought a fifth on the way. He knew he ought to eat something, but he had little appetite. He would have a good breakfast tomorrow. That's what he would do. It would be Sunday, and Sundays were a good day for breakfast.

FORTY-NINE

The dreams woke him again, but this time he did not get up. He lay amidst a tangle of sweat-dampened sheets and wondered if Marie Griffin would now term him an obsessive.

The girls had been there. Pale blue skin. No eyes, or rather there *were* eyes, but no whites, no pupils, no color. Black hollows, sunken and shadowed, like small vacuums into which every ounce of light and shade had been absorbed. Everything in some sort of stilted monochrome apart from the fingernails. Red like new blood. But even as he looked at the hand that reached out towards him, he saw that they possessed no prints. Smooth, perfectly smooth, front and back. We are no-one, it said. We have no identity. We were here, and then we were gone, and we are now remembered only by you – Frank Parrish. Only you.

There were flickering images – children broken, children tortured, children abused.

Parrish did not sleep again. Perhaps he dozed for a handful of minutes here and there, but all he could recall when he finally stood beneath the shower was how he had wrestled with the sheets and the pillow, doing all he could to find comfort and finding none.

Whatever thoughts regarding breakfast he might have possessed the night before were now well forgotten. He made coffee, he craved cigarettes, he considered calling Radick and meeting with him to discuss any ideas he might have had regarding the case. If Monday's interviews proved to be as non-productive as those they had already held, then they were going to need another direction in which to take this thing real soon. He thought about walking over to Clare's. Check if Robert was home, see if he had plans.

Parrish could hardly remember when he had last seen his son. That was not a good sign. He needed to do something about it.

But Frank Parrish did none of these things. He merely left his apartment and started walking, at first nowhere in particular, but as he crossed the corner of DeKalb and Washington he felt an irresistible need to go back to the location of Kelly's body. He took the long way around Brooklyn Hospital, this time thinking nothing of how he could convince Caitlin to work there, his mind focused on Kelly, the simple fact that she had been strangled and left in a cardboard box.

In the alleyway itself there were no signs that such a thing had ever taken place. There were no shreds of crime scene tape on the handles of the nearby dumpsters. There were no chalk marks on the ground, nothing that would indicate the significance of what had happened only five days before. They were operating on the basis that Kelly had been put in the box and delivered here. That would not have been done in a car. A flatbed, a pickup maybe – something sizeable for sure. And whoever drove it wouldn't have wanted to attract undue attention. A utility vehicle – phone companies, repairmen, something of this nature? Or simply an SUV with a tailgate or a wide rear door.

Did anyone at South Two own such a vehicle?

Parrish thought about the people they had interviewed. Lavelle, Kinnear, King, McKee . . . the others whose names and faces were now a blur. He tried to picture any one of them doing something like this. Did they actually have anything on any of them? And as for Lester Young . . . Hell, as it stood right now, they couldn't even find Lester Young. One fragment of hearsay from Lavelle about McKee, the fact that Andrew King was capable of physical violence, then nothing. On the face of it, McKee seemed the most caring and dedicated of the lot. He'd worked in Welfare South before South Two. He'd known of Jennifer Baumann, but beyond that appeared to have no direct connection to any of the girls. But then no-one in such a position would have been dumb enough to drug and rape and kill his own charges. It all came down to two things: firstly, was the perpetrator an employee of Family Welfare, and secondly, was it a case of direct involvement? Was the South Two employee the killer, or was he passing on details of potential victims to someone outside the employ of the city? That raised one further possibility. If details were being passed out of the system to an external perpetrator, then was the inside man perhaps really a woman?

This last question was so anathema to Parrish that he didn't want even to consider it; not until all avenues had been exhausted with the male employees. Until Monday he had no-one.

And it was with that thought that Parrish headed back to his office to see if some further details could maybe be gleaned from different sources.

Using the internal system, he patched into DMV. DMV gave up the drivers' license details for all of the interviewees. There were no outstanding and prior traffic violations, no DUIs – a rarity in itself. King did not have a drivers' license it seemed, and though McKee did, there was no indication that he currently owned a vehicle. That, however, did not preclude the possibility that he did. Unfortunately the system did not work backwards. If Parrish had had a license plate he could have confirmed the registered driver. The database didn't list submissions by name, and thus he could not determine the license plate of a vehicle McKee might have owned. It would be a matter of sitting across the street, waiting for McKee to leave his house, and then following him to see if he walked to a car parked elsewhere. Either that, or ask the man on Monday. But why was he focusing on McKee? Why not Lavelle? There was nothing to tie any of them to any of this. The strongest connection – and this simply because his name had arisen twice – was Lester Young. They had to find him, if only to eliminate him from the investigation.

Once again, Parrish was chasing vague and indistinct shadows, trying to read signs when no signs were present. It had been foolish not to ask all of them when he'd had the chance. And do you drive? You do? What vehicle do you own at the moment? But this was the way such things happened. This was police work. As the investigation progressed and other circumstances were taken into account, new questions needed to be asked. Going back was difficult, especially with such informal interviews. The subject had cooperated, he had answered all questions asked of him, and to go back a second or third time could be construed as harassment. And if the subject was a perp then you were merely putting him on the alert. Now he knew the threads that were being followed. All of a sudden the car has been extensively valeted, every inch of the vehicle washed, polished, wiped, vacuumed and dusted. It was a matter of trying to determine what was needed without making such a thing completely obvious. Perhaps in his professional capacity alone Parrish was capable of subtlety and discretion. With everything else he was clumsy and insensitive. Like in his marriage. Like with his daughter.

Without a warrant he could not run a search on anyone's credit cards to ascertain whether or not they might have hired an SUV or a pickup. As already established, the box itself had given them nothing.

Parrish sat for a while in silence, eyes closed, breathing as slow as he could manage. If one of the South Two employees had killed these girls, assuming that they were all the same perp, then why would he have changed his MO? Say Melissa *was* the first: why pack her into a trash can and wire the lid shut? Why try to hide her? Then later, confidence increasing perhaps, he decides not to hide them at all? One in a mattress bag, another in a motel room, a third in her brother's apartment. No attempt to hide the bodies. So did that exclude Melissa from the serial, or did it make her the beginning of an evolving pattern? The broken neck was an index, but there was no way now to determine if her fingernails had been painted like the others.

Parrish tried to quell his frustration. He tried to focus on something, *anything*, that would make these things gel. Six dead. Six ghosts. And where were the girls killed? Rohypnol played its part, certainly with some of them, more than likely with them all. They were kidnapped – or lured somewhere – and drugged. Their hair was cut, their fingernails painted. They had sexual intercourse, quite probably unaware of that, and then they were strangled. Snuff movies? Was that it? He recalled the conversations with Swede and Larry Temple. Such people as these were too small for this. Gonzo porn, underage stuff yes, but serial killing for snuff movies? It was not in their repertoire. He thought about who he knew, what lowlifes might have slid across his desk in earlier years. Had he ever run a snuff case? Had he ever heard of one in the Precinct? He couldn't recall one.

This was something new, something out of the regular ballpark.

Parrish rose and walked to the narrow window that looked down into the street. He was unable to define how he felt. Adrift? Without an anchor? Certainly disturbed by the seeming lack of anything substantial throughout this entire case. Yes, he was assuming they were all linked, but not without reason. Yes, he was working on stale cases that had long since been dropped by the original investigating officers. Yes, he had included a case that was way out of precinct jurisdiction, and yet bore all the hallmarks of the same perpetrators.

It was intuition, gut feeling, something so basic and fundamental to this business that it gave substance to his certainty. Like a blind man with an astonishingly acute sense of hearing, Parrish believed that all cops – certainly those that dealt with homicide – cultivated an extended sensory catalog. They sacrificed personal stability for intuition; exchanged marital comfort for an innate conviction that someone had lied; let go of parental skills to make way for the unrelenting persistence necessary to watch someone for three months before they made a move. It was a trade-off, always a trade-off, and though the faculties gained were redundant once your work was over, they were still as much a part of you as your memories of better times.

It was this, and this alone, that gave Parrish the resolve to keep on looking, to keep on asking questions, to do everything he could to bring the girls' murderer to a small and airless interrogation room in the basement of the 126th Precinct. Either that, or to see him dead.

FIFTY

MONDAY, SEPTEMBER 15, 2008

'I'm reassured that you came.'

'Reassured about what?'

'About you, Frank . . . you have more staying power than I gave you credit for.'

'I figured you'd get DTs if I didn't show up.'

'So we're talking again?'

'We were never *not* talking. You were the one who said you didn't want me to come anymore. You were the one who was going to give up on me.'

'I have to apologize for that, Frank. It was actually un-professional of me to say that to you. Sometimes you deal with someone and it becomes so much more than the job. You know what I mean, right?'

'Sure.'

'So we start over. A clean slate. I know you want this to work, Frank, and I think that the only way that will happen is if we *make* it work.'

'I still don't really understand what we're trying to accom-plish here.'

'But you understand enough to know that it might help.'

'Maybe. Yes, sure . . . whatever, you know?'

'So we have talked about your daughter. We've talked some about the case you're working on. The thing we talked most about was your father, and I don't think we ever really came to a conclusion about that.'

'How d'you mean – conclusion?'

'Your conclusion, Frank. Whether or not you feel you have attained some sense of closure about who he was and the effect he had on your life.'

'Closure? That's such a bullshit word, don't you think? What does that even mean?'

'It means simply that you feel you have come to terms with something. That you have reconciled yourself to some-thing—'

'I'm not the sort of person who reconciles himself to things easily.'

'So perhaps we need to talk more about him.'

'I don't know what else to tell you.'

'I have a question . . . just something that I was con-sidering over the weekend.'

'Go for it.'

'Do you think you are how you are as some sort of revolt against him?'

'In what way?'

'The apparency. He *appeared* to be the model cop, but he was actually a very destructive and corrupt man. You appear to be destructive—'

'That would make sense if I was all good inside, but I'm not, believe me.'

'You don't think you're a good man?'

'I don't know what I am, but I know I have a habit of fucking things up. I mean, just look at what happened with Radick and Caitlin.'

'It's not uncommon for people undergoing counselling to start letting go of some of the feelings they have been suppressing, Frank. Not uncommon at all. Your outburst towards your daughter represented not only a desire and an impulse to protect her, but also has to be viewed in light of the fact that right now she is the only person in your family that you feel you can still affect.'

'I'm trying to help her.'

'I know you are, Frank.'

'So how comes it ends up harming?'

'I can't answer that, Frank, only you can.'

'God almighty, are you never allowed to just state an opinion? Why do you have to be so goddamned careful about everything you say?'

'Because our conversations are not about what I think, they're not about my opinions. They're about yours.'

'So you want to know my opinion?'

'That's why we're here, Frank.'

'On anything in particular?'

'Your opinion about your job for starters. Tell me your opinion about what you think you're doing, and why. Tell me your opinion about the people you have to contend with, the victims and the perpetrators.'

'My opinion? My opinion is that everyone has the capacity for evil. It isn't genes and chromosomes, for God's sake. It's situational dynamics, it's environment, and maybe it's even mental illness, and I don't think anyone even has a glimpse into the truth of that. Maybe it's just that some people are naturally destructive, and maybe some have the capacity to withhold themselves and some don't. I think psychiatry and psychology are little more than guesswork. I think they blur the lines. Hell, it used to be easy to tell the difference between the perps and the vics. Then these people, people who were supposed to be authorities on the subject, came along and started to tell us that these assholes were just as much victims themselves. Victims of society, victims of parental abuse, victims of neglect. Christ, if everyone who'd been mistreated as a child wound up a serial killer then there'd be nobody fucking left. Well, as far as I'm concerned these supposed authorities did accomplish something. They convinced us that assholes do bad shit to people not because they're just assholes, but because of the terrible fucking things that were done to them when they were kids. They're telling us it's not their fault, that they're a product of the society we've created. And all the lawyers get on the bandwagon. Prosecutors become defenders. Expert witnesses testify on behalf of whoever writes the largest checks. They even contradict their own testimonials and says it's because there's been further research, and then you find out it's because the defense attorneys just put another zero onto their fee. It all ended up about money. It stopped being about guilt and innocence, and started being about the skill with which lawyers could manipulate juries. Used to be that theories would fall apart in the face of facts. Now the facts have become fluid. The facts can be altered, at least the way that people are given the facts. And this job? What we do?

You have no idea how frustrating this can be. We are fighting a losing battle. The harder we work to bring justice back to the law, the harder the law fights to make real justice un-attainable for most.'

'Do you believe that? Really?'

'Yes I do.'

'So why do you keep doing this?'

'Because I'm no good for anything else. That's the truth. I'm just no fucking good for anything else.'

'And your current investigation?'

'Is the same bullshit as ever. I have to chase up phone records from a two-year-old account. I have to find some guy who used to work for Welfare and now seems to have disappeared. I have to go back to Family Welfare on Adams and interview another twenty employees. I have to try and convince everyone that half a dozen dead girls were all part of the same serial, even when there isn't a great deal of clues to suggest that they were, and even less evidence to prove it.'

'But you're convinced of it?'

'I have convinced myself that I am convinced of it.'

'And your daughter?'

'What about her?'

'Have you spoken to her since you kicked Chinese food down her stairwell.'

'I don't want to be reminded of that, and no, I haven't spoken to her.'

'Have you tried to contact her?'

'No.'

'And your partner?'

'We are still working together.'

'Has he mentioned his transfer request again?'

'No.'

'Do you feel that you can continue working with him?'

'Sure, he's a good guy. He does the job. He doesn't complain.'

'You think you can teach him something?'

'If he wants to learn, yes.'

'Good. That's good.'

'So what now?'

'I want to talk about your father some more. I think we

need to keep on talking about him until you have reconciled yourself to who he was.'

'Really?'

'Yes, I think it's important.'

'I don't. Not anymore.'

'Bear with me. I think there's more to be unearthed about how he affected you.'

'Sounds exciting.'

'Okay, so just think about it for me. We'll meet again tomorrow, and in the meantime just try and remember how he was with you, who he was to you when you were younger, and how your viewpoint of him changed as you grew up. That's the kind of thing I want to discuss with you.'

'Okay . . . if that's what you want.'

'And how are you sleeping?'

'Okay I guess. Not bad, not great. I'm having more dreams than I ever remember having.'

'That's a good sign.'

'Why?'

'Well, in and of themselves, dreams don't mean a great deal. There's no great significance to read into them. I know there's dream analysis and stuff like that, but frankly it's more about the interests and obsessions of the interpreter than anything else. What they do mean is that you are more mentally active than you used to be. If they start being nightmares then you need to start eating better and drinking less.'

'I didn't drink at all yesterday.'

'Well done.'

'Do I get a gold star on my progress chart?'

'Yes, Frank, you get a gold star.'

'See, you do have a sense of humor.'

'It's a rumor, Frank, just a rumor. Now go back to work. I'll see you in the morning.'

FIFTY-ONE

Melissa's phone was still theoretically functional, but the memory card within was beyond salvation. The micro-fine layer of protective material that covered the circuit board had corroded with time, and beneath that the tissue thin layer of metal had peeled away from the board and cracked. Melissa's purse had not been as airtight and waterproof as Parrish had hoped.

With the phone a dead end, Parrish and Radick had no other lines to pursue aside from returning to South Two to interview Supervisor Raymond Foley and the remaining twenty employees. Lester Young also needed to be found, but continuing along that line would have to wait until the interviews were completed.

On the way over Parrish explained his thoughts regarding the SUV.

'Makes sense,' Radick replied. 'No way that box would have gone in the back of a car, and even if it had it would have been one hell of a job to get it out in the confines of the alleyway and then carry it around back. Would have had to have been a larger vehicle – a station wagon with a tailgate would have done it perhaps, or – like you say – an SUV or a pickup.'

It was the first question they asked of Foley. Which of the employees owned an SUV, a pickup, or a large station wagon?

'No idea,' Foley replied. He waved Lavelle through from the outer office and asked him the same question.

'I think there's a few with pickups,' Lavelle said. 'Of course no-one comes to work in their car. They all use the subway. I couldn't be completely certain, but I would be surprised if some of them didn't have SUVs or whatever.'

Parrish and Radick went through the same interview with

Supervisor Foley once Lavelle had left the room. How old was he, how long had he worked there, where had he come from, had he had any direct or indirect involvement in any of the girls' cases – official, unofficial, supervisory, review or otherwise. Parrish asked about marital status, number of kids, home address, Social Security number, and lastly what car he drove. He now planned to add this last question in for everyone. Just in case.

Foley came up clean. Nothing he could tell them bore any relevance to the investigation.

They resumed the employee interviews with Kevin Granger, went on through Barry Littman, Paul Kristalovich, Dean Larkin, Danny Ross, and after a while they all began to look the same, and sound the same, and feel like the same interview played through a loop with a different face saying the words.

By lunchtime they had covered twelve of the twenty. Parrish needed a break. Radick said he couldn't have agreed more. They took a walk down Adams and found a narrow-fronted diner on Tillary. Parrish sat in a booth in back. Radick ordered tuna cheese melts, coffee, a bowl of fries. When it came he ate slowly but methodically. Parrish picked at the sandwich, managed little more than half of it, but he drank two cups of coffee and asked for a third.

They spoke little until Radick broke the silence with, 'I'm reminded of that scene in *All The President's Men*. You seen that movie?'

'Yeah, good movie. Really like that movie.'

'You know when Woodward and Bernstein are going to all the houses, one after the other, asking questions of people who worked under Haldeman and Dean and whoever?'

'Yeah, I remember that.'

'Well, they couldn't get anyone to talk. And Bernstein, Dustin Hoffman right? He says "It's like there's a pattern. Like there's a pattern to the way they're *not* talking". It's like that back there.' Radick nodded in the direction of South Two. 'There's a pattern to the way that we're not finding out anything that we don't already know.'

Parrish shook his head. 'I don't even know what that fucking means, Jimmy. I think maybe you're losing it.'

'Lost it already,' he replied.

'We have to think about interviewing the women as well. Not as the perp, but as a feeder-line to someone on the outside.'

Radick pushed the bowl of fries aside and leaned back. 'I can't think with that,' he said matter-of-factly. 'I just can't get my head around the idea that a woman would be involved in something like this. Killing a man, yes, maybe, but out of jealousy, anger, a heat of the moment thing, but not this . . .'

'Just because such a thing doesn't happen very often doesn't mean that such a thing never happens.'

'I agree, Frank, but six girls? Abducted, drugged, sex acts of one kind or another, and then strangled.'

'The issue here is time, Jimmy. The likelihood is it's going to be a man. We deal with the men first. If that comes to nothing then we start in on the women.'

'Agreed,' Radick replied, and then he paused for a moment, thoughtful, deliberate. 'You know what I've been thinking?'

'Tell me.'

'Snuff movies.'

'I've thought the same thing.'

'Teenage girls fucked and strangled at the same time. Someone's filming it, selling the films. Maybe not even here. Maybe in Europe, England, South America. Keep it out of the local market, you know? I want to talk to Vice. See if any of these girls have turned up in their territory.'

'Yes, we'll do that later. Let's finish up these interviews and then go speak with them.'

Radick paid for lunch. He insisted. Parrish let him.

They walked back to South Two, waited until all the remaining un-interviewed staff had returned from lunch, and began again. The last eight took them through until just after four, Parrish aware of the frustration such interviews engendered, cautious not to rush them for the sake of getting through it. *The next one*, he kept thinking. *The next question, the next person . . . they will give us something else, something new, something that will take us somewhere . . .* But they did not, and it did not come as a surprise to him.

Finally, ragged at the edges and desirous of anything but

four close walls and a series of repetitive questions, Parrish and Radick met with Foley and Lavelle.

'Is there anything else we can do to help?' Lavelle asked.

'I don't believe there is,' Parrish said. 'If we need you or your employees again we'll be in touch. You have been very helpful, and it is greatly appreciated.'

'And can you tell us anything?' Foley asked, rising from his desk. What he was asking was simple. *Are any of the people in my office responsible for kidnapping and killing six teenage girls?* Protocol prevented him from being as direct as he would have liked. That, and the belief that if he was subtle he might glean a greater quantity of information from Parrish.

'We can't tell you anything about the investigation,' Parrish said bluntly. 'That's standard procedure in all such cases. All we can do is thank you for your time and co-operation and let you get back to your work.'

Foley didn't push it. Lavelle merely shook hands and showed them down to the lobby.

'You know where I am if you need me,' Lavelle said, perhaps believing that he had now been an integral part of the investigation, that without him they would have been stymied. To a degree he was right.

Parrish and Radick walked back to the car. They didn't speak on the way. Radick knew where Vice was, but Parrish knew *what* it was. Vice was a dark place, perhaps the darkest of all, and he had hoped – somewhere within the vestiges of humanity he had managed to preserve – that he would never have to walk those corridors again. The things he had heard back then. The things he had seen. It was a different world. A world that ran parallel to his own, parallel to everyone else's, and all but a few had the faintest idea of its existence.

FIFTY-TWO

'What do you want me to tell you? I got everything down here, Frank. Anal, DP, gonzo, necro. I got gay, lesbian, under-age, S&M, water-sports, girls fucking animals, the whole goddamn catalog of human depravity. You think of some-thing human beings can do, and I can pretty much show you it in all its many and varied forms.'

'Teenage snuff,' Parrish stated. 'Girl-next-door, teenagers, straight sex as far as we can tell, but more than likely being strangled during or immediately after. Girl will be passive we believe, as we have traced benzos in a couple of them. Will go back at least two years, perhaps longer . . . and it'll have been made locally.'

'Jesus, Frank, you know how many movies that covers?'

'I have an idea.'

Joel Erickson, Vice Archive Supervisor, custodian of all things celluloid and digital, wore a face for the world. First appearances gave you the genial uncle, the helpful next-door neighbor, the cousin who showed up each Christmas with a different bleached-blonde forty-five-year-old girlfriend. Look a little deeper and the cracks and crevices began to show. The lines were there, and the shadows, and when asked about the things he knew he would smile sardonically and shake his head.

'You don't want to know the things I know,' he would say, and then proceed to tell you.

Joel Erickson was not the sort of man who was invited to dinner parties, and – even if he had been asked – he was not the sort of man who would accept.

'Off the top of my head I can think of three, four, five dozen that would fit the bill just in the last quarter.'

Parrish put the case files on Erickson's desk and pushed them towards him.

Erickson opened them one at a time, perused the picture within, and then closed the file and set it aside.

'All the same,' he said quietly, and shook his head. 'They all look the same after a while. Leave it with me for a few days. I'll take copies of the pictures now, and I'll start looking as and when I get a chance. But you know what it's like, right? Needle and a fucking haystack in the same sentence once again.'

Parrish smiled ruefully. 'I get it, Joel. I'm just asking you to do whatever you can. I got six. I think they're connected, and I think that some of those faces might be somewhere here.'

'Like I said, Frank, I'll do what I can.'

Parrish and Radick waited while Erickson photocopied the pictures. They thanked Erickson for his willingness.

'I got all the willingness in the world,' he replied. 'It's time and resources that are the problem.'

'Let's take a break,' Parrish said as they reached the car. 'Let's go get some coffee or something. I just want to take a few minutes to get oriented.'

There was a Starbucks a block and a half down. Parrish ordered the coffee while Radick found a table near the restrooms.

'Hangs together with a fucking spider's web,' was Radick's comment as Parrish sat down.

Parrish didn't reply until he was seated, until he'd removed his jacket, set down his files, fished his cell phone out of his pocket and set it on the table.

'A spider's web is a very good analogy,' he said. 'I think there's so many more threads to this than we see right now. Either that, or they're all unrelated.'

'I don't think they *are* unrelated,' Radick replied. 'The fingernails, the haircuts, the strangulations.'

'For sure, but how many girls get their nails done, get their hair cut? They're doing that kind of shit all the fucking time, aren't they? All we have that's MO-consistent is the COD, and strangulation as a COD has to be about as common as you can get.'

'I understand that, Frank, but I still think you're onto something. I think they're linked, I think they're all going to tie together, and I think there's one person and he works for South Two.'

Parrish smiled. 'So who do you keep thinking about?'

Radick shook his head. 'I keep thinking about McKee, but I know I'm thinking about him because of the skin mags, and that . . . Well shit, it isn't even anything is it?'

'You're right. It isn't anything,' Parrish replied.

'What did you used to say? Something about how things are often exactly as they appear.'

'But also that the obvious can sometimes occlude the truth.'

'McKee is the model employee for sure, but he was also the most familiar with the cases.'

'But he would be,' Parrish replied. 'He deals with cases of his own, some he supervises, and he even does case reviews for the guys they're training.'

Radick didn't reply. He merely looked down for a moment.

'I'm not disagreeing with you, Jimmy. I'm not saying it *couldn't* be him, but without anything to directly connect him, no info on a car, nothing to . . . Hell, he's no more in the frame for this than any of them.'

'So who do you like for it?' Radick asked.

'I don't *like* any of them for it,' Parrish replied. 'I would love for it to be McKee. I would love for it to be that fucking simple.'

'Why d'you bring his name up then? Why d'you say you want it to be him?'

Parrish inhaled deeply. 'Gut feeling? Intuition? Fuck, I don't know. He came in the room, he sat down, and – I don't know, Jimmy, I just don't know. Something, nothing . . . maybe I just want it to be him so we aren't going round and round in fucking circles. I have no more reason to think it's him than I do any of them. If I'm completely logical and rational then there's nothing, and if I'm not . . .'

He didn't bother finishing the sentence.

'So let's just put some heat on him,' Radick said. 'Let's get him to come down to the 126th and ask him some more questions. We can *ask* him to assist us with the investigation without making it formal, and if he refuses then we have another little flag waving over his head, right?'

'We can do that, yes.'

'Only concern I have,' Radick went on, 'is that if we push him for some more info then he'll take evasive action with whatever evidence might be in his car and his home.'

'The mere fact that we're questioning everyone at South Two has done that already,' Parrish replied. 'If he had things to hide then he'll have hidden them already.'

'But they always miss something, don't they?' Radick asked.

'Not always,' Parrish said.

Radick hesitated. 'Shit, Frank, we're just making this up as we go along. In all honesty, Lester Young is more connected to this stuff than McKee.'

'Sure he is, but Lester Young we don't have. We have McKee, and McKee had skin mags in his locker.'

'So I'll call Lavelle, tell him we want to speak to McKee some more, and that we'll pick him up outside South Two when he's done at work.'

Parrish glanced at his watch: it was a little after two. 'Screw it . . . ask Lavelle if he'll let him out now.'

Radick called, didn't get Lavelle but reached Raymond Foley. Foley didn't have a problem, said McKee could have the time to do whatever was needed. He said he would speak to McKee right away, tell him that Parrish and Radick needed his help with some further information.

'We're up,' Radick said as he ended the call. 'Foley is letting him out now. We're going to go pick him up at South Two.'

'Good enough,' Parrish said. He got up, put his jacket back on, and walked to the counter to get a take-out cup for his coffee.

They were outside South Two within fifteen, and McKee was already there, hands in his pockets, collar turned up against the chill breeze, waiting patiently.

In that moment Parrish felt a sense of urgency about Richard McKee. What it was he could not identify or define clearly, but it was definitely there. That *intuitive* thing, as if his line of sight had suddenly shifted and he could see back of the man. See what he could really be like. See what was potentially within. But, then again, he knew there was no

reason for him to feel that way. Maybe this was just desperation. And there was a fine line between desperation to resolve
a case and the obsessiveness that destroyed careers.

Did McKee look anxious, or was Parrish imagining it?
Perhaps *hoping* he looked anxious? When McKee got in the
car he was already asking questions. *What did they need?
What other questions were there that he needed to answer? Was
he being arrested for something?*

'It's okay, Mr McKee,' Parrish assured him. 'Really, it's
okay. There's a good few people at South Two we needed to
get more information from. You just happen to be the first
because you remember something about these cases. This is
just a helping hand for us, okay? Please don't worry.'

With that McKee seemed a little less nervous, but as they
drove Parrish watched him in the rear-view mirror. McKee
was on edge, no question about it. It was not uncommon for
people to react this way. Questioned about one thing, they
immediately thought of all the things they really wouldn't
want to be questioned about. The simple matter of having
to deal with the police could bring on a lot of stress. It was
simply the potential of the situation. The police possessed
authority, and if they took a dislike to you they possessed
the power to arrest, charge, try, convict, incarcerate, even
execute. It had happened to innocent people, and it would
more than likely happen again many more times before the
law and the justice system started to get their shit together.
When it came to the police, people became a statistic, and it
was this that scared them.

Either that, or they were in fact guilty, and in McKee's case
Parrish had to prepare himself to be badly disappointed.

FIFTY-THREE

An interview room in the basement of the 126th Police Precinct, Brooklyn South, was perhaps one of the most airless and unwelcoming places within which to find yourself. Tiny louvered vents high above the door permitted little more than a minimal escape route for the sweat-drenched air that clouded the room; these same louvers didn't seem to allow any fresh air back in.

Radick asked McKee if he wanted coffee. McKee said yes. Parrish showed him to the chair, and immediately apologized for the room.

'If I had an office of my own we'd be in it,' he said, 'but I'm just your standard government mule.'

'Same with us,' McKee replied. 'Dozens of us in one big open space. Doesn't lend itself to discretion, does it?'

Radick returned with coffee. He sat down between Parrish and McKee at the end of the table, Parrish and McKee facing one another. A few moments of awkward silence before Parrish leaned forward and brought the palms of his hands together as if making a small prayer.

'Richard,' he started. 'I can call you Richard? Is that okay?'

McKee nodded. 'Of course, yes.'

'I wanted to ask you some more about your involvement with Jennifer Baumann and Karen—'

'*Involvement?*' McKee interjected. 'I didn't have any involvement with either of them.'

'I think you said you'd heard of Jennifer, even knew her case officer. If I remember rightly, you said he'd gone to the Probation Service.'

'Yes, I did say that. I knew *of* the Jennifer Baumann case, but I didn't know the girl. Never met her, never spoke to her. Same with Karen Pulaski. The name rang a bell, but I didn't even know she'd been murdered.'

'But now you do.'

'*Do* what?'

'You do know she's been murdered.'

McKee frowned. 'Yes, of course I know she's been murdered. You told me yesterday.'

Parrish nodded. He smiled understandingly. 'Yes, of course I did. I did tell you that. But before I told you that you had no idea that she'd been killed.'

'I knew Jenny Baumann had been killed. I told you I was aware of that—'

'Jenny?'

'Yes, Jenny Baumann.'

'I thought you didn't know her.'

'I don't – *didn't* – whatever. No, I didn't know her. Just her name. Had heard that she was killed, but this was the better part of eighteen months or two years ago.'

'You remember when you heard?'

'Yes, I do. It's not every day that you hear someone has been killed.'

'And do you remember how she was killed? The circumstances of her murder?'

'No, not particularly. Why?'

'I just wondered, Mr McKee, nothing more.'

McKee frowned again, seemingly utterly perplexed by the direction and tone of the discussion.

'I'm sorry, Detective, I really think I might have misunderstood your purpose here,' he said. 'You've brought me here because you think that I might know something else about these girls and the circumstances of their deaths. You asked me to come here and I came voluntarily. I came of my own accord, and I came to help, not to be harassed. I'm starting to wonder whether I need a lawyer.'

Parrish didn't speak for a moment, and then he leaned forward and closed his hands around his take-out coffee carton.

'Do you have a car, Richard?'

'A car? Yes, I have a car.'

'What kind of car?'

'A Toyota. Why?'

'What kind of car is it? A compact? A coupe?'

'No, it's an SUV.'

Parrish nodded slowly. He glanced sideways at Radick.

'And you are single?'

'Yes, I told you that yesterday.'

'I'm sorry. I spoke to so many people yesterday, and after a while I forget specifics.'

'You didn't forget that I knew Jennifer's case officer.'

'You're right, Richard. I didn't forget that, did I? I'm sorry. So let's get back to your car, your SUV.'

'What about my SUV?'

'Wouldn't you say it's generally the sort of car you have for a family? Throw the kids in the back, go away somewhere for the weekend. You know the sort of thing, right?'

'I do throw the kids in the back. We do drive somewhere for the weekend.'

'I'm sorry?'

'When I have the kids. We do go places. We do go to different places.'

'You have children?'

'You know I have children, Detective. I told you in the interview. I told you I had two children. Is that a crime now?'

Parrish laughed. 'It should be for some people, yes.'

'But you *are* single?' Radick interjected.

McKee sighed, a slightly exasperated sound. 'I am single now. I was married. I have two children . . . I say *children*, but they are in their teens now.'

'Divorced or separated?' Parrish asked.

'I said already. I'm divorced.'

'Amicable?'

'When is a divorce ever amicable, Detective? It was noisy, let's put it that way.'

'Who divorced who?'

'I divorced her.'

'Because?'

'Why did I divorce her? What the hell does that have to do with the fact that these girls have been murdered?'

Parrish smiled. 'I'm sorry,' he said. 'I'm divorced too. I also have two kids, perhaps a little older than yours. It's just that so many of us make the same sort of mistakes, and sometimes it's reassuring to know that there are other people who've had the same difficulties—'

'I divorced her,' McKee said. 'She was sleeping with someone else.'

'I'm sorry to hear that.'

'Why? It wasn't your fault.'

'We're off track here,' Radick said, sensing that Parrish had elicited as much as he was going to about the familial arrangements of McKee without instilling a greater degree of paranoia and suspicion in the man. He could see what Parrish was doing, and he knew Parrish would bring the man back to the subject soon enough.

'Yes, we're off track,' Parrish echoed. 'We were talking about the circumstances of Jenny Baumann's death.'

'No, we were talking about why I had an SUV.'

'You're right, we were, but before that, Jenny Baumann . . . not Jennifer?'

'Yes, *Jenny* Baumann,' McKee said. 'It *is* very common, I believe, for girls named Jennifer to be called Jenny.' There was an edge of sarcasm in McKee's tone which Parrish ignored.

'Do you remember how you heard she had been killed?'

'I told you. Lester Young told me about it.'

'And he was her case officer?'

'No, Jennifer was never an active case here. Lester was the case officer for another girl, and there was a potential sexual abuse thing, and Jennifer was believed to have been a witness, someone who could corroborate the girl's story. That was all. As far as I know the case was never pursued by the police.'

'And Lester Young went into the Probation Service.'

'Yes, he did.'

'Did you ever speak with him about Jennifer?'

'No, I did not.'

'And how did you know about Karen Pulaski?'

'I knew *of* her, not about her. As I said yesterday, I had no idea that she had been murdered.'

'Yes, you did say that. So how did you know *of* her?'

'Just in passing. There was a change in the whole administrative system at the start of the year. We used to be Family

Welfare South and Family Welfare North. I was in South, of course. They split each division into eight sections, and now I am South Two. We had to handle all the file transfers, hard copy and electronic. It was a huge job. We divided it up alphabetically and there were enough of us to have only two letters of the alphabet each and I got P and R. It was about three hundred files. Karen was amongst them, but she went elsewhere, not to us at Two. I think she was from Williamsburg or Ridgewood or someplace.'

'It was Williamsburg,' Parrish said.

'Right. Anyway, she was South originally, and now she'd be South Seven or Nine or something.'

'So why would you remember her out of three hundred or so files?'

McKee smiled awkwardly. 'This is going to sound foolish.'

'I don't mind how it sounds, Richard, I'm just curious as to why she stuck in your mind.'

'Because of her name.'

'Her name?'

'Karen Pulaski.'

'Yes, I know what her name is, Richard, I just wondered why—'

'My ex-wife's name is Carole. Her maiden name was Paretski.'

No-one spoke for a moment or two.

'Carole Paretski,' Radick said matter-of-factly.

'Yes, that was her maiden name. That's the name she's gone back to now. I remember looking at the Pulaski girl's file and thinking how similar their names were.'

'And what does she do . . . your wife?'

'She works for a law firm out near Lafayette Park.'

'She's a lawyer?'

'No, she's a secretary.'

'And how long since your divorce?'

'It was final in the early part of 2005.'

'And your kids are how old?' Parrish asked.

'My daughter, Sarah, is fourteen, and my son, Alex, is fifteen.'

'And they live with their mother?'

'Yes, during the week they do. I have them Saturday and

Sunday alternate weekends, and Sunday the other weekends. That's because I work Saturdays every other week.'

'Which is why you were at work this Saturday.'

'Right.'

'Why not have them all weekend every weekend?' Radick asked.

'I need the money. It's still a lot of money I have to give her every month.' McKee looked at Parrish. 'You have the same, right?'

'I did,' Parrish replied. 'They're old enough to make their own way now, but until recently it was a lot of money, yes.'

Radick leaned forward. 'Is there still bitterness and animosity between you and your ex-wife, Mr McKee?'

'Still?' McKee asked. 'We were married for over fifteen years, and I think the first year or two was the only time there wasn't bitterness and animosity.'

'But you stayed together for the kids?'

'We did. We put on a brave face for the world, and we kept it together for as long as we could. It was the last affair she had that was the final straw.'

'You want to tell us about that?' Parrish asked.

'What do you want to know?'

'Anything at all, whatever's on your mind,' Parrish said.

'I don't have anything to say about it. What happened happened. It's over.'

'And she is with someone else now?' Parrish asked.

'I presume so. She's not someone who can ever be alone.'

'But you don't know for sure?'

'The kids tell me this and that. Got to a point where I didn't want to know so I asked them not to tell me any more. I could see what it was doing to them, the constant unpredictability, the instability it caused in the home. It's not a good environment for kids, but what the hell, eh? The law is on the side of the mothers, not the fathers, right?'

'Right, yes. It is.'

'So that's where we are. I see them for a day or two every week. I do what I can to brighten their lives a little. I wait patiently for them to be old enough to go to college or whatever, and then I will see them more frequently and make sure that they get a little bit of stability and sanity in their lives.'

'And you have no wish to get married again?' Parrish asked.

'Married again? No, I don't think so. Hell, what am I saying? I'm a sucker for women. If I got another relationship and it seemed right, and she wanted to get married, then yeah, sure, I'd probably give it another go.'

'But no-one in the crosshairs at the moment?'

McKee smiled at the expression Parrish used. 'No, Detective, no-one in the crosshairs.'

'So let's go back to Jenny Baumann. Lester Young was Family South, and he dealt with her directly.'

'Well, he was present at the police interview, that was all. Jennifer was questioned by the police, and because this other girl was present in the interview they had Lester Young along as her Welfare representative.'

'And you knew Lester?'

'Yes, somewhat. Not a great deal more or less than anyone else at South. There were a hell of a lot of people there, which is why we got this most recent shake-up and the division of the two sections into sixteen units. It was long overdue, and I think that once the confusion has all settled down then it will work a lot better.'

'Let's hope so, eh?' Parrish said. 'Let's hope that these girls can be looked after a little better.'

'I don't think that's entirely fair, Detective,' McKee said, a defensive edge in his tone. 'I think – given the resources and facilities we have – that we do as good a job as we can under the circumstances—'

Parrish raised his hand. 'I'm sorry, Richard. That came out wrong. We're looking at it simply from the view that there are six dead girls, and there's the possibility that they might all be connected through Family Welfare. If they are, and if it's someone within the organization, then there's going to be a great deal more shaking up to deal with. I think it will turn things inside-out and upside-down more than anyone can imagine.'

'I find it so hard to imagine that there's someone within

South Two doing these things. I know most of them reasonably well, and the vast majority have been there at least as long as I have—'

'And if you had to ask some questions, Richard, if you had to make a decision about who it might have been, then where would you go with this?'

McKee laughed nervously. 'I'm not going to even try and answer that question, Detective. That's a terrible, terrible thing to consider.'

Parrish smiled understandingly. 'I really appreciate your time, and your honesty,' he said. 'I think we're done. You want us to have someone drive you back to work?'

McKee inhaled deeply and placed his hands flat on the table. 'No, I'm okay,' he said. 'I'll get some lunch now and head back myself.'

'Okay. If we need anything else we'll be in touch.'

Parrish got up. He shook hands with McKee.

McKee reached the door, and then he hesitated. He turned back and looked at Parrish. 'The Baumann girl,' he said. 'When was it that she was actually murdered?'

'Why do you ask?'

'Because I heard of her death from Lester, but I don't think he ever told me when she died.'

'It was January,' Parrish said. 'Her body was found on the fifteenth of January 2007.'

McKee nodded slowly, and then he reached into his jacket for his pocketbook. From it he took a number of creased and dog-eared photographs, and leafing through them he isolated one. He looked at it closely, and then he smiled as he held it out towards Parrish.

'And this is . . . ?'

'This,' McKee said, 'is a picture of my kids at Disneyland. I took it.'

Parrish took the photo. The kids were visible, but barely. They were way in the distance, appeared to be sharing a few words with a six foot Mickey Mouse.

'And you're showing me this because—'

'Because of the date. My camera prints the date in the bottom right-hand corner of the photos.'

Parrish looked at it. *01-12-07*, it read.

'We were at Disneyland that week. In fact we were there from the tenth to the nineteenth. It was the last holiday I took the kids on.'

Parrish looked at the numerals there in the right-hand corner. He returned the photo to McKee.

'Thank you, Mr McKee,' he said.

McKee returned the photo to his pocketbook. He smiled at Parrish, then Radick stepped forward and opened the door for him.

Radick showed McKee out, was gone no more than three or four minutes, and when he returned Parrish was still standing beside the table with a thoughtful expression on his face.

'Doesn't seem like our man,' Radick said.

Parrish slowly shook his head. 'I'm not so sure, Jimmy.'

'But—'

Parrish shook his head. 'Sometimes the obvious occludes the truth. And sometimes things are exactly as they appear.'

FIFTY-FOUR

'Lester Young,' Parrish said. 'That's who I need now. Ex-employees are going to be numerous, and I really didn't want to go down that route, but at least we know him as Jennifer's case officer. Do a search on City and County Probation Service officers, find out where he worked, when he left . . . do whatever has to be done. I need him found. And see if you can't get a license plate on McKee's SUV. I'm going to run some background on McKee's ex-wife and the kids.'

'You want to speak to Valderas, or shall I?'

'I'll do that,' Parrish replied, 'and I'll chase up Erickson at Archives as well.'

Parrish headed out to find Valderas, located him in the canteen.

'I like McKee,' he said matter-of-factly. 'Him, and another character called Lester Young who was indirectly involved with Baumann and whose name was mentioned by both the deputy supervisor there and McKee himself.'

'McKee is your Welfare guy, right?' Valderas asked.

'Yes, up on Adams. There isn't a great deal beyond circumstantial and guesswork to tie them to anything, but of the candidates we're looking at these are the only ones that give me anything.'

'A hunch. That's what you're telling me, right? That you have a hunch.'

'Well, we know it's more than likely a South Two employee. They're either the perp, or they're supplying the perp with info on these girls. Maybe they're working together. McKee has an alibi for the Baumann murder, but if we're looking at him as a supplier, then it doesn't mean a great deal. Whatever, the simple fact is that there's too many similarities in these cases for it to be anyone other than a

South Two connected person. Secondly, the box where Kelly was found had to have been delivered into that alley in the brief window between the truck emptying the dumpsters and the janitor finding her. Box was too big for a compact, so it had to be a pickup or an SUV. McKee has an SUV.'

'Fine. I understand that, but – like you say – this is nothing more than vague circumstantial stuff.'

'Deputy supervisor at his place of work said he had kiddie porn in his locker. I say kiddie porn, but more like teen stuff, you know? He's divorced, two kids, no current relationship. A bit of a loner.'

Valderas smiled.

'What?'

'Sounds like you.'

'I don't do teenage porn.'

'That we know of,' Valderas replied, and then he smiled sardonically. 'So, in truth, you have nothing but a suspicion, and we would put that suspicion in the realm of intuitive feelings and hunches. We have to, don't we?'

'Well, yes, but there's a—'

'What else are you chasing?'

'I have Joel Erickson down at Vice Archives looking for some of these faces. If we can find a single picture, any footage at all that puts these girls in the hands of the sex industry then we're going to be talking to a great deal more people than we've already spoken to.'

'You think that's what we're dealing with?'

'I do yes. I'm pretty much convinced of it. The roofies, the strangulation, the recent sexual activity, the cosmetic stuff – nails, hair, whatever else. I think this is an unavoidable conclusion.'

'Okay, so keep me briefed on what Erickson finds.' Valderas picked up his coffee cup and hesitated. 'And how's Jimmy Radick doing?'

'He's good, yes. He'll be fine. He's just making whatever adjustments he needs to make from Narcotics to Homicide.'

'Good to hear. I liked the guy from day one. I hope he makes it.'

Valderas left. Parrish got himself a cup of coffee, one for Radick also, and headed back to the office.

*

Four-thirty and Radick had a lead on Lester Young. It didn't look good. By five o'clock he had confirmed that Lester Young, he of Family Welfare, subsequently New York County Probation, had died of a heart attack in December 2007. Five days after Christmas he dropped like a stone while shoveling snow in the front yard.

'That definitely takes him out of the frame,' Parrish said, his disappointment evident in his tone. 'Young was dead three days after Karen, and nine months before Rebecca and Kelly.'

'That's something that's been bothering me,' Radick said.

'What?'

'The spacing. We have Melissa around October 2006. We wait three months for Jennifer, seven months for Nicole. Then it's four months to Karen, another nine months until Rebecca gets killed. Then it's only a week before Kelly is murdered. It's very erratic, no consistency.'

'We should have words with the perp when we find him then. Make a complaint.'

Radick smiled wryly.

'Who knows, Jimmy? You can't rationalize irrationality. It's going to be lunar cycles, some crazy shit like that. These people have their own particular strains of complete fucking madness, and there's no predicting them. After you've got them it all makes sense, but before that? Hell, there's very little you can do to determine what they'll do next or when they'll do it.'

'Okay, so what about the ex-wife? You manage to track her down?'

'Yes, I did. We have a meeting with her at six.'

'Official? Unofficial? Did you tell her we want to talk about McKee?'

'No, I didn't tell her what. She said we were lucky to get her, that the kids are with friends for the evening. She's going out but we have her for an hour or so. I said we'd buy her a drink someplace.'

'Better make a start,' Radick said.

Parrish collected his jacket. He thought about how he would approach Carole Paretski. *We need to talk to you about your ex-husband. We think he might be drugging and killing teenage girls. Do you have any thoughts about that?*

Parrish smiled to himself. It would play out however it played out.

Carole Paretski was a good-looking woman. Diminutive, dark-haired, but fiery-eyed. She looked like she carried a loaded temper and could knock you down with it if she wished.

'Just a legal secretary,' she said, when Parrish asked after her position at Gaines, Maynard and Barrett. 'I went back to work when the kids hit their teens. I needed to. I was going stir-crazy.'

They were in a bar on Lafayette Avenue, a block or so from where she worked.

'And how old are your kids?' Parrish asked. He knew their ages, of course, but he wanted to get her relaxed. Talking about kids was always a way in.

'Sarah is fourteen, Alex is a year older. And both of them are going on thirty-five,' she added ruefully.

'Mine are a little older,' Parrish said. 'He's twenty-two, she's twenty.'

'So you're through the worst of it then?'

'It doesn't stop. They're a full-time job however old they get. You don't stop worrying about whether or not they're making the right choices. You want to interfere, but then you just have to take a moment to look at your own life and ask yourself if you really made such good decisions that you can pass them on. Usually the answer is no.'

'You are too cynical, Detective. You make a very valuable contribution to society, and very underestimated. I understand a little of what you guys have to deal with on a day-to-day basis, and I take my hat off to you all.'

'That's appreciated, Ms Paretski, that really is.'

'Carole,' she said, and then – glancing at Radick – she added, 'So what is it that you wanted to talk to me about?'

'To be completely honest, Carole, we wanted to talk to you about your ex-husband, Richard.'

The shift was immediate. Her whole demeanor and body

language changed. It was something neither Parrish nor Radick could have missed.

'What about him?' she asked.

'You are divorced now, correct?'

'Yes, we are divorced. Have been for three years.'

'An amicable divorce, or was it difficult?'

'Amicable? The divorce itself was quiet enough, I'll say that much, but definitely not amicable.'

'You were married for fifteen years.'

'Yes, we were.'

'I'm sorry to have to ask you about this, but Richard said that the divorce became necessary because you were involved with someone else. Was that right?'

Carole Paretski sneered. 'Is that what he said? Christ, he's a gutless bastard isn't he?'

'Gutless? Why d'you say that?'

She inhaled slowly and shook her head. 'You know something? You're married to someone all those years and you think you know them, and then you find out that they've been lying to you the whole time, and that you have chosen to be completely blind.'

Parrish looked at Radick. Radick said nothing.

'I agreed to the divorce on the grounds of *my* adultery because that was the fastest way to end the marriage. He refused to give me a divorce on any other basis, and I was more than happy to agree to that to get the thing over and done with.'

She paused for a moment, and then looked directly at Parrish. 'Why are you here?' she asked. 'Why are you asking me about Richard? What has he done? Has he gotten himself into some sort of trouble again?'

'Again?' Parrish asked.

'That bullshit that went down back in 2002. That shit that he got into . . . You know, right?'

Parrish frowned.

'The things he was supposed to have said to that girl?'

'Girl?' Parrish asked.

Carole Paretski sighed deeply and closed her eyes for a moment. She slowly shook her head and looked towards the window.

'Of course, you wouldn't know,' she said. 'It was never on record, was it?'

Parrish didn't say a word.

'June of 2002. He was accused of making provocative comments to a nine-year-old girl. No charges were pressed. Her name was Marcie Holland. She was in a playground where Richard used to take Alex and Sarah. This girl told her mother that Richard said something to her. He was questioned at the 11th Precinct, the girl was questioned by a female police officer in her home. It was the girl's word against Richard's, and the girl got scared, and then her mother got scared, and nothing happened. There were no charges, no arrest. End of story.'

'You think he did that? You think he said things to this girl?' Parrish asked.

'I don't know, Detective. According to Richard no, he never said a word to the girl. He was a difficult man to live with. He was stuck in that job. He was driven by that job, spent more time and more energy worrying about other peoples' kids than he did his own. I hardly ever saw him, the kids saw him less. That is how he is. He's driven by something, and he does it to the exclusion of all else. And now . . . well, I don't know what's happening here, but he's in trouble for something else—'

'He's not in any trouble, Carole, he's just helping us with some enquiries about a case that is indirectly connected to where he works.'

'Welfare?'

'Right.'

'And if there ever was a job that one man shouldn't have, it *has* to be that one.'

'I'm sorry, I feel like I'm missing something here. I'm listening to one half of a conversation and trying to figure out the rest. Why do you say that?'

'Because of the sex stuff. You know about the sex stuff, right?'

'The sex stuff?' Parrish asked.

'Yeah, the porn he was into. That's what I couldn't deal with. That was what tipped me over the edge finally, why I divorced him. He said he had control over it. He said he could handle it. He said he wasn't thinking about fucking other women . . . other girls. I mean, they weren't kids or anything, but they were teenagers, seventeen, eighteen, God only knows how old, but sure as shit too young to be in fucking porno magazines. And all I could think about was Sarah, but he gave me his word that he had never had thoughts like that about his own daughter. Her friends, yes . . . Jesus, you could see his tongue on the floor when she brought her friends over. It was disgusting. It was fucking degrading.' She shuddered. 'And then that business with the nine-year-old, Marcie, my God! It went away, but it was *so* fucking embarrassing.'

'Did he do anything else that got him in trouble with the law?'

'No, nothing else. And I don't know what to say. Maybe he didn't say anything to that little girl, and maybe it's completely normal for guys of his age to think about sex with cheerleaders, but it's not the kind of person I am, and it's not something that I could condone. He could come across as the most honest and genuine guy you could imagine, and he took his job so seriously, and he brought work home at the weekend, and he appeared to be the most caring and dedicated guy in the world, but he could also be the most convincing liar in the world. Little things, nothing particularly significant, but a couple of times he looked me dead-square in the eye and told me he'd done something he'd promised to do when I knew he hadn't. And after however many years of putting up with him not being there I finally had enough.' She seemed flustered for a moment. 'God almighty, isn't it enough that I have the worry of him with the kids every weekend without having to deal with this? And I don't even know what I'm dealing with here. Why *are* you talking to me?'

Parrish hesitated. He sensed Radick's unease. He could clearly see how agitated Carole Paretski was, and he wondered just what lines he dared safely cross.

'Richard knew someone who was managing a teenage girl's case a couple of years ago,' he told Carole. 'The guy is dead now, but Richard knew him. The girl in question was murdered back in January of last year, and we are working on unresolved and open cases. This just happens to be one of them.'

'But why talk to me?' she asked. 'What am I going to be able to tell you? You think that Richard had something to do with this girl's death?'

'We follow everything,' Parrish said. 'Doesn't matter how thin, doesn't matter how long ago, we follow everything. We have to. You understand that from your work. Sometimes these things look like some kind of wild chase into nowhere, but when you wind up in court, *if* you ever wind up in court with a thing like this, then defense can pull a case apart because there was one person you overlooked, one person you couldn't be bothered to speak to. You know how it goes.'

For a moment Carole Paretski seemed convinced that this was nothing more than a routine follow-up, but then she turned towards Radick and said, 'That still doesn't make sense. That still doesn't tell me why *I* would have any con- nection to a welfare case that was being managed by some- one who my ex-husband knew.'

'In case Richard said anything to you about it at the time. He was working with the guy, one of this guy's charges was murdered, and we wanted to know whether Richard had ever spoken of it at home. It's not every day that you are indirectly connected to an incident like this, and we have found that people generally go home and talk about it.'

'That doesn't make sense, Detective. The girl in question was murdered when? January of last year? I divorced Richard three years ago.'

'Yes, I know that,' Parrish replied, 'but you see him every weekend—'

'So the guy that originally managed the case. When did he die?'

'December last year.'

'And so you're looking at him for the murder?'

'We're looking at every possibility, Ms Paret—'

'Don't bullshit me, Detective,' she interjected. The fiery eyes were alight. 'Don't piss on me and tell me it's raining, okay? You're straight with me, I'll be straight with you. What do you want to know, and why do you want to know it?'

Parrish was silent a moment or two. He looked right at her

and she returned his gaze unflinchingly. She looked ready to put him through the mill and kick whatever was left over down a storm drain.

'There was a rumor at his workplace that he might have been involved in possession of potentially underage pornography—'

'A rumor? Would've been more than a rumor. I said what I said.'

'How bad?'

Carole Paretski frowned and shook her head. 'How bad does it have to be to be considered bad in your eyes? All of it's bad as far as I'm concerned. Disgusting. The amount of money that's involved in that industry could most likely rescue every third world country out of starvation and disease. It's fucking shameful if you ask me.'

'The things you see in the store. The retail magazines, even the stuff they have on display in sex shops . . . I'm not talking about that kind of thing. I'm talking about juveniles, girls under sixteen—'

'I couldn't tell you. Girls of twelve can look sixteen . . . depends on cosmetics, hairstyles, all sorts of things.'

Parrish thought of Rebecca and Kelly – the painted nails, the cut hair.

'How did he react when you told him you wanted a divorce because he neglected the family?'

'He said he'd try harder. He said he'd be a better husband, a better father, but we'd had fights before, and he'd said the same things before.'

'And how long before you divorced him had you been aware of his interest in pornography?'

'Months, a year maybe. I found some of it in the attic, but I guess that's what really did it. You get the feeling that even if you repaired it, even if you tried to make it work, then you're going to be working on your own. The porno thing? At first he said he couldn't help the porno thing, and then he said he had it under control. He tried to make me think that people who were into that kind of thing had some kind of mental difficulty, and it wasn't something that they could just stop and start as and when they liked.'

'Did you believe him?'

'Good God no, of course not.'

Parrish leaned forward, rested his elbows on his knees, pressed the palms of his hands together and hesitated before he spoke again.

'Ms Paretski – Carole,' he said quietly. 'For no other reason than you're the one person who probably knows Richard better than anyone, I have to ask you: do you think – do *you* think he possesses the capability of harming another human being?'

'You're looking at him for this girl's murder, aren't you?' she said matter-of-factly. 'All this runaround shit is besides the point, isn't it? You think he's killed some teenage girl don't you?'

'We think – we know – someone has killed a teenage girl,' Parrish replied, 'and we believe that it might be someone connected directly or indirectly to Family Welfare. Like I said, and this is no bullshit, we're talking to everyone, we're following every line, we're tracking dirt across everyone's carpet, you know? This isn't something we can fuck about with, Carole. This isn't something that you can talk to your kids about, or call Richard on, and you can never, never bring it up when he comes over to get Sarah and Alex—'

'Well, I'll tell you something right now, he is *not* coming over to get Sarah and Alex, not this weekend, not any fucking weekend—'

'That's the point right there, Carole,' Parrish said. 'That's what we *cannot* do. You can't assume that he has anything to do with this, and we can't afford to have you give anything away. You cannot let him know that we spoke to you, and you cannot give him the impression that you are aware of us speaking to him at his workplace. If he brings it up, then just treat it as irrelevant. Show whatever level of interest you would ordinarily show, and no more. I really need you to work with me on this point, okay? We might be right off-track on this, you know? We might be looking in completely the wrong direction. Like I said before, we're going with everything we can, but we're treading careful because this is a big case and – potentially – something that could go very very wrong if we make a mess of it. You say the wrong thing then, if he *is* guilty of something, well then that would seriously hamper any chances we might have of bringing him in.'

Carole Paretski sighed audibly. She leaned back in the chair and closed her eyes for a moment. 'You're telling me that my ex-husband might be a child-killer but, regardless, you want me to let him come over on Saturday and take the kids off me for two days.'

'It's this coming weekend that he has them for both days, right?'

'Yes, it is.'

'Well, yes, that's what I want you to do, and I want you to do it just like always. We find anything else then he might be a guest of ours this weekend and you won't have anything to worry about.'

'Okay . . . okay . . .'

'So back to the question. Do you think that your husband possesses the capability and potential to harm or hurt another human being?'

Again she closed her eyes for a second, and when she opened them they were flint-hard. 'Hurt another human being?' she echoed. 'I'll tell you something, Detective Parrish, most murderers are fucking cowards. They're liars and they're cowards. Well, Richard McKee is a liar and a coward, and I think if it came down to it, if it meant the difference between self-preservation or not, then yes, I believe he could hurt another human being.'

Parrish was silent for a moment, and then he leaned back in his chair and nodded his head. He wondered whether he was hearing something of substance, or simply the bitter resentment of a betrayed ex-wife. Wouldn't Clare say precisely the same thing about him? Obsessive, married to the job, capable of lying, of hurting people, neglectful? Of course she would, and she would say worse.

'I thought that's what you might say,' he replied. 'I really didn't want to hear you say it, but that's what I believed you were going to say.'

'So what now?' she said. 'You want to look at his porn collection?'

'You what?'

'I have them. The magazines and DVDs. Boxes of the shit

in the garage. I told him I was going to get it destroyed, but I didn't. I don't really know why . . . I just didn't know what the fuck to do with it.'

'We absolutely do want to see it,' Parrish said.

Carole Paretski got up. 'So you can save me a trip to the waste dump. You can come get it from the house right now.'

They left together. Radick called Crime Scene and told them to meet them at the Paretski address. They needed photos of the boxes *in situ* before they took them away.

FIFTY-FIVE

Parrish was disappointed. The boxes of pornography turned out to be two, not twelve or fifteen or twenty. The magazines were magazines, the DVDs were DVDs. It was the kind of thing that Joel Erickson would call 'lightweight'. It was not difficult to see that many of them were well in excess of eighteen years of age, and yet dressed and photographed in such a way as to make them appear younger. It was impossible to know – as with all such photographs – how many were there consensually or there against their will; how many were drugged or drunk or stoned or threatened; how many were being blackmailed or prostituted, or how many had been convinced that if they didn't do what they were told and make like they were enjoying it, then something dreadful would happen to them, their loved ones, their friends . . .

It was impossible to know anything except that Richard McKee was a man who possessed a predilection for young-looking girls. This was not the dark world that Parrish had hoped he would uncover.

Parrish and Radick stood in the corner of Carole Paretski's garage on Steuben Street. Crime Scene had been and gone, pictures had been taken. They had been given clearance to examine the contents of the boxes, and they did so while Carole Paretski hovered by the connecting door to ensure that Sarah and Alex didn't wander through on their way out of the house.

'I told the kids you were bug people. Said that we might have a roach infestation and you were going to check it out. I told them to stay in the house until after you'd gone.'

'Where did he hide these when you were together?' Parrish asked her.

'In the crawl space up here,' she replied, and indicated the passageway that ran from the garage to the roof of the kitchen. 'You can access it through a trap over in the corner.'

Parrish noted the trap, wondered if there was anything else up there that would be of interest. He remembered the permit, the citation from the City for Ordinance Violation.

'I went up there,' Carole Paretski said, anticipating his next question. 'I had a real good look, and there isn't anything else.'

'Are there any other places in the house where he could have hidden things?'

'I'm sure there are. You want to have a look?'

'Most definitely,' Parrish said, 'but I'd have to get a warrant and I'd have to arrange to get it done while the kids were away. I also wouldn't want to leave any indications that we'd been here.'

'If I give you permission you don't need a warrant, right?'

'That's right, yes.'

'So you have my permission, and the kids are away all day tomorrow. You have some people that can do this, then let's get it done.'

'Thank you, Carole. That's much appreciated,' Parrish said.

She didn't say a word in response. She hesitated for a moment, almost as if she wanted to look once more through that dark and narrow window into her husband's soul, and then she turned and closed the garage door behind her.

Parrish and Radick went through the magazines and DVDs. *Barely Legal. Just Eighteen. Teen Dreams.* All the material possessed that same consistent thread, yet none of it was any worse than the usual fare one found on the shelves of drugstores and supermarkets all across the country. Perhaps that was the saddest thing of all – the fact that such material was now nothing more than routine. Girls subjected to the degrading parodies of sex that were so prevalent in such publications. Anal, oral, double penetration, undertones of bondage and S&M; some of them dressed as schoolgirls, as cheerleaders, some of them displaying that flash of fear or anxiety that they would have been forced to hide with wide eyes and false smiles. *No, no, no . . . look like you're enjoying yourself!*

'This is not what I wanted to find,' Radick commented.

'Same here,' Parrish replied. 'The more I see, the more I think we might be dealing with an external connection, someone outside of Welfare. Whoever got Rebecca killed Danny, remember? I don't get that McKee is capable of shooting someone in the head with a .22, but if there's someone in the porn business he's working with then there'll be no shortage of people capable of that.'

'You figure a lot of these girls wind up dead?'

'Dead, or addicts, maybe in the porn business for real, or working as hookers. They all wind up the same way eventually. Very rare to find anyone who makes it out, and if they do they're badly broken.'

'So we go through the rest of the house tomorrow, and then what?'

'We have to find something more than this tomorrow or we have to drop him.' Parrish held up one of the magazines. 'This shit I can buy at the drugstore.' He threw the magazine back into the box. 'This gets us nothing aside from the fact that he likes to read porn. We could never prove that he knowingly purchased magazines featuring underage girls. The fact that he works at Family Welfare is circumstantial; so is the fact that he drives an SUV. In all honesty, we still have nothing.'

'But do you think he's the guy? Do you think there's even the slightest possibility that he might be the guy?'

Parrish closed his eyes for a moment. He then turned and looked upwards, up to the trapdoor, the crawl space within which Richard McKee had hidden his boxes of porn, and he said, 'I can't get away from the fact that it has to be someone at South Two, and right now I have no-one else who even comes close. We've lost Lester Young. Now I want McKee to be the guy. That's all I can say. I really want him to be the fucking guy.'

'And for tonight?' Radick asked.

'I'll get Ms Paretski to sign something that turns this over to us. I'll put it in evidence lock-up. You go home, I'll wrap up here. I'll get Valderas to give us three or four guys, out of uniform, for the morning and we come back and go through this place in detail. I want to see if there's anything beyond circumstantial that connects him.'

'I'll come back to the Precinct with you,' Radick said. 'I have nowhere important to go tonight.'

Carole Paretski seemed relieved at the disappearance of the boxes in the garage.

'What time do the kids leave for school?' Parrish asked her.

'Eight-thirty. Leave it until nine if you can.'

'And you don't have to go to work?'

'I won't go tomorrow,' she said. 'I'll call in. They won't have a problem.'

'I wish everyone we dealt with was as co-operative as you,' Radick said.

She shook her head. She hesitated as the sound of one of the kids running across the upper landing interrupted her. Whichever one it was, they didn't come down the stairs.

'It's like the end of something,' she said. 'I've struggled with this for a long time. I don't know what to think about it now. I try to make sense of it. He worked, he paid for the things that he needed to pay for, but there was always that distance. I thought it was me. You always think it's you, right?'

Parrish started to agree but Carole Paretski wasn't waiting for an answer to her question.

'It's almost like I'm trying to do everything to get rid of that part of my life.'

'And the kids?' Parrish asked.

She shrugged. 'I don't know what to think about them. They don't ask me about him. They never talk about the divorce. They go with him when he comes to take them. They do whatever they do – Chinese meals, movies, going to the mall, and they come back with stuff that he's bought them. Father's day they send cards. They ask me for money to buy him stuff for his birthday and for Christmas. They see what they want to see and they don't look for anything else.'

'And if something comes of this? If we learn that he might have been indirectly involved in something that—'

Carole Paretski raised her hand to silence Parrish. 'We jump off those bridges when we get there,' she said. 'Before that I don't want to know, and I'm not going to ask, okay?'

'Okay,' Parrish replied. 'We'll get out of here now. We'll be back in the morning. Jimmy here will come with some uniforms at nine, and I'll be here a little later.'

Parrish and Radick made their way back to the Precinct in silence. They delivered the boxes to Evidence, where they were bagged and tagged. They divided the paperwork between them, and then Parrish went looking for Valderas.

Valderas didn't have a problem giving them three uniforms, but he wanted something in writing from Carole Paretski, witnessed by at least two of the attending officers, stating that she had given permission for the house to be searched.

Parrish said he would type it up before he left.

Radick took off just before ten. It had been a long day, and already they were a considerable number of hours off-shift. Times like this it didn't matter. Times like this it ceased to be a job, ceased to be anything but something that needed to be done.

Parrish sat at his desk alone. He remembered one of the last things that Carole Paretski had said. *It's almost like I'm trying to do everything to get rid of that part of my life.* Was she co-operating with them because it was a way of getting back at her ex-husband? Was there nothing here at all? A guy who worked too hard, who neglected his family, a guy who liked to read porn, a guy who may or may not have said something to a little girl in a fucking playground however many years before, who happened to own an SUV. A guy who was in the frame for something that had nothing at all to do with him. And was he there simply because there was no-one else? Was he getting too stuck on McKee because that's what happened in this line of work, where desperation for a result could become an obsession?

Parrish thought about how it would be to change things. People *did* change their lives – sometimes the decision as rapid and definitive as a lightning strike. He had seen it happen. They cut out for some distant state – Wisconsin or Nebraska or somewhere – nothing for miles but storm clouds and the promise of more distance. A house built of rough timber on a foundation of disused sleepers and cinder blocks, the only sound that of the wind, or of the infrequent passage of semis on the interstate. Nothing louder than someone breathing in the next room.

Parrish believed that if he did such a thing he would never forget New York. He had seen veterans – ten years retired, the rush and punch of the hunt nothing more than a vague memory, part of some other life now disowned and un-remembered. Parrish *could* do such a thing. He *could* make such a decision. But he knew he would not. He was one of those who would walk away from the building and feel homesick after five blocks.

There was a point where you realized you had done all the changing you were going to do. The person you had become was the person you would always and forever be. In the vast majority of cases such a realization was a disappointment, an anticlimax. In Parrish's case it was a fact and a reality, and he didn't need to avoid it.

For a brief moment he thought to call Eve. He decided against it. He wanted to be alone.

He got up and looked down at the files on his desk. *This is what I do*, he thought. *This is what I will always do. This is my heroin.*

FIFTY-SIX

'We're searching his ex-wife's place now.'

'That's where you took the porn from last night?'

'Yeah, that's right.'

'And she's co-operating with you on this?'

'Couldn't be more co-operative.'

'Does that concern you?'

'What? That she might be helping us to get back at him?'

'They're estranged, aren't they? You said that things hadn't been amicable.'

'When the hell is a divorce ever amicable? Seems an oxymoron to me. An *amicable* divorce. If they're so fucking amicable why don't they stay together?'

'That sounds a little bitter, Frank?'

'Whatever. Fact of the matter is that Jimmy Radick is over there right now with some uniforms and they're going to see if there's anything even vaguely incriminating.'

'Such as?'

'Well, *if* he's the perp, *if* he actually did the girls, then it's not uncommon for such people to keep mementos. Maybe he left something there and hasn't been able to go back and get it. If he's just passing information on to someone outside Family Welfare, then there may be an address book, an old cell phone, something that ties him into this.'

'But the earliest case you have is – when did you say?'

'Earliest one we have on record is October 2006. Melissa. The runaway.'

'But he split with his wife before that, three years ago.'

'Sure he did, but who's to say that Melissa was the first? And he has been back there many times since.'

'Just to collect the kids for the weekend, right?'

'Sure, but who the hell knows what he might have left there. I know it's the longest of long shots but it's not something I can overlook.'

'You think he's your guy.'

'I *hope* he's our guy.'

'But do you think he is?'

'Honestly? I have nothing. Not of any substance. I am interested in McKee solely because I feel certain it's someone from Family Welfare, directly or indirectly. It has to be someone from inside the unit itself. And, truth is, I now have no-one else that even raises an eyebrow from me. '

'And there's no doubt it's someone inside Family Welfare?'

'No, no doubt as far as I'm concerned. There's too much circumstantial evidence to indicate it's any other way.'

'So where do you go with it now?'

'We have to find something sufficiently probative to get a warrant for his current place of residence, his car, access to his finance records, whatever we can get to. I'd like a DNA sample, his prints, some of his hair, you know? I want anything I can get on him that can be used to cross-reference against the samples we have from the girls.'

'Does it frustrate you?'

'Of course it frustrates me.'

'Do you ever feel like stepping over the lines to get what you need?'

'Sure I do. Who doesn't? But you don't, do you? You start down that road and you wind up like my father.'

'You believe that's what happened? That he started out doing things for the good, and it all went bad?'

'With my father? No, I shouldn't think so. I figure that he started out bad and it just got worse.'

'Do you feel any need to tell the world what he was really like?'

'I haven't really thought about it since we last spoke of him, so no, maybe not. Maybe I can just let him rot in hell.'

'Do you consider that's progress? Do you consider that you're carrying a little less baggage now?'

'Hell, you know me. I put down one suitcase full of shit I'm just gonna go pick another one up.'

'You know yourself better than you let on, Frank. I think

you like to project that persona – the troublemaker, the loner, the outsider, the difficult one that no-one can get rid of because he's too good at his job.'

'I wouldn't say that. I wouldn't say that I was too good at my job.'

'And that's the other part of it right there – this false humility. You know how good you are, you just believe that talking about it diminishes the effect it has on others.'

'I don't know what the hell you're trying to say here.'

'I'm saying that you want the world to believe that you're this lonely –

'Sure I'm lonely. Who isn't these days? I have enough loneliness to open a store.'

'Of course you do.'

'What? You're laughing at me now?'

'I'm not laughing *at* you, Frank, I'm laughing *with* you.'

'That's just such a full-of-shit thing to say. I'm laughing *with* you. I'm not laughing. Did you happen to notice that?'

'I'm sorry, Frank. I just hear you say one thing and I know you're really saying another.'

'Well, I suppose that's where a psychology major comes in handy, 'cause it feels to me that what I say and what I mean are precisely the same thing.'

'Okay, agreed. What you say is what you mean.'

'Now you just sound patronizing.'

'I'm sorry. I apologize. I certainly don't mean to sound that way.'

'So what now? We're done for today?'

'You think we're done?'

'Christ, what is it with this can't-answer-a-question-without-asking-another-question bullshit? Far as I'm concerned, we were done the first day I came here.'

'I've upset you, Frank, and I'm sorry. I've said I'm sorry. I know you're on edge—'

'I'm on edge because I've got Jimmy Radick over at this woman's house and I'm not there. I think he'll be fine, but I'd feel a hell of a lot better if I was there, too.'

'I don't want to hold you up from your work, Frank, but it seems to me that what we're doing is a way to make you work better. And you have to learn to delegate. You're not going to always be there. At some point you're going to have to stop doing this, and there have to be some people left behind that can do this job as well as you. If Jimmy Radick can't organize searching someone's house then he has no place as a homicide detective, right?'

'Right, yeah. Sure.'

'So sit back for a minute. Just relax, okay? A few more minutes of your time isn't going to affect what happens out there one way or the other.'

'Okay, okay. So what do you want to ask me now?'

'I want to know what you'll do if there's nothing at the house?'

'What I'll do? I've got a trace going on with someone at Archives for any footage or pictures of these girls in their files. I'm going to have to find a way to get into McKee's SUV. I need to look at his finance records, see if he's received any unusual amounts of money—'

'In case he's being paid for information about these girls from their files?'

'Right. And I need to look at his work attendance records. I need to know if he was at work when these girls were supposedly abducted, or if there were days he was absent from work after they went missing . . . this kind of thing. I just need to start building up a much better picture of the kind of person I'm dealing with.'

'And if he's not your man? If you're spending all this time looking in the wrong direction?'

'Hell, that's police work. That's what being a detective is all about. You keep on looking and looking until there's nothing left to see, and then you look somewhere else. Right now he's the only contender I've got, and until I prove that he's *not* the one, then he continues to be my main source of interest.'

'And do you have a gut feeling?'

'Yes.'

'And what would that be?'

'He's involved. I *feel* that much. I don't know if he's the killer, but I feel he is involved. Hell, he could be involved in something else that makes him look guilty, but there's a feeling about this that I can't shake off.'

'And you trust that feeling?'

'I *have* to. Few times it's been the only thing that's got me through a case.'

'Okay, Frank, we'll leave it for today. I want you to think about how you're approaching this. I want you to avoid obsessing on it, take a few minutes every once in a while to remember that there are other things going on in your life that are just as important as Richard McKee—'

'Such as?'

'Well, if you have to ask me that then I see that we still have a great deal more work to do.'

'Good enough. If that's the way it is then that's the way it is. For me, at this moment, there isn't anything else as important as Richard McKee. The only thing that could come close is Caitlin, and I don't think that she'd even give me the time of day right now. That's something I'll deal with when this thing is finished.'

'And if it doesn't finish?'

'Oh, I think it'll finish, Doctor Griffin. One way or the other it's going to finish.'

FIFTY-SEVEN

It was eleven by the time Parrish arrived at Carole Paretski's home. Across Broadway and east two blocks and he would be outside the home of Karen Pulaski.

Radick was in one of the bedrooms with a uniform. When Parrish reached the top of the stairs he heard Carole Paretski's voice somewhere in the background. It sounded like she was talking on a cell phone.

Radick nodded at Parrish, looked up at the corner of the room and pointed.

Parrish followed his line of sight and saw nothing but a small hole that sat immediately in the corner. It was no bigger than a cent.

'This is the daughter's room,' he said. 'And that hole is man-made. I stuck a pen in it and it goes right through.'

'You're thinking what I'm thinking?' Parrish asked.

'Could well be.'

Radick was out on the landing as Carole came off the phone. 'We need to get up there,' he said, and indicated the attic.

Carole backed up and showed Radick the trap in the ceiling outside the bathroom door. 'It's only half-boarded,' she said. 'He started it, never finished it. There was some bullshit about the permit. Be careful or you'll come through.'

'Did Richard go up there a lot?' Parrish asked her.

'Often enough. He kept a lot of paperwork up there, things from work that he needed to refer to.'

'And why keep them in the attic?'

'Security, he said. Didn't want them lying around the house.'

Radick looked at Parrish. Parrish shook his head almost imperceptibly. *Say nothing*, the gesture said. *Not yet*.

In the crawl space they found it just as Carole had said.

Half-boarded, dusty, cramped. Parrish made his way to the corner where the hole had been pushed through. He lay down, unconcerned about the state of his clothes, and managed to get his eye close enough to the hole to see through it. Right down into the girl's bedroom, no question. Radick had a torch. He scanned along the rafters, found small staple-holes every once in a while.

'A cable feed,' he said. 'You reckon he had a camera up here?'

Parrish was up on his haunches, keeping his head low so as not to hit the roof-beams. 'Christ only knows,' he said matter-of-factly. 'But I'm starting to think that maybe we have a live one here. You like him for filming his own daughter, maybe her friends as well. Daughter has girlfriends around for a sleepover. Dad's up here with a fucking video camera?'

Radick said nothing. He backed up and started down the ladder. Parrish followed him, took a moment to brush himself down. He looked like he'd been dragged backwards through a tornado.

'Something?' Carole asked.

'Nothing to get excited about,' Parrish said, though he *was* excited. He could feel it in his lower gut, in the way his fists involuntarily clenched and unclenched, the way his pulse was moving a little faster, the way the sweat had broken out across his scalp. He *itched* with anticipation. He believed he had McKee – if not for the deaths of the girls, but for involvement, some sort of involvement for sure.

'They won't be much longer,' Parrish told her. 'The uniforms. Jimmy's going to stay here until they're done, and make sure they leave everything as we found it.'

Parrish started towards the stairs. Radick hung back, but Carole followed Parrish down to the kitchen. She cornered him by the back door.

'You think he's . . .'

Parrish smiled wryly, and shook his head. 'I think nothing, Mrs Paretski, I think nothing. In this game I either know or I don't.'

'But you have your suspicions. You have to have suspicions otherwise there'd never be anything to follow up.' She looked anxious; if not concerned for her own welfare, then for the welfare of her kids. Even the suspicion, even the rumor that their father was involved in something like this could have potentially devastating consequences for their well-being and safety. This was the kind of thing that im-pelled families to move state and change their name.

Parrish hesitated for a moment, and then he said, 'Can we sit down for a moment?'

Carole Paretski backed up to the kitchen table and sat down. Parrish followed suit. He took a deep breath and then exhaled slowly. 'Sometimes,' he said, 'there are certain things you can say, and once you've said them there's no going back. I could say a lot of things right now, and frankly none of them would serve any purpose.' He smiled, looked away for a moment. 'My wife used to accuse me of not listening. But I was. That's what I do. I look, and I listen. I pay attention to everything that's going on around me, and sometimes it takes a good while before I see or hear anything that con-nects with something else.' Parrish paused; there were tears in Carole Paretski's eyes. 'I don't know if he's done anything, Carole. I really don't. All I know is that I have a number of dead girls, and the circumstances and nature of their deaths suggests very strongly that they are linked. Aside from that there is only one other connection, and that takes us to Family Welfare. Now, it may be that Richard has nothing to do with this at all – I have no evidence right now that he does – but I'm looking at the people there, and I'm listening to what they're saying, and I'm trying to find one thing that connects to another thing. From there maybe I'll find one piece of this puzzle, and that will give me an idea of the picture I might end up with. You understand me?'

'You want me to say nothing, right? You want me to carry on like nothing has happened? You want me to let him come over here and take the kids away . . .'

'I can only assume that this arrangement was sanctioned by the courts in your divorce?'

'Yes, it was.'

'Then you have no choice, and if you have no choice then . . .'

'But, what if . . .'

295

'*What if* means nothing, Carole. I can't tell you anything because there is nothing to tell you. *If* Richard is involved in this thing, directly or indirectly – and right now it's only an *if* – then all I can tell you is that I will do everything in my power to make sure that he does not harm you, and he does not harm the children. But any indication you give him that we've been here – and I have to stress this with the utmost importance . . . any clue he gets that we have been here will only make my job a lot harder. All I can tell you is that I will work as hard as I can and as fast as I can, and if I find anything that makes me believe you or your children are in danger, then I will act decisively to prevent that from happening. Beyond that, I will also let you know when we have confirmed that he is not involved so your mind can be at rest on the subject, okay?'

Carole Paretski didn't speak for a while, and when she looked up at Parrish there was something in her expression that he saw all too rarely.

'How do you do this?' she asked. 'You have kids. Okay, they're older now. They're more independent than mine, but you are a father. You must feel what everyone else feels. You must see what other people are going through.'

'There's an old saying. It's about working in Homicide. It goes along the lines of "When your day ends, my day starts."'

'That's terrible. I can't even begin to understand what this job must do to you.'

Parrish smiled. 'I can't understand it either, and these days I try not to.' He started to get up.

Carole Paretski reached out and took his hand. 'Seriously,' she said, her voice urgent, emotional. 'Seriously . . . if you find out that he's been involved in anything like this, I need you to tell me right away. That thing that happened . . . when that girl accused him of saying those things to her . . . I think he did that. I *believe* he did that. He got away with it because it was her word against his, but I knew . . . I looked in his face and I knew.' She let go of Parrish's hand to wipe a tear from her cheek. 'I don't know why I didn't leave him then . . . hell, yes I do. I didn't leave him because of the kids. They were eight and nine years old. I was still looking after them, hadn't gone back to work, and there was no way I could have supported them alone . . .' Her voice trailed away, as did her gaze. She looked through the window to the street. Parrish said nothing to interrupt her thoughts.

When she turned back she appeared to have gathered herself together somewhat.

'You need to go,' she said. 'Thank you for your time, and for understanding.'

'Trying to understand,' Parrish replied.

'No,' she said, 'I know you understand, Detective Parrish. If you didn't you wouldn't be here.'

FIFTY-EIGHT

Back at the precinct Parrish debriefed Valderas on where they were at.

'I can't disagree with your suspicions, Frank, but essentially you have nothing.'

'I'm aware of that. I just plan to keep on looking until I have something definite.'

'Just get him back in here for more talking,' Valderas suggested. 'Get under his skin. When you ask the public to co-operate they're kind of obligated, aren't they? Otherwise they just end up looking guilty.'

'I've thought of that . . .'

'So do it. Don't push him too hard, but just enough so if there's something to give way it will. They always cave under pressure. It's just a matter of the pressure being so subtle they don't feel it until it's too late.'

Parrish called Radick, told him to wind things up at the Paretski place and get back to the precinct. He then called Foley, got Lavelle, asked for them to let McKee go early once more. Lavelle didn't question Parrish's request, merely said that McKee could leave at lunchtime. Once Radick returned Parrish sent him over to pick McKee up, and when he arrived it was evident that McKee was on edge.

'I don't know what you want from me,' were his first words when Parrish showed him through to an interview room. 'I've told you everything I know, everything I can remember about these cases, and I just don't see what else I can tell you.'

Parrish said nothing for a few seconds. He took off his jacket and sat down. He asked if there was anything he could get for McKee.

'I just want to go back to work, or go home,' McKee replied. 'What I do *not* want to do is sit here talking to you.'

Parrish smiled. He nodded at Radick and Radick sat down on a chair near the door. He was behind McKee, a position designed solely to unnerve and unsettle the interviewee. McKee glanced over his shoulder at Radick. Radick smiled. McKee turned back to Parrish.

'Tell me what happened in June of 2002, Richard.'

'What? What the hell are you talking about?'

'The little girl, Richard . . . the one in the playground.'

'Oh for God's sake, you can't be serious. That was six years ago, and besides, nothing came of it. It was bullshit, and I don't know it was ever considered anything more than some ridiculous and unfounded fantasy by a naive little girl . . .'

'Tell me what happened.'

'What the hell for? If you know about it then it's on file, and it shouldn't be. I was never arrested, and there was no formal complaint, and I was not charged. It's irrelevant.'

'Humor me, Richard.'

McKee looked back at Radick. Radick was cold, expressionless.

'I used to take the kids to the park. I used to take them every couple of days. I met a woman there, just someone who used to take her daughter. This woman's daughter and Sarah used to play together. This girl, nine, ten years old perhaps, told her mother that I said something sexually provocative to her.'

'What did you say?'

'I didn't say anything, that was the whole point of it. I didn't say a goddamned thing.'

'Okay then, what did the girl *say* you said to her?'

'I don't like the intonation in your voice, Detective, I really don't.'

'What intonation would that be?'

'You know very well what I'm talking about. Your tone implies that what the girl said might have been true.'

'I apologize, Richard. I didn't mean for it to sound like that. I wanted to know what this girl told her mother, that was all.'

'It's disgusting. It repulses me to have to repeat it—'

'Please, sir, if you don't mind.'

'She said . . . she told her mother that . . . Jesus, do I really have to say this? I don't get why I'm here. I really am not very comfortable at all with this, Detective. I cannot see what possible motivation you might have for bringing me here. I am supposed to be at work. You're not charging me with anything, right? Right?'

'No, Richard, we're not charging you with anything. Is there something that you feel we should be charging you with?'

McKee laughed condescendingly. 'You're unreal. What the fuck did you say that for?' He shook his head. 'Enough already. You want me to answer any more questions then I want a lawyer here.'

'This is the last thing we're asking of you, Richard. Just tell me what the little girl accused you of saying.'

'I can't bring myself to say it . . .'

'I read the reports, Richard,' Parrish interjected, all-too-aware that he himself was now lying. 'I read the complainant's statement.'

'So you know what I'm supposed to have said. Why are you asking me to repeat it?'

'Because if it's so untruthful, if you really didn't say those things, then I believe you could talk about it quite rationally, quite calmly, and though I appreciate that it might be dis-tasteful to you, I still believe that we could discuss this quite amicably—'

McKee looked away for a moment. He sighed audibly and then he looked back at Parrish. 'Apparently – and this is only the little girl's imagination – I am supposed to have told her . . . I am supposed to have told her that I wanted her to sit on my face.'

'That was all?'

'That I told her I wanted her to sit on my face so I could put my tongue inside her.'

'And you didn't say this to her?'

'God almighty no! Jesus, what kind of sick bastard do you think I am?'

'I don't know, Richard, I really don't know.'

'There! You did it again! You're taking something I say and

turning it round to make me look like some sick pedophile. Jesus, this is unbelievable! This is verging on harassment now. I really don't know what kind of authority you think you have to do this, but I want a lawyer here right fucking now.'

'No authority, sir, just a simple request for assistance from a member of the public—'

'Bullshit! That's just so much bullshit!'

Radick got up suddenly as someone outside knocked on the door. He opened it, shared a few unintelligible words, and then turned back to Parrish. He nodded. Parrish got up, excused himself, and left the room.

Valderas was in the corridor. 'Got a call from Joel Erickson at Vice Archives. He thinks he might have found one of your girls.'

Parrish's heart skipped a beat. 'Okay, okay,' he said, and then was caught in a moment of indecision. 'Can you call him back for me? Tell him to hold on, I'll be there as soon as I can. I need to finish this.'

Valderas said he would call Erickson. Parrish returned to the room, and at once noticed the change in aspect in McKee. As with all interviewees and interrogation suspects, the moment that any words occurred outside of their earshot they believed those words related to them. You came back in, they wanted to ask what was going on, what was it about, but they couldn't. To show any concern for what might be going on outside was to demonstrate a reason to be concerned.

'So, Richard, you refuted the allegation made by this girl?'

'Of course I did. It wasn't a matter of refuting it. I didn't have anything to prove. It was her word against mine.'

'And she was how old?'

'I don't know – nine, maybe ten years old.'

'Same age as your daughter at the time.'

'Meaning?'

'Meaning that the girl who accused you of saying these things was about the same age as Sarah was at the time.'

McKee took a deep breath and exhaled. 'Yes, about the same age.'

Parrish leaned forward. 'Tell me something, Richard . . .

have you ever had any kind of impulse or urge towards younger girls?'

McKee laughed awkwardly, smiled, shook his head too quickly. 'Christ no, what do you take me for?'

'Cheerleaders, sophomores, college girls . . .'

'Enough,' he said emphatically. 'Enough, enough, enough—'

'Is it true that when the Family Welfare offices moved there were a number of pornographic magazines found in the locker that you used?'

'No, of course not,' McKee interjected – once again a little too quickly.

'And that those magazines featured images of girls that couldn't have been more than sixteen or seventeen years old?'

'No. Not at all. Who told you that? The only person I ever knew who had magazines like that was Lester.'

'Lester Young?'

'Yes, Lester Young.'

'You know that he's dead?'

'Dead?'

'Yes, he died of a heart attack in December last year.'

'No . . . no, I didn't know that.'

'Well, being dead he cannot deny any allegations.'

'Implying, once again, that I might be lying.'

'Implying no such thing, Richard.'

McKee shook his head. 'You don't have the right to do this, Detective Parrish. I'm going to make some kind of formal complaint against you. You bring me in here on some sort of pretext that I might be able to help you with this investigation, and you actually bully and harass me—'

'You are free to go, Mr McKee,' Parrish said matter-of-factly. He stood up, took his jacket from the back of the chair and started to put it on.

'What?'

'You are free to go. We appreciate your time, we really do. You have been most co-operative, and we are sorry for any inconvenience we might have caused you. If you do honestly feel that you have a mindful cause for complaint, then please ensure that you make a statement to the sergeant at the front desk and he will find someone for you to talk to.'

McKee was speechless. He stared wide-eyed at Parrish, then looked at Radick.

'Jimmy . . . can you make sure Mr McKee is safely escorted back to the lobby.' Parrish paused for a moment, and then he extended his hand.

McKee took it involuntarily.

'Thank you again for your time. You have been most helpful.'

Parrish left the room. He made his way upstairs to his office and waited for Radick.

Minutes later Radick appeared; he was smiling, shaking his head. 'Jesus, the guy was a fucking mess. He didn't know what the fuck was going on.'

'Good,' Parrish replied. 'The more unsettled he is the better.'

'You really are starting to think it's him, aren't you?'

'I was unsure,' Parrish replied. 'I was unsure until I asked him to repeat what he was supposed to have said to that little girl.'

'He was embarrassed, Frank—'

'He wasn't embarrassed, Jimmy, he was turned on.'

FIFTY-NINE

Erickson looked serious. He sat behind his desk with an expression that Parrish had seen all too many times before. Something had punctured the veneer and reached him. The more years in Vice, the more years in Homicide or Narco, the tougher the veneer became, but every once in a while there was something of sufficient force to get through. Evidently, whatever he had found had possessed that force.

'Sit down,' he told Parrish and Radick. 'I found your Jennifer. A picture we've managed to isolate as originating in January or February of last year.'

'Jennifer was dead by mid-January 2007,' Parrish said.

'So January it is . . . and it might have been the day she died.'

Radick's eyes widened.

Erickson leaned forward to his desk and picked up a thin manila folder.

'How much of this kind of stuff have you dealt with?' he asked Parrish.

'Did three years in Vice, '96 to '99.'

'And you?' he asked Radick.

'Narco, Robbery-Homicide, and now this.'

'But you've seen some shit, right?'

Radick nodded. 'I've seen some shit.'

Erickson opened the folder. He removed a single picture and slid it across the desk to Parrish.

It was Jennifer, no question. She was gagged with a black scarf, but her hair was back from her face and she was twisted around, looking back over her shoulder at the camera. Her eyes were wide with – what? Fear, horror, pain? As was routinely the case with many such pictures the faces of the male participants were out of view. Jennifer had her hands tied behind her back, and from the look of her fingers and wrists it appeared she had been tied roughly and with far greater tension than was necessary. Her hands were significantly paler than her forearms. On her upper left thigh was a series of dark bruises, one of them carrying a thin line of blood at the edge. Her face appeared to be bruised also, and to Parrish it looked like the right cheek beneath the eye was swollen.

'Is this what we're dealing with?' Radick asked. 'Girls kidnapped for torture, for rape, for pornography?'

Erickson nodded. 'If money-lending is the first profession and prostitution the second, then pornography is the third. Ask Parrish. He did three years in Vice. He'll tell you.' He indicated the photograph in Parrish's hand. 'This is toy town stuff compared to most of what we see.'

'I think the roofies came later,' Parrish said, almost to himself.

'You what?'

'Rohypnol. We found traces of rohypnol on the more recent cases. This one . . . hell, this one looks like she was beaten into it. I think whoever's doing this got smarter, started drugging them.' He turned to Radick. 'You see her fingernails?'

'Red,' Radick replied. 'Just like the Lange girl.'

'You want me to keep looking for more pictures?' Erickson asked.

'For sure, yes,' Parrish replied, and then, 'Can you tell where it came from?'

Erickson shook his head. 'Almost impossible. A magazine definitely, but they all use the same processing facilities, the same kind of paper, the same printers. And then there's the strong possibility that it was a movie still that was then printed for a magazine. Two for the price of one, you see? The digital evolution has done us no favors. Now you don't even get negatives or film stock numbers. Now it really is the case that anyone with a hard-on and a camcorder can do this shit for no money at all.'

'This is good,' Parrish said. 'This is progress. We can keep this?'

'Let me give you a copy. I need the original.'

'Give me half a dozen, would you?' Parrish said, and handed the picture back.

At the 126th, Parrish secured the assistance of one of the uniforms who had been at the Paretski search. His name was Landry. Parrish asked if he had a strong stomach.

'Strong enough for what?'

Parrish showed him the picture. 'Need you to go through all those magazines and DVDs we took from the woman's house and find anything that's similar to this.'

Landry took the picture. He didn't wince, he didn't frown. He just looked at it like it was someone's holiday snapshot. 'I can do that.'

'They're in the Evidence Room. Tell them I sent you. Any difficulty call me.'

'And we're going where?' Radick asked as Landry walked away.

'Back to see an old friend.'

Larry Temple – the Swede Thorson tip-off – was not pleased to see Frank Parrish and Jimmy Radick.

He opened the door with that crestfallen expression of philosophical resignation. Whatever he might have done in the past, however he might have overcome his own demons, the shadow of his sins would follow him for ever.

Parrish did not believe for a moment that Temple was clean, but if Temple co-operated then he would restrain himself from turning the apartment inside out.

'You were here a week ago,' Temple said matter-of-factly.

'Eight days,' Parrish replied. He walked on through to the sitting room. Again Parrish was struck by the remarkable cleanliness and order that prevailed.

'I have a photograph,' Parrish said. 'I want you to look at it very carefully. I want you to think about the girl. Look at her face. I need to know if you recognize her. I want you to look at the image as well. Tell me if you recognize the style, who might have taken the picture, or made the film that the picture came from. You understand?'

'And what the hell makes you think I would even know about this kind of thing?'

'What kind of picture do you think I'm going to show you, Larry?'

'Some kind of porn, more than likely. Probably something really sick, some S&M shit maybe?'

'The fact that this is the conclusion you jump to answers your own question.'

Temple scowled. 'Oh for Christ's sake, just show me the thing already.'

Parrish slipped one of the color copies from the folder and handed it to Temple.

Again, just as with Landry, there wasn't the slightest hint of a reaction. Parrish wondered when everyone had become so desensitized. Was the whole world inured to this shit?

'It's from a film,' Temple said. 'You can tell by the blurring at the edges. Someone's freeze-framed an image from a film and printed it off from their computer.'

'The girl?'

Temple shook his head. 'Hell, Parrish, they all look the same. You've seen a hundred, you've seen them all. College cuties, bangs, ponytails, barrettes, white socks, cheerleader shirts. It's all straightforward stuff.'

'You call this *straightforward*?' Radick asked.

Temple smiled wryly. 'You've never done Vice, right?' He shook his head. 'You should speak to some of your colleagues in Vice. This? This is lightweight compared to some of the stuff going around.'

'So who is she, Larry?' Parrish asked.

'Who is she? Christ almighty knows.'

'I don't mean her name, I mean *who* is she? What happens to put a girl into a situation like this? What are the mechanics of it?'

'You know the story. You've been around long enough. Cutie wants to get into the movies. Maybe she gets a habit. Something happens, she winds up in someone's sights, and it's all over. Once these people get their hooks in they'll fuck you until you die, figuratively and literally.'

'And this? This is for real, or this is staged?'

'Looks real enough to me. She's one of your dead ones, isn't she?'

'She is, yes.'

Temple sighed and shook his head. 'Poor thing.'

'But you buy this shit, Larry,' Parrish said, and then realized that not only was he getting angry, he was also pursuing a futile line of discussion. You can't rationalize irrationality. Some of the worst serial killers ever were some of the most sympathetic when faced with photographs of their own victims.

'I want you to ask around, Larry. I want you to keep that. Show that picture to some people. Make some inquiries. You find anything, you let me know.'

'And why the fuck would I want to do that?'

Parrish hesitated. He clenched and unclenched his fists. He counted to five, and then he leaned forward until his face was mere inches from Temple's.

'Because fundamentally you're a good person, Larry. Because secretly, in your heart of hearts, you understand that every single one of these girls have mothers and fathers, brothers, sisters, cousins, whatever. They had lives, and then – as you so poetically put it – someone fucked them to death. You're going to do it out of basic goodness, and to go some small way to earning yourself the right to still be called a human being. That's why, Larry, and Jimmy here is going to give you his card, and if you hear anything or see anything that you feel might be helpful, then you are going to call him. Are we connecting with one another, Larry?'

Larry Temple – awkward, pained – nodded his head.

Parrish didn't wait to be shown the door. Radick handed over his card, and followed him out into the hallway.

It was en route back – the atmosphere in the car stilted and uncomfortable – that Parrish took a call from the precinct.

'Landry thinks he has something,' was all he said as he ended the call.

Radick put his foot down.

SIXTY

There was no question that it was an image from the same film. There was no question that it was Jennifer. A tiny advert in the back of one of Richard McKee's magazines shouted *S&M TEENS!!*, and then gave a PO Box where you could send twenty-five dollars. By return, and in discreet packaging, you would receive a copy of *HURTING BAD*, and if you mailed your request before March 31st, 2007, then you would get a free copy of *EAT ME BEAT ME*.

'It's her, no question,' Landry said. 'Third or fourth magazine I went through.' He shook his head. 'And this is some sick shit they advertise in the back of these things, let me tell you.'

'You don't need to,' Parrish replied. He looked more closely at Jennifer's frightened face. 'Call the magazine,' he told Radick. 'Tell them we need details of this company, who booked the ad, the usual.' Parrish turned the magazine over, and Radick noted the title. Buried in the small print, he found the name of the company – Absolute Publications; some place out in East LA.

Radick was gone no more than ten minutes. He came back shaking his head. 'Out of business. No longer exists.'

'It'll exist,' Parrish said. 'It'll just be under another name and working out of another office. Try the offices of the East LA Postal Department; trace the PO Box number.' He turned back to Landry. 'Get me six color copies of the ad, blow them up a couple of times so we can see her more clearly. Drop those off in my office, and then carry on going through this. See if you can find anything else.' He walked to the door. 'You did good, Landry, real good.'

Back in his office Parrish took stock of these developments. He felt certain that he was heading in the right direction. Eight hundred and fifty thousand teens went missing every year in the US. The percentage of those that ended up in the sex industry? He didn't know, would never know, but it would be significant. He believed that these girls had gone this route. Not only Jennifer, but also Melissa, Nicole, Karen, Rebecca and Kelly. And what better source than the soon-to-be-adopted, the unwanteds, the children that haunted the edges of society? Caught somewhere between dead junkie parents, new families and the state, what better resource than the comprehensive files of Family Welfare to scout for new blood? Parrish wanted it to be McKee. Since that moment in the interview room, the moment he'd seen the flash in the guy's eyes. *I told her I wanted her to sit on my face so I could put my tongue inside her.* What he would give to get into the guy's apartment, his car, his bank records, his work-space. He looked at Jennifer's picture. *Hurting Bad.* Jesus, the depths these people fell to. More accurately, the depths they were dragged down to by others.

Radick received a call from Larry Temple a little after three. They were no more than a minute or two on the phone, and then Radick went to find Parrish.

'He said that someone came back with the same film title as the one Landry found.'

'Anything on who would have made the film, where we could get a copy?' Parrish asked.

Radick sat down. 'Temple said to tell you it was supposed to be a ghost. He said you'd know what that meant.'

Parrish closed his eyes and shook his head.

'What is that? What's a ghost?'

'It's what they call a film that is supposed to be a snuff movie. They film the whole thing – the beating, the torture, whatever they do, but they cut it off before they actually kill the girl. The cut version goes out as a regular S&M flick, but the long version, the one where the girl is murdered . . . well, that is sold on in an entirely different way.'

'Jesus . . .'

Parrish exhaled slowly. He leaned back and looked out of the window. 'Makes sense, doesn't it? Based on what we have. They're kidnapped, abducted, whatever. They're drugged, forced into sex acts which are filmed. They are then strangled on camera. The bodies are dumped in motel rooms, trash cans, dumpsters, on stairwells, and in the case of Rebecca she is strangled and left in her brother's apartment. Danny is then shot in an alleyway.'

'Suggests that she got away, maybe?'

'No. I think she was filmed in Danny's apartment, and they strangled her there. Laking put the apartment as primary. We're not dealing with Stanley Kubrick here. The quality of the cinematic experience is not first on their list of priorities. We're dealing with real lowlifes, scumbags extraordinaire. I think they made the film there, they strangled her, Danny comes back, sees what's happened, does a runner. They chase him down, shoot him, and it's all over.'

'And you think McKee could have done this?'

'I think McKee could be our supplier. He's the one inside Family Welfare. He knows what the girls look like. He has a picture. He can even visit with them, for fuck's sake. Sometimes adoptive parents and children in care are seen so many times by so many people they don't remember who the fuck they've spoken to. Even if he didn't see them in person he knew where they were, he knew where they lived. He could have followed them, taken more pictures, filmed them on his cell phone, for God's sake. Then he passes them over to whoever, and they do the abduction, the film, the killing. He gets a finder's fee, he's not directly implicated in anything but a circumstantial way, and no-one's the wiser. The only connection between them is the red nail varnish, the change of clothes, the fact that they were adopted, and welfare. It's a thin link, and thus it has gone on for at least two years without anyone being aware of it.'

'Maybe,' Radick said.

Parrish smiled sardonically. 'Like I said, it's always a maybe until it's not.'

'So we need to get into his house.'

'Which we're not going to do without substantive, probative, probable cause-type evidence. Like you said, all we have right now is a maybe.'

'We get Lavelle to give us the names of the cases McKee is working on currently—'

'He's too smart. He's not going to go for anyone that he's directly connected to, that's for sure. I think where he has had some direct connection to any of these girls – meeting with the prospective parents, reviewing a case file for a colleague – all of those have been coincidental. I think he stays well away from the cases he's assigned.'

'So where?'

'To tell you the truth, I don't know right now, but I'm working on it, Jimmy, I'm working on it.'

'Never seem to be investigating the death of a rich guy's daughter, do we? All victims are not created equal, right?'

Parrish frowned. 'Where do you hear that?'

'I don't know . . . heard it somewhere along the line. Why?'

'No reason. It was something my father used to say. Fire Department says the same thing. They never seem to be putting out fires in rich folks' houses.'

'We made the society—'

'Made a fucking mess of it is what we did.'

'No argument there, Frank, no argument there.'

SIXTY-ONE

Seven o'clock and Parrish was frayed at the edges, torn at the corners. He'd sent Radick home an hour or so before. He called Eve from the office. Her voicemail spoke to him once more. He had not spoken back for two weeks. He wondered whether she'd finally had enough of his shit and was screening out his calls. Going over there was out of the question. She was working, that was all. She was hard at work, doing what she did, saving her money for the time she'd move out to Tuscarora and grow phloxes behind a white picket fence. Parrish smiled to himself. As if.

He stopped at Clay's en route home. He had a couple of shots, a single glass of beer. He walked to a pizza place and ordered a pepperoni, Monterey Jack, jalapeño. He ate half of it in the kitchen at home without even removing his jacket. By eight-thirty he knew where he was going. It had never really been in question; it had simply been a matter of how long he would wait before he did it. He called the precinct, got a message from the desk. The priest had called again. Third time. What the fuck was his problem? Parrish got a uniform to find McKee's address for him. He lived down on Sackett Street, maybe eight or nine blocks from Kelly. The fact that McKee was half that distance from Caitlin raised the hairs on the nape of Parrish's neck, and it was that reaction – the definite feeling that he seemed to be looking at something with substance – that gave him the motivation to look further.

He took the subway through Pacific and down to Union Street. He walked Union and took a right on Bond, a left onto Sackett, and found McKee's house. What he had expected to see, he did not know. What he actually saw was a plain and unremarkable building – red brick up to the lower window frames, wood beyond that to the roof. Three steps up to a wooden canopy-type porch and the front door. There were drapes in both lower windows, the single upper window too, and Parrish presumed that there were two bedrooms, one of them looking out over the rear of the property. There was no sign of a car, no incorporated garage, no front yard to speak of. This was not a man with money; or it was a man with money but very conservative and unimaginative tastes. This was the house of someone who did not believe his home should make a statement, at least not to the outside world. The feeling it gave Parrish was of a man who wanted to remain anonymous, even invisible. Had Parrish not been looking for the property he never would have noticed it.

Now he believed he was creating all manner of things when there was nothing there. He walked back to the end of the street. He buried his hands in his pockets and looked back the way he'd come. All the houses were innocuous. In all truth, there was no single building that stood out from the rest. Richard McKee was nothing more than someone with a mild curiosity for younger girls, not so uncommon for a man in his early forties who did not appear to have an ongoing relationship. This was another assumption: neither he nor Radick had asked McKee whether or not he was in a relationship. They had asked if he was married, and he had said he was not, that he had been but was now divorced. He had implied that he was single, but not directly said so. Yet Parrish had assumed it to the point where he had written it in the notes. A simple mistake. Simple, because McKee had not said what everyone says when asked such a question. *No, I'm not married, but I'm in a relationship . . . have been for a while. We talk about getting married, but I don't think either of us has the courage!*

But he hadn't said that. Hadn't said anything like it.

Parrish walked back and looked at the house again. There were lights on in all three front windows of McKee's house, two on the ground, one above, the light beneath the porch canopy also. There was a storefront set back from the sidewalk thirty yards or so away, and here he waited for a while. He didn't know why he was there, he didn't see what good it would serve, but the mere fact that he was in the vicinity of Richard McKee gave him some sense of purpose. What would he otherwise do? Sit home, watch TV, drink? It struck him then that he had not been drunk for a while – a couple of days perhaps? A couple of shots at Clay's, that was all he'd had. He hadn't bought a fifth en route home, emptied it within the hour, gone out for another. Progress? Maybe. Progress towards what? He hadn't a clue. Marie Griffin would be pleased, but he wasn't in it to please Marie Griffin. Aside from the drinking there was the other thing. The thing he'd felt, the thing he'd not expected, and that was some-thing he would speak to her about in the morning. Whatever she was doing to him . . . well, it wasn't therapeutic from any perspective, except possibly the simple benefit of talking to someone who listened. Sure, she asked too many questions. Sure, she answered every answer with another damned ques-tion. But when he spoke she was quiet. She didn't interrupt. She didn't seem to have an agenda. She was perhaps the closest to a friend he had. Sad, really fucking sad, but the truth.

When the door opened and McKee came down the steps from the porch Parrish froze. He hesitated for a second, and then he backed up and pressed himself into the shadows. McKee was unaware of anything save where he was headed. No jacket, just jeans and a sweater. Going out? Parrish didn't think so.

Parrish waited until McKee was fifteen yards from the house, and then he went after him. They walked for no more than a minute, and then McKee turned right into a side street. Parrish crossed over. He looked back the way he'd come. Why, he didn't know, but he did. He entered the side street slowly, tentatively. McKee was out of sight. Parrish hurried down and reached the end. The alleyway opened out into a complex of small garages. The SUV. This must be where McKee kept his car. The light wasn't good, but Parrish heard the metallic sound of a door being raised, the squeak of un-oiled hinges as it was slid back. Parrish moved carefully. He caught sight of the open garage. He counted down. Right-hand side of the block, fourth garage from the end.

McKee backed out, reached up to pull the door down again. Parrish quickly retraced his steps and was soon out on the street – breathless, anxious, even a little frightened. He hadn't felt scared for a good while. But he did feel scared, for real. He was still on pay-hold, he was still unable to drive, he was still being watched every step of the way as he worked. Maybe even Radick was keeping tabs on what he was doing and reporting up the lines. To be caught harassing a potential witness, a suspect in a murder case; to be seen hanging around the guy's house, following him down to his lock-up . . . End of story. He'd be looking for another job by the end of the month.

Parrish left hurriedly. He was a block and a half away by the time McKee emerged onto Sackett Street. Parrish took the subway home. It was only when he reached his apartment that he realized what he had to do, why he had to do it, and what would happen if he did. More to the point, what would happen if he didn't. He wouldn't be able to live with himself. And considering that he lived alone, well that would mean he was really fucked.

He was wired. He knew he wouldn't sleep. He walked to the liquor store and bought a bottle of Bushmills. He drank a third of it and lay on the couch watching *The West Wing*.

SIXTY-TWO

'Well, just describe it as best you can.'

'It's real simple. It was like . . . well, it was like the feeling that someone was relying on me.'

'But people rely on you all the time, Frank.'

'Yes, I know that, but they rely on me in a professional capacity. You're a police officer. You're a detective. They see you arrive somewhere and they think you know all the answers to all the questions. This was different.'

'How so?'

'Well, she lives alone. With her kids, of course, but she doesn't have a guy there as far as I can work out. We went through her place with a fine-toothed comb and I didn't see any evidence of another guy. She divorced McKee back in 2005. That's three years ago. Maybe there's been boyfriends or whatever, but I kind of get the idea that she's concentrated on the kids. Two of them. One of them's fifteen, the other's a year or so younger. She worries about them. She sees him take them away every other weekend, and I can imagine she's anxious until she gets them back. She knows he's a creep. I think she stayed with him for all the same reasons that so many people stay together. Routine, predictability, financial security, the fact he – whoever *he* might be – is the father of her children. Some of the same reasons me and Clare stayed together, you know? Anyways, I think she was relieved to get him out of her life, but he's not out of her life, and whatever fears she might have had for the safety of her own kids has resurfaced due to our involvement.'

'And you feel responsible for her state of mind?'

'I feel a little responsible for her worry, yes, but at the same time I feel like she is making me responsible for resolving it.'

'But you *are* responsible for resolving it, Frank.'

'Yes, I am, but only if he *is* the guy. Only if McKee *is* the guy can I do anything to resolve her worries. If he's not the guy then she's left with him, and there's nothing she can do about it. And then worst case scenario, he is the guy but we miss the boat on him and he goes after the daughter at some point.'

'You're certain he's the guy now?'

'Certain as I can be. Certain as you ever get in this job. I think he's either the perp or . . . actually, I think it's more likely that he's involved in the supply line.'

'And you have confirmed that one of these girls was filmed in some kind of S&M thing?'

'Yes.'

'And the others?'

'I don't know. Maybe they went the same way. I think this is snuff movies. I think they are killed on camera. This movie that Jennifer was in – I think there's an edited version which went on the open market, and then there's a rumor that the full version, the version where she is actually killed, is out and about there somewhere.'

'Let's go back to his ex-wife. What's her name?'

'Carole. Carole Paretski.'

'Are you attracted to her?'

'Jesus no. What the hell do you ask me that for?'

'Frank, don't react. Just think for a moment. Are you attracted to her?'

'Attracted? Let's not even go there, eh? I have a job to do, that's all. I am concerned for her state of mind. I don't like to think that she is carrying all that worry for the welfare of her kids.'

'Are you attracted to her vulnerability?'

'Hell, that's a bit fucking deep for this time in the morning, isn't it?'

'Listen to me, Frank. I believe that we've made a little progress. I don't know if you feel that way and I'm not asking you to tell me, but from what I see you are a little less wound-up. You seem a little less tense. You don't talk about your father anymore. You don't talk about your ex-wife or your own kids. You're talking about things that are now outside your immediate personal sphere. The cases you're working on, the way this particular case is progressing, and now you bring up your concern for someone who you consider is a victim of this terrible, terrible situation. This tells me something, Frank.'

'And what would that be, Doctor Marie?'

'Don't be sarcastic, Frank, please.'

'Okay, okay . . . so what does it tell you?'

'It tells me that we might be starting to turn the corner. People come here and they talk about themselves. Endlessly, for hours and hours and hours they talk about themselves. When they start to talk about other things – external situations, things that are happening now as opposed to things that happened in the past, and especially when they start to express a concern for the well-being of others, well that tells me a great deal about where their attention has turned.'

'So I'm all better now?'

'Frank! Listen to me, Frank. I'm trying to explain something to you here, something that might have a little positivity to it, and you have to come back at me with a wisecrack—'

'Look, Doc, for me it's real simple. My life is a fucking mess. Let's be straight with one another. I was thinking about this only yesterday. I wanted to come here today. Probably for the first time in all the days we've been talking, I wanted to come here and tell you about what I was feeling. It was really simple. I thought to myself "Oh jeez, how about that? That's something I can tell Marie Griffin about tomorrow". And you know what else I thought? I thought that maybe what was happening here was no more complicated than what happens when you get to talk about shit with your friends. But I don't have any, you see? I don't have any friends. I have work colleagues, I have a partner I've known for about three hours, I have a daughter who thinks I'm a pain in the ass, a son who doesn't even call to let me know he's still alive, an ex-wife who's a bitch in stilettos, and you. That's what I have. You happen to be the closest I got to a buddy. So I talk about stuff to you. I told you about my father, my mother, about this that and whatever. It's no big deal. I happen to be drinking a little less, but I believe that has more to do with the fact that this case has really got to me. I want to know who is drugging and strangling teenage girls. I want to know if there's a snuff movie out there where Jennifer Baumann gets the life choked out of her while someone's fucks her in the ass; and I want to know what kind of sick fuck thinks this is the kind of thing he wants to watch while he beats off. That's what I want, and right now that's *all* I want—'

'Frank, listen—'

'No, hang on there a minute. You listen to me. That's what you get paid for. I like you, Doctor Griffin, I think you're a good person. I think you care for people and your job is important. I also believe that a great deal of happiness comes from doing something worthwhile in life, and I can clearly see that what you are doing is worthwhile, at least in your own eyes. My job is something entirely different. I get paid to find people like Richard McKee and make them feel an awful lot worse. If someone like Carole Paretski feels better because her scumbag pervert ex-husband is behind bars for the rest of his life, well that's a secondary thing. It's good, it's fine, but it's not the reason for doing the job. We're on the other side of two entirely different fences. My world isn't yours, and yours isn't mine, and I don't think there's a great deal of hope that they'll ever meet—'

'Frank, I don't understand why you're suddenly being so defensive and aggressive.'

'I'm being defensive and aggressive because I'm kind of worn out with being told what I think and what I feel, Marie. That's the truth, and whether you like it or not that's the way it is. You know the prayer we say around here? It's really simple. Lord God, just grant me one more day. That's what we say. We also know that our day starts when someone else's day ends. We also know that we cannot escape the power of small things. The truth is small, and so are the lies. Sometimes the smallest lies are the ones that kill us. You know what else I used to say to myself? It was like a little chant, a reminder of where I was at and how my life was going. I used to say that every day in every way I was *not* getting better. It was my attempt to remind myself that I needed to change, but you know what? I never fucking did.

I also know that no-one ever got better from drinking but I still do it. Am I self-destructive? Does that make me a born loser, because I am doing something that I know is no good for me, and hell it might even kill me if I do it enough? Sure it does, but you know something else? It doesn't matter, because when I finally hit the deck, when it's all over and the lights are going out, I'll know that because of what I did there are some people out there who are still alive. People who don't even know that they came this close to a bad and unnecessary end. I sit on the subway sometimes. I sit there and look at people and I wonder who isn't going to make it to Christmas. Well, some of those people are alive now because I took some scumbag off the streets and put him in a six by ten and they threw away the key.'

'Frank—'

'We are the brightest lights, Marie. We believe that here. We *have* to believe it. But the problem right there is that we also cast the darkest shadows. That's what we have to carry, and we carry it every day. People live and die by what we do. Always have, always will. It's a burden sure, but we carry it and we try and smile the best we can, and right now I really don't give a fuck what my father did or didn't do, and how that might have damaged me. It doesn't matter, and I'll grant you that, okay? I think you have managed to take my attention away from the past and direct it more towards the future. Well, perhaps not the future. We're not very good at future. Maybe you've helped direct it towards the present, and the present is right there, right there in front of me on DVDs and in magazines, in the sickening image of a teenage girl left with a broken neck in a cardboard box behind a dumpster. Someone did that. Someone is going to go on doing that. I think I know who that person is, and I'm going to do everything in my power to make sure he never does it again.'

'And what happens if you collapse, Frank? What happens if the pressure and responsibility costs you your relationship with your kids, and your health and sanity as well?'

'That's the drill, Doctor. That's what we do. I think it's called an occupational hazard.'

'*You* are the occupational hazard, Frank. You just can't see it.'

'Too busy looking elsewhere.'

'Well, I'm going to recommend—'

'Nothing, Marie. You're going to recommend nothing at all. I'll come back tomorrow, and maybe I'll be in a different mood. But if you do or say anything that causes me to be taken off this case . . . well, I don't know what I'll do. If you really are concerned for my mental welfare then you won't do anything to jeopardize my work on this case. I am only so far away from the truth . . .'

'I wasn't going to say that, Frank. Who the hell do you think I am? All I was going to say was that once this case was over I was going to recommend that you take some paid medical leave. I think you should get out of the city, go up-state maybe. Perhaps Robert and Caitlin could go with you. Do something outside of what you've been doing for the last God-knows how long.'

'Well okay, we'll talk about that when this thing is done.'

'Deal?'

'Deal. Now I have to go.'

'I understand, but do something for me, please?'

'And what would that be?'

'Take a moment every once in a while to remember that there is more to you than a homicide detective. Like what you were talking about, what you felt towards that woman.'

'And what good would that do?'

'You might be surprised. Like you said, sometimes we cannot escape the power of small things.'

SIXTY-THREE

Parrish asked Radick to go over to Erickson at Archives and help look for any more pictures of the dead girls. It was a diversion and Radick knew it, but he did not question it.

'You doing something useful?' he asked Parrish.

'Perhaps.'

'Something you have to do alone?'

'Something it's better that I do alone.'

'You think I wouldn't be able to handle it?'

'Jimmy, please . . . I just bawled out the doctor. I'm not in the mood for square-dancing. Go help Erickson. I'll call you. Whatever I might be doing is no more or less important than finding more evidence about what happened to the girls. Let's just leave it at that.'

'How long do you need?'

'Couple of hours.' Parrish looked at his watch. 'Meet me back here at noon, give or take.'

Radick left without further questions. Parrish was gone ten minutes after – heading right back to Sackett Street and the garage lock-ups where McKee stored his SUV.

The street was empty. Windows looked back at him vacantly. He walked purposefully. Worst thing he could do was appear to be a stranger. In his pockets he carried two screwdrivers, a box-cutter, a torch, a key-ring with a collection of metal strips attached to it, some of them straight, some of them angled, others hooked or turned at the end. He also had a bunch of generic car keys. They were all routine tools for any car thief. Down back of the alley Parrish waited for a few seconds to ensure that no-one was arriving, leaving, or currently using their garage. It was quiet, so quiet that even his own footsteps on the gravel, even his own hurried heartbeat, seemed inordinately loud. Three minutes is a hell of a long time to wait when you are simply waiting. Half a dozen times Parrish knew he should walk away. Walk away right now. Just go, don't look back, don't even think about doing what he was planning to do. But he simply had to remember how Rebecca had looked when he'd found her on the bed in her junkie brother's apartment. Sixteen years old. Red fingernails. Petechial hemorrhaging back of the ears, visible in the whites of her eyes.

Parrish pulled on a pair of latex gloves, and then walked quickly to the garage. Within moments he was inside, had drawn the door back down and closed it. God, he hadn't even been smart enough to call and ensure that McKee was at work. It was Wednesday. Less of a chance that McKee would take a day off mid-week? Days off were usually Mondays and Fridays, trying to extend the weekend as long as possible. That counted for shit in the face of what he was doing. McKee could take a day off whenever he wanted.

Parrish stood in the dim silence of the lock-up. He breathed deeply. He tried his best to quell his heart, his pulse, but it was no good. He was out-of-shape, scared, already so far in over his head that there would be no way out of this if he was caught. Harassment, B&E, invasion of privacy, violation of all the protocols regarding search and seizure and probable cause. Whichever way it went, if he was caught he was fucked.

In back of the garage, there between the front bumper and the wall were the usual cans of paints, toolboxes, painting tarps, a folding bicycle which looked like it hadn't been unfolded for years. There was a spare tire for the SUV, a box of light bulbs, a bag of wire coat hangers, other such things that should have been thrown out but never were. Aside from that it was just the car.

Parrish cupped his hands against the glass and looked through the front nearside window. He found the alarm light in the dash. It was off. Sure, he could disable an alarm, but it took thirty, forty seconds, and the newer the alarm the longer that stretched. The likelihood that anyone would hear it out here . . . well, better not to have to contend with that possibility.

From the bunch of keys Parrish selected the three or four that he felt might best fit. Second key he was in. The door opened soundlessly. Once again he paused for consideration of his actions. Now it wasn't just B&E. Now it was far more serious. If he went through the guy's car – irrespective of whether or not anything was found – he was committing a serious offence. If he did find something there would be nothing he could do about it. It would be inadmissible in any investigation, any police precinct, any court of law. And he would be prosecuted to the full extent of the system. That much he would have earned. He knew that whatever he might find he would be unable to use it, but that wasn't why he was there. He was there simply to try and find something to confirm his suspicions. He *wanted* McKee to be the guy. He *needed* him to be the guy . . .

A sound. Was that a sound? Something outside?

Parrish's heart stopped. He heard himself swallow. He glanced down at the thin strip of light between the ground and the lower edge of the garage door. From outside would it look like the door had been left unlocked? Would whoever was out there notice it? Security? Did they have a security patrol during the day, some guy who got fifty dollars a week to just drive by and check that the doors were all secure?

Parrish tried to remember if the door had made a sound when he'd opened it. Had it squeaked? Would it make a sound if he tried to close it? He left it. He backed up and crouched down behind the front bumper. He watched the strip of light along the ground. He waited for the shadows of someone's feet to appear. He tried to breathe silently. He tried to vacate his mind completely. What would he say? He could just barge past the guy and run like a motherfucker, hope he wasn't caught. He could flash his badge, take the guy completely by surprise, tell him that this was part of an undercover operation and swear him to secrecy. Security guards – hell, they all were wannabe cops. That would work. Sure it would . . .

Parrish silenced the internal voice. He wouldn't be caught. The guy wasn't security. He was no-one. He was walking down here because he was lost. He would see it was a dead-end, turn around, disappear. That's what would happen.

Parrish waited.

There seemed to be no sound at all, and then suddenly he

could hear footsteps again. The sound of someone walking on gravel. Where was the gravel? Was it just at the entrance to the complex, or was it all the way down? He couldn't remember. He closed his eyes. He clenched his fists. He thought about how much he would have to drink to get over this feeling.

And then there was nothing.

He didn't even hear the footsteps recede into silence. They were there, and then they were gone. It was not so much that he heard silence, but that he *felt* the absence of anyone out there.

Parrish came out from behind the bumper. He stood up and flexed his knees. He realized how much he was sweating and took off his jacket. He walked to the garage door and stood there for at least two minutes. He could hear nothing but the odd car passing in the street beyond.

Parrish backed up, got into the car, and started looking through the glove compartment, the well between the seats, beneath the seats themselves, under the rug in the foot-well. He climbed into the back, pushed the seats forward, looked behind them and underneath them, searched through the bundle of maps in the rear door wells. Once he was done, he got out the car to check the trunk.

It was here that he found the files. A metal file box, to be exact. Big enough for legal, maybe two inches deep. It was locked. He went slowly, carefully, insuring that he left no scratches around the lock or on the smooth metal surface of the box. It opened within a minute, and he stood looking at the files for quite some time before he reached for them.

Seven files, all of them Family Welfare-stamped, a couple of them from CAA, the others from Child Services. Inside each one were current notes, all of them handwritten, all of them initialed *RMcK*. Four boys, three girls – the youngest nine, the oldest seventeen. Were these McKee's active cases? Were these visits he would be making? Did all Welfare staff have a secure box in their car to carry active case files for when they made visits? Parrish had no idea. Such a thing seemed entirely plausible, and from the notes it seemed that each of them were current cases . . .

And then Parrish looked again. Two of the boys were black,

as was one of the girls. The second girl was twelve, brunette, perhaps Mexican, Puerto Rican. The last girl, sixteen years old a month or so before, was blonde. She was a pretty girl, and from the brief scan that Parrish made of the file he learned that she had been adopted by a family in South Brooklyn more than nine months earlier. The most recent comment in the file came not from McKee, but someone else. Someone with the initials *HK*. HK? Was there someone they had interviewed with the initials HK?

Parrish put down the files. He had his notebook with him. Did he still have the names that Lavelle had given him? He went through his pockets, found the list, unfolded it and straightened it out on the surface of the box. HK . . . HK . . . Harold Kinnear. Yes, he remembered him now. The older guy. Had been in the department for thirty years. What had he said? Something about the more civilized and sophisticated we became the less able we were too look after our kids.

This was not McKee's case. Jesus Christ, this was *not* McKee's case.

Parrish turned the list over. He wrote down the girl's name – Amanda Leycross, her date of birth – 12 August 1992, and the name and address of the couple that had adopted her back in January. Martin and Bethany Cooper, Henry Street, South Brooklyn. Parrish knew Henry Street, no more than three blocks from Caitlin, maybe half a dozen blocks from McKee himself. Take Williamsburg and Karen out of the equation, put all the locations on a map – Family Welfare Two, the Kelly Duncan crime scene back of Brooklyn Hospital, Sackett Street, the Coopers' place in South, Danny Lange's apartment on Hicks – and they tracked a circle, a circle that went all the way around this part of the city, as far north as Brooklyn Bridge, as far west and south as the Brooklyn-Queens Expressway. McKee had boxed himself in. Was this the commuter that the FBI profilers spoke of, always traveling out to the crime scene, dumping bodies far enough away not to attract attention? But when you added them all up, when you put them all together . . . then you saw a different picture entirely?

And Amanda Leycross? Was she next on the roster? Or was

she dead already? Or was this just another file of another case that McKee was helping out on, reviewing, supervising? Had Parrish missed the game completely? He could not afford to think that. Not yet. Not until he knew who Amanda Leycross was and why McKee had her file.

Parrish had to get out, and quickly. He closed up the files, returned them to the box, relocking it carefully. He set it back precisely where he'd found it, grabbed his jacket then closed and locked the car and walked to the door.

He counted to five, opened it swiftly, banged it shut behind him, locked it and walked towards the alleyway. He was out on the street within seconds, walking back the way he'd come towards Union Street. His heart didn't stop pounding until he was on the subway. He looked again at the piece of paper upon which he'd written the girl's name. Amanda Leycross. Sixteen years old. Blonde, innocent, pretty as hell. Would she be number seven?

SIXTY-FOUR

'How was Archives?'

'Un-fucking-real, Frank. An hour, that's all I could handle. I don't know how those guys can spend their working days looking at that stuff.'

Parrish smiled. 'They get hardened to it.'

'That supposed to be a wisecrack?' Radick didn't wait for an answer. 'And where did you go?'

'To check on something.'

'Where?'

'It's better we close this line of questioning right now, Jimmy,' Parrish replied.

'Frank . . . you can't put yourself at risk, not in your current situation—'

'Jimmy, enough already.'

'One fuck-up, Frank, and—'

'Jimmy, I said enough. Okay?'

Radick sighed and shook his head. 'You ever take any of this shit seriously? Does it ever cross your mind that maybe, just maybe, they might get a skinful of your attitude and kick you out?'

'Kick me out? I'm a fucking institution, Jimmy. They kick me out and the whole place will fall apart.'

'You really believe that?'

'No, of course I don't believe it. You think my ego's that big?'

'Sometimes I wonder.'

'Sit down, Jimmy.'

'I'm gonna get a lecture?'

'Just sit the fuck down, Jimmy, okay? Just sit down and listen to me for a moment.'

Radick sat down. His expression was one of patient resignation.

'Now listen to me,' Parrish started, 'and listen to me carefully. I have a name. Where I got this name from doesn't matter. I don't want you to ask about how I came by this information, but it relates to a girl. She's sixteen, she was adopted about nine months ago, and she went to a family in South Brooklyn. This is someone I want to follow up on. Whether she's someone or not . . . whether she's got a place in this thing I don't know, but I want to follow up on her—'

'Whether or not she's got a place in this thing? Are you serious? You have the name of some girl and you think she might be a potential victim. Is that what you're saying?'

Parrish hesitated.

'Frank? Tell me what the—'

Parrish nodded.

'And where the fuck – may I ask – did that lead come from?'

'No you may not ask.'

'You gotta be kidding, Frank. You can't just come to me with a piece of information like that and say, "This is what we're going to do, but I'm not going to tell you why we're doing it". You can't run a homicide investigation like that.'

'So what do you suggest, Jimmy? I have a feeling about this, I really do. I have this idea that she might be in the line-up for this guy, and I cannot shake it. You think we should just sit on our hands and wait for this motherfucker to kill someone else? '

'*This* motherfucker? Presumably that means McKee, right?'

'Sure.'

'Frank, we have nothing, and I mean *nothing* probative that suggests McKee is the guy. This is one hundred percent circumstantial.' Radick stood up and walked to the window. 'Christ, Frank,' he said exasperatedly, 'you have any idea how much of a nowhere this case is right now?'

'I'm not waiting any longer, Jimmy. This is bullshit. You know as well as me that this is the guy—'

'Frank, we don't *know* anything, not for sure—'

'Christ, Jimmy, get some balls on this thing man! We know it's someone at South Two. That's a connection you just cannot ignore. We know the guy likes teenage porn and all that shit. He has an SUV. He has the freedom to move. He's not in a house with a wife and kids. There's no-one there to keep an eye on what he's doing day and night. He's a free agent. He's a fucking commuter, that's what he is, just like the Feds say in the profiling material. He's out there collecting up teenage girls and selling them on, or making fucking snuff movies himself. That's what he's doing, and I fucking *know* it.'

'Okay, so he's the guy. Say he *is* our guy. What do we do now? We follow him every which way? You think we're gonna get a judge to sign a surveillance authorization, a wiretap . . . you really think we've got enough to sway a judge on this?'

'No we haven't, and that's why we're not going to do this on official lines.'

'You what?'

'We are gonna do it. You and me. We're gonna do it by ourselves. This is what it takes sometimes, Jimmy. This is the sort of thing you have to do sometimes to make one of these cases open up—'

'You're not serious.'

'I am serious, Jimmy, as serious as I've ever been. I can't live with this . . . I just cannot live with the idea that this guy is going to get another one when there's something we can do to stop him.'

'So what? You want to follow him out-of-hours? You want us to tail him, see where he goes, what he does?'

'No, I want to find out if this girl is still alive, and if she is I want to keep an eye on her.'

'This mysterious girl that you think might be his next victim?'

'Yes.'

'The girl that you just *happen* to know about? The one that you somehow magically know about but you won't tell me *how* you know about her? *That* girl?'

'I could use a little less sarcasm here, Jimmy.'

'And you, Frank . . . you could use a little more sense, don't you think? So say this is the next victim. Say that this is the girl he's gonna do next. We intervene. We stop him. Then where is our case, eh? We start to write reports, we start to answer questions, we go to the Grand Jury and they start

331

to look under the lid of this thing, right? What are they going to see, Frank? What are they going to find out about that you haven't told me? We're partners. We're supposed to work together, to know everything that the other one is doing. Isn't that the way it's supposed to work?'

'Jimmy—'

'No, you hear me out on this one, okay? I'm sat before the Grand Jury. They ask me how come we knew about this girl as a potential victim. How did we know? Where did the intel come from? What am I going to say? "Oh shit, I don't know. I just figured Frank was the boss and he knew what he was doing. I'm just his kid brother. I just did what I was told to do, Your Honor". You think that's going to work out okay for me, Frank?'

Parrish raised his hand. 'You're right. It's okay. Just drop it.'

Radick smiled knowingly. 'Oh no, Frank. We're not going that route.'

'What route? What are you talking about?'

'You think I don't see right through that tone? That dismissive tone? "It's okay, Jimmy, just drop the thing". You think I'm stupid? I know exactly what that means. That means you're going to do this by yourself. You're going to leave me out in the cold and just go ahead and do whatever the hell it is you want, right?'

'Jimmy, you really think I'd—'

'Yes, Frank, I do. Just like you did with your last partner, and look where the fuck that got him—'

Parrish shot to his feet. His fists were clenched. He looked at Jimmy Radick with an expression of such anger.

Radick raised his hands. 'I'm sorry. I apologize. I didn't mean to say that. I meant to say—'

'Whatever the fuck you meant, Jimmy, you don't have one single fucking idea about what happened . . .'

'I know, and I said I'm sorry, it was out of line. I'm upset, Frank. I'm as pissed about this situation as you are, but I just don't see how you can even consider doing this thing. You can't just decide to follow some girl in the hope that she might turn out to be bait for you. It doesn't work that way, Frank, and you know that better than anyone. You need to tell me where the hell you got this girl's name from, and if it turns out that you did something illegal to get it . . . well, then—'

'Well what, Jimmy? You going to run tell Valderas? Or maybe Internal Affairs? Is that what you're gonna do?'

Radick didn't reply. He leaned back in his chair and closed his eyes for a moment. When he opened them he asked Frank Parrish to sit down.

Parrish did so.

'Look. This isn't complicated. Until we have something substantive, something beyond circumstantial against McKee, we are out on our own. We cannot do a search and seizure, we cannot put surveillance on him, we cannot get a wiretap. We were flying close to the wind taking that stuff out of the ex-wife's house, but she owns the property now, and as far as the law is concerned anything that is a remnant of the relationship that is in that house is legally her property so she was within her rights to turn it over to us. We're covered on that. The hole in the fucking ceiling is circumstantial. The thing back in 2002 is circumstantial and bears no relation to this case. The fact that he works at South Two and used to work at family South is circumstantial. The fact that he has an SUV is . . . well, it's worth nothing at all. This thing you have now, this name – however the hell you came by it – this is something else entirely. As your partner, as a fellow cop, I cannot allow you to do anything that will either jeopardize the case or jeopardize your position in the department. I am here to work with you, Frank, but I'm also here to look out for you, to keep you coloring inside the lines. You know that, right? You understand that I am the last partner you are ever likely to get, because if something goes wrong then it's more than likely going to be your fault and you are going to get canned.'

'Thanks for the vote of confidence.'

'You're welcome, Frank.'

'So tell me, Sherlock, what the fuck do you plan to do?'

'We have to find the film company. We have to do that. We have to get a handle on who is producing these things, and that might require collaboration with the LAPD. It's their territory. It's California someplace, this East LA connection. That's where ninety-nine percent of this shit comes from. That is the belly of the beast when it comes to the sex industry. We need to speak to them, and we need to get their help in finding whoever it was that made the film with Jennifer in it. Then we might have something. One lead connects to another which connects to another, and we might wind up with McKee himself, or whoever McKee is the finder for. That gives us a line into his finances, his house, the rest of his life, and if we get that and he *is* our man, then it'll all end happily ever after.'

'You've spoken to Valderas about this?'

Radick shook his head. 'No, but I will.'

'Okay. Make up a submission report for whoever we send it to, and speak to Valderas.'

'And if we end up going to LA, we're going together. Okay?'

'Okay,' Parrish replied. 'Together.'

SIXTY-FIVE

Parrish left after one. He told Radick he had a dental appointment, that he wouldn't be too long. 'I keep missing them,' he said. 'Figured I should make the effort at least once a year.'

Parrish did not go to a dentist appointment. He took the subway out through Bergen, got off at Carroll, walked three blocks down 1st Place and took a right on Henry. He walked right past the Coopers' house. Inconspicuous, ordinary, nothing striking about it, but what had he expected? He slowed down thirty yards away, walked back as if he was trying to find a number, and then he crossed over and stood at the corner of Carroll and Henry. There was a convenience store there, a mailbox and some newspaper vending machines. He went into the store and bought a sandwich and a bottle of Coke. He stood on the corner. He ate his sandwich. He watched the house for more than an hour. He saw no-one leave and no-one arrive. Just before three he was ready to give it up when his attention was caught by two girls coming down from the corner of President. He stepped back, closer to the wall, and he watched. Twenty yards away and he knew the girl on the right was Amanda Leycross. She had not changed from her case file picture. Schoolbags, cell phones, multi-colored laces in her sneakers, a blue streak dyed through her blonde hair. She was a regular kid. Sixteen years old. She was doing most of the talking. The other girl seemed content to listen. They passed right by Parrish and went into the convenience store. They were no more than a couple of minutes, and then they headed across the street to the Cooper's house and Amanda said goodbye to her friend, who carried on up Henry and then took a left.

Amanda looked like the others. That's what struck Parrish with the greatest force and certainty. She looked like the others, and it was a moment before he put his finger on what it was. They were normal girls. That was all. They weren't outstandingly pretty or tall or short or thin or fat or anything else. They were blonde, and they were normal.

Parrish could feel his heart racing, his pulse beating in his temples. He dropped the empty Coke bottle in the trashcan outside the store, and he headed back to the subway station. He knew. If he had ever been uncertain then it was in that moment that his uncertainty dissolved completely. He *knew* it was McKee, and he knew that Amanda Leycross was next.

Parrish was back in the office by four. Radick greeted him with, 'Valderas has taken the paperwork to Haversaw. He says we should be able to get the help we need from LA.'

'But no word about a week or two for us in the sunshine?'

'Dreaming,' Radick replied.

'Did you even suggest it?'

Radick didn't answer the question. He merely rolled his eyes and then asked after Parrish's dental appointment.

'I don't floss enough,' Parrish said.

They waited for word back from Valderas but it didn't come before six. Radick said he had a thing going on. Parrish let him go.

It was in the silence of the office, Radick gone, the other detectives out doing whatever they were doing, that Parrish's thoughts turned back to Caitlin. He would have to rebuild the bridge. She wasn't going to do it. As far as she was concerned time away from her father was time away from questions about where she was going to wind up working. When was he going to accept that she was an adult, she had her own life, that she was going to make her own decisions and there was little he could do about it? Never, that's when. That was the thing with fathers and daughters. That was just the way it was. The brightest of all his days, the darkest of all his nights.

He lifted the phone to call her, decided against it. Last time he'd seen her was six days prior. That Thursday night, the way he went for Radick, how he proceeded to kick take-out food all down the stairs. He closed his eyes as a sense of quiet shame came over him.

Parrish lifted the phone again and called a different number. This time she picked up.

'Eve.'

'Frank. How are you?'

'I'm okay, Eve, I'm okay. I've called a few times.'

'I know, Frank, I've seen your number. I've been busy, you know? Real busy. I have a thing tonight, an hour or so and I have to leave.'

'Could I come over?'

'You driving yet?'

'No.'

'You take the subway, Frank, and by the time you get here it'll be time for you to leave.'

'I can get a cab.'

'I have to get ready, Frank. I need to take a shower, dry my hair, get changed.'

'Tomorrow?'

'Tomorrow I'm working, Frank, and then Friday I'm going upstate to see my mom for a little while.'

'You're giving me the brush-off—'

'It sounds like it, Frank, but I'm not. It'd be good to see you, but things have been a little crazy . . .'

'For me too, Eve, for me too.'

'But you're okay? Everything's okay with you?'

'It's fine.'

'I know that tone, Frank.'

'Go to work, Eve. Call me when you get back.'

'You're not going to give me anything are you?'

'You don't want my hardships, Eve. Jesus, I don't even understand why you put up with me.'

'Because I know you. I know what you're trying to do. I saw what happened to you when Mike was killed—'

'Enough already. We're not having this conversation again.'

'That's what you always say, Frank, the point being that we never really *did* have that conversation in the first place.'

'Go to work, Eve. Have a good time with your mom. Call me when you get home.'

'Now who's giving who the brush-off?'

'Take care, okay?'

Parrish leaned forward and hung up the phone. He felt that pain in his lower gut. He knew what would kill that feeling, and he knew exactly where to get it.

SIXTY-SIX

'How much did you drink?'

'Who says I drank anything?'

'I'm not a fool, Frank. Look at you. It's easy to see when you've had a bad night.'

'Half a bottle maybe.'

'And what started you off? You were doing better with that.'

'I thought about calling Caitlin and I couldn't. I then called a friend who I was hoping I could see and they had plans already.'

'Loneliness?'

'God knows. Something. I got to thinking about my father. I got to thinking about how many wrongs make a right. I got to wondering whether this case would ever break.'

'Where are you at now?'

'No further forward really. We need to get inside his house, his bank account. We need to get a helluva lot closer than we already have, that's for sure.'

'And you have no leverage to do that?'

'No, not yet.'

'Did you do something you shouldn't have?'

'Like what?'

'Did you cross a line, Frank? Did you talk to someone you shouldn't have? Did you get some information from someplace—'

'Everything we talk about here is confidential, right?'

'Of course it is. You know that.'

'Even though you are a department counsellor?'

'Yes, even though I'm a department counsellor.'

'I have your word on that?'

'You don't need my word, Frank, it's the law.'

'I still want your word.'

'Then you have it.'

'Then the answer to your question is yes, I got some information.'

'From someplace you shouldn't have been?'

'Yes.'

'You shouldn't be doing that.'

'I don't need to be reminded of that.'

'Your father—'

'My father and I are nothing alike, Marie. Let's get things into perspective here.'

'You don't think he started down that route by doing something he shouldn't have? Planting evidence. Shoot an unarmed guy and then stick a knife in his hand. You don't think they all began that way.'

'You think my father did something like that and then it got worse and worse?'

'That's the way it starts, Frank.'

'Not with my father. Like I told you, he was the worst you could imagine right from the get-go.'

'Okay, we're not talking about your father anymore—'

'He and I are different, okay?'

'There's no need for you to be defensive.'

'Say it.'

'Say what?'

'Say that me and my father are different.'

'Of course you're different. No two people—'

'You know what I mean, Marie. Say it.'

'Okay, Frank, okay. You and your father are different.'

'Good. Okay. So what was your next question?'

'This information you got – irrespective of where you got it from – did it make anything clearer?'

'Yes.'

'It confirms your suspicions about this – what was his name?'

'McKee. Richard McKee. And no, it doesn't confirm anything, it just gives me another lead to follow.'

'But you still have nothing probative, nothing that tells you he is definitely your guy?'

'No, I don't.'

'So how does that feel?'

'Feels like bullshit. That's what it feels like. Feels like so many other situations I've been in. You know something but you can't do anything about it.'

'Like your father.'

'Yes, like my father.'

'And if you *were* your father, what would you do?'

'If I was my father . . . Jesus, I don't know, maybe go over there, beat the crap out of the guy, tell him the game was up and extort as much money out of him as I possibly could. Either that, or kill him.'

'You think that's what he'd do?'

'Yes, more than likely.'

'But you're not him.'

'No.'

'So what are *you* going to do?'

'I'm going to follow the rules and color inside the lines and say "Please" and "Thank you" to everyone I meet—'

'Really, Frank. What are you going to do.'

'I'm going to get him in again and ask him some more questions. I'm going to put some more pressure on him and see if we can't make some cracks show. That's what I'm going to do.'

'Today?'

'Yes, today.'

'What makes you think he'll co-operate?'

'The simple fact that perps like to be as close to the police as they can be. Either they're scared and they want to see what we've got, or they're arrogant and they want to see how they can continue to outwit us.'

'And which category does your guy fall into?'

'Both. I think he's a good bit scared and he's arrogant as well. I think he's done this before, many times, and he's got away with it, and now he's wondering whether his lucky streak has come to an end, or if we're just chasing everything we can in the hope that we get something.'

'You think he'll crack?'

'In here? No, I don't think so. But you put enough pressure

on these guys and they start to fuck up. They get over-cautious and that's when things go wrong.'

'But how will you know what he's doing if you're not following him? I presume you have nothing that warrants surveillance.'

'That's right.'

'So—'

'If I happen to be over that side of the city, and I just happen to see him—'

'That's illegal, Frank.'

'So is abducting girls and strangling them on video.'

'I don't know what to say.'

'You don't have to say anything, and if you are good to your word then you *won't* say anything.'

'I'm good for my word, Frank. That's not the problem here. The problem here is whether you are.'

'My oath as a police officer?'

'Exactly.'

'Let me worry about that, Marie. Right now it seems to me that the end will justify the means.'

'I could apply that to the situation I have with you.'

'Sure you could, but if you go blab your mouth off then I'll get suspended again, and then McKee will do whatever the fuck he likes because no-one is really interested in the guy but me.'

'Maybe there's a reason for that.'

'He's the guy, believe me. He *is* the guy.'

'I hope you're right, Frank, I really do. But what I hope even more is that you get him legally and legitimately, and you don't go dig an even deeper hole for yourself than you already have.'

'I think I'm at the bottom, Marie. Dig any deeper and I might just wind up on the other side.'

'That's precisely what I'm worried about. I'm worried that you're going to wind up—'

'Like my father?'

'Yes, Frank, like your father.'

'I wouldn't worry about that.'

'Why not?'

'Because there's one fundamental difference between us,

Marie, and it's real simple. Everything he did, he did it for the wrong reasons, whereas—'

'Whereas you're doing it for the right ones?'

'Yes.'

'You know he would have had exactly the same viewpoint.'

'Maybe so, but he would have been wrong.'

'Be careful, Frank.'

'Now what good did being careful ever do for anyone?'

SIXTY-SEVEN

'On what pretext?' Radick asked.

'Doesn't matter what pretext. Hell, just tell him we have a couple more questions, should be the last ones we ask him, but we believe we're getting closer to Young. Tell him that we really think Lester Young might have been Jennifer Baumann's killer.'

'And he'll go for it?'

Parrish smiled knowingly. 'If he's half the man I think he is he'll go for it.'

Radick called Family Welfare. He had the call put through to McKee direct. They were on the phone no more than a minute.

'He'll come after work.'

'How did he seem?'

'Puzzled. He didn't protest coming down here, but I get the idea he's more curious than guilt-ridden.'

Parrish got up from his chair and walked to the window. He seemed elsewhere and then turned slowly to face Radick. 'You know something, Jimmy? If this isn't the guy then I'm going to quit.'

'You what?'

'What I said. If McKee isn't the guy then I'm quitting. I'm a pain-in-the-ass to everyone, you know? They keep me because of past successes, not because they can't do without me. They keep me because they know that sooner or later I'm going to do something irreparable and they'll have to throw me out. That's a lot cheaper than trying to buy me off with an early pension or something.'

'I don't think that's what they expect, Frank.'

Parrish sat down again. He smiled patiently. 'I've been dancing round these motherfuckers for years, Jimmy. I don't do things the way they want them done. They know it, I know it. They need people like you. Smart, organized, methodical people who know where the lines are and can stay inside them. People who can get the job done within the system. I've been trying to do the job *despite* the system.'

'Hell, Frank, we all have the same frustrations—'

'Yeah, I know, but you guys don't take it personally. That's the difference right there. I take it home. I wear it like a fucking overcoat. I took it out on my kids, my wife . . . and you know, just about everything went to shit. You know where I went yesterday?'

Radick raised his hand. 'Don't tell me, Frank. I don't want to know.'

'Jimmy, you do, believe me—'

Radick leaned forward. He looked at Parrish unerringly. 'Frank. Hear me now, and hear me good. I don't want to know. Don't tell me. You tell me you'll regret it, okay?'

'What the hell is that s'posed to mean?'

'Frank, just believe me when I tell you that *I do not want to know*, okay?'

'Suit yourself.'

'Thank you, Frank.'

'So between now and the golden boy arriving?'

'I'm going back to Archives,' Radick said. 'I'm going to keep on looking for any more pictures of these girls.'

'Good man. I'll wait here, go back through the notes, try and put something more comprehensive together, and see if I can chase up this LA thing with Valderas.'

Radick got up. He walked to the door, reached it, paused, and turned back slowly. 'And can I ask you to stay inside the lines, Frank?'

'You can ask, Jimmy.'

'Then that's what I'm doing. I'm asking you, Frank, for your own sake, and for the sake of this case. Stay inside the lines.'

Radick was gone for more than three hours. When he got back he looked like crap.

'There is something seriously wrong with this fucking planet, Frank. The stuff they have over there . . .' He shrugged off his jacket and dropped into his chair.

'Seen it all,' Parrish replied. 'I stopped asking questions about why people were so fucked up years ago.'

'But all that shit, man . . . Jesus, what the fuck is that all about?'

'It's an addiction, Jimmy, just like smack or coke or booze. It's an addiction. Some people are just wired up that way and no-one knows why.'

'Un-fucking-real,' Jimmy exhaled.

'Sad thing is that it's very real indeed.'

'You get any word back on this submission to LA?'

'Not a sound. Valderas . . . Jesus, I wouldn't want his job. I've been chasing him around the building all afternoon. Finally cornered him in the canteen.'

'And?'

'And he says that Haversaw is going to speak with someone who'll speak with someone else's assistant-fucking-deputy something-or-other, and we might get word back by Monday. That's if we're lucky.'

'Christ, it makes me wonder how the fuck we ever get anything done around here.'

'Let's go get a room for McKee, okay? That is something we can do.'

McKee arrived promptly. He showed up in the lobby, informed the desk sergeant that he was there to see Detectives Parrish and Radick, and when Radick went down to get him he was seated quietly in the foyer reading a newspaper. He smiled when he got up. He extended his hand. He seemed pleased to see Radick. Radick – in all honesty – could not see the guy making snuff movies.

They reconvened in the same interview room. Parrish was already seated by the time Radick and McKee arrived. Parrish got up and greeted the man warmly. Parrish appeared calm, measured, self-assured. McKee seemed the same.

Radick took his chair near the door, McKee's back to him, Parrish facing him and to his left.

McKee began by asking what other possible questions Parrish could have for him. He made it clear that he was not willing to be subjected to any inappropriate questions, that he had already sought legal advice, that he had the phone number of a lawyer and he would call him given the slightest provocation.

Parrish began by apologizing to McKee. 'I cannot expect you to understand the pressure we are sometimes under,' he said. 'But I do appreciate your co-operation, your time, your willingness to assist us. If you want a lawyer present now then please call him.'

'I have nothing to hide, Detective Parrish,' McKee said. 'I think you know this by now. However, as I said before, I will not be bullied or harassed.'

'All I can say is that I am sorry for the trouble and upset we've caused you. You are not under arrest, and these interviews are being undertaken because you have been so helpful.'

'In what way?' McKee asked.

'Because we're still around the edges of this thing,' Parrish replied. 'Because we're still looking at the possibility that Lester Young might have been connected to this matter.'

McKee's eyes widened. 'I would find that really hard to believe,' he replied. 'I knew Lester for a long time, and I always held him in the highest regard.'

'I appreciate that, Mr McKee, but we cannot avoid the conclusive evidence that the disappearances and deaths of these girls are connected to Family Welfare. We just cannot get away from that. Two girls perhaps, three unlikely, but seven girls—'

'Seven? I thought there were only six?'

'Yes, sorry. You're right. Six girls. So, as I was saying, six girls go missing and wind up dead, and each of them is connected. That's far and away beyond the bounds of any coincidence.'

'I agree,' McKee replied. 'But Lester Young? He died back in December last year, and there have been murders since then, haven't there?'

'Yes, there have. But let's get off that for a moment. I wanted to ask you whether you had heard of something called Absolute Publications.'

McKee frowned. 'Absolute Publications? What is that?'

'It's a publishing firm, Richard.'

'Well yes, I gathered that, but what do they publish? Why might I have heard of them?'

'I'm not saying you have heard of them. I was just wondering *if* you had.'

'No, I can't say I have. What do they publish?'

'Well, I don't know for sure about everything that they publish, and as far as I know they're out of business now.'

'But you must know something otherwise you wouldn't ask me about it.'

'Well, I know that they publish pornographic magazines, Richard. I know that much about them.'

McKee opened his mouth to speak. He closed it again. He glanced back over his shoulder to Radick but said nothing. When he looked back at Parrish he seemed pale, a little worried.

'You *have* heard of them?' Parrish prompted.

'No,' McKee said suddenly. He spoke too quickly. He knew it. Parrish knew it.

'Richard?'

'Okay, so I used to read magazines like that—'

'Used to?'

'Christ, man, I'm a single guy. I've been divorced for three years. I don't get out much. I don't go on dates . . .' He looked embarrassed, awkward.

'I know exactly what you mean,' Parrish replied. He smiled reassuringly. He was trying to make McKee feel alright about reading stroke mags. He was trying to make it safe to talk.

'I mean, it's not against the law or anything—'

'Depends what's in them, Richard.'

'Meaning?'

'You know what I mean.'

McKee was silent. He did that about-to-speak-and-then-say-nothing thing a couple of times, and then he looked away towards the door.

'Did you go and see my ex-wife?'

'I can't answer any questions, Richard.'

'You went and saw her, didn't you? She told you that I used to read stuff like that. What did she do? Did she keep some of those things? Did she show you some of the magazines that I left there?'

'I can't answer that question, Richard.'

'Bitch!' McKee snapped suddenly. 'Fucking bitch!'

'Richard—'

'Jesus, man, the fucking divorce is done. It's over. What fucking right does she have involving herself in this—'

'Involving herself in what, Richard?'

'This case you're investigating. What the hell d'you think I'm talking about?'

'We just contacted her because we felt that she might remember you mentioning something in passing—'

'What? What are you talking about?'

'Back then. When you worked with Lester Young. One of these dead girls was connected to one of his cases, and you knew him, and we asked her whether she remembered you mentioning something about it at the time.'

'And?'

'I can't tell you what she said, Richard, you know that.'

McKee frowned. 'What the fuck is this? What's going on here?' He took his cell phone from his pocket. 'I'm calling my lawyer—'

Parrish paused for effect. It was obvious what he was doing, but he did it anyway. 'Do you think you need to call a lawyer, Richard?'

'Oh come on! Jesus Christ, this isn't fucking *Law and Order*.'

'No, it isn't, Richard, it's a great deal more serious than a TV show.'

'You know what I meant. Cut the bullshit theatrics, for Christ's sake. You think I have something to do with these disappearances, these murders? Is that what you think?'

'I'm looking at this with no preconceptions right now,' Parrish replied. 'I'm trying to maintain as open-minded a viewpoint as I can.'

'Bullshit, Detective, that's bullshit and you and I both know it.' McKee leaned forward. When he spoke again his voice was louder than normal, each word stressed carefully as if he was explaining something to a foreigner. 'I. Am. Not. The. Man. You. Want. You understand me? I am not who you are looking for.'

Parrish acted as if McKee hadn't spoken. 'My father was a cop, you know that?'

'No, I didn't know that, Detective. I would have no reason to know that.'

'Well, he was, and he used to say something. It was a long time before I really understood what he meant. He used to tell me that not all victims were created equal. You understand what that means?'

'Of course I do.'

'Well, you're a smarter man than me.'

'I can do without the sarcasm, Detective. You have to appreciate that I work with victims too.'

'I know you do, Richard, and that's why this case is possibly more disturbing than most. It's not just about young girls being abducted and murdered, it's about what happens to them between the abduction and the killing.'

'I have no idea what happens to them.'

'They wind up in magazines and films, Richard, that's what happens. They wind up in the sort of magazines that are published by Absolute, and other companies of that type. But those images, those stills you find in those magazines are not what we're really concerned with. What we're concerned with is the films that are made. You know the sort of thing I'm talking about, right?'

'Not personally no. I know *of* sex movies. Who doesn't? I don't watch sex movies if that's what you're asking.'

'I find it hard to believe that someone who buys and reads the kind of magazines that you do doesn't also watch films, Richard.'

'Well, I'm not saying I haven't ever watched films like that, but certainly not recently.'

'And can you recall the titles of any of the movies you might have seen in the past?'

McKee looked down at his hands, at the cell phone on the table in front of him. It was then that he seemed to notice how he was twisting his fingers together nervously. He placed them flat on the table. He looked back at Parrish without flinching. 'No,' he said emphatically.

'You're sure?'

'I'm sure.'

'What about a movie called *Hurting Bad*? You ever heard of that movie?'

'No, I haven't.'

'No need to hurry with this one, Richard. Take your time. Think about it.'

'I don't need to think about it. I have never seen a movie called *Hurting Bad*. I presume this is some kind of S&M thing. I don't watch that kind of thing.'

'I thought you said you didn't watch sex movies at all.'

'I don't. I didn't. Jesus, you know what I'm saying. When I used to watch sex movies I never used to watch *that* kind of movie.' McKee paused. He tried to smile. 'Look,' he said. 'I am not the man you are looking for. I understand what you're trying to do, and if I was in your position then I would probably be doing the same thing. I would really very much like to go now. There can't be any more questions you need to ask me. I have co-operated with you right down the line. I have come of my own volition. I have tried to be as helpful as I could. Anything more than this and we're heading in the direction of harassment, wouldn't you say?'

Parrish was silent. He looked right back at McKee until McKee started to fidget awkwardly.

McKee broke the deadlock. He laughed nervously. He got up from the chair. He retrieved his phone, buttoned his jacket. 'I have to go,' he said. 'I really have to go now. I'm sorry that I couldn't be of greater assistance to you, but I have things to attend to. If you need to speak to me again then you should understand that I will most definitely bring my lawyer. Not because I have something to hide, but because I am ignorant of the law and I don't want to be railroaded into something that—'

Parrish looked up. He smiled sympathetically. 'Railroaded, Mr McKee? What on earth gives you the impression that anyone's trying to railroad you?'

'Come on, Detective, we're not in kindergarten. I may not be a lawyer, but I have dealt with lawyers and with people from Child Services and County Adoption for most of my working life. I do know something. I am not a complete idiot.'

'No-one is suggesting that you are.'

'Then why are we doing this, eh? Why are you bringing me down here to answer questions that I have no answer for? Why am I the focus of your investigation?'

'What makes you think you are?'

'Jesus Christ, it's obvious. The stuff you're asking me, the fact that you've spoken to my ex-wife—'

'But you might not be the only person we're speaking to, Mr McKee. You might be one of several people at Family Welfare we're talking to. We might have visited any number of ex-wives and girlfriends and mistresses and God-only-knows who else in an attempt to make some sense of this. What gives you the impression that you are the focus of this investigation?'

'Nothing.'

'Have we charged you with anything?'

McKee glanced at Radick. He turned back to Parrish. 'No.'

'Have we even implied that we are looking at charging you? Have we suggested you bring a lawyer? Have we read you your rights? Have we even bothered taking notes or recording our conversations?'

McKee took a deep breath and exhaled slowly. 'No, Detective Parrish, you have not.'

'Then I find it difficult to understand why you are so paranoid.'

'I am not paranoid.'

Parrish smiled. 'I think you've been watching too many *Law and Order, Special Victims* episodes Richard, I really do. These things don't start and finish in an hour. A case like this – six dead girls over the better part of two years – doesn't tie up neatly with a bow. First line of questioning in any case like this is the family of the victim. In all of these cases, without exception, the immediate family are divorced, estranged, unreachable, unwilling to speak, and in many instances they are dead. These girls were all adopted, or on their way to being adopted. They all had a fresh start waiting for them, and then someone took that away, you understand?'

'Yes, I do.'

'So, as a parent, as a homicide detective, I find myself in a situation where I am damned if I will let this slide by. I have six dead teenagers, and from what I can see right now it looks like they were abducted for the purposes of pornographic exploitation, and when their purpose was served they were killed. I could be wrong. I could be far wide of the mark, but I don't think so. I start to ask questions, I start to dig a little deeper, I find a connection to Family Welfare, to Child Services, to the CAA. I start to talk to the employees and I find someone who was indirectly connected to these cases, or had at least some degree of access to their files, and he has a history of . . . let's just say he has an issue on his record, a small note that suggests he might have run into some difficulty regarding this area of predilection. You get me so far?'

'Yes, I do.'

'So we go speak to his ex-wife, and she tells us that he had a certain taste for a certain type of pornographic literature. She says there's still some in the house. Would we like to take it away? She is concerned that the kids might find it. We say we'll take it off her hands, and from what we can see there is nothing overtly illegal about this material, though there are some images that could be of girls who might have said they were older than they in fact were. This kind of thing happens, Richard. I'm sorry to say that it's not uncommon. We are interested, Richard, that's all, and though this could be about as far from you as you can get, it would still be very remiss of us not to follow it up with some degree of persistence and tenacity. You see where I'm coming from?'

McKee nodded. 'There are other people at Welfare that you are talking to?'

'I cannot answer that question, Richard.'

'Okay, so am I the only person you are talking to about this case?'

'No, Richard, you are not.'

McKee looked momentarily relieved. He stepped forward and sat down again. 'So I don't need a lawyer?'

'Your decision, Richard, really. I cannot tell you whether you need a lawyer or not.'

'But you're not planning to charge me with anything, right?'

'No, unless there's something you feel we should know that we haven't covered?'

'No, of course not. I haven't done anything that I could be charged for.'

'Well if that's the case then you're fine, Richard, just fine.'

Parrish got up. McKee followed suit.

'Thank you again for your time,' Parrish said.

McKee tried to smile. 'Not at all. I would say that if you need anything else then let me know, but I'm hoping that you don't need anything else.'

'So do I, Richard, so do I.' Parrish shook McKee's hand. 'Detective Radick here will show you out.'

SIXTY-EIGHT

'You are walking a very fine line, Frank. You are right on the edge with this guy.' Radick took off his jacket and sat down.

Parrish smiled sardonically. 'Well, you know what they say?'

'What's that?'

'If you're not close to the edge then you're taking up too much room.'

'It's not a matter for humor, Frank, I'm serious. He shares a few words with the wrong type of lawyer and we could find ourselves on the end of a harassment suit. I am also concerned that we might just have caused some more trouble for Carole Paretski.'

'I don't think he's stupid enough to say anything to her. He upsets her any further and she's just going to co-operate with us even more, and I think he realizes that.'

'Nevertheless—'

'I know, Jimmy,' Parrish interjected. 'But don't you just love the cat-and-mouse. He think he's fooled us. He thinks that we're just questioning him in the general line of the investigation.'

Radick frowned. 'We are . . . aren't we?'

Parrish seemed taken aback for a moment. 'You don't have any doubts, do you?'

'Doubts about what?'

'About McKee? About McKee being the guy?'

'Christ, Frank, of course I have doubts.'

'You're not serious, surely?'

'Of course I'm serious. We don't have anything on this guy. I've been there for every interview, Frank, and I don't see anything but some poor schmuck who's wife dumped him because he had a thing for cheerleaders—'

'You missed the signs, Jimmy, you missed the signs.'

'Signs? What signs?'

'It's fine. Don't worry about it. You couldn't see his face while we were talking.'

'I heard what he had to say though, Frank. So what are you talking about – signs?'

'His eyes, his hands, the way he reacted when I backed off. You see how relieved he was?'

'Jesus, Frank, I think I'd be relieved if all of a sudden I got the idea that the guy that was harassing me about being a multiple murderer told me that he wasn't really that serious about it.'

Parrish was shaking his head before Radick had finished speaking. 'No, Jimmy, those were the signs. These guys don't think the way we think. They just don't. It's good that they don't otherwise we'd all be doing that shit. It's like I said before, they're arrogant. They pretend they're not, but they're arrogant. They have whatever they're into, the girls, the snuff movies, the torture sex, all that, but there's an element of it that tells them they have to challenge the police. They have to prove to themselves and the rest of the world that they're smarter than everyone. They don't want to get caught. Of course not. But you know something? There's a tiny little bit of them that does want to get caught. Why? Because they want the recognition. They want the world to know what they did, how long they got away with it for . . .'

'Hang on a minute there, Frank. As far as I can see we are not any closer to nailing McKee for anything than we were a week ago. So he's a loser. So he likes to read stroke mags. So fucking what? You know how many people read that shit? That isn't against the law. Like it or not, that's the truth. There's no way we can prove that any of the girls in those mags were underage when the pictures were taken, and compared to some of the stuff I've been looking at in Archives it's pretty mild. Even if we did prove it we wouldn't have a case against McKee, it would be a case against the publishers. Second thing is this movie. So there was an ad for the movie in one of the magazines. We have a picture of Jennifer doing things that no seventeen-year-old should be doing against her will, but we have no proof that she did it against her will. Hell, Frank, we don't know anything about the circumstances of their disappearances or their murders. We just know they went missing, and then they were dead. Jennifer could have done those pictures weeks before she went missing, months even, and she could have done it willingly. We don't know. That's the thing here. We have no proof.'

Parrish was smiling, almost to himself. 'Which is where the intuitive certainty comes in, Jimmy. There's a line they cross, and once they cross that line you know you're into something—'

'What the fuck are you talking about, Frank? Lines? Intuition? Jesus, man, listen to yourself. We do not have a case against Richard McKee. He has not been charged because we have nothing to charge him with. He has not been advised to get a lawyer because he doesn't need to get a lawyer. If I didn't know you I'd think you were harboring some irrational obsession about this guy. Fact of the matter is that I do know you, and I still think it's an irrational obsession. Leave the guy alone. You heard what he said. Next time we ask him down here for questioning he's gonna bring a lawyer—'

'I'm not going to bring him down here for more questions.'

'Thank fuck for that.'

'I don't need to. I've got all the information on him I need.'

'What?'

'He's the guy, Jimmy. I mean it. You can hear me out on this or you can call me crazy. *He is the guy*. It's more obvious to me now than ever. In fact, the more you talk to me about leaving him alone the more I understand how fucking clever he's been.'

'Aah for Christ's sake, Frank, will you just drop it? What are you going to do? Apply for an arrest that will get turned down? Try and get a search warrant for his house?'

'No, Jimmy, I'm just going to wait for him to make his next move, and we'll be ready.'

'You're serious aren't you? You really believe that Richard McKee has abducted and killed six teenage girls in the last two years.'

'I do, Jimmy, I do. And I think that very soon he's going to go after number seven.'

'Why, Frank? Why in God's name would he do that if he thinks we're onto him?'

'Because we've got him excited, Jimmy. We've got him all excited again. He's got to prove to himself that he can outwit us, and like I said before, the more we talk to him about it the more turned on he gets. He's gonna go for another one. I know it. He's gonna do it, and it'll be soon.'

'Jesus. If this is what it's going to be like then I don't know that I can go on working with you, Frank. Seriously, this is getting to be too much.'

'Not yet, Jimmy, not yet. Don't bail out on me yet, okay? A little while longer. A few days, a week maybe. Hang in there with me on this one. If I'm wrong then I'll quit, like I said. If I'm right then I'll quit anyway, but you'll get a blue ribbon for your first case in Homicide and Valderas will love you.'

'A week, Frank. I can agree to that. A week longer on this case, and then we go elsewhere. We start looking at some of the other things that are backing up behind us.'

Parrish nodded and extended his hand. 'Deal,' he said. 'A week, and if we haven't nailed McKee for his involvement in six murders then we'll drop the case completely.'

'You're serious?'

'I am.'

'Okay,' Radick said. 'A week it is.'

They shook. Radick leaned back in his chair. He looked out of the window for a moment and wondered if Frank Parrish was his karma for sins in another life.

SIXTY-NINE

Parrish was home by seven. He should have eaten but he had no appetite. Twice he picked up the phone, and twice he put it down again. He paced the kitchen, paused ahead of the refrigerator, opened the door and looked inside. He closed the door again and resumed pacing.

At twenty to eight he picked up the phone once more and dialed a number. He stood with his eyes closed as it rang. Just as he was about to hang up it was answered.

'Hello,' he said. 'It's me.'

There was a hesitation at the other end, and then, 'Jesus, that voice is a blast from the past.'

'It's been a long time, Ro—' and then he cut himself short. No names. Not on the phone.

'How have you been?'

'Better,' Parrish replied.

'And I can only assume that the request I made last time we spoke has fallen on deaf ears?'

'Look, it's not that simple. I'm stuck. Really stuck.'

'As you were last time, or have I got that wrong?'

'No, you're not wrong. This is important—'

'You know the deal. I helped you out last time and I shouldn't have done. Christ, I shouldn't even be speaking to you.'

'But it's been three . . . no, four years. You ever consider how many times I could have called you in the last four years and I never did?'

'I know. I understand that. But you know something? That's the way it should be.'

'I need your help.'

'I can't give you any help.'

'Listen to me . . . I *need* your help.'

There was silence at the other end. Parrish could hear

breathing, that was all. 'Look,' he went on. 'If I didn't think it was serious, I mean *really* serious, then I wouldn't call you. You know that.'

'How serious?'

'Six. Another one imminent. I'm sure of that.'

'Men, women—'

'Teenage girls . . . snuff movies, I think.'

'Oh, what a wonderful world we live in.'

'So?'

'So what?'

'Will you help me?'

'Depends entirely on what you mean by *help*.'

'Meet me. An hour. Maybe less. I just need someone outside the loop to talk to. I need to tell you what we've got . . . well, what we *haven't* got actually, and see if there's any way out of this.'

There was silence once more. It seemed to go on until midnight.

'This is not good.'

'I know,' Parrish replied. 'I'm sorry. If there was someone else I could talk to—'

'Did you do something that means you can't go through standard channels?'

'I did something. It doesn't relate to standard channels. I know something that can't go on record. It may be nothing . . . I don't know what the fuck it might or might not mean. I'm in a jam, you know? I'm in a fucking tight spot and I need to know if there's a way out.'

'There probably isn't, knowing you.'

'I know, but I have to try.'

'Jesus Christ, you really are—'

'I know. A pain in the ass. A liability. I've said that if this doesn't fold in a week I'm quitting.'

'Oh, it's one of those moments is it?'

'I'm asking you. I'm *begging* you to help me out on this.'

'Time is it?'

'Quarter to eight.'

'You still live where you used to?'

'Yes.'

'Meet you at the second place we met. Half past eight.'

The line went dead in his ear.

Parrish stood for a moment with the receiver in his hand. He could hear the thudding of his own heart. It was another minute before he hung up.

SEVENTY

Parrish wondered whether he'd even visited the diner in the previous four years. He couldn't recall, not clearly. Situated on the corner of Park and Ryerson, a stone's throw from the expressway, it was no more than half a dozen blocks northeast of his apartment. He walked, and even taking his time he was there at quarter after. He took a booth in the back right-hand corner, ordered coffee, and waited.

'I cannot stay long,' was Ron's opening gambit.

Parrish smiled. 'I don't expect you to stay long.'

Ron sat down, and it was then that he perhaps first looked at Frank Parrish properly, because he said, 'You don't look so good.'

'I've been better.'

'You still single?'

Parrish nodded.

'You need someone to take care of you, Frank. You don't look well.'

Parrish shrugged. 'Been better, been worse.'

'You want a refill?'

'Sure.'

Ron beckoned the waitress, asked for coffee for himself, a refill for Parrish.

'So whose nightmare are you chasing these days?' Ron asked.

Parrish laid out the facts that he possessed – quickly, succinctly – and in doing so reminded himself that he had very few facts at all.

'Sounds like the cosmetic alterations, the hair, the nails, whatever he's doing . . . that's your signature, right? However, we don't have all the answers at the Bureau. You do know that, right?'

'I know, Ron, I know. All I'm hoping for is perhaps a

different angle. Something I can go after this guy with. Something that might crack the façade and get me inside.'

'There's a lot of assumption on your part,' Ron replied. 'Sounds to me that you really don't have anything on him at all.'

'I get that, but I feel so certain it's—'

Ron raised his hand. 'Looking at it purely with a view that he *is* the guy, okay? Taking all of these six cases as victims of the same guy, he's more than likely a commuter. He's going out to different locations to get his victims. He does whatever he does, and then he dumps them. If he is making films then I doubt very much that he's using his own house. He could be. A basement maybe, an upstairs room that he considers secure, but from what you've told me I get the impression he's not working alone.'

'I thought about that.'

'And these girls all look similar. Blonde, pretty, slim, good-looking kids, right?'

'Yes, they are.'

'And what does his daughter look like?'

Parrish shook his head. 'I actually don't know. I saw a picture of her, but it was from a while back and it wasn't very clear.'

'Tell you now, she's either going to look a lot like the victims or she's gonna going to look precisely the opposite.'

'Explain.'

'Anger-retaliatory is a tough call on this, Frank. The victim symbolizes someone, usually someone you want that you can't have, or someone that the perp believes has wronged him in some way. Anger-retaliatory victims are mostly unplanned and very violent. Your guy is a planner, and as far as the violence is concerned, well, he just doesn't make the grade. The anger-excitement thing? That comes out of a need to terrify, to cause as much suffering as they possibly can before killing the subject. They go at it like it's a military operation. Everything down to the last detail. Where, when, how, everything rehearsed time and time again before the actual event. If your guy is selecting his victims from files, especially if he is ensuring that none of the victims can be directly connected to him from a professional standpoint, then he is a planner. That takes it out of the realm of anger-retaliatory.'

'You get crossovers between the categories, right?'

'For sure. These categories are not cast in stone, Frank, they're loose outlines. There's no single killer that's the same as any other, believe me.'

'And the thing you said about the daughter?'

'Well, that would be an interesting thing to know. The possibility that he has been filming the daughter from the crawl-space above her bedroom. He could have a fixation on his own daughter, an incestuous thing. Well, he can't fuck his own daughter so he goes after girls that look like her. And in order to convince himself that he's not an incestuous pedophile, he makes these cosmetic alterations so they look slightly different and slightly older. How old's the kid?'

'Fourteen.'

Ron leaned back in the chair and shook his head. 'Thing is you just don't know what the fuck is going on with these guys until you get them, and then you only get what they want to tell you. Whatever information we have managed to collate over the years at the FBI is bound to have question-able elements in it. After all, we are dealing with some of the world's best liars.'

'And what if the daughter doesn't look like the victims?'

'So if his daughter is a bespectacled, overweight brunette, then he's upset that she doesn't fit the acceptable social model. Maybe she's had difficulty at school, maybe she's been excluded from things because she's not the cute blonde that he hoped she would be. Then it becomes a matter of revenge against all those that made her feel differ-ent and unwanted.'

'If she looks like her mother she's going to be the former, not the latter.'

'Okay, then he's fucking his daughter by proxy. Here we get into the destroy-what-you-have-created thing, but at the same time empathizing enough with the victim so as not to go overboard on the torture and pain thing. That could ex-plain the rohypnol. If they're drugged they can't fight back, if they don't fight back you don't have to restrain or hurt them.'

'I think the first ones were hurt,' Parrish interjected. 'This movie, *Hurting Bad* – well, I think the title gives away the game, don't you?'

'Like I said before, Frank, you have no way of knowing how this thing evolved. He could have been working with someone on the first ones, and then gone solo because he didn't like the pain thing. He could have started out hurting them and then graduated to a more sophisticated way of doing what he needed to do—'

'*Needed* to do?'

'Sure. It's never a want with these characters. Always a need. They can't control it. It resolves something. Always. Beneath everything, when you get right down to the core truth of what's going on with these guys, there's always some difficulty, some problem, some deeply-inlaid issue that they're resolving by doing this. And the other thing that makes me feel that we've got something very personal going on here is the strangulation.'

'Meaning what?'

'Strangulation and suffocation are non-invasive. It's not a gun, it's not a knife, it's not beating someone's head in with a hammer or a brick or something. There's no blood, there no actual visible physical damage aside from a few bruises perhaps. Strangle someone, suffocate them and they look pretty much the same, at least for a little while. You can sit them up, lie them down, put them in a chair, talk to them, explain yourself, even fuck them some more. You can have them be around you without being constantly reminded of the fact that you just took their life from them.'

'And he would do this?'

'Absolutely he would. These guys hold on to the victims as long as they can, right until the point that it becomes unavoidably obvious that they are dead. They rigor up, they start to decompose, then they ain't the sweetheart anymore and they have to go. Oh, and the fact that he's strangled at least one of them with a scarf implies guilt, implies a desire to be as gentle as possible, and also removes him from the physical reality of killing by insuring that he does not have to have physical contact with the victims as they die.'

Parrish nodded. He wanted more coffee but he didn't want to break the flow of what he was being told.

'I think if you managed to get a look inside the guy's house, that's assuming that he is the guy, then I believe you would find an exceptionally well organized, immaculately clean place. This is the kind of guy that arranges his canned goods alphabetically and by expiry date.' Ron smiled drily. 'But, of course, you are not going to have a chance to look inside his place, are you, Frank?'

Parrish shook his head. 'Way it's going right now I don't see that we're going to get a chance to look at anything. He's got us boxed out, Ron, seriously boxed out, and there's nothing probative that gives me probable cause for a search and seizure, a further interrogation—'

'You know where he lives. Go and see him at home. Go tell him that you wanted to speak to him about how he's co-operated, that you are very grateful for his time, and that you wanted to apologize for any degree of harassment he might have felt.'

'I have considered that, but I don't want to tip my hand any further, and I sure as hell don't want him to slow up on his plans.'

'The proverbial rock and a hard place,' Ron said. 'Do we go after the guy and blow any possibility of securing a conviction, or do we wait until he moves again and risk losing another victim?'

'Right.'

'There is one thing that is puzzling me, and that's the timescale. Tell me again.'

'First one, at least the first one that we're tying to this pattern, was back in October 2006.'

'And that's the Baumann girl, the one you found the picture of?'

'No, the first one was the Melissa Schaeffer girl, the one we found in the trash can. Jennifer Baumann was the second one, and that was January of 2007. Third was August, fourth was December, and then there was nine months until Rebecca Lange at the start of this month—'

'And the last one was the girl in the box back of Brooklyn Hospital ten days ago.'

'Yes, that's right.'

Ron was silent for a moment, and then he leaned forward. 'I think you've missed some, Frank . . . not *you* specifically, but I don't think you have all the victims. The pattern doesn't make sense. Three months between the first and second, then seven months, then four months, then nine months and then a week?' He shook his head. 'I'm thinking that there are other girls outside of the Family Welfare connection. Either that, or perhaps you have a cycle that isn't based on predetermination.'

'Meaning?'

'Situational dynamics, Frank. Situational dynamics, and also something that the profilers are looking at now that's called the Exceptional Human Experience.'

Parrish frowned.

'It's not complex. Situational dynamics you understand. Simply the environmental, familial, social and educational factors that contribute to the person becoming who they are. There's a pattern to these things. Physically and sexually abusive parents or relatives, social alienation, a complete collapse of self-worth. They start off torturing animals, then they graduate to arson, then it's arson and manslaughter, then murder. Some of them have a pattern within themselves, and that can manifest itself in both who they kill, and in most cases *when* they kill. Lunar cycles, harvest moons, every seven Sundays, whatever. Then there's this new idea creeping in. This EHE principle. This works on the basis that every serial killer is continually trying to stop themselves from killing further. It's like the alcoholic who has to stop drinking, the kleptomaniac who has to stop stealing . . . that underlying knowledge that what you're doing is wrong, and the battle that rages inside the person. This Exceptional Human Experience thing is simply something that occurs in the individual's life that tips them over the edge of self-control. It empowers the impulse to kill to such a degree that they cannot stop it. It overwhelms their power of choice completely, and they have to go find a victim. The need has been externally generated, they seize the opportunity, and the original situational dynamics help them rationalize their actions. They don't have to deal with the guilt until after the fact, and by then it's too late. Someone else is dead. That could be the case with your guy. There is no pattern. He just holds himself back as long as he can, and then he explodes. That is a possibility. However, I do believe that in this case it's simply that there are other girls and you've missed them as part of the serial. We have well in excess of three quarters of a million child disappearances a year in the US, and we find a depressingly small percentage of them.'

'I don't want to hear that.'

'Hear it. Deal with it. This is the nature of the beast, my friend. I don't have to tell you that.'

'So what do I do? Where do I go from here?'

Ron smiled. 'You tell me what you're not telling me.'

'There isn't anything I'm not telling you,' Parrish replied. He felt the knot in his lower gut tighten a good deal more.

Ron lifted his coffee cup and drained it. He made as if to get up.

'What are you doing?'

'I'm leaving, Frank, what the fuck do you think I'm doing? You ask me to meet you, I meet you. You want to tell me something, I listen. I ask you to tell me everything and you bullshit me. You and I did a good thing four years ago, and you helped me out. Okay, so maybe we didn't follow the rules precisely, but we did it and we got the guy. But we said back then that neither owed the other anything. That's what we agreed. No debts, no dues, nothing. I'm not down here for the good of my health. This is all off-the-record. It has to be, just because of the nature of what we do and who we are. The FBI owes the NYPD nothing and vice versa. When we collaborate it's because we want to, not because we have to. I've sat here and listened, and now we're done and I'm going home.'

Parrish looked up at Ron. 'I think I might know who he's after next.'

Ron paused for a moment, and then he sat down heavily. 'And now you're going to tell me that you're the only one who knows this, and that the way you found this information could get you suspended, perhaps even fired.'

'I'm already on pay hold,' Parrish replied. 'I don't have a drivers' license. They're waiting for me like vultures. One more fuck-up and I'm out on my ass. It's cheaper this way. They don't have to pay me off or give me a full pension.'

'Jesus Christ, Frank, what the fuck is it with you?'

Parrish smiled sardonically. 'If I knew that I'd market it 'cause I know everyone would love to have a little.'

'What did you do?'

'I looked someplace I shouldn't have.'

'And what did you find?'

'A file on a girl that looks like the others.'

'And was it one of his own cases?'

'No.'

'In his house?'

'His car.'

Ron inhaled deeply and sighed. 'Fuck,' he said, and the single syllable was said with such certainty and emphasis that it hit Parrish like a physical blow.

Perhaps then – in that split-second – he knew that he'd pushed things so far off-kilter that there was no going back.

'I don't know what to tell you,' Ron said. 'Whatever it is that you might have found out . . . well, you know as well as I do that you can't use this information, not only because it was gained illegally, but because it wouldn't do you any good. Any arrest or interrogation secured on the basis of illegally obtained evidence is useless, Frank. You know this.'

'Of course I know it, but it was something I had to find out. I had to reassure myself that I wasn't chasing this guy for nothing.'

'And what has it proved? Nothing, right? He's supposed to have Family Welfare case files. He's meant to have that stuff. It's his job, isn't it?'

Parrish shook his head. 'I don't think this girl was his day job, Ron, I think it was part of his extra-curricular plans.'

'All of this based on nothing but coincidence, circumstantial evidence, and the incontrovertible certainty of gut reaction.'

Parrish hesitated. He didn't want to sound foolish, but he did. There was no escaping it.

Ron looked at his watch. 'Persistence, Frank. Persistence, hard work, stubbornness, and an unrelenting willingness to stay late, work harder still, persist even more. Those are the primary reasons cases get resolved. You know that. I don't even know why I'm here. I cannot sanction anything. I cannot give you any information you don't already have. I can give you suppositions, theories, perhaps confirm one or two suspicions you might have regarding rationale and motivation, but aside from that I am useless.'

'But you're a G-Man,' Parrish said. 'You're one of Hoover's superheroes.'

'Hoover was a closet transvestite, paranoid control freak, but we don't put that in the brochures.' Ron paused for a moment, and then he leaned forward. 'I'll tell you one thing more, and that's all I'll say. They keep mementos. Always, invariably, they keep mementos. I could tell you to not cross the lines, Frank, but you already did that. It didn't get you anyplace, but you did it anyway. Seriously, you're in so fucking deep already you're pretty much all done and finished. And if you make a decision to push this further? Well, what can I tell you that I already haven't? There will be mementos, and they will be close to him, and however much he knows he should get rid of them, he won't. Whatever you want to do with that piece of information is entirely up to you.' He moved out along the seat and stood for a moment looking down at Parrish. 'As is always the case, this conversation never happened. Your secret is safe with me because you never told me, okay? Whatever you do now is your call, not mine.'

Parrish didn't respond.

Ron reached out and gripped Parrish's shoulder. 'You take care now. Find the truth for sure, but don't kill yourself in the process.'

He left. Parrish watched him go. He asked the waitress for a refill and a danish, and then he called the Precinct and got Carole Paretski's number.

She picked up on the second ring.

'Ms Paretski? Frank Parrish. I just need to know something. Your daughter . . . Sarah, right? What does she look like?'

He paused, listened.

'No, of course not. No danger whatsoever. I just need to know for a physical profile analysis thing we're doing.'

Parrish nodded, and his expression changed subtly.

'A little taller than average, slim, blonde hair, blue eyes . . . your regular cheerleader, right?'

Parrish closed his eyes and nodded.

'Yes of course I will. Yes, absolutely. You take care now, Carole.'

He set his phone on the table, and he lifted his coffee cup. He held it in mid-air as he considered what to do next. There wasn't really any consideration at all, it was simply a moment of reflection. As Ron had so eloquently put it, he was useless for anything else. The case they had worked on together four years before had resulted in a man's life being saved, perhaps two men. The simple fact was that those potential victims had never even been aware of what was happening around them. They had been targeted, and then the threat against them was removed silently, swiftly, expertly. They were none the wiser. Parrish *knew* that Amanda Leycross was McKee's next intended victim. He needed to remove the threat without Amanda Leycross ever realizing what had happened, what might have happened, the fact that she was spending her days being watched, considered, targeted. To live one's life knowing that a killer had almost taken that life away from you . . . well, such a thing would not rest easy in anyone's mind. Was there something about you that made you a victim? If you had been chosen once, then would you be chosen again?

No, Amanda Leycross needed to walk right through this unscathed and unaware.

Parrish got up. He left behind half a cup of coffee and a danish barely touched.

Perhaps it was true that some things were so well-hidden they would never be known, that some cases would never be solved. Perhaps all victims were not created equal. Maybe there were people all over the city who wouldn't make it to Christmas. The Leycross girl would not be one of them.

There were mementos. Always. Invariably. They would be close to McKee. Parrish had to find them. And if that meant the end of his career then so be it.

SEVENTY-ONE

'I slept fine, better than I have done for a while.'

'And how much did you drink?'

'Last night? Last night I didn't drink anything.'

'This is good, Frank. This is progress.'

'I believe so, yes. And I have to tell you that I feel more settled in myself.'

'How so?'

'Like I've resolved some things. It's hard to explain. Perhaps it's nothing more complicated than spending all this time talking about stuff. It's all baggage, right?'

'A lot of it, yes.'

'And you carry it around and around and around, and when you actually get a chance to put the suitcases down and look inside them you find that you've been carrying a lot of worthless crap.'

'Some of it has value, surely?'

'Perhaps some of it, yes, but mostly it's your own unfounded fears about what other people might think, and what other people really meant when they said something, and the rest of it is indecision.'

'I must say that you sound a good deal more positive today than almost at any time since you've been coming here.'

'Well, like I said, I feel like I've resolved something important.'

'Do you want to tell me what that is?'

'Not really, no. Well, I'll say that I have an idea about where I should go from here, what I should do with myself—'

'Career-wise you mean?'

'No, nothing as dramatic as that. More like my attitude

towards what I'm dealing with, where to go with the current case.'

'You feel it's going to break?'

'Yes I do.'

'What has happened? Have you made some good progress with your case – this man you suspect?'

'I have, yes.'

'That's good. Really good. I'm very pleased to hear it. It highlights the pattern we spoke of before, the point where you start to think about things other than the internal. I believe that you're now at the stage where we can – we should – start really talking about tomorrow as opposed to today, about your plans, the direction you're going in. This relates to your life, how you'll deal with your kids as they make their own lives – their careers and marriages or whatever. I also think we need to start looking at whether or not you are going to spend the rest of your life alone, or if you need to start considering the possibility of a new relationship.'

'Is this a roundabout way of asking me out on a date, Doctor? Because, you know, if you want to go on a date you only have to say so.'

'Frank . . .'

'I know, I know, I'm only kidding. I get what you say. It makes sense, but it's Friday now. I think you should give me the weekend to get this thing all wrapped up, and then we'll start talking about all that stuff you were just saying.'

'Did you listen to what I was saying?'

'Of course I did. Jesus, Marie, what do you think I am? Ignorant?'

'No, Frank, I don't think you're ignorant. I just think we need to start tackling these issues, and seeing as we've made some progress I don't want to backslide.'

'I'm not going to backslide. I'm not planning on drinking myself into a coma this weekend, if that's what you're worried about. This thing is going to end, and once it has you're going to get a hell of a lot more of my attention.'

'So the weekend?'

'Sure, the weekend. Skip our session tomorrow, Sunday is

as it is, and then we'll get together again on Monday morning.'

'Right. If that's what you want to do, then Monday it is. And have a think about what I've mentioned. You know – the future, where you go from here, new relationships . . . okay?'

'Okay.'

'Excellent. Have a good weekend, Frank.'

'I plan to.'

SEVENTY-TWO

'You okay, Frank?'

Parrish looked up. He'd been staring out of the window, unaware of anyone else in the room. Radick was looking at him quizzically.

'Okay? Sure I'm okay. Why d'you ask?'

Radick shrugged. 'You seem elsewhere.'

'I was thinking about my father.'

'What about your father?'

Parrish smiled drily. 'Nothing. Nothing about my father, Jimmy.'

What could he have told Radick? *My father was a crook. He was the best of the best – apparently – but really he was a fucking crook. A good one sure, but as corrupt as they came.*

Parrish had left Marie Griffin's office an hour before. Since that time he'd thought of nothing but his father. The Mighty John Parrish. He remembered when he was killed, what they reported as having happened, what had *really* happened, and he remembered also how he'd felt in that moment. There was no other way to spell it. Frank Parrish had been *relieved*.

September 30th, 1992. Eleven days time and it would be sixteen years since it happened. Sometimes it felt like yesterday, other times it felt like an entirely different life. Parrish had been twenty-eight years old, married the better part of seven years, Robert was all of six, Caitlin just four. Clare had been more of the woman he married, less of the nightmare she became. Later, after the divorce, Parrish had asked himself whether his father's death had been a significant factor in the beginning of the marital dissolution. Clare and John had been close. John Parrish called her *the daughter I never had*. She took his death badly. She had to be sedated after the funeral, and then she spent a month moping around the house in sweats, her hair unwashed, chain-smoking, drinking vodka after lunch. She snapped out of it soon enough. The kids pulled her through far more than he had. He had yet to be made Detective; that wouldn't come for another four years. He was still busting his hump, taking on extra shifts, doing the legwork and groundwork and donkey-work that he'd been told was the road to success. Bullshit. Making Detective was as much about *showing up and not fucking up* as anything else.

The events of that day were clear in his mind, as clear now as they had been a decade and a half earlier. Whoever hit them hit them both. John Parrish and his long-time partner, George Buranski. George used to come over with his wife, Marie. Marie was all bouffant hair and cheap perfume. She brought angel food cake every time. She made it herself, and it tasted like crap. How someone could make angel food cake taste that bad Parrish didn't know, but somehow she managed it. They'd stay a few hours, Marie talking to Frank's mother, Katherine. Cop wives together. They knew precisely what John and George were discussing in back of the den, out in the yard with their Buds and burgers, sitting in front of the house in George's car like there were listening devices planted in the living room and the kitchen. Paranoid as hell, the pair of them. Sometimes George left with a brown paper grocery bag stacked with fifty-dollar bills. Sometimes he brought one with him and left it behind. Frank knew to say nothing, ask nothing, look nowhere but straight ahead. He knew to say *Thank you, Marie* when she gave him a bottle of Crown Royal for his birthday, another for Christmas. That was the best these people could do. Tens of thousands of dollars, and all they could come up with was Crown Royal and angel food cake. Cheap bastards.

So September 1992. Things had been on the upslide for years. The money was coming in, very little of it was going out. The Saints were cleaning up left, right and center. The Brooklyn Organized Crime Task Force was into everything that was worth being into. IAD did their periodic check-ups; IAD gave them a clean bill. And then something went bad. To this day Parrish had been unable to work out precisely what had happened, but it related to a bank on Lafayette near the Classon Avenue subway station. The Saints never did their own grunt-work. They weren't the workers, they were the management. Parrish had looked into it a little later, carefully peering round the edges of the internal investigation. His father had been involved. People were obviously concerned about what Frank might know, what Frank might say. Last thing they needed was the cop-son of the most decorated anti-organized crime, OCCB/BOCTF veteran spilling his guts on Channel 9. He got looks and comments in the corridors. *You okay there, Frankie? Everything alright at home, Frankie? Hey, Frankie, how's your ma doing? She holding up?* It went that way for a moment or so, and then they figured he was good. He wasn't gonna bust open like an overripe watermelon. He was going to keep it in-house, under wraps, close to his chest.

It was then that he'd started looking. Carefully at first, checking out what had been reported about the heist that took place that Wednesday afternoon at East Coast Mercantile & Savings. It wasn't a major league bank. Routine day-to-day traffic, three ATMs in the street, one inside; four tellers, a loan advisor, a mortgage guy and a business consultant. Beyond that there was a manager, an assistant manager, a duty security guard. He was an ex-cop called Mitchell Warner, right out of Brooklyn's 15th, and evidently he had been their inside man. Of course that small fact never came to light, but reading between the lines – taking into consideration that Warner was in the restroom when the heist kicked off, the fact that they knew he was in there and had someone waiting outside the door for when he exited, and most of all the fact that he was found in his car with a *self-administered* .25 caliber bullet in his head eight hours after the fact . . . well, road signs were road signs and they led only one way as far as Frank Parrish was concerned.

The heist was carried out by four men. It went according to plan. They entered the bank at eleven forty-one a.m., exited at eleven fifty-six. Across the street was a barbershop, and it was from there that an off-duty cop called Richard Jackson had seen them. He came out with his hair wet and his .38 drawn. He was not on the Saints payroll, couldn't have been, for if he had been he would've known to leave well alone. This was official business, no question about it, and the last thing they needed was some gung-ho jarhead uniform gatecrashing the party. But gatecrash it he did, and got a gut full of double-ought for his trouble. He was thrown back through the plate glass window of the barbershop, and the four men were away like Thunderbolt and Lightfoot. Had it not been for the dead cop it would have wound up another unsolved matter for Robbery. The Feds would have trodden on everyone's toes, but they would only have trodden so long. They were as underpaid and overworked as everyone else. No, it was definitely the dead cop that soured the pie. All of a sudden Richard Jackson was a hero, an off-duty cop in a barbershop that tried to do the right thing. He didn't have a radio, couldn't call for back-up, had asked the barber to call 911, which he did. But 911 responses were always minutes, never seconds, and the speed at which these things unfolded meant that by the time they got to the scene most of the damage was done. Whoever was going to get shot was shot already. Whoever was going to die had already done so. In that instance it was Jackson, and whoever might have come along from IAD and Robbery to make it go away couldn't. Not this time.

And as far as killing two cops were concerned, it was easy enough. Someone calls some business in for the Task Force, John Parrish and George Buranski are dispatched, another member of the Saints is waiting for them and that's the whole show. The Unit has the emergency call-out on file, and whoever made that call was smart enough to use a phone booth and pass it through the switchboard so it couldn't be traced. So now there were two dead cops in a derelict house near Ferris Street. Frank Parrish could only later surmise that his father and George Buranski were the go-betweens. They had dealt with the bank crew, with the security guard; they had made whatever arrangements were required, and they were the ones who could have connected the job to Internal Affairs, the Brooklyn Task Force, the head of the unit himself, Captain James Barry. So they had to go. John Parrish and George Buranski were good officers. They would be sorely missed. They would be buried with full honors, and their wives would receive the pension that was due them. The last chapter was written, the book was closed. The security guard from East Coast Mercantile, ex-cop Mitchell Warner, so overwhelmed was he by his dereliction of duty, said failure resulting in the death of a fellow officer, that he took his own life only hours later. Frank Parrish knew that Warner no more took his own life than Richard Jackson had, no more than his own father and George Buranski.

It had been a business matter, all of it, and business such as this was kept in-house for the good of everyone.

James Barry, ex-head of the Brooklyn Organized Crime Task Force, had long-since retired. The Task Force, at least in that unholy incarnation, had been disbanded back in 2000, but their legacy lived on. You caught sight of it every once in a while when some old-hand mobster was dragged in. He would ask to speak to so-and-so or such-and-such, believing still that the right word in the right ear would see them home for fettuccine and cannolis with the grandkids. When informed that so-and-so or such-and-such was retired or dead, they would start to sweat.

Frank Parrish's legacy was a dead father, a dead mother, the ghosts of the past, a sense of guilty conscience that he had been a part of that – at least indirectly – and that people were dead that shouldn't have been because of John Parrish. Talking about it with Marie Griffin had been important in more ways than one. Did he believe that it had had some inherent therapeutic value? No more than the value anyone would gain by talking about something. Did he believe that he had *let go*? Did he hell. He'd lived in the shadow of John Parrish his whole life, and the shadow was still very visibly there. Did it matter? No more than any other detail of his fucked-up life. Clare. Robert. Caitlin. Jimmy Radick. Richard McKee and the snuff movies. He'd meant what he'd said to Radick. If he was wrong on this one then he was going to quit. He was not wrong. He couldn't be. Not again.

SEVENTY-THREE

Friday dissolved somewhere. Parrish was uncertain where it went. He and Radick talked around in circles until lunchtime, and then they both went down to Archives to see if there was any further evidence of Absolute Films and the work that they had undertaken to further Jennifer's short-lived cinematic career.

Erickson gave them unlimited access. 'Knock yourselves out,' he said, and left them to it.

Parrish – no stranger to such material – was nevertheless reminded of the very darkest edges of human depravity and degradation. At what point did people become uncontrollably driven to do such things to one another? And why? For sexual satisfaction? Dominance? Power over life and death? And at what point did it become necessary to cross the line . . . He did not know, and neither, he believed, did anyone else.

Everyone has thoughts – cruel, destructive, wicked, vindictive – thoughts sometimes harbored for months and years against people whom we believe should suffer ignominy and retribution for some wrong they have perpetrated. But these remain just thoughts. We withhold ourselves from action, perhaps because we have our own built-in censor; or perhaps because we believe in the fundamental balance of all things and are concerned for the harm that might come our way if we enact our own strains of viciousness.

But those who *did* terrible things, thought Parrish, were only a tiny minority when measured against the vast majority of those who only *thought*. Thought was no sin. Action, when directed against the peace and dignity of the individual, of the society – that was the sin. It was there in the law books. It was in the moral structure of the community. It was woven into the very fabric of society. And yet now, here, sitting with Radick in a basement office of Vice Archives, reminded of what had happened to these girls, he fixed his resolve on his intended course of action. The single shot of Jennifer had been enough. And perhaps Richard McKee was not guilty of all the sins of Man, but he was sure guilty of something . . .

Guilty enough to warrant the extraordinary measures that Parrish was going to take? He believed so.

They'd had enough by four, both of them. They boxed up the material that Erickson had left and returned it to the rightful storage unit. They had only scratched the surface.

'It's endless,' Radick said as they were exiting the building. 'We could go on looking for ever, and maybe find nothing, and then if whoever's doing this doesn't take another girl, or if he does but we don't know, then I guess we're never going to find the truth.'

Parrish – tempted then more than at any other time to tell Radick his suspicions, to give him the name of Amanda Leycross, to tell him what he planned to do and the action Radick should take if it all went horribly wrong – said nothing. Radick would only try and convince him otherwise, and Parrish knew he didn't want to be convinced. It was now no longer a question of *if*, but merely when. Tonight, tomorrow night, sometime before Monday morning for sure. As he had told Marie Griffin, he needed only a day or so to wrap this thing up. What he should have added was that this thing was going to end: *one way or the other*. But she would have asked him what he meant, would have delved into his thoughts the way she had been doing for the previous two and a half weeks. Seemed so much longer. Seemed like a month, two, six. Seemed like an eternity. Things had changed. There was no question about that.

He now realized how much of his father he had carried with him all these years. He realized how little he'd understood Clare or the kids, what they wanted and how he had failed to provide it. He had begun to appreciate that existence was a collaborative thing. It didn't work single-handedly, at least not the way he had managed it.

He was not so selfish as to consider that the people he knew would be better off without him. That was so much self-pity and shallowness. That was the sort of thing you told people when you wanted them to feel sorry for you. No, he didn't believe that. He believed that people, in general, were better *with* him – strangers for example; he did well with strangers. And he did well with the dead. He was dogged and persistent enough to make someone else's death a matter of priority. The old saw: *My day starts when your day ends.* He now believed that. The time with Marie Griffin had given him a sense of balance, an understanding of his own small but necessary place in the woof and warp of things. He was not wrong about the present case. He had convinced himself of this much at least. And if he was wrong, well – as he had vowed so unequivocally to Radick – *if* he was wrong then it wouldn't matter because he wouldn't have the job anymore. It was that simple.

At half-past five Parrish told Radick to call it a day.

'Only if you will,' Radick replied.

'I am,' Parrish said. 'I'm out of here, I've had enough. We're back on early shift next week . . . not that shifts make a lot of difference, but it means we get the weekend at least.'

'Man, have I looked forward to this.'

'You got anything planned?'

Radick shook his head. 'Nothing particular. Eat, sleep, watch TV, eat some more, sleep more than that. The last two weeks have been a bitch and I really feel like I need to recharge, you know what I mean?'

Parrish smiled understandingly. 'I know exactly what you mean. See you Monday, Jimmy.'

'Take care, Frank.'

Parrish watched him leave, waited until he saw Radick's car pull away and turn down Fulton. He knew in his bones that Jimmy would be seeing Caitlin this weekend, and he also knew that there was nothing he could do about it . . .

Parrish was leaving the room when the phone rang. He glanced at the phone, hesitated, but it was his desk, and that meant the desk was calling up with a message. Erickson? Maybe Radick calling from his cell phone with a final thought? Parrish stepped back and lifted the receiver.

'Frank, that you?'

'Yeah, what's up?'

'You got a priest on the way . . . sorry, I couldn't stop him. He asked if you were up there and I said yes, and he was gone before I had a chance to stop him.'

'Oh for Christ's sake—'

'Taking the Lord's name in vain, Frank?'

Parrish turned at the sound of voice behind him. There, in the doorway, stood Father Briley.

'I got it,' Parrish told the desk sergeant, and he hung up.

'Father—' he started.

Briley raised his hands in a placatory fashion. 'Fifteen minutes,' he said. 'I just need fifteen minutes of your time. I've been trying to reach you, but for whatever reason my messages haven't arrived.'

Parrish couldn't lie to the man. 'Your messages arrived, Father, I just didn't return them.'

Briley nodded. 'I understand that. Perhaps we didn't part on the most amicable of terms.'

Parrish smiled. 'Compared to the conversations me and Clare have had recently I'd say we parted the best of friends.'

'I need to talk about—'

'My father?' Parrish interjected. 'I can't, Father, I really can't. I have spent the last two weeks talking about my father with a counsellor here, and I've kind of had enough.'

'There's things you don't know, Frank.'

'And I am sure, Father Briley, that there's things that you don't know either.'

Briley looked down at his shoes. 'Can I sit, Frank? Can I sit down for a minute?'

'Look, I appreciate your concern, but I really have to go—'

'Like I said, Frank, fifteen minutes . . . fifteen minutes to let me tell you something that your father made me swear I never would.'

Parrish started to speak, an automatic response, and then he registered what Briley had said, and indicated a chair. They both sat, and for a few moments they just looked at one another in silence.

'It started with Santos,' Briley said. 'You might not remember him. Jimmy Santos? He would have been around when you were five, six, seven years old.'

'I know the name,' Parrish said. 'He was a dirty cop. Armed robbery. Got busted, did time, came out and went to the dark side.'

'He was the one who helped sew up the airport,' Briley said. 'He named names, had information on which police they needed out there, and your father took money from him to expedite those transfers.'

Parrish shook his head. 'I don't want to hear this, Father, I really don't—'

'Yes you do, Frank, yes you do. You just think you don't.'

'He was a crook, okay? What more is there to know? He took money, he took bribes, he lost paperwork and evidence, he was involved in armed robberies, Christ only knows what. I know enough already, enough to see that he and I are so different . . .'

'You love your kids, Frank?'

Parrish stopped and looked at Briley.

'You don't need to answer that question. I know you love your kids. And your father loved you. More than you know. More than you can imagine. He made mistakes. He crossed the line and took some money from Jimmy Santos, and once he did that they had him. Santos was a bad man, through and through. He could have kept his word. He could have maintained your father's anonymity and just used him to get the police he wanted out at the airport, but no. Jimmy Santos wanted to be the big man. He wanted to be in everyone's good books. He told the people he worked for about your father, and they came for him. Your father was a sergeant in 1967. He was a good cop. He was making an impression. He took a few hundred dollars to expedite some paperwork, but aside from that he was a good cop. He had policing in his blood, and he was never going to do anything else. These people saw that in him, and they saw a man rising in the ranks, someone they could use to get cases dropped, to get evidence mislaid, to get reports lost from files before they got to the DA—'

'What are you saying?' Parrish asked. 'How the hell do you even know this?'

'Because he told me, Frank. He came to me regularly, once

a month, sometimes twice or three times. A tortured man, haunted by his conscience, but left without a choice—'

'Excuse me, Father, but that is such bullshit. Everyone has a choice. I made mine, he made his. His choice was to be a corrupt—'

'It isn't a choice when it comes to the lives of your children.'

Parrish looked back at Briley.

'Like I said, they had him from the moment he started dealing with Santos. And Santos gave him up to them. He went like a lamb to the slaughter. They had enough leverage because of the money he'd already taken. Santos played him right into their hands, and then they threatened you . . .'

Briley left the last statement hanging in the air.

It was seconds before it registered with Parrish, and then he slowly shook his head. 'No,' he said. 'I don't understand why you're trying to do this. I really don't get what's in it for you, but that is just so much horseshit . . .'

'There's nothing in it for me,' Briley said. 'You came and saw me. I could see your father in you. I could see you torturing yourself about something. Guilt about your kids, about Clare, about . . . I don't know. I know a drinker when I see one. I work in a predominantly Irish-Catholic community, Frank. Give me some credit, eh? I see a man tearing himself to pieces about something, and I know that there's something that might help him, and you think I'm going to hold onto that? Well, I'm sorry, Frank. John is long gone, God rest his soul, and even though I swore to him that I would keep my silence, it seemed to me that not knowing was perhaps more destructive to you than knowing . . .'

'Knowing what? Knowing what exactly?'

'That he was not the man that you think he was. That he was not corrupt . . . well, he was corrupt, but he was threatened. They threatened you, Frank. They didn't threaten him, they didn't threaten your mother, they threatened *you*. If you don't do what we want, John Parrish, we are going to kill your son. We are going to kill your only child.'

Parrish was shaking his head. 'No,' he said. 'Fuck . . . Fuck it, no. That is something I do not believe. You didn't live with him, Father Briley. You didn't see the money that came in and out of the house—'

'Not his money, Frank, *their* money. He had to hold it, him and his partner. You remember him, George Buranski? He had three kids, three little girls. You remember them? They got to them both, Frank, him and George, and they used them every which way they could, and after the bank robbery, the one where that off-duty cop was killed, they started to figure that your father's loyalty to the department might be greater than the leverage they had over him. You were no longer a child. You were a cop yourself by then. Your father knew you could take care of yourself. And these people got scared that John Parrish and George Buranski knew too much, that they might finally turn them over, and . . . well, that's when they killed them, Frank. Gunned them down in the street like dogs.'

Parrish felt sick. Light-headed. He wanted a drink. He *needed* a drink, and he wanted to be elsewhere. He was in a state of shock and confusion, and he did *not* want to listen to this, could not at this moment deal with it. This was not the truth, *could* not be the truth. His father was a bad man, a corrupt man . . . This was a certainty that could never be taken away.

'He told me everything, Frank. I saw him three days before he was killed. That was the last time I spoke to him, and then I was there to administer last rites, and I delivered his funeral, remember? And I said what I said, and I looked at the picture they had of him up there near the coffin, and I believe I was the only one who understood what had really happened to your father.'

'So why now? Why tell me this now? Why not tell me five years ago, ten years ago?'

'Because he made me promise. Your father made me promise that I would never say a word to you.'

'Why? Why would he do that?'

'To protect you. For the very same reason that he did all those things for all those years . . . to protect you.'

'From what? What the hell did he have to protect me from?'

'From yourself, Frank.' Briley paused, leaned forward. 'You

ever hear the old saying about vengeance? That if you head out for vengeance you should dig two graves?'

'Yes, I've heard that.'

'He knew you could get to these people. He knew you could find out who Santos worked with all those years ago, find out whatever you wanted. You were right there, a cop just like him, and anything you needed to know about the Task Force and the OCCB was right in front of you. He didn't want you to know because he didn't want you to spend your life trying to get back at them. He knew that if you went down that road you'd be dead in a week.'

Parrish was shaking his head. 'This is too much. I cannot . . . Jesus Christ, this doesn't make sense . . .'

'Makes perfect sense, son. John was not the man you thought he was. He was your father, first and foremost he was your father, and though he made some very bad decisions, he also decided never to put you in harm's way. He knew he was wrong. He knew what he'd done was no good, but he kept his word as a father. That was one of the last things he said to me. He said that if the truth ever came out then at least he kept his integrity as a father.'

Parrish stood up, his jaw set, his expression inscrutable. 'I need you to leave now,' he said quietly. 'I have work to do. I have things I need to be doing—'

'Frank, seriously—'

'Enough,' Parrish interjected. 'Please, Father, I've heard enough. I don't want to hear any more. He was not who you think he was. He was dangerous. He was fucking crazy. That's the truth, and you won't convince me otherwise—'

Briley stood up. 'Frank, listen to me—'

'No, Father. I've done all the listening I want to. I need you to leave now. I really do.'

Briley was silent for a moment, hurt and disappointment in his eyes, and perhaps a sense of failure that he had not accomplished what he intended.

'I wanted you to know so you would stop killing yourself with guilt,' he said. 'There is nothing for you to be guilty about. Your father did what he did for you.'

Parrish looked down. He spoke without raising his head. 'I'll not ask you again, Father. Out of respect for you I will not throw you out of the building, but one of us is leaving the room right now and I think it should be you.'

'Very well, Frank,' Briley said. 'I am sorry for all of this. Perhaps I should have told you earlier . . .' He shook his head. 'I believe I knew your father better than anyone, and he was not the man you think he was . . .'

Parrish looked up. He said nothing. His eyes were like flint, hard.

Briley nodded, then turned and left the room.

Frank Parrish stood where he was for a good five minutes, his breathing shallow, a fist of emotion in his throat, his heart racing, a thin line of sweat beneath his hairline.

He willed himself to move, he willed himself to forget all that Briley had said, but he was seething with tension, with conflict, with a sense of betrayal, and he felt rage boiling up inside him. He closed his eyes and breathed deeply, again and again, forced himself to focus on what he was about to do. Focus on that and nothing more. He had something to do. Something important. Something right. Something positive. He had already spent too long delving into his own past, his own thoughts. And where had it gotten him? Nowhere. He had broken things apart to look inside, and the only result had been more damage. With Caitlin, with Clare, with Radick. How long could he go on apologizing for his own existence? How long could he go on saying sorry for everything that came out of his mouth? Wasn't it time just to trust his intuition, his own sense of certainty, and to do something about what had happened? People were dying. Children were dying. Someone had to stop it, and it had to stop now.

It was that thought above all that moved him. He closed the door behind him and hurried down the back stairs to the basement.

SEVENTY-FOUR

Eleven minutes, that was all, and the car pool supervisor stepped out of his office and crossed the garage to the restroom on the other side of the building. Parrish hurried across, entered the office, snatched the first set of keys he could reach, and then walked along the bank of unmarked cars until he found the plate that matched. A beat-to-shit dark blue saloon, unremarkable and innocuous. Parrish got in, started the engine and pulled out of the garage. The supervisor would assume that someone had borrowed the car for the weekend. He would express his annoyance at the offender on Monday morning, *if* he was the guy on shift when the car was returned. Such 'loans' were a common occurrence, and there was little that could be done to stop them.

Parrish took a left on Hoyt and made his way south-east. He forced himself not to think about Briley, about his father. He willed himself to shut all of it out of his mind until he was through with this. He needed to see Caitlin, and prayed that she would be home. He *had* to make things good with her. Clare could think what the fuck she liked, and Robert would think whatever he wanted regardless of what any of them said or did. It had been a month now since he'd seen his son, and they could go another six months without speaking, and yet when they collided once again it would be as though they had spoken only the day before. Robert's nonchalant and unconcerned attitude had always seemed an issue, certainly for Clare, but now, after all this talk with Marie Griffin, it seemed to Parrish that his son's attitude might actually serve him better than the over-serious, *responsible* viewpoint that parents so often tried to foist off on their kids. Robert was Robert. It would be good for him or it wouldn't, and no end of fatherly discussions and advice would change Robert's mind. If he went ahead and spent the rest of his life accomplishing not very much of anything at all, and yet he was happy accomplishing nothing, then so be it. Most times it was the over-achievers who experienced disappointment and stress. *Cynical bastard*, Parrish thought as he pulled over a block and a half from Caitlin's apartment block.

Parrish couldn't remember her name, the girl who opened the apartment door.

'Mr Parrish,' she said cheerfully, evidently remembering his.

'Hi there,' Parrish replied. 'I was after Caitlin.'

'She's not here.'

'She's studying?'

'No, I think she's working tonight. She's doing a long-weekender at the University Hospital. You know where that is, right? Up where Atlantic meets the expressway?'

Parrish knew exactly where it was: a block from Hicks Street, a block from Danny Lange's apartment and a dead girl that seemed so long ago.

'Yes,' Parrish said. 'I know where it is.' He hesitated, almost as if he had something else to say.

The girl looked awkward. 'Was there anything else you needed?'

'No,' he said, and smiled as best he could. 'I'll go on up there and see her.'

He drove back up Smith and took Atlantic. He pulled over on Clinton and walked the rest of the way. The hospital receptionist was helpful but relatively clueless. The student nurses could be anywhere in the building, she told Parrish. She could put an announcement on the system perhaps? Was it important?

'Sir?' she prompted as Parrish stared off into the middle-distance without answering her question.

He turned back and shook his head. 'Not so important as to disturb her while she's working.'

'You want to leave a message?'

'Yes, a message. Sure. Tell her that her dad stopped by. That he said he was sorry for everything and that he loves her.'

The receptionist smiled. 'I'll make sure she gets it, sir.'

Parrish left the hospital. He drove home, parked a block

away, spent an hour making sandwiches, a flask of coffee, collected some tape cassettes of Tom Waits, Gil Scott-Heron, Kenny Burrell, and dumped the lot in a holdall. He changed out of his shirt and tie into a plain dark sweatshirt, a loose-fitting jacket, a pair of jeans. He took a torch, his keys, an unmarked and untraceable .32 caliber revolver he had picked up on a bust several years before, and then he stopped at the door as he was leaving and looked back at the nondescript room. Had he not lived there he would have believed the place empty, waiting for tenants. He had become his job. He was defined by dead strangers. Depressing, but true.

Frank Parrish locked the door behind him and made his way out to the street.

SEVENTY-FIVE

'He needs to know, Caitlin. Seriously.'

Caitlin Parrish, seated there in the University Hospital canteen, shook her head slowly. 'Not yet,' she said. 'He needs to suffer a little longer. He needs to really, really miss me and then he'll forgive me anything.' She smiled coyly.

Jimmy Radick leaned back in his chair and crossed his legs. 'You are a wicked daughter,' he said.

'I know him, Jimmy, believe me. He can be very possessive, jealous almost. It was something that Mom used to run into frequently. He even resented the way that my grandfather used to talk to her.'

'How old were you when he died?'

'Grandpa John? When was it, now . . . 1992 . . . I would have been, let me see, four, four and a half.'

'And how the hell would you have known what your father thought of your grandfather when you were four and a half years old?'

'Because we girls have extra-sensory perception when it comes to such things.' She smiled. 'Because my mom told me, that's why.'

'But that's just your mom's take on things, Caitlin. There are two sides to everything.'

'Look, Jimmy, you have to understand something here. As far as my father is concerned, my mother is numero uno bitch of all time. He wants you to think of her that way so you forgive him for being such an asshole to her. He was never there, always working—'

'You know what it's like. It'll be the same for you when you're full-time nursing—'

'It wasn't the shifts, Jimmy, it was the broken promises. Anyway, we're not here to talk about my parents' fucked-up relationship, we're here to talk about us.'

'Yes, and I think Frank needs to know. This creeping around, meeting each other when we know he's not going to come visit you. He's my partner, for God's sake—'

'And you've only just started working together, and you and I have only just started going out together, and I want both these relationships to settle somewhat before we start upsetting everyone.'

'You think he'll be upset?'

'I think he'll be concerned.'

'Because of our age difference?'

'I'm twenty, you're twenty-nine. When you're sixty, I'll be fifty-one, no big deal. No. Age isn't what he'll have a problem with. It's the fact that you're a cop.'

'But so is he.'

'Exactly! He doesn't want what happened to him and Mom to happen to his daughter. It's bullshit, but it's the way he thinks. He used to lecture me – well, maybe *lecture* is too strong a word – but one time he made me promise that I'd never date a cop.'

'And now you're dating his partner, *and* doing it behind his back.'

'Leave it as it is,' Caitlin said. She reached out and took Radick's hand. 'We've been going out for a little over two weeks. Everything's new, everything's exciting. Give me a month and I won't care what you do . . . in fact I'll probably be all too eager for you to tell my dad because I'll be looking for a reason to dump you.'

Radick laughed. 'This inspires me with great confidence.'

'Anyway, we'll talk about it some other time. I've told the girls at home that I'm on a long-weekender here just in case he comes around to the apartment. I don't think he will, I think he needs at least another week to deal with his shame, but you never know.' She glanced at her watch. 'I've got two hours and then I'm done. Come pick me up. We'll go eat some place nice, and then you can keep me in handcuffs at your apartment for the weekend, okay?'

'Sounds good to me.'

Caitlin leaned forward and kissed Radick. 'Eight o'clock, Detective,' she said, 'and don't be late.'

SEVENTY-SIX

Richard McKee was in his house. He was there for the night. Frank Parrish was going to sit in an unofficially loaned car half a block down the street and watch that house. As and when McKee went out he was going inside. If he was caught it would all be over. If he found something incriminating, well, he would be impotent as far as offering probative evidence was concerned. He had no real justification for the search, but in his own mind he did, and such justification was as good a warrant as he needed. His probable cause was a suspicion that he could not ignore, a sense of duty, a *need* to know for sure and for certain that McKee was the guy.

There was a single light on in the lower half of the house; then, a little after nine, a light went on upstairs as well. Parrish had kicked the seat back to stretch his legs. He knew he was here for the duration. He knew that what he was doing was beyond all bounds of protocol and procedure. At eleven the lower light went out. A second light went on upstairs, and was switched off fifteen minutes later. McKee had showered perhaps. The drapes moved in the one remaining lit window, and then the light went out and there was the flicker of a TV. What was he doing? Watching Drew Carey reruns? Parrish smiled to himself. He was watching himself choke Jennifer and Karen to death while he fucked them. That's what he was doing.

The house was in darkness by a quarter of midnight, and Parrish moved to the back seat of the car. He loosened his belt and untied his shoes. He would stay awake, no question. Plenty of experience, no shortage of practice. He could sit still for hours. He had a plastic bottle to piss into, his flask of coffee, his food. He could put on the music later, just quiet, just there in the background to help him focus, and he was set. No different from any other stakeout, except this time he was alone.

Parrish woke with a start. His mouth tasted like stale cheese and copper filings. He squinted at his watch. Twenty past three. McKee's house was still in darkness. How long had he been asleep? Had he really slept, or had he just dozed for a moment? He sat up straight, reached for the flask and filled the cup. Still surprisingly hot, the coffee took the bad taste from his mouth and warmed him. The interior of the car was bitterly cold. Parrish scooted over into the front passenger seat. He turned the key in the ignition, switched the heater on, inched open the window to allow a through-draft, and settled back. Maybe he wasn't so good at this. Maybe he had lost the edge.

He felt a sudden sharp twinge in his lower gut. The sensation hadn't bothered him for a few days and he'd forgotten about it. It eased momentarily, and then came back with a vengeance. Like teeth and claws in the base of his stomach, and just as he was about to open the door and stand up it passed again. He massaged his abdomen. He took a couple of deep breaths. He poured out some more coffee and drank it slowly.

By the time daylight started to edge its way over the city, Parrish felt more alert. He had not slept again, and he felt sure that McKee had not left the house while he was asleep earlier. Perhaps he would wake soon. Perhaps he would go out for the day. Was he working today? Or was it this weekend that he had the kids? When the kids came over did they stay home, or did he take them out – movies, the zoo, crazy golf, whatever doghouse-dads did with part-time kids to make themselves feel as though they were being paternal and positive?

Parrish found it difficult to believe, but the previous Saturday – September 13th – had been the first time he'd met Richard McKee. He remembered the conversation he'd had with Carole Paretski – the fact that this was the weekend when Richard had the kids for both days. He also remembered what she had asked him, whether he wanted her to let

Richard take the children. Yes, he had told her. Leave everything as it is. Don't alert him to anything out of the ordinary.

Did Carole usually bring them over, he wondered, or did McKee go and collect them? If he went out to get them, then they could go for a day out from Carole's house and Parrish would be none the wiser. However, if Carole delivered them and then McKee took them out it was unlikely he would be back for several hours. Hell, there was no certainty of that either. He could drive them down the road for pizza and come right home again. The whole thing was a mess of uncertainty, and the uncertainty of McKee's schedule was only important if he intended to break the law.

Parrish thought to call Carole Paretski, ask her what the arrangements were for the pick-up. But he couldn't do that. She might mention such a conversation to Radick if they had to see her again. Parrish now seriously began to question what he was doing. Perhaps he should abandon it, he thought. Perhaps he should just start the engine, pull out, drive home, get a proper meal, a good sleep, see how he felt about the situation later . . .

But he couldn't. This wasn't going away, and if he didn't do something about it then he would never know. If he didn't break this thing wide open one way or the other then he would be haunted by it for the rest of his career. People did get obsessed by the unsolved cases. He'd heard of it, it was not uncommon. A thousand murders, all but two or three of them solved, yet hardened, weather-worn veteran homicide detectives would spend the rest of their lives wondering and worrying about the ones that they missed. Especially if kids were involved. Kids got under your skin and lived with you for the rest of however long. The cases that woke you up at night were the ones that you had to finish, come what may.

Parrish resolved to stay. It was a few minutes before five a.m. It was unrealistic that McKee would be out to get the kids before seven earliest. He set the alarm for seven on his cell phone and curled up on the back seat. He was asleep within minutes, dreaming, and what he dreamed seemed only a reflection of his waking thoughts in some grotesque funhouse mirror.

The girls were there – all of them and more – and he knew that if he did not give them closure they would indeed follow him for the rest of his life.

SEVENTY-SEVEN

At first Parrish was disoriented, uncertain where the sound was coming from, what it meant.

He snatched his phone from the edge of the seat and held it close to his face. The alarm. He switched it off, but it took a good fifteen or twenty seconds for him to remember where he was and what he was doing. He sat bolt upright. McKee's house was right there to his left. There was now too much daylight to determine whether any internal lights were on, but the upstairs drapes were still closed. The house looked still and silent and unchanged.

Parrish took several deep breaths. He felt dizzy and nauseous. He wanted a drink, knew that it would have been the worst idea of all, and resorted to the tepid dregs of his coffee. He was hungry too, but there was no food left.

Something shifted at the edge of his field of vision.

The left half of the drape had moved – just a few inches, but it had moved. McKee was still in there, and now he was awake. Parrish suddenly felt a resurgence of purpose. He looked at his watch. Six minutes past seven. Would he leave to collect Sarah and Alex . . . Sarah and Alex what? McKee or Paretski? Had Carole Paretski initiated the final act of ignominy and humiliation against her ex-husband by changing the kids' names to hers? And if he was going to collect them, when would he leave? Parrish simply had to wait. That was all he could do.

An hour passed. He pissed in the plastic bottle, managed to spatter his hands and the knees of his pants. He felt like a bum. He could only begin to imagine what the inside of the car smelled like. Lucky it wasn't his. Lucky if he returned it with no-one the wiser. In truth, he knew he was fucked. He knew that whichever way this came out he would be up before Valderas, Haversaw, Internal Affairs perhaps. There would be an inquiry – the polite and politically correct name for a ball-buster of an investigation. Would he walk away unscathed? Not a prayer. Would he lose his job once and for all? Most likely. And in considering such a scenario, the only thing that galled him was the possibility that he would be officially castrated before he had a chance to nail McKee. This was the case that he needed. This was the one that would save his self-respect.

If he could break this thing then perhaps he would no longer carry the burden of guilt about his father, the fact that he said nothing, the fact that he could have done something about what was happening and didn't. And now this bullshit from Briley . . . He didn't understand that. He couldn't grasp why a priest would want to defend his father. But then, if what Briley had said was true . . .

Parrish shook his head. He could not allow himself the luxury of such a thought. He needed to hold onto his own certainty. John Parrish had been a fuck-up. People were dead because of John Parrish. People were alive because of Frank.

Was that what it was all about?

He turned the rear-view and looked at himself. Unshaven, tousle-haired, exhausted. He looked like crap and felt no better.

Eight-thirty a car pulled up outside McKee's house. Parrish's heart quickened. *Yes!* he thought as he saw Carole Paretski exit the vehicle. She stood on the sidewalk as Alex and Sarah climbed out of the car and walked to the stoop. *Carole Paretski, I fucking love you!*

He looked at Sarah. How old did Carole say she was? Fourteen, fifteen? Not much younger than the girls that had been killed. And Carole had been right in her physical description – Sarah was tall and slim, blonde-haired, an attractive girl. Parrish thought of the hole in the corner of her bedroom, of her father lying in the dust up there, wiring that thing up, recording his own kid, her friends . . .

Parrish waited just as they did. Sarah knocked on the door, stepped back, glanced at her mother, seemed for a moment to glance back at Parrish but her gaze didn't linger or hesitate.

She raised her hand to knock again, and this time the door

opened. Carole Paretski stood with her arms folded for a moment, and then she hugged and kissed each of the kids and waited as they went inside. She shared a few stone-faced words with her ex-husband. He nodded, turned to close the door, but she said something that caused him to turn back and frown. A moment of recognition perhaps, a businesslike smile from McKee, and he stepped back inside the house and left the door open. Moments later he returned with a sheet of paper. She searched her purse, handed him a pen, he signed the paper at the bottom, folded it and gave it to her. What was it? Permission for the kids to do some activity at school? An approval for music lessons, a medical appointment, an orthodontist's bill? It didn't matter. Business was done. Carole turned back to her car, Richard went inside, closed the door, and Parrish sat there for a minute with his heart doing double-time. Carole Paretski took one more look at the house, and then she got in the car and pulled away. Parrish wished that Michael Vale was with him. His partner would have understood. His partner would have done this with him. Had his partner been alive he wouldn't be playing uncle to Jimmy Radick.

The house was still and silent again. Parrish took a deep breath and set himself to waiting once more.

The wait was not long. Forty minutes at most. McKee left the house alone, walked down towards the end of the street, and minutes later he pulled up outside in the SUV. He went to the front door, opened it, called the kids, and then locked the front door once they were in the car.

They drove away, all three of them. They just drove away and left Frank Parrish sitting across from the empty house.

Parrish didn't hesitate for long, but it seemed a small eternity. He knew now that things had reached the point of no return. If he moved he was going inside the house; if he got inside the house then he would not be coming out unless he had something certain and probative. He needed the mementos that Ron had spoken of with such certainty. He did not dare consider that he was wrong. Such a possibility was far too uncomfortable to contemplate. He felt as if the entirety of his career now came down to this decision. He was here because of his own intuition, his own self-belief – professional and personal. He was here because he felt sure that Richard McKee, he of Family Welfare, South Two, was a child-abductor, a rapist, a sex killer. These were peoples' children, peoples' daughters who had, at one time, been loved and cared for, and then the harshest of realities had intervened . . .

Parrish reached for the door lever and got out of the car. He took his holdall, his keys, his flashlight, his .32.

He hurried across the street, and with a skill and efficiency that belied his sense of panic, he had the front door unlocked and was inside the hall within thirty seconds.

He stood still for some time, waiting for his heart to resume something approximating a regular pace. It didn't completely manage that, but it got close enough for him to move.

SEVENTY-EIGHT

'What's her name?'

'I think her name is Eve, maybe Evelyn, I'm not sure.'

Radick frowned. 'I tell you something, he's never given me any indication that he has something going on with someone,' he said.

Caitlin Parrish reached up and touched her forefinger to Jimmy Radick's lips. 'That's because you don't have the female's intuition. We see things that men don't see.'

Radick smiled. 'Is that so?' He shifted sideways a fraction.

Caitlin put her right leg over his thigh and her hand on his chest.

'It is so. I can tell. A couple of times I've just picked something up.'

'And who is she?'

'I have no idea.'

'So how do you know her name?'

'Well, I don't. Not as such. There was a Post-It next to the phone at his place one time. This was like a year ago maybe. It just said Eve and then a date, that was all.'

'And your extraordinary powers of female intuition led you to believe that this was the girl your father was seeing?'

'No, it was how he reacted when I asked him who Eve was. He looked directly at me and said it was just a work thing, but there was this flicker in his expression, like he didn't want me to ask.'

'You think he'd be embarrassed if he thought you knew he was going out with someone?'

'No, not embarrassed. Dad doesn't get embarrassed. But he's old-fashioned, and he still thinks of me as his little girl. You saw how he was when you guys came over the first time, all that worrying about what I'm doing, what my friends are like, when I'm going out, how long I'm staying out for, where I'm going to work. I mean, to be completely honest, it gets a bit claustrophobic sometimes. He does get a bit obsessive.'

'I know about that.'

'What?'

'Well, this case we're on. I mean, I really don't see it, but he has a guy for these killings. He has really zeroed in on this guy, and I can see why Frank might consider him a suspect, but I really don't see how he can be so sure. It is a bit obsessive, like you say.'

'That's just his nature. Mom used to say that sometimes he was so certain, even when he was wrong, and there was no way you could convince him otherwise. Some people are just like that, and Frank Parrish is one of them.'

Radick looked thoughtful, was quiet a moment, then asked, 'What's the deal with his drinking?'

'He's always been that way. I don't think he's gonna kill himself from it, but it's certainly an issue for him. I always put it down to the stress of his job, but recently I've started to have other ideas.'

'Like what?'

'Well, I know he's my dad an' everything, but we've done this whole thing in work, like basic psychology stuff, and one of the classes we took was about drug and alcohol dependency. It talked about how people can start drinking out of some imagined inadequacy, you know? I thought about Dad, and then I thought about his dad, my grandfather—'

'John Parrish.'

'You know about John Parrish?'

'The guy's a fucking legend. OCCB, Brooklyn Organized Crime Task Force, more commendations than any other officer in the precinct's history.' Radick smiled.

'Yeah, and he and my grandma had a marriage that lasted forever. He had one son, and that son followed in his footsteps, right into the police department. As far as cops are concerned, the best validation of your parenting skills is if your son goes into the department alongside you, and that's what Frank did.'

'So you think he feels inadequate because he's always having to live up to the John Parrish reputation?'

Caitlin turned her mouth down at the corners. 'I don't know, but it sounds plausible. I . . . well . . . it hasn't exactly been straightforward with his career, has it? And his marriage was a fuck-up, and his kids are doing whatever they're doing. I don't know when he last saw Robert, but Robert is about as far from what Granddad would have approved of as you could get. John Parrish was your regular all-American tough guy, a real John Wayne type that thought you were a fag if you didn't drink a quart of sourmash and go out picking fights with someone three times your size.'

'I know guys like that. A dying breed, but they still make 'em every once in a while.'

'Well, my brother is like your artistic type. He's studying engineering, but I think he'll wind up a graphic designer or an interior decorator or something. I mean, he's not a fag or anything – not that I would have anything on it if he was – but he doesn't go around biting trees and wrestling pickup trucks.'

Radick shifted again. He moved his leg upwards until he felt the warmth between Caitlin's thighs. He reached up his hand and stroked away a lock of hair from the side of her face.

'It's hard for me to consider that your father feels inadequate,' he said.

'Why?'

'Because he's so sure of everything he does. This job is not what I thought it would be . . . not exactly . . .'

'How d'you mean?'

'It's slower. It's more methodical. There's a hell of a lot of waiting and looking and more waiting after that. I figured it might be a little more fast-paced.'

'You wanna do Starsky and Hutch shit, right?'

Radick smiled. 'It's a job of patience and persistence, and being able not to get frustrated when you don't get what you want.'

'Dad's spoken to me about it,' Caitlin replied. 'He told me one time that he worked on a case for fourteen months. He got a compelling witness, someone who would stand up in court. He got wiretaps and search warrants and hard evidence on a multiple homicide case that would put the guy away for like two-fifty or something, and then the guy had a stroke and died thirty-six hours before they were scheduled to bust him. He said that a lot of them went like that – not that the perp always dies, but that there's some glitch or some legal technicality that makes the whole thing fall over.'

'You said perp.'

'Yeah, a perp. You know what a perp is, right?'

Radick laughed. 'A cop's daughter. Here I am, lying in a bed with a cop's daughter, and we're talking about busting perps.'

Caitlin smiled. She wriggled out from under Jimmy and sat on the edge of the bed. 'You want some coffee?' she asked.

'Sure,' he said.

She hesitated for a second, and then she looked over her shoulder at Radick.

'You think he's going to be okay?' she asked.

'Okay? How d'you mean?'

'Like, he's not going to do anything stupid on this case is he? This guy he's obsessing about for the killings?'

Radick shook his head. 'Frank? No, I don't think so. He knows how close he's come to getting fired from the department. I don't see him doing anything to risk that.'

Caitlin nodded and stood up. 'You're right,' she said. 'He wouldn't jeopardize that, would he? He doesn't have Mom, he sort of doesn't have me and Robert anymore, but hell, even when he had us we always came second.' She seemed pensive for a moment, and then she smiled. 'He's a cop, nothing more than that. Not a bad thing, but just the way he is. Without his job I don't think there'd be any reason for him to get up in the morning.'

Radick watched her as she walked from the bedroom. She looked great. Best-looking girl he'd ever dated. This one was a keeper, no doubt about it. One in a million.

He smiled to himself and turned over. He hoped Frank was okay. A weekend alone. He hoped he stayed off the sauce, sitting around the house obsessing about Richard McKee and dead teenage girls. Radick respected the man, no question. Respected him, but would do everything he could not to wind up like him. Some things you could admire from a distance without ever wanting to become them.

He listened to Caitlin making coffee in his kitchen, and then wondered if he should call Frank on the cell. Maybe later. Just to make sure he was okay. Just to make sure he wasn't planning anything crazy.

SEVENTY-NINE

It was very much the house of a single man. The refrigerator was barely stocked, same with the kitchen cabinets and the freezer in the back utility space. Three bedrooms, a large one at the front of the house, two smaller rooms on the left and right of the passage that led to the bathroom. It was meticulously clean and neat, just as Ron had said it would be.

Frank Parrish walked around looking for the obvious, and when he was done with the obvious he looked for everything else. He walked the carpets in all the rooms with his shoes off, feeling for indentations and ridges – the index of uneven floorboards, a trap, a hatch of some sort. He tested beneath the linoleum in the bathroom, and then carefully tugged back the plastic paneling on the side of the tub to see if there was anything behind. He went through every room, every section of upper-floor ceiling to determine if there was a trap for the attic. There wasn't, but that didn't necessarily mean that there was no crawl space; it was simply a matter of determining how such a space could be accessed. The smaller rooms had the kids' backpacks on the beds. These were stopover rooms for their weekends there. McKee's bedroom he checked more thoroughly than all of them. Here was the TV, the DVD player, a collection of discs in a unit beside it. Action movies, regular stuff, nothing of any interest, but he did check inside each box to ensure that the advertised disc matched the one within. He went through the wardrobes, checked for false bottoms and tops, looked under the bed, lifted the mattress, pressed along the edges to make sure that nothing had been hidden there. He came away with nothing but frustration.

Parrish headed downstairs, beginning to feel a nagging sense of doubt. The kitchen also gave him nothing; he pulled back the freezer and washing machine, but however closely he looked he saw only a freezer and a washing machine.

In the back yard there was nothing but a flagstone path, a small section of grass, a couple of yards of scrubbed earth.

Parrish stood for a while looking out of the kitchen window.

Think. If I was him, what would I do? Where would I keep things that I didn't want anyone to find?

He went back to the sitting room. He moved the sofa and table away from the walls and tugged up the carpet a good three or four feet towards the center of the room. He up-ended the sofa and used a screwdriver to loosen sufficient staples to get his hand under the canvas backing. He felt nothing but padding and wooden struts. But there was something here. He knew it. He just *knew* it.

Parrish replaced everything as he'd found it. He wondered if there was an inspection pit in the floor of McKee's lock-up garage, or if the man had another property, a trailer somewhere outside of the city, a safehouse, a bolthole, a private fucking cinema . . .

The cupboard beneath the stairs was narrow and awkward, but Parrish managed to take everything out of it – paint cans, a vacuum cleaner, a box of blankets – and he kneeled in there and tapped the walls. They were all solid, no doubt about it, even the underside of the risers above his head were solid wood. No paneling, no false ceiling, no secure box padlocked and wedged against the wall. Parrish put everything back. He sat on the hall carpet and felt that overwhelming sense of disillusionment and failure he had been dreading. He tried to resist it, to slow it down, but it was upon him.

And with it came the sound of an engine, a car engine, and it slowed as it reached the front of the house, and for a second Parrish believed that it couldn't be happening. The car stopped.

Parrish got up and hurried to the front door. Through the spy hole he saw McKee's SUV, McKee exiting even as he looked, and Parrish felt his heart stop dead. He ran back to the kitchen, grabbed his holdall, his flashlight, his screwdriver, and rushed back to the under-stair cupboard. He crammed himself in there, pulled the door to as best he

could even as he heard the sound of McKee unlocking the
front door.

'Stay there!' McKee shouted. 'I think it's in the back.'

Parrish willed his heart to stop beating. He felt dizzy,
frightened, utterly panic stricken. His pulse surged errat-
ically; he felt it in his temples and his neck. His legs were
beginning to protest the awkward space, the onset of cramp,
that sudden and unbearable pain that would force him to
move, to fall forwards out of the cupboard and into the
hallway.

He shifted his foot. It touched the door and the door
inched open a fraction. There was no handle inside, nothing
to grab onto and close the door again.

McKee hurried past. Parrish saw his legs as he went
through to the kitchen. He closed his eyes and held his
breath.

He heard the sound of cupboards opening. He willed the
cramp to go with everything he possessed. The pain was
building slowly, his muscles tightening with every second.
There was nothing he could do to stop it. Any moment now
it would grip him like a vice, and it would take everything he
possessed to not make a sound, to not move.

'Got it,' he heard McKee say, and then he was coming back
down the hallway, and for a split-second Parrish believed
he might just walk right on past the open cupboard door, the
door that had been firmly closed when he left the house
earlier that morning.

But McKee did not walk past. He slowed, and then he
stopped. Here was a precise and meticulous man. Here was a
man who didn't leave doors ajar.

Parrish imagined the frown, the moment of curiosity,
McKee's certainty that he had last seen the door shut tight,
and then he would reach for the door. He would open it, and
there he would find Detective Frank Parrish of the New York
Police Department's 126th Precinct crouching beneath the
stairwell with a flashlight, a screwdriver, a holdall full of tools
and keys and assorted housebreaking equipment. What
would he do? What could he possibly say? *Hi there, Mr
McKee . . . well, let me say first and foremost that this isn't what
it looks like?* McKee knew him. He knew his name. There

R. J. Ellory

would be no point in running. If he ran, what would he say later when McKee reported the incident? *McKee's a liar. I was never in the guy's house . . . ?*

The kids, Alex and Sarah, sitting in back of the SUV waiting for their dad, their *innocent* dad, to come right on out with whatever they'd forgotten, would see him.

Parrish could see the headlines. He could hear the IAD investigators. He could feel the shame and humiliation that he would suffer until his final dismissal. He knew this was it, this was how it would end, caught crouching in a cupboard after having committed felony B&E and an illegal search of a suspect's house. Not only that, but McKee would sue the PD, then he would sue Parrish for harassment, mental cruelty, Post Traumatic Stress Disorder, and while Parrish reached the very lowest level of his life, McKee would be exonerated and rewarded for his undue suffering . . .

Parrish closed his eyes. He held his breath.

McKee kicked the door shut with his foot and hurried out of the house.

Parrish waited until he heard the car pull away and then he let out an anguished gasp of pain.

It was then that he realized he was trapped beneath the stairs.

EIGHTY

Carole Paretski had thought long and hard about the discussions she'd had with Detective Frank Parrish. There was something unspoken – she knew that. And though she believed that Parrish's partner was unaware of it, she knew that Parrish suspected her husband of so much more than reading stroke mags and watching *Barely Legal* porn films. She had misjudged the man she'd married, considered that he'd become someone else, and that did nothing but fuel the fundamental concern she felt for her daughter.

Sarah was fourteen. She was becoming a woman. She was pretty and bright and blonde, and she trusted her father without question. Richard had never given her any reason to do otherwise, but Carole believed that Richard harbored dark thoughts about Sarah – the kind of thoughts that grown men should never harbor about teenage girls, especially not their own daughters. There was an aura of malevolence that she felt around her ex-husband. She *sensed* it, and she trusted her own instincts. That malevolence was directed at her, and not only because she had divorced him, but because she was the one that withheld Sarah from him. She was the mother and, as is usual, the courts had not only granted her custody, but they had directed Richard to pay alimony. To Richard's mind, it was as though the courts had believed her more reliable, more ethical, more honest, a better parent than he, and for this he resented his ex-wife. Carole believed that Richard would not have been at all concerned if she came to harm. He would never do anything to her directly, he was too much of a coward. But if she were to disappear from the scene then he would be only too pleased. Since the divorce she'd tried to imagine him otherwise, but it was not something that she could so easily escape. The meetings with Parrish had reminded her of everything that she disliked about her ex-husband, and the thing she liked least of all was that he still had access to the kids.

At nine-thirty that morning she concluded that the only way to allay her fears was to go over there. She had a key, had always had a key – one of those things she had insisted on when they'd at last concluded the visitation rights. Each possessed the other's house key for use in case of emergency. They were still parents, and despite the divorce, despite the animosity and acrimony, despite everything that had gone between them and everything that was yet to come, Alex and Sarah were still their most important consideration.

Richard had taken them out for the day. She knew that. He was taking them to the mall, the movies, a restaurant. He'd told them that the week before. He had more money than she did, and he lavished gifts on them. He bribed them for affection. Alex and Sarah didn't see it that way. They saw him as a loving father, and every once in a while he would drive it home by subtly implying that how it was at weekends would be how it would be if they lived with him full-time. They had been too young to be aware of what an asshole he was, and though she had no question that Alex and Sarah loved her, they were still tempted. As far as Carole was concerned, Richard had gone to the dark side, and the dark side was where he would always be.

Before she left she thought about what would happen if she was found in his house. If they came back early, having forgotten something perhaps? What would she say? She went up to Sarah's room and found her iPod. She was always leaving it behind. Okay, so she didn't use it that much these days, but it wasn't so long ago that she wouldn't have been seen without it. *I just brought Sarah's iPod over. I thought she might want it.* That would do. It was better than nothing.

Carole Paretski took her purse, her keys, her jacket, and left the house. It was a good thirty-minute drive south-west, all the way from Steuben, across Washington, Flatbush and down Fourth. Being Saturday, the traffic wasn't as bad as it could have been, and she crossed the Gowanus Canal a little before ten. She felt nervous, afraid even, but there was a question in her mind that had to be resolved. Was his house full of this stuff? The same kind of stuff that Parrish and his partner had taken away? Were her kids spending weekends with a man who watched child pornography and wanted to fuck teenagers? She shuddered at the thought. If he touched Sarah . . . Hell, if Richard touched Sarah she would kill him. She would drive a kitchen knife into his eyes and castrate him. She would douse him in gasoline and let the mother-fucker burn to death.

Carole Paretski came out from the junction too quickly and someone blared at her. Surprised, she pulled over suddenly, her heart racing. What was she doing? This was crazy behavior. But would she say that if something happened to Sarah and she had done nothing to prevent it? They were out – all three of them. She had the house key. She just had to know. She *needed* to.

She pulled up outside the house on Sackett Street. She paused for a moment. There was nothing else to do. She flipped the door lever and climbed out.

EIGHTY-ONE

Robert Parrish sat at the kitchen table and looked at his mother defiantly. He had long since tired of the complaints and bitterness that seemed to hover at the edges of every conversation about his father.

'He *would* understand,' Robert said once again, and rolled his eyes exasperatedly. 'The fact that you and he seem incapable of even having a civil conversation these days is beside the point. It's my education, it's my life, and I do actually have a say in it.'

'But you've done two years, Robert, *two years* of the course, and now you want to drop it and do something else entirely.'

'Yes.'

Clare Baxter sighed. She closed her eyes for a moment, and then reached for a cigarette. She lit it, smoked it rapidly like a teenager, shaking her head every once in a while as if she was battling with some internal conflict.

'I'll speak to him,' Robert said.

'No,' Clare replied, '*I* will speak to him. *I* will deal with this, Robert.'

'You're just going to try and convince him to make me do what you want. The thing you seem to forget, and this is not the first time, is that what you want and what I want are not the same thing.'

'You think I don't have your best interests at heart?'

'I think you have your own best interests at heart—'

'That's a dreadful thing to say—'

Robert sneered. 'What's the matter? You can't handle the truth?'

Clare Baxter gritted her teeth. She ground her half-smoked cigarette into the ashtray and got up from the table. She needed to do something – *anything* – to distract herself.

Otherwise she would more than likely slap the disrespectful—

'I am going to speak to him,' Robert said, interrupting her
thoughts.

Clare reached the sink. She turned back towards him and
took a deep breath.

'Your father is a drunk, Robert. That's a truth for you right
there. You say I can't handle the truth . . . well, let me share
a few home truths with you about the marvelous and
wonderful Frank Parrish.'

Robert started to get up. 'I don't want to listen to this shit
anymore Mom, I really don't—'

'Sit the fuck down, Robert! I'm serious now. You sit right
there for a minute and listen to what I have to say. You can
do that much at least. What you do after that is entirely up
to you. You go over and see him. Go tell him you're going
to quit engineering halfway through the course. Graphic
design? Jesus, you really believe that there is work out there
for you—'

'What the fuck do you want from me, eh?' Robert snapped
back. 'You want me to go on doing something that I don't
like and can't do?'

'Well, if you can't do it that's probably got more to do with
your own attitude than anything else—'

'It's not about attitude, it's about purpose. I've done
enough of it to realize that I don't want to spend the rest of
my life in the guts of filthy fucking machines in dirty
factories, smelling like a fucking—'

'Enough!' Clare snapped. 'We don't need to scream and
shout at one another, and I certainly don't see the need for
you to use that kind of language to me.'

Robert took a deep breath. 'Okay,' he said quietly. 'Okay,
this is the way it is. I am not going to carry on doing
engineering. I am going to quit the class and do graphic
design. This is what I want to do. If I told Dad he would say
okay, that's fine, if that's what you want to do and you're
sure—'

'Your dad would just say what he thought you wanted to
hear—'

'No, Mom! Dad would treat me like an adult and respect the fact that I have power of choice.'

Clare hesitated, and then something just came over her and she let it go. 'Robert, listen to me. He's a drunk. He is in trouble at work. He's always in trouble at work. You know they took his driver's license off of him and put him on pay-hold. He doesn't know that I know this, but I do. His last partner was killed in the line of duty, and there was an internal investigation to determine whether Frank contributed to that situation—'

'And the internal investigation decreed that every action he took was in-policy, that he demonstrated the exact procedure and protocol for that scenario—'

'You sound like a police manual.'

'No, Mom, I sound like someone who's taken the time to talk to his father about what really happened with him and Michael Vale. You want to know what happened?'

'No, I really don't, to tell you the truth—'

'Well, I think you should. I think that's the least you should do. Listen to what someone else has to say for a moment instead of being so eager to hear your own voice.'

'How dare you—'

'No, Mom, how fucking dare *you*! He's my father and I love him, and here's a blind-sider for you, Caitlin loves him too. We respect him for who he is and what he does. You never worked before you got divorced. He supported you and us, and as far as we're concerned he did a damned good job of it. You only started working after he left, and that was because you had to. You didn't have a fucking choice. Well, let me tell you something. He did have a choice about what he could have done. He didn't become a cop because he wanted to. He became a cop because he *needed* to, because he felt it was the right thing. He had a sense of responsibility, which is more than I can say about you . . .'

That's when Clare Baxter lost it. She took two swift steps forward and raised her hand to slap her son, but even as her hand arced towards him, Robert stood up. The chair fell over backwards. He caught her arm by the wrist before it reached him. They stood there for a moment – deadlocked, a stand-off – and then Robert leaned forward, inches taller than his mother, and said, 'I'll do what I want, Mom. That's the simple truth of it. I will do what I want when I want how I want, and there's not a goddamned thing in the world you can do to stop me.'

Robert released her wrist and stepped away. The look in her eyes told him that she was not going to challenge him anymore.

He picked up his chair, set it straight, took his jacket from the back and put it on.

He walked to the door and hesitated. He looked back at her and half-smiled. 'Tell you something, Mom. I love you, and I respect you. And I understand your frustration with Dad, but believe me when I tell you that you are one hell of a bitch sometimes.'

Robert Parrish, looking more like his father than he ever had, left the house on a high. Half an hour and he'd be at his father's apartment, and he would have a story to tell.

EIGHTY-TWO

It had taken a few minutes for Frank Parrish to extricate himself from the cupboard beneath the stairs. Thankfully the blade of the screwdriver had been slim enough to fit in the gap between the latch and the striker plate, otherwise he might have had to break the door to get out. He stood in the hall for a while, and then he sat on the floor with his back against the wall. He massaged his thighs, his calves, flexed his knees, and waited until circulation fully returned to his legs, but they still hurt like hell.

He stood carefully, leaning against the wall for balance, and then he walked up and down the hallway a few times until he felt that his legs were once more his own. His stomach hurt. He could feel it a little more than before.

It was then, as he closed the stair cupboard door once more, that he paused. He reached out his hand and pressed against the floor. Almost imperceptibly, but unmistakably, it gave. Overtaken by a sudden feeling of urgency and agitation, he hurriedly pulled the contents out of the cupboard again. A toolbox, a vacuum cleaner, a pair of kid's sneakers, a bucket of paintbrushes and three cans of paint, a blanket, a shoebox. Beneath these things, there on the floor, was the small section of carpet, cut perfectly to fit snugly in the space. Parrish took a screwdriver and used it to lift the corner of the carpet, and saw linoleum beneath. He kept tugging until the section of carpet came away entirely, then he used the screwdriver once more and lifted the linoleum. He saw the edge of a floorboard and, pulling back the floor covering a little further, he discovered that the board had been cut horizontally. As had the one beside it. And the one beside that.

His heart racing, Parrish tugged at the linoleum. It had been stapled at the back edge and it tore fractionally. He cursed, and used his screwdriver once more to ease out the staples. He pulled them free, the linoleum came away complete, and he put it beside him in the hallway. The cut boards – three of them, side-by-side – now gave the impression of a two-foot wide trapdoor. Parrish levered the screwdriver beneath the nearest board and prized it up. He saw them right away, and there was no mistaking what they were . . .

Reaching out to lift the other board he heard a car slow and stop outside the house. His heart froze. He heard the car door open. Hurrying, desperate, panic-stricken, he replaced the first board, the linoleum, stuffed the carpet back in the cupboard, after it the sneakers, the cans of paint, the bucket of brushes, everything he had taken out of there. He pushed the door to with his shoulder, snatched his bag and his torch from the floor and turned to run up the stairs.

Frank Parrish made it to the uppermost riser just as someone put a key in the front door lock and turned it . . . just as he realized he'd left his screwdriver behind.

EIGHTY-THREE

Carole Paretski paused in her ex-husband's hallway and waited for a good three or four minutes. The house was utterly silent. She went on through to the kitchen, the utility space, and right to the rear door that led out into the yard. She headed back to the front of the house and began looking for anything that seemed out of place. She looked in every DVD case, amongst piles of magazines and work-related documents. She went through Richard's bureau – opening drawers and rifling through them, ensuring that she put everything back exactly as she'd found it. She walked around the edges of the room, pulling back the carpet and looking beneath for any sign that floorboards had been loosened. She tried to think what she would do if she had something important to hide. Where would she put it? How would she make it as secure and concealed as possible?

She did the same in the hallway, even started to knock the lower risers of the stairwell to see if any of them sounded less solid than the others. There was nothing.

The last thing she checked was the under-stairs cupboard, and it was here that something struck her as odd. Richard was meticulously neat, always had been. What she believed would have been very orderly was somewhat random. A screwdriver on the floor, the section of carpet haphazardly tossed in there, cans of paints, a spilled bucket of brushes, a pair of Sarah's sneakers just thrown in there as if they were to be discarded.

Carole frowned. She started to lift things out one by one and place them on the hallway rug behind her. The section of carpet came out last, evidently cut to fit in the space, evidently supposed to belong there, matching the hallway carpet exactly. She started to put it back – why, she didn't know – but she did, and it was as she pressed it down that she felt the floorboards move beneath the linoleum. She paused. She looked back to her right for the screwdriver, and using the tip she lifted the edge of the linoleum and started to pull it back. She tucked the screwdriver into her back pocket, carefully lifted the whole section out and placed it behind her. She paused for a moment, and then she lifted one of the boards.

Frank Parrish stood silently at the top of the stairs. Someone was down there, and from the angle he could not see who it was. It had sounded as if they were searching the place, much as he had done, but that didn't make sense. Who else would have come over to look through the house? Someone with a key, evidently. Who would have had a key? Only person he could think of was Carole Paretski. Or perhaps a girlfriend that McKee had withheld from them? Then it struck him: the accomplice. It had always been there at the back of his mind, the feeling that McKee had not worked alone. Had the accomplice come over to remove evidence, take something away, collect something that McKee had promised him? Was their relationship such that they trusted one another with house keys? Of course it was. Hell, they kidnapped, drugged, raped and murdered teenage girls together.

Parrish eased out his .32 and took a deep breath. Perhaps half a dozen risers down the stairwell and he would be able to see who was in the hallway. He raised one foot, and then lowered it ever so slowly to the right edge of the uppermost riser. He released his weight as carefully as he could, praying that the risers did not creak, that they were solid and secure and silent. With all his weight on his right foot he gripped the banister and started to move his left. He could feel his heart thudding in his chest. What would he do? Arrest the guy? He could do nothing else, and yet the arrest would be invalid. *He* would be the one arrested shortly thereafter. Illegal search, B&E, the whole works. Whatever the consequences, it didn't matter. McKee's accomplice was down there removing all the evidence and Parrish had no choice but to stop him.

He lowered his left foot silently, exhaled, inhaled once more, and lifted his right foot again.

*

The horror and dismay that engulfed Carole Paretski as she lifted one image after another from the box beneath the floorboards was immeasurable. Teenage girls, they had to be, and they were dying. There was no question in her mind that these girls were being tortured and killed. Their eyes staring back at the camera – wide and terrified and bloodshot. Their faces reddened, blue in some cases, as something was tightened around their necks and they were choked into lifelessness. Naked, kneeling, prostrate, tied, handcuffed, some of them bruised and bleeding, some of them already unconscious as her ex-husband fucked them. There was no doubt in her mind that it was Richard. His face was not present in any of the images, but she had spent sufficient years living with him, sleeping with him, had carried and given birth to two of his children . . .

She knew what she was looking at, and every fear that had ever possessed her was realized in that moment.

Beneath the pictures were DVDs, dozens of them, and as she looked through them – handwritten titles that were more often than not just a single girl's name – she began to appreciate the breadth and depth of what he had been doing. Frank Parrish had walked her around the edges of it, unable to tell her the truth. There was something about how he had asked questions, something about his manner, that had done nothing but exacerbate her fears. And now here she was – kneeling in the hallway of Richard's house, in her hands the evidence that the police needed – DVDs and photographs of some of the very worst things that she could imagine, her husband guilty of far worse than she could ever have believed.

The DVDs slid from her fingers. They scattered across the floor, and as she watched them go she saw something that struck her with such force she was unable to breathe.

Sarah and friends – August, September, October 2004

Carole picked up the DVD. Sarah? Her daughter? It couldn't be. It wasn't possible.

She got up suddenly, and walked through to the sitting room. She snatched the DVD remote from the coffee table, switched on the TV, waited for the DVD tray to slide from the front of the machine and then she dropped the disc in.

Even as she pressed the play button her heart was hammering through the front of her ribcage. Even as she saw the jagged black and gray lines at the start of the images she knew . . . she just *knew* . . . and there she was, Sarah, her own daughter, with a couple of school friends on a sleepover.

She fast-forwarded the images, and she found what Richard had been looking for. The three of them getting changed into their nightclothes. She closed her eyes. She felt the overwhelming grief, alongside it the sense of relief as she began to understand what would happen to him, that now he would be out of their lives for ever, that he would never, never be able to do anything to Sarah again.

As the TV started up Parrish moved more quickly. Maybe whoever was down there had just come over to watch some of the DVDs. Maybe that was the arrangement he had with McKee. On the days McKee was out of the house the accomplice could come over. Or maybe they watched these things together, but Saturdays – when McKee was out with the kids – the accomplice had free rein to come around and party all by himself.

The feeling of vindication he had experienced when he saw the pictures that McKee had hidden beneath the floorboards more than compensated for any sense of guilt he felt about breaking into the man's house. The man was scum, the lowest of the low, and this was where the game ended. How he would do it he didn't know, and in that moment – as he reached the bottom of the stairs, as he turned with his gun ahead of him towards the front room of the house, he didn't care. It was now over – for Melissa, Jennifer, for Nicole and Karen and Rebecca and Kelly. For all those that would have followed in their wake, the nightmare was finished.

Frank Parrish – feeling a greater sense of resolve and clarity than he could ever recall – reached the sitting room door.

Was that the front door?

Carole stopped dead. She froze for a split-second, and then she backed up and pressed herself against the wall behind the door. The sound of the TV almost drowned out the beating of her heart. She squinted through the gap at the edge of the doorframe, and she saw nothing but a gun. She couldn't believe what she was seeing, but she could not negate her own eyes.

Did Richard own a gun? Had he obtained a gun from somewhere? Had he come into the house while she'd been watching the DVD, seen the mess spilling out of the cupboard, and was even now planning on shooting the imagined burglar?

Carole reached for the screwdriver in her back pocket and held it tightly. She hesitated for a second, looked through the gap one more time to see Richard take another step forward, and knew she had to do it. She knew that this was her chance to be rid of the bastard for ever.

Stepping forward suddenly, her left hand brandishing the screwdriver, she grabbed the door handle and used it as a pivot to swing herself around the edge of the door. She had her full weight and strength behind her, and even as Frank Parrish stepped across the threshold of the room he saw nothing but a flash of silver, the shape of an arm, and then there was a pain beyond description in the middle of his body. It was not the pain that made him drop the gun, but the sudden and unexpected shock. The gun clattered to the ground, and he dropped to his knees, and he looked down to see the handle of a screwdriver protruding from his upper abdomen, right there beneath his ribs, and when he took a moment to look up he saw Carole Paretski looking down at him with a look of such surprise he couldn't help but smile.

The smile lasted no more than a second. His system went into shock, he started to hyperventilate and shake, and had Carole Paretski not had the foresight to grab his shoulder then Frank Parrish would have fallen forward and driven the screwdriver all the way into his stomach. Internal bleeding kicked into overdrive as he passed out without a sound.

EIGHTY-FOUR

Robert was in his father's apartment no more than five minutes before he picked up the phone and called his cell. It rang out. He called the Precinct and asked for Frank Parrish and was told that Frank was not on duty that weekend.

He wondered where his father could be, and then thought of Eve. He searched for Frank's phonebook, couldn't find it, and then noticed the cell phone at the side of the bed. He had switched it off, left it behind, and Eve's number would definitely be there. He found it without delay, called it, got the voicemail and left a message.

'Hi, Eve, this is Robert, Frank's son. Was wondering if you knew where he was—'

'Robert?'

'Oh, hi there. How ya doin'?'

'I'm good, yes. How are you?'

'Fine, fine, no problems. Was after my dad.'

'I haven't seen him, Robert, not for a while.'

'Okay. If you do see him, or if he calls you, let him know to give me a call on my cell.'

'I'll do that, Robert. You take care now?'

'You too.'

Robert hung up. Way cool. Dad's hooker friend. He put Frank's cell on the kitchen table and opened the refrigerator. There were four cans left of a Schlitz six-pack. He pulled one out, cracked it, sat down at the table and drank his beer. He figured he'd hang out for an hour or so, maybe watch the tube, play some records, and then he would head home. That was unless Dad showed up, and then they'd maybe go get a burger or something. He hadn't seen him for some weeks, and it would be good to catch up.

*

Caitlin Parrish was drying her hair when the phone rang. Instinctively, she picked it up just as Radick was coming through to tell her he didn't want to answer it in case it was Frank.

She asked who it was, what they wanted, and even as Radick stood there watching her, even as she listened to the caller at the other end, she visibly paled.

Radick frowned, tilted his head to one side.

'Yes,' she said, 'of course we will. We're on the way now.'

She hung up, looked at Radick, looked back at the phone.

'What?' he said.

'It's Dad,' she replied, the shock evident in her voice.

'What about him? What's happened?'

'He's at Holy Family Hospital. He's been stabbed.'

Clare Baxter had smoked three more cigarettes after her son had left the house. She also poured three quarters of an inch of Crown Royal into a glass and drank it straight. She stood in the kitchen and wondered whether it was her or the rest of the world. Probably the rest of the world.

Frank would agree with Robert. Robert would be smug and condescending. Fuck the pair of them. Frank always agreed with Robert and Caitlin simply because he felt so guilty about being such an absent father. And he had been an absent father, regardless of what Robert and Caitlin believed.

She poured another drink even as the phone rang. At first she thought it might have been Robert calling to apologize, but he was too much like his father to dream of such a thing.

It wasn't Robert, it was Caitlin, and even as Clare listened to her, even as she registered what she was being told, she felt the glass slipping from her fingers. The sound of it exploding when it hit the floor snapped her into action. She hung up, grabbed her coat, and hurried out of the house. If the traffic was with her she could make it to Holy Family Hospital in fifteen minutes.

Robert tossed the empty beer can towards the trash and missed. It bounced off the back wall and skittered across the floor. He left it where it was. He needed a smoke. He didn't have any with him. Where was the nearest store? He'd take a

426

walk, grab a pack, then head back and see if Dad had returned. If not, he would leave him a message and go home. Maybe he'd go see a movie. It was Saturday. Saturday wasn't for studying.

Robert got up, dropped the can in the trash and headed for the door. His cell rang, and thinking Eve had gotten a message to his father he punched the button without looking at the screen.

'Dad?'

'It's Caitlin. Listen to me. Dad's been hurt. He was hurt in some incident. I don't know details, but he's over at Holy Family Hospital. You know where that is?'

'What? What are you fucking talking about?'

'Listen to what I'm saying, Robert. I don't know any more than this. Dad is at Holy Family Hospital. It's on Dean Street down near Atlantic Avenue. Get over there now. You got your car?'

'No, I haven't.'

'Get a cab, whatever. Just get there, okay?'

'Okay, yes . . . I'll get a cab. Jesus, Cait, what the fuck—'

'I gotta go, Robert. See you at the hospital.'

The line went dead. He stood there for a second, and in a moment of inexplicable consideration he picked up the land-line receiver, hit *Last Number Redial*, and waited for Eve to pick up.

He told her what had happened. She asked him where he was.

'At Dad's apartment. I'm still here.'

'Wait there,' she said. 'I'm coming to get you.'

Radick drove. They were there within ten minutes. Caitlin rushed up the steps and hurtled into Patient Registration.

Radick called the Precinct. He spoke to Valderas, told him that he knew nothing but the simple fact that Parrish had been injured and had been rushed to Holy Family. Valderas said he was on his way and hung up.

Radick hurried up the stairs after Caitlin and had his badge out by the time he reached the desk.

Caitlin had already found her father in triage, was there to share the briefest of words with him before he was rushed into surgery. He was delirious, drifting in and out of consciousness, but when he saw her he smiled, told her she looked good, asked her if she had enough walking-out money. He told her that he'd finally managed to get her into a local hospital. Then he fell unconscious again and the nurses took him away.

EIGHTY-FIVE

Valderas called Marie Griffin, picked her up enroute. By the time they arrived at Holy Family Hospital Valderas had secured at least a few details of what had happened on Sackett Street from the attending officers. He knew that both Carole Paretski and Frank Parrish had been in Richard McKee's house. From what he understood, Carole Paretski had every right to be there, but Parrish – predictably – did not. Whether they had gone there together or separately he did not know. He guessed the latter. Carole Paretski was under arrest; she was being held at the 11th, and as soon as the lead detective there had some further and better particulars he was going to call Valderas. When it came to the wounding or murder of a fellow officer, the territorial lines seemed to disappear and everyone co-operated one with another.

Aside from Jimmy Radick, Valderas didn't know the people that had gathered in the waiting room.

'This is Caitlin, Frank's daughter,' Radick told him.

Both Marie Griffin and Squad Sergeant Valderas expressed their concern for Frank, their willingness to do anything to help.

'And this is Mrs Clare Baxter,' Radick added, and Valderas shook hands with a stone-faced woman who looked like she resented their presence.

'Frank's ex-wife,' Radick added, and Valderas remembered a conversation he'd had one time with Frank about this woman. He allowed nothing in his expression, but smiled as sympathetically as he could, and once again iterated his desire to do anything he could to help . . .

'So what have you been told?' Valderas asked Radick.

'Very little. Stabbed once, but deep, and somewhere in the upper abdomen. They took him right into surgery.'

'I spoke to him before he went in,' Caitlin interjected. 'He was delirious. He didn't really say anything about what happened.' She paused, looked at Jimmy, then at Valderas. Her expression said everything that needed to be said: she was fighting with her emotions; she looked ready to burst; she looked terrified.

'Do you know what happened, Sergeant?' she asked.

Valderas shook his head. What he did know did not belong in a conversation with the man's daughter. If Parrish had gone over there alone then he was going to get busted out of the PD, no question. Already on pay-hold, already without a driver's license . . . and that prompted another thought – the fact that Parrish might have been the one who took a car from the pool. One was missing, and in that moment Valderas would have put his paycheck on it being Frank Parrish. So it would be theft of PD property, driving without a license, B&E, illegal search, harassment of a witness . . .

Valderas turned at the sound of the door suddenly crashing open.

'Robert!' Caitlin said, and rushed towards a young dark-haired man. The likeness to Frank was unmistakable. This was the son.

Following him was an elegant brunette, mid-thirties perhaps. Great looking, very self-assured, but again that telltale strain in her face of dealing with something she didn't understand.

Caitlin and Robert hugged, and then he asked her what was happening, how Dad was, if he was okay, if he was going to make it.

'I don't know enough, I don't really know anything,' she said.

Clare Baxter was with them then, and though she said nothing she was obviously sincerely concerned for what was occurring, perhaps more for the mental state of her children than the physical state of her ex-husband.

Caitlin introduced Robert to Valderas, to Jimmy Radick, to Marie Griffin, and then Robert turned and nodded at Eve. She came forward, perhaps a little tentatively. She was evidently out of place, felt as much, but didn't want to be anywhere else in the moment.

'This is Eve Challoner,' Robert said. 'Dad's friend.'

Eve smiled, shook hands with everyone. She said nothing.

There were seven of them there – the ex-wife, the kids, the daughter's lover, the psychotherapy counsellor, the squad sergeant and the hooker – all of them waiting for word back from Surgery. Frank Parrish had been stabbed, seriously wounded by all accounts, and there was nothing they could do but wait.

Valderas and Griffin were the first to sit. Eve followed suit, and then Robert sat beside her as if he felt some obligation to be the link between her, his family, and Frank's professional life. Caitlin sat beside Robert, Jimmy Radick beside her, and Clare Baxter paced the room like she was caught between staying and leaving. After a moment she said, 'I need to smoke,' and left the room. She had been gone no more than four or five minutes before she walked back into the same awkward silence she'd left behind.

'Anything?' she asked Caitlin.

Valderas perceived tension between the mother and the son. Was it because he'd brought Eve, someone he could only imagine was Frank's current girlfriend? Was there still something there between Frank Parrish and Clare Baxter? Or was it purely the son and the mother? Valderas didn't know, couldn't guess. He didn't really care, he was just trying to fill his mind with things that weren't about whether Frank Parrish would die, and beyond that – if he survived – how it would be his job to kick Frank Parrish out of the NYPD.

And then there was the case Frank had been working on. Already he'd heard from the lead at the 11th that something had been found at the McKee house. 'Something heavy,' was all that he'd been told. 'Soon as I get anything else I'll call you,' the detective had said, and Valderas had thanked him. It would be ironic if Parrish had broken the case. Parrish and this Carole Paretski working in consort. Had they found the guy? Was McKee their guy?

'What can we do?' Robert asked suddenly. 'Caitlin?'

She shook her head. 'There's nothing we can do right now, except wait.'

Robert frowned. 'You're a nurse, aren't you? Can't you go through there and ask them what the fuck is going on?'

'No, I can't, Robert. I just have to wait like everyone else.'

Robert stood up. 'This is bullshit,' he said loudly.

Eve reached out and touched his arm. 'Sit down,' she said.

Robert sat down.

'Does anyone know where he was?' Radick asked. 'What he was doing?'

'All I know is that Carole Paretski was involved,' Valderas said, 'and that stays inside this room, okay?'

'Who the hell is that?' Robert asked.

'She is the wife of a man Frank was looking at; a case he's working on. That's all I know, and that's all I can say.'

'And she was with him when he was stabbed?' Caitlin asked.

'I don't know any details,' Valderas replied. 'All I can tell you is that Frank is here and she is being held at a local precinct.'

'Was she the one who stabbed him?' Eve asked.

Valderas shook his head. 'Like I said, I don't have any details—'

'Can't you call someone?' Clare Baxter asked. 'Can't you find out what happened?'

'I have to let the arresting officers and assigned detectives do their jobs, Mrs Baxter, just like your daughter has to let the doctors and surgeons do their work here. I'm waiting for a call to let me know what they've found out. Soon as I hear anything I'll obviously let you know what I can.'

'So we just wait,' she replied, stating the obvious. She walked to the door and stood there looking out through the porthole window.

'He's done something crazy, hasn't he?' Caitlin said. 'This case he's working on . . . he got frustrated and he went and did something crazy, right?' She was looking at Valderas but her question seemed to be directed at anyone. Her anxiety was evident in her face, her hands, her whole body. She was trying to persuade herself that it was all going to be okay, that her father was going to pull through, that he would come out the other side of whatever he had gotten himself into.

'Caitlin, we just don't know what happened,' Radick said, and in that moment everyone present understood that there was something deeper here than a cop and his partner's daughter.

Clare Baxter turned back to look at Jimmy Radick. Valderas frowned, Marie Griffin, too – almost unnoticeably. Eve glanced at Robert, Robert looked at Caitlin, then at the man beside her, and they all understood that these people weren't strangers. No-one said anything; there was nothing that needed to be said.

'Whatever happened,' Valderas said, 'it happened because he believed he was doing the right thing.'

Clare Baxter made a sound. It was dismissive, perhaps, even condescending. *I lived with the man,* that sound said. *I lived with him, I carried his children . . . so don't you come here and tell me what to think about someone that you don't even know.*

'Shut up, Mom,' Robert said. 'Just shut the fuck up. '

Caitlin's eyes were wide. 'Robert!'

'And you can shut the fuck up too,' he snapped. 'You don't know him. Jesus, none of you do.'

Clare Baxter, her face like a deflated balloon, walked slowly to the chairs on the other side of the room and sat down.

The silence was oppressive, uncomfortable, electric.

'I know him,' Eve said, and with those three words she not only broke that silence but everyone in the room turned and looked at her with a quizzical expression. 'I know him, as well as anyone else I know, that's for sure.' She paused, then she smiled, and then seemed to laugh to herself as if remembering some half-forgotten moment. 'Last time I saw him he spent three hours trying to talk some kid out of killing his girlfriend. He gave it his best but the kid killed the girl anyway . . . killed the girl and then killed himself.' Eve looked up. She looked at each of them in turn. She returned her gaze to some indefinite space in the middle of the room, and she smiled pensively. 'They were in a bathtub. The boy had already cut the girl's leg, in her thigh, you know? She was bleeding very badly. Then he cut her throat and then he cut his own throat, and Frank spent however long trying to wrestle the kids out of a bathtub full of blood to save their lives. But he didn't do it. He tried his best but he didn't do it.'

'Frank is a good cop,' Valderas interjected. 'He has his issues, he has his difficulties, but he's one of the best.'

'Like his father,' Radick said.

Valderas smiled knowingly.

'What?' Caitlin asked.

'Nothing,' Valderas replied.

'No, tell me,' she said. 'Tell me what made you smile.'

'It was just the old crew that Frank's father used to belong to. They were called the Saints of New York. They were the ones who helped get organized crime out of New York. No question about it, Frank came from good stock.'

Marie Griffin opened her mouth to say something, and then she closed it. She wanted to say something, wanted to tell them about Lufthansa, about the unsolved deaths of Joe Manri and Robert McMahon, about what Frank Parrish really felt about his father, but she could not.

'He's a good detective,' Jimmy Radick said. 'I mean, we've only worked together for – what? – nearly three weeks, but I've learned a hell of a lot—'

'Does Frank know you're sleeping with his daughter?'

Radick looked up at Clare Baxter.

'Mom! Jesus Christ, what the fuck is your problem?'

Clare Baxter was angry. Her eyes flashed as she looked at Valderas. 'Is that even allowed in the New York Police Department?'

'Mrs Baxter, it's none of our business. We don't regulate the personal lives of officers, except where the law is being broken—'

Radick was speechless. What was it with this woman? Did she just hate Frank? Did she hate her kids? Was she jealous, perhaps afraid of something? He made a mental note that if Frank came through this he would congratulate him for divorcing the crazy bitch.

'Yes, Mom, it's none of your business,' Caitlin said. 'We're talking about Dad here, not you. Be content just for one second not to be the center of attention, okay?'

Valderas glanced at Marie Griffin. She didn't even raise an eyebrow, she didn't need to. Everything that needed to be said was there in her eyes. The whole fucking family was nuts. No wonder Frank Parrish had a hard time at work.

'And who the hell are you?' Clare Baxter said, turning on Eve.

Eve smiled. 'I'm Eve,' she said. 'Eve Challoner. I'm a very, very expensive escort, but Frank comes over to see me every once in a while and gets it for free.'

Clare Baxter sat open-mouthed and incredulous. Robert laughed. Valderas smiled. No-one spoke for at least a minute.

Clare Baxter made a performance of hunting through her purse for cigarettes. She found them, and then flounced out of the room like a petulant child.

'Jesus,' Robert said. He turned to Eve. 'I'm sorry about that,' he said. He looked at Valderas, at Griffin, at Radick. 'She's stressed, man, seriously stressed. I don't know what the fuck is going on with her, but she is worse than usual.'

They all nodded. No-one spoke. It was understood.

'Is there anything else you can tell us about what happened?' Caitlin asked. Her question was directed at Valderas.

Valderas shook his head. 'Like I said, I know very little about what actually happened. I'm waiting for more info, and as soon as I get it I'll tell you.'

'So is he really good at his job?' Caitlin asked. 'Is he really a good detective, or are you just saying that because we're here and he might die?'

'Cait—' Robert started.

'No, Robert, I want the truth. I want to hear the truth from someone who knows him professionally. You've known him a long time, right?'

'Sure have,' Valderas said. 'I knew him before he became a detective.'

'So?'

'So what?'

'So is he good?'

'One of the best,' Valderas replied.

'So what the fuck is it with the driver's license and the suspended pay? What the hell did he do?'

Valderas shook his head. 'Frank isn't one for rules and regulations,' he said. 'Never has been. Frank is old-school. He gets frustrated with the system, as we all do, but he gets more frustrated than most. You get cases where you know the truth, but there is nothing you can do about it. Charges

435

get dropped, guilty people make plea bargains with the DA's Office, cases fall apart on technicalities, criminals go free to do the same thing all over again. He struggles with it, and every once in a while he does something out of line and he gets reined in. It is not an easy job, let me tell you, and I feel the frustration and disillusionment these guys experience. Unfortunately, the system is the system, and however much we complain about it it's all we have until something better comes along.'

'Is he going to lose his job now?' Robert asked. 'Did he do something wrong?'

'I don't know, Robert, I really don't.'

'This is a tough thing to come back from,' Caitlin said.

'He's dealt with tougher than this,' Valderas replied.

'Michael Vale,' Eve said. 'He dealt with Michael Vale.'

Antony Valderas turned slowly and looked at the woman. There were tears in her eyes. Her mascara was smudged.

'Yes,' Valderas said. 'He dealt with Michael Vale.'

'He never told me what happened,' Caitlin said.

'He didn't tell me either,' Robert added.

'I know what happened,' Eve said.

Valderas nodded. 'So do I.'

Caitlin and Robert looked at one another. 'So?' they said, almost as one.

'You want to hear what happened when Michael Vale was killed?'

'Sure,' Caitlin said.

'Abso-fucking-lutely,' Robert added.

Valderas looked at Eve Challoner. 'You wanna tell them?' he asked.

'Let's both tell them,' she replied.

EIGHTY-SIX

'You are a fucking loser. Jesus, Mike, what the fuck is this?'

Frank Parrish held up a polystyrene cup of coffee, and from a small hole in the base a continuous stream of liquid dribbled into the bin beside his desk.

'High quality utensils, ably provided by the New York Police Department. You want another one, go get it yourself.'

Parrish did so, returning in a moment with a new cup.

'So what's the news today?' he asked Vale.

'We go back and check on that thing from yesterday, the girl from the Heights, and then we spend the rest of today and tomorrow looking busy. I have a weekend away planned, and I want to get out early. Last thing I need right now is another case starting up.'

'Where you going?'

'Upstate,' Vale replied. 'Last time Nancy and I had a week-end away was like . . . Jesus, it must be three years ago.'

'You had that wedding. Who was that – your nephew or someone?'

'Someone else's wedding doesn't fucking count. You have to go on up there and be on your best fucking behavior. I hate that shit. Anyways, it's been too fucking long, I know that much, and she's stir crazy. I get something that stops me going she's gonna go find a lawyer and take *him* away for the weekend.'

Parrish laughed, he drank his coffee, and he didn't even hesitate when the phone rang on his desk.

Less than twenty minutes later they were back of a generator unit behind a block of apartments on Baron Street. The place was filthy. Broken-down cars, the seats burst open, the body-work rusted and pitted with holes. Broken bottles, a burned-out brazier, needles and used diapers and garbage strewn back and forth around the place. It stank, and Parrish and Vale hunkered down behind the car while the first-response uniform told them what was going on.

'Far as I can tell, there's one guy. He's down in the basement with most of the residents. There's about thirty of them. He says he's got a grenade—'

'A what?'

'I know. Like I said, a grenade. He's ex-military himself, says his brother was in Iraq and gave him a working grenade as a memento. Says he's going to use it.'

'What's he want?'

'Wants his girlfriend to bring his kid back. Apparently she took off with the kid yesterday, won't answer his calls, has now switched her phone off. I think he was up all night doing crank and he's lost the plot completely.'

'And he says he's gonna use the grenade and kill some people?'

The officer shook his head. 'Not just some. He says he's gonna kill all of them. The apartment block has an oil-fuelled heating system. He's down there with the oil tank, and three jerry cans of gasoline. He says that if he lets the grenade go then everyone is going to die.'

'Fuck this,' Vale said. 'This is federal. This is kidnapping, terrorism. This isn't our jurisdiction. They need to get out here with a hostage negotiator.'

'We're onto that already, but he just sent a kid out—'

'There are kids down there?' Parrish asked.

'About eight or nine of them, as far as I know.'

'Jesus fucking Christ,' Parrish said. 'So he sent one of them out?'

'He did . . . sent them out with a message. Said he wanted to talk to a detective in the next five minutes or he was going to kill one of the hostages. Oh yeah, he has a handgun as well. From what the kid said it sounds like a semi-automatic. What do they get in the military now – maybe a Beretta, a Glock perhaps? The kid said it was square and long, not like a revolver.'

'Fuck it,' Parrish said. 'Let's just go down there and shoot the asshole in the head.'

Vale stood up. He brushed down the backs of his pants. 'I'll go down there,' he said. 'Come with me, stay close, we'll take it from there.'

Parrish got up. The pair of them started walking to the car for vests.

Vale looked back at the young officer still crouched back of the black-and-white. 'And get the Feds down here, for God's sake. Tell them what's going on. Tell them we need a negotiator.'

The officer nodded, walked around back of the car and reached for the radio.

It was not a good set-up. The basement was more a utility room, no more than fifteen by fifteen. It housed an oil tank, a rack of shelves loaded with various tools and repair equipment, in back a door that led through to the boiler room. The hostages – thirty-four in all – were seated in a huddle against the right-hand wall. There were men, women and children. One girl, couldn't have been more than twenty or twenty-one, was carrying a baby. The first question on Michael Vale's mind was how this guy had managed to get thirty-four people down into the basement. He must have gone through the apartment block with his gun and his grenade and herded them all down here like sheep. Un-fucking-real.

'You alone?' the guy said. He was white, heavy built, buzz-cut hair, the top half inch of his right ear missing. He looked like the doorman at a KKK meeting. In his right hand he held a Sig, in his left the grenade. The pin was still in, but that didn't mean a great deal, for he had looped a piece of string through it and put that string around his neck. One sharp pull and the pin was out. He didn't have to use his gun hand to activate the grenade. He'd thought this thing through. This was premeditated.

'What's your name?' Vale asked.

'You on your own or is there someone back of you?'

'My partner's back there.'

'Well, bring him the fuck on down here, motherfucker. Can't have him left out of the party, can we?'

The kid's eyes were hot and spiked. He was still cooked on whatever he'd been doing.

Parrish had heard every word, and he came on down.

'Guns,' the kid said, and nodded towards the floor. Both Vale and Parrish produced their service semis and lowered them to the concrete floor.

'Ankles,' the kid said. 'You first,' he added, and waved his gun at Parrish.

Parrish leaned down and lifted each pant leg in turn. There was no ankle holster.

Vale did the same, took a .38 snub-nosed from the holster and put that on the floor also.

'Lift your arms and turn around slowly,' the kid ordered. 'I wanna see waistbands, wanna see under arms, wanna see everything.'

Vale and Parrish did as they were told.

'Now kick those guns over here – slowly, okay?'

Vale did as he was asked, and the kid used his foot to put the guns behind him in the corner.

The kid – satisfied – told Parrish to sit on a step halfway up. 'And sit on your hands,' he added. 'I see you move I'm gonna shoot someone in the fucking face, okay?'

Parrish backed up a step, sat down, put his hands beneath him.

'What's your name?'

'Frank Parrish.'

'And you?'

'Michael Vale.'

'I'm Karl. That's all you get. Just Karl. My girl's name is Laney, my son's name is Karl junior. They live upstairs at 13B. Everything you wanna know about them is in the apartment – pictures, phone books, her computer, the fucking lot. That's what you got. You gotta find her and my kid and you gotta bring them back here to talk to me, or everyone goes sky-fucking-high, okay?'

'When did she go?'

Karl frowned. 'Yesterday.'

'And does she drive . . . does she have a car?'

'Sure she does . . . why?'

'So we can gauge how far she'll have gone.'

'Shit, man, she won't go far . . . she'll go see that motherfucking Ramone. Either that or her mother, fucking bitch.'

'Who is Ramone?' Parrish asked.

Karl looked surprised. He scowled at Parrish. 'I was talking to you, motherfucker? Was I fucking talking to you? Mind your own fucking business, you cocksucker . . . I'm talking to your buddy here.'

Parrish raised his hand – palms up, a conciliatory gesture.

'Anyways, who is Ramone? I'll tell you who Ramone is. Ramone is a wetback motherfucker asshole who's been fucking my girl, that's who he is.'

'And where does he live?'

'I don't fucking know. I only found out about it yesterday.'

'What happened? You found out she was cheating on you?'

Karl laughed – a sharp and sudden sound.

The baby started crying.

Karl turned and raised his gun. 'I said for you to shut the fucking baby up, lady!'

'Karl!' Vale said. His voice was commanding and definite. 'You have to let the baby go,' he said.

Karl turned and looked at him. The gun was now directed at Vale's chest. 'You what?'

'We have to get the baby out of here. No questions. No bullshit. No fucking around. There are more than enough people here to get what you want. The baby, the mother . . . in fact all the kids need to be out of here now.'

Karl was silent for a moment.

'Hey, man, say one of them was Karl Junior. This is not a good scene. This is not what people want to see on the TV. They wanna see some guy, he's got a beef, he's cut up by his girl, you know? He's gonna make a stand, he's got something to say, but he's a father, right? He understands what's happening. He proves how good a father he is by letting all the kids go—'

'You!' Karl said, and he pointed the gun at Parrish. 'You take all the kids outside. You come right on back, okay? No bullshitting me. You come right on back . . . you got one minute to get all these kids outta here, the mother too, and then you come right on back or your buddy's gonna be breathing out a hole in his fucking head, you understand me?'

'Absolutely,' Parrish said. He stood up. He came slowly down the steps as Vale stepped to the left.

'Get up, kids,' Parrish said. 'Get up quickly. Come with me. We're going up the steps and out of here now.'

The mother with the baby helped corral the children – all eight of them, and she and Parrish escorted them up and along the corridor that led to the basement exit.

Vale was left in the basement with Karl and his remaining twenty-four hostages.

Parrish was back within forty-five seconds. He returned to the step and sat down.

'So you were telling me who Ramone was. You were telling me what happened.'

'Ramone? I don't know who the fuck Ramone is. She said if I hit her she'd tell Ramone. She didn't even mean to fucking say it. I know it. She said his name and then she knew she was in it deep, man, in it real fucking deep. I told her I'd find the motherfucker and put a half dozen caps in his ass. She told me that he was over the street at this house, and I went to find out what the fuck was going on. She lied to me, man. There wasn't no fucking Ramone over the street. I come back here and she's taken off with Karl Junior. Fucking bitch!'

Karl was angry and agitated. He started waving the gun at the hostages. They crouched closer. They let out exclamations of fear. Some of the women were crying, but trying to suppress it. He was pissed, they knew that, and they didn't want to piss him off even further. They only wanted to get out of there one way, and that was alive.

'So there was no Ramone?' Vale asked.

'No,' Karl said. He stopped waving the gun and turned back to the steps.

'You wanna know what I think?' Vale asked.

'Not really no.'

'I don't think there is any Ramone—'

'What? What the fuck you talking about, man?'

'What I said. I don't think there is any Ramone. I don't think there's such a person. Girl like Laney isn't gonna go for a guy called Ramone. C'mon, man, take a look at it. Look at you. For God's sake, man, as American as they come. You've done service, right?'

'Yeah, sure have. Done my time in the military.'

'A girl who goes with a solider, has his son, calls him Karl junior . . . shee-it man, she isn't gonna go for some wetback cocksucker called Ramone, is she? Get your head straight, man. She's just bullshitted you to get a bit of space. She's over at her mother's place, right? Is that where she goes when she's pissed with you?'

'Yeah, man, she does. She goes over there and tells the old bitch what an asshole I am.'

'Hell, man, they all do that. It's how they make themselves feel less guilty for holding out on you. It'll be something simple, man. She's taken some of your money. She's had some guy ask her out and she hasn't told you about it. You did something that pissed her off and she's got mad and taken off, and she's probably all ready to come right back at you and say sorry.'

Karl didn't respond.

Vale took a half-step closer to Karl. 'How old's your son?' he asked.

Karl looked up. 'How old? He's five, man, five years old.'

'And you guys have been together how long?'

'Me an' Laney? Eight years we been together, eight fucking years.'

'And how many times has she run off like this?'

'Aah, man, I can't even remember how many fucking times she's done that.'

'See?' Vale said. 'It's the same as always. You guys just need to get your heads straight. You need to stop cranking up so fucking much for starters, and then you need to spend some time together, talk about this shit, get it worked out.'

Karl closed his eyes for a moment and breathed deeply.

Vale took another half-step forward.

Parrish watched him do it, felt the indescribable tension in his gut, in every nerve and sinew and muscle. Vale wasn't a negotiator. He wasn't trained to do the shit that he was doing.

Karl opened his eyes. He seemed not to notice that Michael Vale was a foot closer than he had been.

'You're right, man. This is just so much bullshit.'

'Look, Karl. I can't get you out of this with nothing. You

got a weapon there. You got a fucking grenade, for God's sake.' Vale smiled. 'That's fucking impressive by the way. All the years I've been doing this and that's a fucking first for me. Work o' genius, a fucking grenade of all things. Anyways, like I said, you got a weapon there, you got a grenade. You let all the kids go. That was real fucking smart even if I say so myself. You got some people down here who are a bit shaken up, but right now no-one's been hurt—'

Vale was interrupted by his radio.

The sudden burst of static was loud in the confines of the room. Karl took a step backwards and raised the gun. 'What the fuck?'

Vale raised his hands. 'It'll be news about Laney,' he said calmly. 'Let me find out what's happening, okay?'

Karl paused. He looked at Vale, then at Parrish, then surveyed the hostages. 'Go,' he said. 'Answer the thing.'

Vale unhooked his radio and held it up. He pressed the button. 'Vale here,' he said. 'What you got for us?'

'We got the girl, Detective. She's here. She says she's willing to see the guy now. The boy is here too.'

'Good enough,' Vale said. 'We'll be up in a little while. I don't want to see anyone up there. Everyone stay well back. No guns, okay? No sharpshooters. None of that bullshit. We're gonna be coming up unarmed and ready to talk.'

He released the button on the radio and switched it off. He lowered it gently to the ground and kicked it towards Karl.

Karl watched all of this in silent surprise, as if he couldn't believe that he was getting precisely what he wanted.

'So, like I said, there ain't much here on you. Possession maybe, though I figure that's your service sidearm and you have a right to own it. You got kidnapping, but like for what? An hour?' Vale smiled. 'That ain't nothing to get excited about—'

Karl pointed his gun at Parrish. 'He takes everyone up. You stay down here with me.'

Vale didn't hesitate. 'Everyone. Up on your feet.' He looked back at Parrish. 'Frank . . .'

Parrish nodded, got up, stepped to the edge of the stairwell and indicated that the hostages should walk right on past him and up the stairs.

The crowd seemed to hesitate as one, as if they couldn't believe that they were coming out of the basement alive.

'Go!' Karl said. 'Get outta here!'

They hurried then, almost falling into one another.

Parrish waited until they were all out safely, and then he walked back to the top of the stairwell.

'What can you do for me?' Karl asked.

'Up to the DA,' Vale replied. 'We get you a Public Defender, a good one, we get you a psych eval, a drug counsellor, the best we can find, and maybe we're looking at . . . you ever been down before?'

'No.'

'Arrested?'

'Aggravated assault . . . charges were dropped.'

'How long ago?'

'Five, six years.'

'And how long were you in the military?'

'Four years.'

'You went overseas?'

'Iraq,' Karl said. 'Was honorably discharged for medical reasons.'

'Mental health reasons?'

Karl hesitated, and then he nodded slowly.

'Then I think you're gonna walk this, my friend,' Vale said, and for the first moment since this nightmare began he realized how utterly terrified he had been, and how he now believed that he might come out of this alive.

'Your partner up there . . . tell him to get the fuck out the way.'

'Frank?' Vale called up.

'I'm here, Mike.'

'Go on up. We're coming out.'

Vale looked back at Karl. 'I need the gun,' he said.

'Fuck you, I'm keeping the gun.'

'You can't go out there with a gun, Karl. They see you with a gun and they're gonna shoot you.'

'You get the gun, I keep the grenade or no deal.'

Vale stood there for a moment. He was out in left field. He didn't know what the hell he was doing.

'Okay,' he said, 'but once you're outside you're gonna give that thing to me before anyone sees it.'

It was Karl's turn to hesitate, and then he nodded and agreed. 'Okay,' he said. 'Deal.'

Karl gave Vale the gun and Vale put it on the floor. He kicked it back with the others and turned to make his way up the stairs.

'Hey, man,' Karl said.

Vale turned.

'You got kids?'

Vale nodded. 'Three,' he said, 'but older than yours. They're in their teens.'

Karl nodded, but said nothing.

Michael Vale went first. He took the stairs slowly, used his body to block any attempt Karl might make to run. He wanted to get the kid out into the daylight, out where everyone could see, get that grenade off of him before he put him down on the floor and cuffed him.

The door was up ahead, and Vale could see Frank Parrish back near the car. As he approached the door he realized how many squads and unmarkeds had gathered. The hostages were nowhere to be seen, but in their place was a small army of police officers, all of them crouched behind opened car doors, handguns and rifles at the ready. A tactical bomb unit had been deployed and the oversized white and blue truck was parked back across the street.

It was then that Vale saw the girl. She was way back near the car. She had the kid with her, was holding him in her arms. Vale felt a sense of accomplishment, of clear-headed resolve, and his heart – triphammering like fury – only then started to slow down. He knew he would not feel the effects of this for quite some time. He thought about the weekend upstate. He thought about his wife, his kids. He thought about everything that could have happened here, and how it had not.

She started shouting then. Laney.

'Asshole! You fucking asshole, Karl! You're a fucking useless asshole, Karl, and I was gonna give you another chance, but you're such a fucking asshole you don't deserve it.'

Vale felt his heart miss a beat. He was aware of Karl behind him.

Vale raised his hand. Why, he didn't know. She perhaps couldn't even see him, but he did it anyway.

Shut the fuck up! he was thinking. *For God's sake, shut the fuck up!*

'Bitch,' he heard Karl say behind him, and it wasn't even a word, it was just a sound, an expression of vehemence and hatred and jealousy and bitterness.

'Fucking asshole!' she screamed even as Frank Parrish reached her, tried to hold her, tried to quieten her down, shut her up.

'You think you're gonna see Karl Junior again, well you're fucking mistaken, my friend! Seriously fucking mistaken!'

And Karl said *Bitch* again, and Vale turned, and he opened his mouth to say something, to placate the man, to tell him that she was just upset, that she would settle down, that everything was going to be fine . . .

And Karl held out his hands, and in one of them was the grenade, and hanging around his neck was a loop of cord, and attached to the cord was the pin, and Michael Vale knew then that it was all over.

He stepped forward and put his arms around Karl Emerson, and he hugged him tight to limit the breadth of the blast.

Two and three days later pieces of them were still being found thirty yards away.

EIGHTY-SEVEN

The first person Frank Parrish spoke to when he came out of surgery was his son. 'Gimme a couple of hours we'll go shoot some hoops,' he said. Robert told him he was full of shit.

'I met Eve,' he said.

'Cute, huh?'

'Way cute. Monster fucking cute. You gonna shack up with her or what?'

Parrish smiled. His words slurred a little, and he had the glazed eyes of a man jacked on painkillers. 'In another life maybe . . . she has her thing. She is what she is. No-one's going to change her.'

'She's like you then. Maybe that's why you get on.'

'Won't be like that for long. They're going to kick me out on my ass.'

'For what you did?'

'For what I did.'

Robert leaned forward and gripped his father's hand. 'I'm gonna drop the engineering—'

'I figured you might.'

'You okay with that?'

'You can do what the hell you like, Robert, you know that.'

'But Mom—'

'Tell her to go fuck herself.'

'She's pissed, Dad, real pissed.'

'She's always pissed, Robert.'

'So what the hell happened to her? How come she's like this?'

'She spent a few years married to me. Enough to ruin anyone for life.'

'You're so full of shit.'

'Yeah, I know. I take after my kids.'

*

448

Caitlin came a while later. Frank told her they weren't putting chairs on the tables yet, which she didn't really understand, but she figured it meant that he wasn't ready to die.

It was dark outside, and she sat beside his bed, and she reached out and took his hand.

'You want some water or something?' she asked.

He did not answer her question, but he did say, 'Been a long time since there was anything out in front of me.' He tried to smile, but it just looked like he was hurting more. She told him not to say anything, to close his eyes and go to sleep again, but he shook his head and said, 'Always been a day late and a dollar short. You know that? That's one thing you can rely on as far as Frank Parrish is concerned. I'll be one of those people who stays the same no matter what happens.' He closed his eyes. There were tears on his cheeks and Caitlin brushed them away with the ball of her thumb. 'You think it's come up on you quick,' he said, 'but it hasn't. It's been coming for years, an inch at a time. You don't notice it until it's right there in front of you, and you still think you've got a chance to change it but you haven't—'

'Dad . . . please . . .'

Frank Parrish squeezed his daughter's hand. He looked at her intently. 'You think I'm dumb? I'm not dumb, Caitlin. I know what's going on with you and Radick.'

'I don't think you're dumb, Dad . . .'

'Make sure he looks after you, okay? He's a good man . . . young, green as grass, but he's a good man.'

'Dad . . .'

'Tell Jimmy Radick that if he hurts you I'll kill him . . .'

Caitlin smiled.

Frank closed his eyes. He was asleep before she could answer.

Valderas came the following morning. Parrish asked about Carole Paretski, told him that under no circumstances did he intend to press charges. Under *no* circumstances. He was somewhere he shouldn't have been, she had every legal right to be present in the McKee house, and he was an intruder.

'Did they get the stuff in the house?' he asked.

'Yes, Frank, they got the stuff in the house. And had she not been there none of it would have been admissible.' Valderas shook his head. He sat down on a chair beside Frank's bed. 'Jesus Christ, Frank, I don't know that you could have done anything crazier—'

Parrish smiled with difficulty. 'Hell, Tony, I was planning on just shooting the guy in the head and being done with it.'

'Well, it was good you went with Plan B then.'

'So what happened?'

'Well, she called 911, obviously. She'd just fucking stabbed you with a screwdriver – your own screwdriver, I might add. By the time they got there you were out of it. They saw the stuff she'd found, they called the PD, and by the time I found out about it you'd gone and she was under arrest. Anyways, I told the guys there what the deal was, and they were waiting for McKee when he got back with the kids. They didn't try and contact him in case he did a runner.'

'And where are the kids now?'

'Ironically, they're with Family Welfare. Carole Paretski will get them back today . . . we already figured out how you were wrong and she was right. Regardless of whether or not you press charges, there isn't a DA in the country who would take her to court under the circumstances.'

Parrish smiled, and then he grimaced in pain.

'You need to rest,' Valderas said.

'I know, I know, I will,' Parrish replied, and then he looked at Valderas directly and said, 'I'm fucked, aren't I? That's it now. The car, the break-in, everything. It's completely fucked, right?'

Valderas hesitated, and then he slowly nodded his head. 'Yes, Frank, it's completely fucked.'

'But you've got McKee, right? You've got him.'

'For how many things we don't know yet, but yes, we've got him. He was shipped over to us as soon as Haversaw got word of what had happened. The 126th will take the bust.' Valderas smiled sardonically. 'Despite you and your efforts, Frank, we will take the bust. Anyway, McKee opened up like a can of worms. He's making noises about giving up other people who were also involved—'

'What people?'

'This outfit called Absolute Films. Some other crew of psychos. Links to the West Coast, LA, Vegas as well, I think. He's going to rat them all out for a deal of some sort.'

'And who gets the murders?'

'Oh, he'll get the murders, at least two of them. He was the one in a whole bunch of those pictures. The earlier ones we don't know, and right now it looks like there might be a great deal more Missing Persons cases getting resolved. The Danny Lange shooting we don't know about yet, but someone's gonna hang for that one as well. Maybe McKee'll get life instead of the death penalty if he gives everyone up.'

'It was a bad, bad scene.'

'And we touched the edges of it, Frank, just the edges of it. The girls you knew about were not the only ones. That's something we're sure of now. And it goes back before Jennifer, most definitely. I mean, shit, the guy worked in Family Welfare for years. He had names, pictures, addresses, phone numbers. He could approach these girls without drawing attention to himself in any way. It was his job to get up close and personal. That's the real thing here, that's the really sad thing about all of this. They already had two strikes against them, and then they ran into Richard McKee.'

Parrish was quiet for a time. He had so many questions, but the pain was making its way through the wall of painkillers, and he was exhausted.

'So you're gonna manage to clean up the city without me?' he said eventually.

'No, Frank, not a fucking prayer. Without you it's all gonna go to hell in a hand basket.'

Frank Parrish smiled. 'You better believe it,' he said. He closed his eyes for a second.

'Hang in there, Frank. You got one more visitor. A priest.'

'Oh for Christ's sake—' he started.

Father Briley appeared back of Valderas. 'I heard that Frank Parrish, and if you don't stop taking the Lord's name in vain you are going to burn in Hell . . .'

EIGHTY-EIGHT

Marie Griffin looked at Frank Parrish for some time before she spoke. The light from the window behind her cast a fine halo through her hair.

'So this is the end of the line for you.'

'Seems that way,' Parrish replied.

'It's hard to imagine that we met less than six weeks ago.'

'I know, I know. Doesn't it seem so much longer.'

'Wiseass. Jesus, you don't let up, do you, Frank?'

He smiled wryly. 'It's just the way I was made, Marie.'

'So what did they give you?'

'They gave me a Congressional Medal of Honor, and they said I should run for Mayor.'

'Frank—'

'They didn't prosecute. That's what they gave me. They let me off the hook for all the shit that I did.'

'But you're out of the PD.'

'I am.'

'With nothing?'

'No, Marie, not with nothing. They gave me sixty-five percent of my pension, and there's a possibility that when I actually reach retirement age they'll give me some more. But hell, I ain't gonna hold 'em to it.'

'And you didn't blackmail them?'

'Blackmail them?'

'Give me everything I want or I'll go to the newspapers about John Parrish, the OCCB, the Saints of New York?'

Parrish leaned forward. He took something from his jacket pocket and held it in his hand for just a moment. Then he reached forward and put it on her desk.

'What's that?'

'Take a look.'

She reached out and gathered it up.

'A rosary,' she said.

'It is.'

'It has a picture attached to it. This is a little kid . . .' She paused and frowned. 'This is you, right?'

'It is.'

'And this came from where?'

'My father's priest. He and I had a few words before I went into McKee's house. He told me some things about my father. Then he came to visit in the hospital and brought that with him.'

'And he got it from your father.'

'It was in my father's hand when the priest gave him the last rites. It was in his hand when he died.'

'And this priest . . . he kept it for you?'

'No, he kept it for himself, but then he thought I would have more use for it.'

'Does this resolve something for you, Frank?'

'Maybe. A little. I haven't figured it all out yet.'

'So you're letting go of him? Of the ghost of John Parrish.'

'I'm not thinking about him in the same way, if that's what you mean. All this shit happened a long time ago. What was the truth and what wasn't, well, it doesn't mean anything now. Stirring all of that up would simply give people a reason not to be confident in the police department now, and that wouldn't do anyone any good.'

'That's a very responsible viewpoint to take.'

'It's common sense, Marie. I don't think it's anything but common sense.'

'And you?'

Parrish shook his head. He looked away towards the window and sighed. 'I will just take some time to let things sink in. Was he who I thought he was? Was he someone different? I don't know Marie, I just don't know.'

'But now you're a civilian.'

'Yeah, I'm a civilian, just like you.'

'And how is that?'

'Well, I got out of hospital two weeks ago, and most of those two weeks I've spent answering questions and writing reports about this whole case, so I really don't have a handle on it yet. I'm drinking less because the doctor says I have to . . . oh yeah, I also had a stomach ulcer I didn't even know about, but hell, as soon as I'm fixed up I'll be back on a bottle and a half a day.'

'Whatever you say, Frank.'

'So you'll have to give me a little while, you know? You'll have to give me six months to find my feet and get oriented.'

'And where does the case stand now? Wasn't there some question about admissibility of evidence?'

'They got around that because Carole was there when the evidence was found. She had a key that he'd given her and that gave her legal access to the property.'

'So they've got McKee, no question.'

'So far they've got seven of them. They have McKee on first degree for Kelly Duncan, Rebecca Lange and Nicole Benedict. It looks like Melissa Schaeffer, Jennifer Baumann and Karen Pulaski were killed by one or other of his buddies. They also have the guy that shot Danny Lange. McKee just opened his mouth and started talking, and he's a good way from done yet. This thing went back before Melissa, that's for sure, and there were others in between during the last two years as well. They didn't only take girls that went through Family Welfare, they took them from wherever. From what we can work out it was a set-up that already existed before McKee got involved, and when he showed up he just came with another feeder line for the party.'

'And they were making snuff movies?'

'They were making everything you could imagine. They catered to every taste you can think of. The sad thing is that they were a relatively small operation, all things considered. There are bigger organizations out there doing worse things and more frequently. I really cannot bear to think how many of our runaways are buried in the Hollywood Hills and the desert outside Vegas. Anyway, they've got seven of them, McKee of course, and then some other guy he hooked up with on the internet, and then there's the people from the film company in LA. McKee is up for three counts of first-degree murder, and then endless counts of accomplice to murder, kidnapping, rape, pandering . . . the whole lunchbox, you know? They've thrown the book at him. But because he gave up everyone else he's gonna get consecutive life-terms instead of the death penalty.'

'How do you feel about that?'

'I feel okay. I feel like he should spend one hell of a long time thinking about what he did, and I'm hoping that a three hundred and fifty-pound gang member called Bubba is gonna take a shine to him in the joint.'

'And what about the fact that this case only scratches the surface?'

Again Parrish was silent for a time, his expression reflective. 'I think that's something that we all come to terms with very early on. If you spend your time and attention worrying about all the ones that you didn't get, then you go crazy. You deal with what you've got in front of you, you deal with it the best you can, and you hope that somewhere else there are people who are working as hard as you to make things right. Maybe that's the one thing I've managed to be philosophical about all these years.'

'And McKee's ex-wife?'

'She's good, you know? She can't tell me sorry enough. She came to see me in the hospital, and I've seen her a couple of times since I was released. She's a good woman. She's happy to have the asshole out of her life, and now she knows her kids are safe.'

'He really filmed his own daughter?'

'Yes, he really filmed his own daughter.'

'And how are Robert and Caitlin?'

'Robert thinks I'm a hero, Caitlin thinks I'm going to drink myself into an early grave.'

'And what do you think?'

Parrish shrugged his shoulders and smiled. 'I'm forty-four years old. I've been a cop for eighteen years. I don't know anything else.'

'Maybe you could go into the private sector? Investigator's work, maybe?'

'I don't think so, no. I'm the sort of person who needs a system and a structure around me otherwise it all falls apart.'

'Well, for someone who says they need a system and a

structure around them, Frank, you spent an awful lot of time defying it, don't you think?'

'You're not IAD. I don't have to answer that.'

'So – I hope I'll hear from you. I hope you will let me know what you're doing and how it's going.'

'You'll forget, Marie. A week from now it won't matter where I am and what I'm doing.'

'Oh, I don't think so, Frank Parrish. I think you've earned yourself a name.'

'Well, you know what they say. One crowded hour of glorious life is worth an age without a name.'

'It's been good knowing you. Good talking with you.'

'And I was never really in therapy was I, Doc? Not for real.'

'No, Frank, you were never in therapy.'

'Thanks for your time.'

'You're welcome.'

Frank Parrish paused at the door. He turned back and looked at Marie Griffin.

'All that stuff we spoke about – you know, my father, my marriage, my kids? I think it was good. I think it helped me.'

'And I think it taught me something, Frank,' Marie Griffin said.

'And what was that?'

'That even when people do things the wrong way they can still be doing them for the right reasons. And about your father? The truth is that he's dead. Physically, spiritually, emotionally . . . every which way he's dead. And whatever he might have called himself, and whatever people might have thought about him, it's guys like you that are the real Saints of New York.'

Frank Parrish nodded an acknowledgement. He smiled once more, and then he closed the door ever so gently behind him.